For Moriah, Melissa, Ming
致敬莫立娅，梅丽莎，明

To My Grandchildren, and their Grandchildren
献给我的孙辈，以及他们的孙辈

A Special Thanks:
特别感谢

To the city and people of Beijing, for giving me the sublime space and temperate time in which to write.
北京这座城市和人民给了我绝佳的空间和静好的时间从事写作。

George Randolph Barlos
乔治·兰道夫·巴洛

BRUISE ART
瘀伤艺术

By

George Randolph Barlos

【美】乔治·兰道夫·巴洛 著

沈茵茵 译

中国戏剧出版社
CHINA THEATRE PRESS

图书在版编目(CIP)数据

瘀伤艺术：汉文、英文 /(美) 乔治·兰道夫·巴洛著；沈茵茵译. -- 北京：中国戏剧出版社，2024.10
书名原文: BRUISE ART
ISBN 978-7-104-05474-0

Ⅰ.①瘀… Ⅱ.①乔…②沈… Ⅲ.①幻想小说—美国—现代—汉、英 Ⅳ.①I712.45

中国国家版本馆 CIP 数据核字(2024)第 065326 号

BRUISE ART
瘀伤艺术

责任编辑：赵宇欣
责任出版：冯志强

出版发行：	中国戏剧出版社
出 版 人：	樊国宾
社　　址：	北京市西城区天宁寺前街 2 号国家音乐产业基地 L 座
邮　　编：	100055
网　　址：	www.theatrebook.cn
电　　话：	010-63381560（发行部）　010-63385980（总编室）
传　　真：	010-63381560

读者服务：010-63381560
邮购地址：北京市西城区天宁寺前街 2 号国家音乐产业基地 L 座

印　　刷：	四川科德彩色数码科技有限公司
开　　本：	787mm×1092mm　1/16
印　　张：	20.75
字　　数：	350 千
版　　次：	2024 年 10 月　北京第 1 版第 1 次印刷
书　　号：	ISBN 978-7-104-05474-0
定　　价：	198.00 元

版权专有，违者必究；如有质量问题，请与出版社联系调换。

前言

Bruise Art—new art form created and developed by George Randolph Barlos in 2015 involving the use of the Eastern 'cupping/bruising' technique. Beyond the traditional therapy, Bruise Art, as art form, uses a series of bruises on the skin arranged and manipulated to create various works of art in the form of images, patterns, and designs. The cupping bruises are the brush strokes, the body's skin the canvas. The random markings of the therapeutic technique are thus transformed into an intentional and new art form, that is, Bruise Art.

Bruise Art
瘀伤艺术

  瘀伤艺术——作为一种新的艺术形式，由作者乔治·兰道夫·巴洛于 2015 年运用东方的"拔罐"手法创造、开发而成。瘀伤艺术超越了传统的治疗目的，成为一种艺术形式。通过在皮肤上制作出一系列瘀青印迹，创作出不同形状的画像、图案和设计。拔罐造成的瘀青相当于画笔，皮肤就是画布。原来用于治疗的随机瘀青印迹被改造成一种自觉的新艺术形式，即瘀伤艺术。

  Bruise Art is written in the form of a novel combined with memoir, or 'Nov-oir'. In the case of Bruise Art, where the fiction story ends and memoirs begin is always at issue, part of the point and purpose of the author's use of the combination. Barlos provides tantalizing hints in the form of 'Truth about the Fiction' notes at the end of the book. However, for the most part readers are left to their own devises to determine which depictions are delicious real revelations and which are writer's creative imaginations. Those lines are purposefully blurred, playing back and forth, one to the other, at times the two becoming the one.

《瘀伤艺术》是一部结合了个人回忆录的小说。在本书中，哪些是虚构情节，哪些属于回忆，并无明确边界，这是作者故意采用的混合写法。作者在本书结尾"与小说相关的事实"部分，提供了一些引人无限遐想的线索。当然，在大部分内容上，读者还是需要靠自己来决定哪些描写是鲜活的现实，哪些是作者的创造性的想象。它们之间的界限被故意模糊，来回反复，时而你中有我，时而合二为一。

Bruise Art—A philosophy and lifestyle that involves the constant testing of oneself as a means to greater enlightenment, toward the realization of one's highest reasonable potential. Just as the therapeutic cupping/bruising technique challenges the body's immune systems, and thus creates a positive and health-enhancing reaction, so the intentional challenging of oneself in life choices and in the setting

Greater Enlightenment
拓展觉知

of higher goals and aspirations, serves as a pathway to greater knowledge, enlightenment, and life successes otherwise unrealized. It is the living of life within the framework of the art of self-testing, of 'bruising' oneself, that is the essence of the 'art of the bruise', Bruise Art.

瘀伤艺术作为一种表现人生哲学和生活方式的艺术形式，它关乎一个人持续不断地拓展自己的觉知，最大限度地实现自身潜力。拔罐产生瘀青的手法挑战身体的免疫系统，激发一种正向的、健康的反应。与此相应，它有意识地向自我提出人生挑战，不断设定更高的目标和抱负，也是一种获得更广袤的知识、觉知，取得意想不到的成功的方式。挑战自我、令自己"伤痕累累"的生活方式，就是瘀伤艺术，也是其精神实质所在。

To use the power of the pen in intense combination with other creative arts to ① rejuvenate oneself, ② write a great story, ③ provide a retrospective of the author's design work, ④ document the author's life for his descendants, ⑤ help save American culture by exposing the primary source of police corruption (Hint: Not racism), ⑥ significantly enhance harmonious relations between the 'East' and 'West', ⑦ provide a tool for Chinese—English language education, ⑧ allow the author the possibility of **'digital immortality'** through reverse engineering of information provided in the *Bruise Art* novel/memoir/illustration series so that posterity may recreate him in **digital/AI (Artificial intelligence) form.**

作者精心构思这部小说是希望可以用笔下的文字与其他创意艺术紧密结合，以期达到以下目的：①焕发自身活力；②撰写一个好故事；③回顾作者自身的设计作品；④为作者的后人留下其文字记录；⑤揭示美国警察腐败（并非种族歧视）的问题；⑥加强东西方的和谐关系；⑦为中英语言教育提供读本；⑧通过对《瘀伤艺术》这本小说（回忆录）中的信息进行回溯处理，使作者的后代有条件通过**数字化或人工智能手段**重塑其人，使其获得"**数字化永生**"的可能。

The fictional character of Jackson Bartholomew is the aspirational alter ego of the author, George Randolph Barlos. At times Jackson's story closely resembles the real-life experiences of the author; At other times it varies greatly, depending on the needs of the novel and of the overlapping requirements of the memoir. The novel/memoir's interweaving of the author's story with Jackson Bartholomew's exploits 'helps to pull the author along' in the directions he aspires to go.

杰克逊·巴塞洛缪（下文简称杰克逊）是作者乔治·兰道夫·巴洛虚构的人物，代表着作者希望构建的第二自我。在杰克逊的人生经历中，有些部分与作者的真实经历极其相似，有些部分则大相径庭，因此，这是一本具有回忆录性质的小说。作者将自己与杰克逊交织在一起，"有助于带领作者"走向他希望达到的方向。

The use of the aspirational alter ego character is also a means to prompt the author to continue his personal development as an international designer, creative writer, American pop culture participant, and police culture reform activist/advocate. The literary devise of having a revered central character turn up missing or dead at the beginning of a story is to allow for a review of a dynamic life and is well suited for a memoir turning into novel, with intentions on a film; *Think Citizen Kane, The City of Your Final Destination, or The Great Gatsby.*

乔治·兰道夫·巴洛是一名国际设计师，创意作家，美国流行文化参与者，美国警察文化改革活动家、倡导者，书中的主人公——这个虚构的第二自我也是作者对其个人成长与发展的一种激励。小说以一位声名卓著的核心人物失踪或者死亡作为故事开篇，意在回顾一个充满活力的生命。如同《公民凯恩》《终点之城》《了不起的盖茨比》，这部回忆录性质的小说，最终或将搬上银幕。

Jackson Bartholomew at Masada, Israel
杰克逊·巴塞洛缪在以色列马萨达

The 'Great American Novel' is the concept of a novel that shows the culture of the United States of America at a specific time (In this case, the early 1980's to the 2020's). It is presumed to be written by an American author who is knowledgeable about the state, culture, and perspective of the common American citizen.

在美国小说界一直对一个概念特别着迷——"Great American Novel"（"伟大的美国小说"）。作者将其定义为刻画某一特殊时期（在本书中，指20世纪80年代到21世纪20年代）美国文化的小说。因为作者是一位美国作家，他对美国国情、文化、普通民众的观点有着深入的了解。

The author uses his literary work to identify and exhibit the language used by the American people of the day, and to capture the unique American experience, problematic, aspirational and otherwise, especially as it is perceived for that time. In historical terms, it is sometimes equated as being the American response to the 'national epic'.

作者运用自己的文字，寻找和展示当代美国民众使用的语言，捕捉那个特定历史时期独特的美国经历，不论其定性为问题丛生、充满希望还是其他。从历史的视角，或可将这部小说等同于美国文化的回响。

2023年10月

TABLE OF CONTENTS
目录

Episode One BEGINNINGS
第一篇 开端

Scene One Dreams   003
第一幕 梦境

Scene Two Invitations   037
第二幕 邀请

Scene Three Highway One   055
第三幕 一号公路

Scene Four Santa Cruz   085
第四幕 圣克鲁斯

Scene Five Jasmine   109
第五幕 茉莉

Scene Six Moriah   127
第六幕 莫立娅

Scene Seven A Toast to Jackson   137
第七幕 为杰克逊干杯

Scene Eight The Vagus   147
第八幕 迷走神经

Scene Nine Surveillance   167
第九幕 盯梢

Episode Two INTERVIEW WITH ARTIFICIAL INTELLIGENCE
第二篇 与人工智能的访谈

Scene Ten   Inside the Geodesic Dome   171
第十幕 圆形穹顶之内

Scene Eleven J.B.—AI   175
第十一幕 人工智能杰克逊

Scene Twelve J.B. Retrospectives—Creations   213
第十二幕 杰克逊·巴塞洛缪作品一览

Scene Thirteen Pop Culture Phenom   249
第十三幕 流行文化现象

Scene Fourteen Renaissance Man, Rebirth, Reincarnation   267
第十四幕 文艺复兴人、重生、轮回

Scene Fifteen Truth About the Facts   291
第十五幕 事实真相

Scene Sixteen "Stick With Us, Samuel"   309
第十六幕 "坚持住，塞缪尔"

Facts about the Fiction   313
附一：与小说相关的事实

Films with Thematic Connections to *Bruise Art*   317
附二：与《瘀伤艺术》主题相关的电影

Episode One

BEGINNINGS

第一篇
开端

Scene One　Dreams

第一幕 梦境

"Dreams and half dreams." a woman's whispering voice, repeated, the warm pressure of her naked bottom on my lower back. "Art of the bruise, world in transition, rebirth, reincarnation, separation and reunification..." I love that part." Then how does it go? 'Traditional to popular, religious to secular.' Nice thesis, doll."

"梦境,半梦半醒之境。"一个女人的声音反复呢喃,她裸露的臀部暖暖地贴在我后腰上。"瘀伤的艺术,变化的世界,重生,轮回,分离,重逢……"我喜欢这样。"然后呢? '从传统到流行,从宗教到世俗。'好棒的论文,宝贝儿。"

"What? Go away." I 'sleep mumbled' the words, face in pillow. "I'm dreaming!" She knew about my dreams, full on, vivid; how I believed in them, used them, tried to shape them to my will. She also knew that forcing me to think about the structure of my thesis project might force me to wake up.

"什么,走开啦。"我头埋在枕头里,睡意未消地咕哝着,"我在做梦呢!"她知道我的梦境,一清二楚,活灵活现。她知道我相信这些梦境是真实的,我利用它们,试图依着自己的意愿来塑造成这些梦。她还知道逼我去思考论文的结构会迫使我醒来。

"Don't you like to hear lines from your own thesis? How about this, 'Bruise Art'! Come on, get up. Today's the day. My parents. We've got a lot to do. Samuel! Get up!"

"你不想听听自己写的论文吗?这个怎么样,'瘀伤艺术'!来嘛,起床了。今天是大日子。我父母要来了,有好多事情要做。塞缪尔!起来!"

I'd trained myself to have the capacity to move within the transition space between the dream state and 'awake'. I had a talent for it. Half-dreams the best, filling the void with the widest spectrum of information, unexpected combinations, bits of knowledge, forgotten subparts; then reassembled, put back together, useful arrays, epiphanies, poetic phrases, vignettes. Even with Havanna on my back, reciting chapter titles from my thesis project, I could force the drift, find a way back in. The view of the old bridge returned, crumbling, Ponte Vecchio, heart of Florence. Something there, someone, just beyond. Couldn't quite see it. Close. Jackson again? Had to be.

我已经练就了这样的能力,在介于梦境和"清醒"之间的混沌状态中游走。我有这个天分。半梦半醒是最佳的状态,其虚空之境充斥着涉猎最广的信息、意料之外的组合、知识的碎片、遗落的部件，在其间重新组装、拼接，成为有意义的排列组合，犹如圣灵显现，诗意迸发，光晕炫目。即使哈瓦娜趴在我背上诵读我论文中的章节标题，我也能够进入这种游离状态，也能把自己找回来。那座老桥的幻影重现、坍塌，佛罗伦萨市中心的维琪奥桥。在那边有什么东西？什么人？看不清楚。近了。又是杰克逊？一定是他。

"Not today. No dreaming, and no damn Jackson Bartholomew." she said, blowing a sharp breath into my ear.

"今天不行。不要做梦了，去他的杰克逊·巴塞洛缪。"她说着，往我耳朵里猛吹了一口气。

"Stop! Not pleasant!" I said, humping up my back to buck her off. "Seriously ... not."

"别闹！难受死了！"我弓起背想把她翻下去。"说真的……不好玩儿。"

She held on, riding it out, knees pressed into my ribcage. She knew I had the capacity to go back in, to help the dream, pull with it, harder, from the other side, all the images mixing, scenes forming, dissolving, reforming. I could see it, Jackson, on the bridge, then in the water, the moment he fell over ... or jump?

她顽固地骑在我背上，膝盖顶住我的肋骨。她知道我有本事重返梦境，在那里边继续纠缠，越陷越深，所有幻象混合，场景浮现、消失、再浮现。我能看到杰克逊，在桥上，之后又在水里，他跌入水中的那一瞬间……抑或是跳入？

"Obsession works, sometimes. Not today." she said, rocking back and forth, the feel of her body moving on mine, rhythmic, enough to take me away again; The bridge, the images of Jackson, fading. I concentrated, hard, forcing it, the scene of him sitting on the stone wall. The crowd noise came up, filled in. This time he was already falling, arms flailing out as he tossed backwards, the body disappearing with a loud 'plop'; no splash, no rippling, like a Chinese diver's entry into an Olympic pool. The surface of the dirty green water held steady, odd, too calm, considering the weight of the body, the distance fallen. Jackson Bartholomew gone, escaped, captured, something, somewhere, under, within the wet voluminous dank of the Arno River.

"执着有时候管用，但今天不行。"她说着，前后摇晃，我感觉到她的胴体在我背上有节奏地晃动,足以将我再次唤醒。桥和杰克逊的画面正在消散。我努力迫使自己集中精神,捕捉他坐在石头墙上的那一幕。人群的喧闹声越来越大,充斥于耳。这一次他已经在下坠,身体向后倒的时候双臂摇摆,随着"扑通"一声巨响,他消失在水中,没有水花,没有涟漪,如同中国跳水运动员在奥运会泳池入水的那一刻。浊绿的水面纹丝不动,考虑到体重和坠落的高度,这水面过于平静了,透着古怪。杰克逊·巴塞洛缪是消失了、逃跑了,还是被抓住了?在阴暗深沉的阿尔诺河里,某个地方,有什么东西?

"A few more minutes. That's all. Come on ... please." I mumbled into the pillow, loud, enough to get out, urgent.

"再给我几分钟,仅此而已。拜托……求你了。"我头埋在枕头里咕哝着,声量大到能够听见,这很要紧。

"Damn you ... All right. Then that's it. When I come back ... up and at 'em. Okay?!"

"该死的家伙……好吧,那就这么着,等我回来……你已经准备好去迎接他们,听到了吗?!"

Samuel
塞缪尔

It took more time than usual, to get back in. Havanna had pulled me away, too far. Maybe not, no way back in, to the familiar, repeating dream. Relax, concentrate. Good, there, I was ... good, back in ... dream repeat. Everyone'd seen it, this one, compilations, replays of videoclips from Jackson's own real-time documentary, interviews of Jackson, news clips from the day he disappeared, several iconic photos of the exact moment of his fall off the Ponte Vecchio; All of it together, now emblematic pieces of collective popular culture memory. It had become my dream-mind's own short film, re-reset, it playing, once again.

　　我用了比往常更长的时间重新进入梦境。哈瓦娜把我拉得太远了，或许回不去那个反复出现的熟悉场景了。放松，集中精神。好了，就在那里，我又回来了，太好了……梦境又回来了。所有人都看过这些东西——杰克逊本人的影像合集，他的纪实纪录片的片段，关于他的采访，他失踪当天的新闻报道剪辑，他从维琪奥桥跌落瞬间的几张照片，这些东西全都成了流行文化集体记忆的标志性片段。它已经成为我头脑中迷梦之境的影片，不断重设、重播，一遍又一遍。

　　Jackson Bartholomew(J.B.), the world-famous American novelist/creative genius, (55, John Grisham meets Tom Ford; with the look of Daniel Day-Lewis). Him in frantic departure, on his private plane, headed for one of his over-the-top, self-promotion marketing trips. He's frustrated, shouting, "Why haven't we 'gone viral. It's been over a month!" He's planning something, special. A spectacular event on the Ponte Vecchio, 'Old Bridge' crossover of the Arno River, in the historic heart of Florence, Italy. The 'go viral at any cost' mindset has him livestreaming, everything. His entire trip from Silicon Valley to Los Angeles, to the airport in Florence, to the iconic foot bridge in the heart of Tuscany, and then the event itself. All of it, including the kickoff event on the bridge, to appear simultaneously, Facebook, Instagram, Twitter, TikTok, his own extravagant podcast and website, even old-school network television; Jimmy Fallon already there, setting up for a simultaneous interview, *Saturday Night Live* and the *Tonight Show*.

　　杰克逊·巴塞洛缪（下文简称 J.B.）是世界知名的美国小说作家和创意天才，时年 55 岁，堪称约翰·格里森姆（美国畅销小说作家——译者注）和汤姆·福特（美国著名时尚品牌创始人——译者注）的集合体，外表酷似丹尼尔·戴—刘易斯（美国著名电影演员——译者注）。他登上私人飞机，在忙乱中启程，踏上一场声势浩大的推广之旅。他火冒三丈，大声嚷嚷："我们怎么还没火起来？都过去一个月了！"他在策划一桩很特别的事情。他要在意大利古城佛罗伦萨市中心，横跨阿尔诺河的维琪奥桥——在"老桥"上演壮观的一幕。他要"不惜一切代价火遍全网"，把一切活动都做成直播。从硅谷开始，在洛杉矶、佛罗伦萨机场、托斯卡纳大区中心的标志性步行桥，最后是这次活动本身。所有一切，包括桥上的启动仪式，要在脸书、instagram、推特、TikTok、他炫酷的个人播客和网站，甚至老派的有线电视上同步直播。吉米·法伦（美国知名脱口秀主持人——译者注）已经准备就绪，在《周六夜现场》和《今夜秀》栏目中对他进行现场采访。

"It's all about promotion." Jackson shouts, his eager entourage gathered tight around him. They're in a private plane. "*Bruise Art*, my novel/memoir ... it's got to be, going to be, the 'Great American Novel'." I'm not waiting for someone else to call it that. I'm making it. Then talk about each of the spin offs, all things connected, their plans for the J.B. product line of fashion and jewelry, handmade in Tuscany (limited edition), mass production in China. "It'll work, once we trigger it ... today." he tells them.(Nothing new for me in this part of the 'dream-half-dream'. The scene had played and replayed in my mind so many times, each part seen thousands of times, millions of views, all media forms, after his spectacular fall into the Arno, his bizarre disappearance. I searched for something more, yearned, some clue, revelation, what lay beyond ... beyond what was already known.)

"全都要靠营销！"杰克逊对紧紧环绕在身边的随从人员大声说道。他们在私人飞机上。"《瘀伤艺术》，我的小说兼回忆录，注定、必将成为'伟大的美国小说'。我不要等着别人来给它定义，我正在成就它。"之后他大谈这本小说的衍生品——一切与之相关联的东西：关于J.B.品牌线的时尚和珠宝，在托斯卡纳的手工制作（限量生产），在中国的批量生产，等等。"这些都会实现的，一旦我们将它启动……就在今天。"他对他们说。（这部分的半梦境对我而言没有什么新的信息。这个场景我在脑子里已经循环重播了无数次，且他在阿尔诺河坠落并神奇失踪之后，每个环节我也都在各种媒介上观看了成千上万次。我在寻找更深的东西，我渴望找到一些线索、启示，一些已知现象之外的东西。）

Then his young assistant speaks up, Jasmine Xi'an (25ish, refined, Stanford grad student, Hologram—AI Technologies) is fretting. He might miss another promotional event, something back in LA. Her famously pregnant declaration: "You can't be in two places at the same time." Jackson answers, "We're working on that one, aren't we?" Jasmine nods approval. The exchange suggests, foreshadows, another Jackson Bartholomew extravaganza, their Hologram—AI project, cutting edge, never seen technology.

他的年轻助理说话了。茉莉·席安，25岁上下，精致，斯坦福大学全息兼人工智能技术专业毕业。她忐忑不安。他可能要错过在洛杉矶举行的另一场推广活动。这是她常说的意味深长的一句话："你不可能同时出现在两个地方。"杰克逊回答道："我们正在为此努力，不是吗？"茉莉点头同意。这次对话预示着杰克逊·巴塞洛缪的另一场大秀，他们的全息—人工智能计划是一项前所未闻的尖端技术。

Jackson's demeanor changes. It's the scene from his documentary footage. He's suddenly troubled. Moriah. He tells someone to get her on the phone, then cancels. He'll do it later. (Endless pop culture speculation on this one ... what did he want to tell her.) Instead, Jackson turns to Jasmine, side commenting about De Vinci and Michelangelo, the significance of the bridge, the fabled Ponte Vecchio, "It's the same place where both sold their sketches. Renaissance men in full-on self-promotion. Perfect place for me, for this."

杰克逊的举止变了。这是他纪录片中的场景。他突然显得心烦意乱。莫立娅。他叫人拨通她的电话，又取消了。他稍后会再打。（对此流行文化圈猜测无数……他想跟她说什么呢？）他转向茉莉，大谈达·芬奇和米开朗琪罗，以及维琪奥桥的重要意义："这两位都在桥上卖过自己的手稿。文艺复兴人物的自我营销。对我来说、对这个计划来说这里真是个完美的地方。"

My dream—view switches, out of the J.B. private plane, now at the ancient bridge, the stone structure crossing of the Arno River, the iconic old bridge. The scene is already chaotic, crowded, cameras, the extra chaos laid over the usual thick throng of tourists. Someone shouting, "Jackson Bartholomew! He's coming!" There he is, arriving, pushing through. It's the same scene seen, so many thousands of times, by everyone, in all corners of the globe. Nothing new, not yet. Me still looking, examining for something different, even a detail. Now, Jackson climbing, as before, up on the stone low wall. Standing, just behind the bronze bust of Benvenuto Cellini; The best place to command the moment, address the crowd, to place himself in clear sight of hundreds of cameras, tipped-off media. Once again, Jackson Bartholomew is expertly marketing himself, achieving 'fame transferred into wealth'. Mass self-promotion by the modern Renaissance man, at the peak of his creative powers.

我的梦境视角变了，从 J.B. 的私人飞机转到了那座历史悠久的桥上。这座横跨阿尔诺河的古老石桥是个标志性建筑。场景热闹喧嚣，人头攒动，相机闪耀，原本游客就熙熙攘攘，现在更添一层喧闹。有人大喊："杰克逊·巴塞洛缪！他来了！"杰克逊出现了，他从人群中挤过来。这一幕，全世界各个角落的人都已经看了无数遍。还没发现什么新鲜东西。我还在寻觅新的线索，哪怕是一个细节。就在这时，杰克逊爬上了石头矮墙，他站在本韦努托·切利尼（意大利文艺复兴时期的雕塑家、画家——译者注）的青铜胸像后面。这是把控全场、向群众发表演说的绝佳地点，他清清楚楚呈现在上百个镜头和事先安排好的媒体面前。杰克逊·巴塞洛缪再一次娴熟地推销着

Jackson Bartholomew on the Ponte Vecchio—Florence, Italy
杰克逊·巴塞洛缪站在意大利佛罗伦萨的维琪奥桥上

自己，实现了"名利双收"。这是现代的文艺复兴人物在他的创作巅峰面向大众进行的自我营销。

Then the local Italian police, white helmets, light blue uniforms, my dream mind already anticipating the next familiar scene, as though I were watching a favorite old movie. The view from above and to the side, the 'white hats' frantic, pushing through the crowd, calling to Jackson, pleading, coaxing the famous man to please come down. Then it starts, the final scene, Jackson playing with the crowd, walking, balancing, teetering, comically on one leg, then the other … then, it happens, he falls. Slow motion, 'train wreck'. Each time, even for me, hard to believe, it's happening, again. The long lanky body piercing the water's surface, head long, disappearing, inch by terrible inch, an artistic canvas, two-dimensional abstraction, submerging, into the dank green of the Arno River. Jackson, gone, never seen again.

接下来，戴着白帽子、穿着浅蓝色制服的意大利警察出场了。我脑海里已经预见到下一个熟悉的场景，就像在看一部我喜欢的老电影一样。从俯瞰和平视的角度，我看到"大白帽"着急忙慌地推开人群，一边大叫杰克逊，连求带哄地请这位著名人物从墙上下来。最后一幕开始了：杰克逊挑逗着人群，在墙头走动，耍平衡，左摇右晃，他还两腿轮流玩起了金鸡独立…… 之后就发生了那事。他掉下去了。慢动作。即使我看了无数次，每一次重看仍然很难相信。他那具颀长的身躯刺破水面，一头扎进去，一寸一寸地消失不见，就像一幅平面抽象画，沉没在阿尔诺河浊绿的水中。杰克逊消失了，从此不再露面。

Tumult! Dream—view switching again. Speeding up. Screams, searching, dragging the shallows, divers, witnesses. Talk about 'going viral'! The world is transfixed, beyond popular culture, everyone, everywhere, 'twenty-four-seven'. Full-press coverage, investigation, speculation, outrage; the obsessive reportage itself is covered as a major story. Where is he? How is it possible that one of the most famous men in the world could completely disappear, without a trace, in front of everyone, in the crowded middle of Florence, Italy, and off the Ponte Vecchio? "Not possible, yet it happened." The closing words of one commentator, signing off from the scene, his own body leaning precariously over the exact place on the low wall, at the center of the bridge, where Jackson's body fell off, over, in.

Ponte Vecchio, Florence, Italy—'Jackson Bartholomew's Fall'
意大利佛罗伦萨维琪奥桥——"杰克逊·巴塞洛缪的坠落"

骚乱！梦境又变了。快进。尖叫，搜寻，浅滩拖捞，潜水打捞，询问目击者。还担心火不起来。全世界都惊呆了，这事儿超出了流行文化范畴，每个人，每个地方，7天24小时。媒体全方位报道、调查、猜测、愤怒。对这事没完没了的报道本身都成了新闻故事。他在哪？！全球最有名的人物之一，就这样在意大利佛罗伦萨人头攒动的维琪奥桥上一跃而下，在世人眼皮底下完全消失无踪，这怎么可能？"不可能，但这事儿就发生了。"记者以危险的姿势靠在桥中央的那堵矮墙上，就在杰克逊跌落水中的那个位置，以这句话结束了现场报道。

Then, warm, moist, soft. Grey. Dream faded. Something pulling me, away from the center, to the dream's edges. I felt it, twice, at the same time, within the dream, and without. Dreams contained 'duality', something viewed caused by an external action in the 'real world', or the reverse. For years I'd practiced, within dreams, on the edges of them, from different angles, perspectives, until I had the ability of self-awareness, to know what was happening while in the midst of a dream. That's the ultimate, to understand while it happens, then to react, control it, orchestrate. In that 'duality', the feeling came on again, someone's flesh, originating from outside, irritating, suctioning, rhythmic. On the dream side, it became someone standing behind me, a woman, watching, with me, as I watched the scene on the bridge. Dark hair. Not Havanna. Her quiet, Italian. A playing at my neck, the same spot. I struggled to ignore it, needing to concentrate, to decipher the crazy panic of the people gathered. I managed to change perspectives, move my viewpoint, this time from within the thick crowd, looking out. I wanted detail, something hidden inside the larger images.

之后，温暖，湿润，柔软。像灰色一样，梦境消散了。有东西将我从梦境中央拉扯到边缘。我同时可以感受到梦境内外的两种状态。梦有"双重属性"，在梦中看到的可能是外部"真实世界"的行动的结果，但也可能相反。我已经练习多年，在梦中，在梦的边缘，从不同的角度、不同的层面解读，直到我拥有自我觉知的能力，即使在梦的中央我也能知道发生了什么事。事件发生的时候能够准确觉知，其后采取行动应对，对其加以控制和调动，这是最高段位。在"双重性"里，这种感觉又来了，某人的身体，来自外界，烦人且有节奏地要将我拽出去。在梦境这一侧，仿佛有一个人站在我身后，这是一个女人，跟我一起观看桥上的这一切。这不是哈瓦娜。她很安静，深色头发，是个意大利人。有人在逗弄我脖子的那个部位。我极力排除这个干扰，我需要专注，解析喧嚣疯狂的人群。我更换了视角，将视线从拥挤的人群中看出去。我需要细节，

Man Underwater—Samuel's Dream Sequence
水中的男子——塞缪尔的梦境系列

那些隐藏在大幅图景中的东西。

There it was, again, a man's hand, underwater, palm up, clinching, river bottom silt bleeding through fingers. Streams of sunlight playing, dancing, illuminating particles. Small objects, perhaps gold or silver, metallic, tumbling, turning, delightful, like shinny pieces of confetti falling, in slow motion. Then something behind me, to one side, distracting. The feeling on my neck again, pleasurable, taking me away, out. Havanna, fingers digging in, her thighs pressed against my ribs, hard, ruthless, restricting. Pressure, then more, too much.

它又出现了。在水下，这是一个男人的手，掌心朝上，拳头紧握，河泥从指缝中漏出。几缕阳光透下来，跳跃着，照亮了水中的微粒。细小的颗粒焕发出金色、银色金属光泽，翻滚旋转，十分喜庆，仿佛慢放的闪闪发亮的节庆彩纸。突然我身后有事物分散了我的注意力。又是脖子上那个部位，愉悦的感觉将我拉了出来。哈瓦娜的手指捏着我，大腿死死地顶着我的肋骨，让我动弹不得。好疼，又来了，受不了了。

"Damn! I'm out." I shot a hand back, behind, under her, between her legs. Fully out! Dream lost, beyond grey. My breathing restricted, something at my neck, the quick way to end a dream-half-dream. Wish I'd never told her that.

"该死！我出来了。"我伸手朝后打她屁股。完全出来了！梦境遗失在灰色地带。脖子受制，呼吸受限，这是快速结束我半梦境的方法。当初真不该告诉她这窍门。

"Havanna! What in the hell are you doing?" I said, rubbing at the soft skin just below my ear, the spot still wet from her mouth. "I was in the middle of it, the dream. You know it's important to me."

"哈瓦娜！你搞什么鬼啊？！"我揉着耳朵下面那个地方，她湿润的吻痕还印在上面。"我正在那个梦境中央。你知道这对我有多重要。"

"Oh? Sorry. Don't mind me, I was ... just a little, how do you say, making some 'Bruise Art'." she said, pulling back onto her haunches, a seated position on my back, the way you sit astride an animal about to buck.

"哦？抱歉啦，别理我，我只是在做那个，叫什么来着，'瘀伤艺术'而已。"她说着直起腰背，跨坐在我背上，就像跨骑在一只准备跳起来的动物背上一样。

"What? Come on now." I stretched to the small hand mirror on the side table. "My god! That's a full—on hickey. What's wrong with you?" I said, on my stomach, still with hopes of getting back in, another try at the sequence, the man in the water.

"什么？别闹。"我伸手拿床头柜上的手持镜。"上帝！这绝对是一块瘀伤。你有毛病吧？"我继续趴着，希望重回梦境，顺藤摸瓜，找那个水中的男子。

"I don't understand. What's the problem?" she shrugged. "I like them. They're erotic."

"搞不懂你，怎么了吗？"她耸耸肩，"我喜欢，很色情啊。"

"A bruise on the skin, maybe, depends, but on you ... not high on my

Havanna
哈瓦娜

neck! Damn it Havanna. Everyone'll see it. What about your parents? For God's sake!"

"皮肤上有吻痕也许很诱惑，但因人而异，比如说在你身上，而不是在我脖子上！该死，哈瓦娜，这下每个人都能看见。你父母会怎么想？我的天啊！"

"You know?" she said calmly, "you haven't been paying me enough attention lately. I'm not talking about sex. You got to get your mind right, Gringo. My parents are coming. Do you hear me? Hey, dream boy? My parents."

"你知道吗？"她平静地说，"你最近心思都没在我身上。我不是说感情。你得保持头脑清醒，美国佬。我父母要来了，做梦男孩听到了吗？我的父母要来了。"

"What does that have to do with this?" I felt at the slight raise, the welt on my neck.

"这两件事有什么关系啊？"我摸着脖子上轻微隆起的吻痕。

"It's my mark. You're mine, for the next two days, as long as it lasts, as long as my parents are here. You promised, and now you're not cooperating."

"那是我的标记。在接下来的两天里，只要它还能保持，只要我父母还在这里，你就是我的。你保证过，现在却一点也不配合。"

"You're crazy."

"你个疯子。"

"Just think of it as a part of your thesis project, you know, 'Bruise Art', Jackson Bartholomew, all that."

"你就把它当成论文的一部分好了，'瘀伤艺术'，杰克逊·巴塞洛缪那一套。"

"Cute. Wrong kind of bruise, by the way." I pushed up, twisting my body to face her, muscled legs resisting, the pressure grabbing at my ribs. "Damn, that hurts you know. And this, how am I going to cover it up?"

"真机灵。可惜你这瘀伤是错的那种。"我挺起身，转过来面对着她，她大腿抗拒着，把我的肋骨顶得更紧。"疼死了你知道吗？还有这个，我可怎么遮起来啊？"

"Don't know, but you're going to take a break, today and tomorrow. No more Jackson, bridges in Italy, visions, dreams. Time to get up. There's a lot to do."

"不知道，不过你今明两天要放下这些。不要去想什么杰克逊，意大利的桥，幻觉，梦境。起来了，还有好多事要做。"

"I don't like it when you order me around. You're so Latina. This isn't Cuba." I said, pulling the sheet over my head.

"我不喜欢你支使得我团团转。你真够拉丁范儿的。这儿可不是古巴。"我把被子拉起来盖住头。

"Oh, racist, and sexist, at the same time, with a bad accent! And first thing in the morning? Are you kidding me right now? Come on, let's get going, zou ba, vamos!" she said, sliding in and out of the three-language game. "My parents will be here in the morning. Tomorrow morning! You can wear the shirt with the high collar I bought you."

"噢，种族歧视、性别歧视，你都占了，口音还那么难听！一大早就来这个？你在逗我玩吗？来吧，我们得走了，走吧，快走！"（原文分别用英语、中文和西班牙语表达——译者注）她又开始玩三门语言转换的把戏了。"我父母一大早就到了，明天早上！你可以穿我给你买的那件领子很高的衬衫。"

Her long black hair tickled my shoulders as she leaned forward, kissing my neck softly, then sucking hard, quick.

她俯下身体，黑色长发扫得我肩膀发痒，轻轻吻我的脖子，突然快速用力地嘬吮。

"Don't do that! I'm warning you!" I said, pushing her away, but not off, the pleasure of her setting in, picturing her ... with me.

"别这样！我警告你啊！"我把她推开，但不是推下去，脑子里浮现出她坐在我身上的画面，着实美妙。

"Come on, sweet Samuel ...

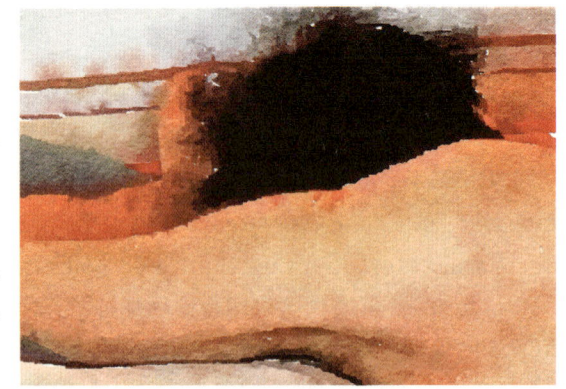

Samuel on Pillow (Adaptation in Watercolor)
塞缪尔趴在枕头上（水彩处理）

'first king of Israel'. It's a fine summer day in the land of Hollywood, but you still have classes to go to today. I want everything perfect, before they get here. No procrastinating."

"来嘛,甜蜜的塞缪尔,'以色列第一个王'。今天是好莱坞一个美好的夏日,但你还得去上课。我希望他们到达之前一切都准备完美。不要拖拖拉拉。"

"May the Songs of Solomon play upon your ears, the wisdom of the ages fill you to overflowing ... and it was Saul, not Samuel."

"愿雅歌奏响于你耳际,岁月的智慧令你心灵充盈满溢……而且那是扫罗,不是塞缪尔。"

"Oh my God, where did that come from?" she said, pulling the sheet from my grip. *"The Bible?"*

"天哪,那是从哪来的?"她把被子从我手中扯下来,"《圣经》吗?"

"It's from the novel, Jackson's *ode to Moriah* ... of course."

"当然是杰克逊的小说啦……《莫立娅颂歌》。"

"Should've guessed." she said, her lips curling up at the edges. The most delightful expression. No resisting it. You had to forgive her everything. Havanna, Cuban father, Mexican mother, equal portions, Spaniard and Aztec. That 'conquistador combination' a specific genre of female beauty: Tall, sharp-edged European face and body combined with soft, filled-out curves of the indigenous. Her name perfect, 'Havanna' something longed-for, missing, not quite attainable, Taino people, 'ago', passed. Her hair lay jet, in soft waves about and over her shoulders, longer than most women's these days, some of the strands making their way down to the small of her back, just at the point where her waist expanded into two smooth rounds. Her skin shown young, peached, her father's bloodline come down from the Pyrenees. Eyes wide, spherical, soft. She knew her beauty, an entitlement long since internalized. She'd drop her chin, open her eyes wide, speak in quick flashes of island Spanish. Beautiful. Ruthless.

"早该猜到了。"她说着,嘴角上翘,这愉悦的表情,令人难以抗拒。她做什么你都会原谅。哈瓦娜,古巴父亲,墨西哥母亲,拉丁和阿兹特克血统的均衡结晶。她是"征服者集合体",是女性美貌的独特类别,她那棱角分明的欧罗巴脸庞和高挑身材,混合了当地人柔润丰满的曲线。她的名字"哈瓦娜"(古巴首都哈瓦那——译者注)完美诠释了那种令人渴望却遗失无踪的东西,遍寻不得,泰诺人,从前的,逝去的,种种。她乌黑的长发披散在肩头,比时下女性流行的长度还要长,几缕发丝从背上垂下,恰好及腰。蜜桃色的肌肤闪耀青春光泽,显示出她父亲的血统是从比利牛斯山脉延续下来的。她温柔的双眼又大又圆。她对自己的美貌心知肚明,那仿佛与生俱来的特权。她会压低下巴,抬起双眼,语速很快地讲西班牙语,美艳又无情。

"Stop!" I said, pushing her up enough to slip my arm further under, then the other, my forearms and palms holding her bottom. Leveraging her head down, her head hitting hard; An odd thud sound, forehead hitting.

"打住!"我把她推起来,胳膊和手掌伸到她臀下,把她放倒。她前额重重地砸到枕头上,砰的一声。

"Oww! Idiota! Ni sha!" she said, the sweep of her hair engulfing us. "That hurts!" She shouted into my ear, then went for the mark on my neck.

"哎哟!笨蛋!你傻啊!"她甩头,浓密的长发将我俩包围。"好疼!"她冲我耳朵吼,又埋头去嘬我脖子上那个印迹。

"My ear for heaven's sake? Don't do that!"

"我耳朵聋了!拜托!别这样!"

"Why not? I own you." She had a hand on each of mine, pressing them back against the bed above my head. Her lips lowered on mine in a full kiss, confident, a young woman knowing her beauty, using it. I pulled her in with my leg, down, our bodies aligned. She could feel me, arousal, her skin moistening at my forearm.

"怎么不行?你是我的。"她双手分别按住我的双手,死死摁在枕头边,俯下头给了我深深一吻。一个年轻女人,对自己的美貌充满自信,并且知道怎么使用这个武器。我用双腿夹住她,身体缠绕在一起。她能感到我的兴奋,我能感到前臂环拥下她肌肤的湿润。

"I had the dream again ... Jackson, in Florence." I said, holding her mouth almost on mine, a hand behind her head. "I needed it, that last piece, to see it.

You interrupted."

"我又做那个梦了,杰克逊在佛罗伦萨。"我一手托着她的后脑勺,她的双唇几乎跟我的贴在一起。"我需要最后一个碎片,要看清它。你打断了我。"

"Damn! Okay ... You're going to go there? Have it your way. Get up! Come on, get up." she said, pushing back, angry. "We've got to get going. Everything's got to be perfect today, especially for my father." Using my body and the bed as springboard she bounced, upward and back, athletic, landing lithe, atop a pile of quilts ... exotic, Havanna.

"该死!好吧,你还要做梦吗?悉听尊便。起床了!来吧,起来。"她生气了,抬起身来。"我们该出发了。今天一切都要完美,尤其是对我老爸来说。"她拿我的身体和床当跳板反弹坐起,动作轻盈矫健地坐在被子堆上。哈瓦娜风情万种。

"Yeah, I remember, your father, the guy that suggested you dump me. How did he put it? 'Why will I ever buy the cow when I can get the milk for free?' How dare he compare his daughter to a cow!"

"啊,我想起来了,你那位劝你把我甩掉的父亲大人。他怎么说来着?'我不花钱也能喝到牛奶,干吗还要买那头奶牛?'他怎么能把自己的女儿比作一头奶牛?"

"No, the 'milk' is the point. He was right. You're very lucky to have gotten any at all." She slapped my legs with double rapid motions, like a massage therapist finishing in a flurry. "Get up."

"不对,'牛奶'才是重点。他说得没错。你能喝到牛奶,应该说非常万幸。"她快速拍打我的大腿,就像按摩师最后结束时的手法。"快起来。"

"Okay, but first ..." I held her at the ankle, pulling, playful.

"好吧,不过首先……"我抓住她的脚踝,戏谑地轻轻拉扯。

"Calm yourself. We don't have time, not now." she said, still pausing to brush her toes over my groin. "Come on Gringo, get up. Your damn thesis class is this morning, water polo practice after that. Then, back here boy, to do everything."

"你冷静一点。我们现在可没时间。"她说着,还一直用脚指头碰我的大腿。"起来了,美国佬。你那该死的论文课不是今天早上吗?然后还有水球训练。记得回来把所有活儿都干了。"

"Everything?" I said, mocking, trying to hold on to the long leg.
"所有吗？"我逗她，去抓她的大长腿。

She leaned forward, bending it, letting me pull her in, just enough to gain leverage, then push back hard, burst of air forced from my lungs. The cast-iron head frame banged violently on the wall behind me.
她任由我把她拉向前，俯身压腿，刚好够保持平衡。然后她突然推开我起身，我长呼一口气，身后的铁架床头撞到墙上砰然巨响。

"Hey, we have neighbors." she complained.
"嘿，咱们可有邻居。"她抱怨道。

Havanna turned the lamp to its brightest, pulled on my t-shirt, the 'UCLA' rippling over her breasts, skin glimmered in even shades of tan, natural, nubile. She'd stood out her whole life, midnight eyes, lips turned up just before each smile. She knew instinctively when it was that I focused on her, looked at her, acknowledged her beauty.
哈瓦娜将台灯调到最亮，她套上我的T恤，UCLA（加州大学洛杉矶分校的英文缩写——译者注）四个字母在她胸前起伏，肌肤闪耀着古铜色、自然、性感且匀称有光泽。她永远出类拔萃，眼神如夜色深邃，双唇在微笑前总是噘起。她本能地知道我关注她哪个地方，眼睛看向哪里，我欣赏她的美貌。

"Okay ... I'm up, Cuban princess."
"好吧，我起来了，古巴公主。"

"No 'princesses' in the people's Cuba." she said.
"人民的古巴没有公主。"她说。

"Well, I mean before the Castros, or maybe after; either way."
"呃，我的意思是卡斯特罗以前，或者之后都行。"

"Get up, zou ba, andiamo!" She pulled the curtains back from the French doors, allowing the milky LA light to flow in, her slender form pausing, displaying, silhouetted under the thin cotton fabric of my shirt.

"起来,走吧,我们走!"(原文分别是英语、中文和意大利语——译者注)她把法式门上悬挂的窗帘拉开,洛杉矶乳白色的阳光洒进来,她苗条的身材在薄棉T恤里一览无余。

"Your Chinese is getting better. You and your language game." I said, mocking.

"你的中文越说越好了。你和你的语言游戏。"我逗她。

"Mandarin. You've got to be kidding me. No one could be more obsessive than you. I'll be glad when it's over ... the Jackson thing. You'll finally be able to move on, do something else."

"是普通话。你就逗我开心吧。没有比你更执迷的人了。那个杰克逊的破事儿什么时候了结了我就开心了。那样你才能往前走,做点别的。"

Havanna's apartment near UCLA—Westwood, CA
哈瓦娜在UCLA附近的公寓——加州威斯特伍德

"He's the perfect subject for me. You've got to admit. The novel, film development, manipulation of popular culture, the dream sequences, even the themes of 'rebirth'. Then the pure success of it all. Nothing like it, before ... or since. That's what I want to be, do."

"他对我来说是个再完美不过的题材。你得承认这一点。小说、电影、被操纵的流行文化、梦的序列，甚至是'重生'这个主题。然后这一切都成功了……没有什么比得上这个，以前没有，之后也没有。这才是我想成为的，我想做的。"

"Come on, let's go. Your thesis will explain it all, someday. Right now, we got stuff to take care of, before they get here."

"来吧，咱们走。总有一天你的论文会解释一切。而眼下，在他们到来之前，我们有很多东西需要搞定。"

I was obsessed. The right word for it. What else could I be, should I be? I'd totally immersed myself in him, his novel, designs, projects. It wasn't just my obsession. The rest of popular culture had it as well. Every generation has something, someone, that catches fire, takes their imagination. In the era of social media, Internet, instant communication, it all could be amplified, sped up, to make it possible, that a single person could be so quickly famous in every corner of the world, at one time, from nowhere to everywhere. There had to be a 'hook' though, some special thing to catch the mind, bend it toward that 'thing', that person, some bit of 'magic' to take you in, convert you to its cult. That was true in every new religion, movement, all the more in our world so dominated by the 'popular'. Jackson had managed to create several of them, several 'hooks', all working together at the same time, to reel you in.

我是着迷了。这个词很贴切。除此之外我还可能是什么，还应该是什么？我已经完完全全沉浸在他这个人物里面了，包括他的小说、设计、项目。我有我的执迷，其他的流行文化也是如此。每一代人中都有一些事情或人物蹿红，激起大众的想象。在社交媒体、互联网、实时通信时代，这一切会被放大、加速，一个人有可能瞬间从籍籍无名变得世人皆知。当然，这需要有一个"诱饵"，靠某种特殊的东西来抓住人们的思想，将他们引向那个事物、那个人物，这就需要一点点"魔法"来勾住你，使你变得对此狂热和崇拜。每一种新宗教、新运动皆是如此，在"流行"统率一切的当下更是如此。杰克逊已经成功地创造了一些"诱饵"，它们共同发力，把你拉进去。

Even so, Jackson Bartholomew had a love-hate relationship with the popular culture, the 'someone' that created him. On one hand he played them all: Internet, social media, LA, California, the new rich. On the other, he wanted his work to be taken seriously, especially the writing. He had no less ambition than to have his single work of fiction, his novel-memoir, on the list of 'Great American Novels'.

即便如此，杰克逊·巴塞洛缪与成就了他这个"人物"的流行文化，也存在一种爱恨交织的关系。一方面，他是互联网、社交媒体、洛杉矶、加州新贵中的一分子；另一方面，他希望自己的作品能够被当成严肃作品来看待，尤其是其写作的部分。他最大的野心就是自己唯一的虚构类作品——他的小说能够进入"伟大的美国小说"的行列。

Very hard to put your finger on it, analyze it, put down on paper some equation that explained how to get there, to that 'Bartholomew' level of success. Fortune, happenstance? "Pure extract of luck." Jackson called it. Nothing like that could happen without it, the creation of a new genre, and simultaneous dominance of the old, it all injected into the heart of popular culture, in America, China, worldwide. He 'caught a wave', rode it all the way in.

想要弄清、分析"巴塞洛缪式"的成功模式和道路并且付诸文字，那可是大费周章的事。幸运，还是偶然？"纯属运气。"杰克逊这么说。没有运气是不可能打造出这样的新流派，完全压倒旧传统，灌注到全球流行文化的内核。他"抓住浪头"，一路冲了下去。

Then, he was just gone. One day, gone. Missing, like the person in the magical box after the magician waives a wand. Theatrical location, the Ponte Vecchio, center of Florence. It seemed staged, had to be. He tittered, tottered, fell back, off the edge. Plenty of video of it, everyone watching, him standing on the ancient stone wall, just behind the bust of Benvenuto Cellini. (Appropriate it be Benvenuto, himself a bigger than life Renaissance character, writer of his own memoir, self-created popular culture figure within his time, mercurial phenomenon.) Someone said they'd seen a flash from the far bank just before Jackson fell. No telling anything for sure, with no body recovered. One moment, in the middle of one of the most celebrated public spots in the world, his own event, mid-day, then, 'disappeared', everyone left to gawk in the naked sunlight, more police arriving, searching, dramatic dragging of the river bottom. Tires and shoes coming up, shards from broken pottery, keys, thousands, all sorts of little keys from the endless supply of lovelocks place on the metal fence surround at the Benedetto bust; But no Jackson, not a sign of him, nothing.

然后，他突然消失了。就一天，就消失了。仿佛魔法师挥一挥魔法棒，盒子里的人就消失不见了。佛罗伦萨市中心的维琪奥桥，多么戏剧性的地点。一切像是策划好的，一定是。他摇摇晃晃，跟跟跄跄，从桥上摔下。大量的视频显示，所有人都看着他站在古老的石墙上，就在本韦努托·切利尼胸像之后（本韦努托·切利尼真是太搭了。这位文艺复兴时期的著名人物也写自传，将自己打造成当时年代的流行文化人物，多么变幻多端）。有人说在杰克逊落水前，看到远处河岸有一道闪光。当然这并不说明什么，因为没有找到尸体。在一个全世界最知名的公共场所的中心，他自己操办活动，在光天化日之下瞬间"消失"，所有人目瞪口呆，一拨又一拨警察前来开展搜寻工作，夸张地撒网式搜索河床。捞上来的都是轮胎、鞋子、陶瓷碎片、钥匙，成千上万各式各样的小钥匙，桥边金属围栏上拴着的密密麻麻的爱之锁。就是没有杰克逊，一丝痕迹都没有。

Just not right. Couldn't be like that. Had to be another explanation, something everyone's missing. Odd, no body, so quickly. The Italian courts investigated, ruled it suicide. A full commission report, hundreds of pages. When something like that happens, the public doesn't accept it, can't afford to. Think Monroe, Kennedys, Michael Jackson, Elvis Presley. They're just too big, too important, too famous, over popular, too central to their lives, to be dead without a good explanation, without some greater reason than 'random'.

这不对劲。不应该是这样的。一定有另外一种解释，所有人都漏掉的线索。很奇怪，没有尸体，一切太快了。意大利司法部门进行了调查，认定是自杀，还出了一份上百页的警方调查报告。公众对这类结果并不买账。想想梦露、肯尼迪家族、迈克尔·杰克逊、猫王。他们都太大牌、太知名、太耀眼、太流行，太以他们的自我为中心了，他们的死也需要一个好理由，需要某个比"偶然"更站得住脚的理由。

"Are you dressed yet?" Havanna shouted from the bathroom.
"你穿好衣服了吗？"哈瓦娜在浴室里喊。

"Sure babe. Just waiting for you. Got to shave." I said, pulling on some shorts, up to the door, easing the crack open.

"当然，宝贝儿。等着你呢，我得刮脸。"我边说边穿上短裤，走到门边，轻轻拉开一条缝。

"Ah yes, the water polo body." She let her finger linger across my chest. "Look, I understand about your project. You've got to finish it. Almost done, right? At some point you've got to let it go though. It can't be everything, all the time. You got to move on. Just saying."

"啊，水球运动员的身材。"她用手指缓缓划过我的前胸。"听着，我知道你得完成这个项目。快完成了，不是吗？不过，到了某个节点你得放下。它不能时时刻刻占据你的所有。你得向前看。我就是说说。"

As the words left her lips I felt it, familiar now, a stopping, sinking, as though my chest suddenly emptied, contracted. My heart missed, there again, not doubting it, first one beat, then several, then more. I leaned over, breathed deep, coughed hard, hit myself with my own clinched fist, shock. It helped. Did it again. Started back then, the beats thick at first, then lighter, the feeling receding, disappearing.

她话音未落，它又来了，那熟悉的感觉，突然停顿、下沉，好像我的胸腔瞬间被掏空、收紧。我的心跳消失，又回来了，毫无疑问，开始一下，然后几下，之后更多下。我身体前倾，深呼吸，用力咳嗽，握拳捶打胸口。起作用了，再来一次。心脏仿佛重启了，一开始跳得很密集，之后慢下来，这感觉慢慢退散，直至消失。

"Damn, what the hell was that?" Havanna demanded, her eyes intense, demanding.

"见鬼，那是怎么回事？"哈瓦娜两眼紧盯着追问。

"Like before. Worse this time." I said, still bent over, checking pulse on my neck.

"之前的老问题，这回更糟糕。"我还弯着腰，手指按在颈上检查脉搏。

"What're you talking about, 'before'?"
"你说什么，'之前'？"

"It's happened a few times. I told you about it. Not this bad." I said, hitting myself in the chest.

"发生过几次。我跟你说过的啊。但是没这么糟。"我边说边捶着胸脯。

"Don't pound yourself like that." she said, checking my chest, then my neck for pulse, just above the bruise mark she'd made earlier. "A heart problem, at twenty—five?"

"别这么捶自己。"她检查了一下我的胸部,又探了探颈上的脉搏,就在她嘬出瘀青印的地方上去一点。"25岁就出现心脏问题?"

"Defective material." I said, faking a joke. "It's not really a heart problem. Something with the nervous system. Vagus nerve, I think. It can be fixed easy enough. Laser. In through the arteries, a couple of zaps and its done. Quick, a 'procedure'."

"零件有毛病了。"我假装开玩笑,"并不是心脏真的有问题,是神经系统问题。迷走神经,我觉得是。治疗很简单啦,激光什么的。从动脉穿过去,滋滋弄几下就完事了。快得很,就是走流程。"

"Well, get it done man, right away. I don't want you checking out when you're with me. You know, those old guys that die in the middle of sex, the police showing up, the woman trapped underneath."

"那就快点去做吧,哥们儿。我可不希望你跟我亲热的时候挂掉。你知道吗?有些老头子亲热到一半死了,警察来了,女人还压在下面呢。"

"You're so worried about me."
"你可真够关心我的。"

"Why didn't you tell me about it?"
"你以前为什么不告诉我?"

"I did, just not completely. That's exactly why. I knew you'd either overreact or not care at all. Somehow, you managed to do both."

"我说了,只是没说全而已。这就是原因。我就知道你要么反应过度,要么一点儿不在乎。没想到你某种程度上两头都占了。"

"Are you going to be okay while my parents are here?!"
"我父母在这儿的时候你不会有事吧？！"

"It's okay. I'm sure I'll get through the weekend." I said, not daring to mention that Jackson Bartholomew had a similar affliction.
"没事的。我保证能活过这个周末。"我没敢提杰克逊·巴塞洛缪也有类似的症状。

"Are you sure? No kidding around. I really do care about you. You know that. What about when you out surfing? If that happened out there... "
"你确定？别跟我开玩笑啊。我真的很在乎你。你知道的。那你冲浪的时候呢？如果冲浪的时候你出那样的状况……"

"No, never does. Not sure why. Maybe the cold from the ocean."
"不会的，永远不会。说不上来为什么，也许是海水太冷。"

"Well, get it checked." she said, shaking her head, big sister.
"好吧，去检查。"她摇着头说，像个大姐姐似的。

When I finished in the bath, she was standing at opened French doors, at the balcony, looking east, to the bright white spire of the old Fox Theatre. Her profiled, beautiful, soft silhouette, perfected within the stream of LA light, film-like, as though a scene from one of those exquisite black and whites, early thirties.
我洗漱完毕出来，她站在法式门外的阳台上，望向东边福克斯剧场白得发亮的尖顶。洛杉矶的阳光将她的轮廓勾勒得完美柔和，仿佛20世纪30年代那细腻的黑白电影中的一幕。

"Someday you'll be in a movie." I said, coming up behind her. "I'll escort you to the opening. It'll happen for you. You'll be a great actress. Right there, at that theatre."
"你总有一天会演电影的。"我走到她身后说，"我要护送你去首映式。它专门为你开幕。你会成为一位伟大的演员。就在那边，在那个剧院。"

"You really think so?"

"你真的这么想?"

"Your movie opening should be at the 'Fox', all that history, Audrey Hepburn, Marilyn Monroe, and you seeing it every day, from here. Just a matter of time, it'll be 'Havanna'. No need for a last name. Everyone'll know you." I knew she loved to hear that, to imagine herself famous, rich, the center of it all, a 'one name star'.

"你的电影首映礼就应该在'福克斯',你每天从这里都能看见,过去是奥黛丽·赫本、玛丽莲·梦露,有一天将会是'哈瓦娜',只是时间问题。不需要冠父姓。所有人都知道你。"我知道她爱听这个,想象自己成名、变富,更重要的是她是一位"明星"。

Fox Theatre—Westwood, CA
福克斯剧场——加州韦斯特伍德

"I'm already twenty." she said, feigning, pulling me to say more.
"我都 20 岁了。"她装模作样地说,引诱我再说点漂亮话。

"You'll be the new, 'it girl'. Maybe one of the women in Jackson's novel, turned movie."
"你将会成为新的'那个女孩'。也许是杰克逊小说改编成电影里的那个女人。"

"God! Jackson? Again? Always Jackson. What makes you think his book will ever be a film?"
"老天!杰克逊?又来了,总是杰克逊。你凭什么认为他的书会拍成电影?"

"He would have made it happen, if he'd lived. He almost got it there. Talk about going viral, millions of hits, all media, all the time, that first week after he disappeared. A lot of people believed there was already a movie, the thing in Florence a part of a plan, him staging it. Either way, in one pop-culture manipulation, he re-marketed his book, to continue as a best seller, to be considered the 'Great American Novel' for heaven's sake, and, set up expectations for a film. Genius. Reportedly, he'd already planned another big 'scene' ... Moriah, in evening gown, his J.B. designs, a massive flash-crowd produced in hundreds by app; him in Armani, taking her arm, limo, red carpet. Iconic. Fake, yeah. Movie inside itself, performance art, for a specific effect. He designed everything, after all."

"他会拍成电影的,如果他活着的话。他几乎已经成功了。想想他失踪后一周的流量,上百万点击、全媒体、全时段。许多人没准儿相信电影已经在拍了,在佛罗伦萨那一幕就是计划的一部分,由他自己出演。不管怎样,作为流行文化的一记推手,他把自己的书又推广了一波,使之持续畅销,而且看在老天的分上,还成了'伟大的美国小说',同时,推高了人们对电影的期待值。真是天才。据说他本来在计划另一个'大场面'……通过 APP 招募组织几百位粉丝搞个大型快闪活动,莫立娅穿着他设计的 J.B. 牌晚礼服,而他本人穿着阿玛尼,挽着她步出豪华车走上红毯。太典型了,太能装了。这本身就是演戏,是为了某种特殊效果的表演。说到底,他的所有行为都是策划好的。"

"How long does it take to have a novel become a film?" she asked, moving the subject back to her, dark eyes fixed on the theatre spire a block away. "You'd have to dress the part. If you're going on the red carpet with me. No jacket and jeans. Gucci maybe."

"把一部小说拍成电影需要多长时间？"她把话题拉回到自己身上，黑眼睛盯着一个街区之外的剧院尖顶。"你得穿得像样点，如果你要送我走红毯，可不能穿夹克、牛仔裤。穿古驰还差不多。"

"I like them, but too much, color splashed everywhere." I nuzzled into the thick hair at her neck.

"我喜欢古驰，但有点过，花里胡哨的。"我把鼻子埋在她颈后的浓密头发里。

"You can start now, by upgrading your look, including today. Get something better than that on." she said, tugging playfully at my shorts. "And wear the necklace I got you in Taxco."

"你现在就可以开始升级改造自己的形象了，从今天开始。换件比这好点的衣服，"她戏弄地扯了扯我的短裤，"戴上我在达斯科给你买的项链。"

"You sure It'll go with my ensemble?" I asked.

"你确定项链跟我的着装搭吗？"我问道。

"People'll notice you more, I guarantee it. That's the most important thing. Count how many times it happens. You'll see."

"你会更引人注目的，我保证。那才是最重要的。你看看回头率就知道了。"

"You know I clean up well. I can be that person, the Ryan Gosling kind of thing." I said, pulling the necklace off the bedside table, laying it over my head to let it fall down onto my chest. "Don't worry about tomorrow. It'll all go great. I promise, everything done, everything. You know me, even if I put things off, in the end, I do what I need to, what has to be done."

"你知道我捯饬一下还是不错的。我能成为瑞安·戈斯林（美国著名电影演员——译者注）那样的型男。"我说着，从床头柜上取下项链挂在胸前。"别担心明天。会很棒的，我保证，所有事情都会办得好好的，所有一切都没有问题。你了解我的，即使拖拖拉拉，我最终总能完成该做的事。"

"You better, or you'll be in deep mierda, shit, gou shi." she said, pushing back into me, forcing me to prop her up. "You don't want to see me when I'm mad."

"你最好把事情办好,否则就是臭狗屎(原文分别用中文、英语、西班牙语表达——译者注),"她往后倒入我怀里,我把她搂住,"你可不想看见我生气的样子。"

"Is that a line from a movie? You're right about that. I don't want to stereotype here, but, man, what a Latina."

"那是电影台词吗?你说得没错。我对此没有成见,可是天啊,你可真是不折不扣的拉丁范儿。"

She turned her head, presenting her neck, offering it up for my kiss. "You better put on a robe. That could get you arrested." she said, feeling me, behind her.

她扭头露出脖子让我亲吻。"你最好披上睡袍。那样可能会被捕的。"她能感觉到我在她身后。

"You too. That guy down there is looking."

"你也一样。楼下这家伙盯着看呢。"

"At me? Are you sure? Maybe he's checking you out." she said, waving down at him, letting her robe open, laughing, pulling at me with the other hand, trying to show me off.

"是看我吗?你确定?说不定他在盯着看你呢。"她说着朝那人挥手,大笑着任由睡袍敞开,另一只手拽着我,对他显摆起来。

I remember that singular moment, the kind that grows in your mind, comes to symbolize a person, your time with them. We were unaware, everything before us, things in place, her parents on the way. The light hit just right, warm, milky. Us playful, happy, relevant. 'The pleasure of not knowing', Jackson called it. Los Angeles provides a lot of those moments. That was ours.

我记得那个特别的时刻,那种铭刻在你脑海的片段。你跟那个人在一起的时光,都变成那个人的符号。对即将到来的一切,我们毫不知情,万物安好,她父母在路上。阳光正好,温暖、和煦。我们嬉闹、快乐、活在当下。杰克逊将其称为"不谙世事的快乐"。在洛杉矶拥有许多这样的时刻,那是我们的时光。

The LA morning light, desert sand in the air mixing with sea fog, eastern light from over the mountain ridges; That exact combination, geographic, atmospheric recipe, provides the flat of land between the surround of mountains and the Pacific an endless cinematic milky haze, dreamy charm filtering everything through the prism of old Hollywood. If you think about it that way, everything becomes connected under its cinematic production palette, everyone in the city a part of the film process, extras to the stars, those present, those fading. Havanna and I were a part of it, even if just 'wannabes'.

在洛杉矶的晨曦中，沙漠扬起的沙砾混合着海雾，阳光从东边的山脊照射过来。在地理和气候条件的结合作用下，这片被山脉和太平洋环抱的土地始终氤氲在乳白色的雾霭中，一切仿佛经过旧式好莱坞的棱镜过滤，散发出银幕般梦幻的魅力。用这种眼光来看，这里的一切都在电影工业的调色板上相互关联，不光是明星，当红的也好，过气的也罢，每个人都是电影制作过程中的一分子。哈瓦娜和我也是其中的一部分，哪怕我们只是"想成为明星"的那些人。

"Make sure you get back early from class. No detours." she said, turning into me under the long white robe, guiding me in, toward her.
"你保证下课一定早回来，不许干别的去。"她转过身钻进我的长浴袍，将我向她拉近。

"Yeah, got it. Hundredth time you've told me."
"好的，知道啦。你说八百遍了。"

"Just making sure. No second chances. It's my father."
"我就是要确保万无一失。没有第二次机会，这可是我父亲。"

"Hello Havanna, Sammy!" A blond perky girl shouted up to us, waiving.
"你好，哈瓦娜、萨米！"一个充满活力的金发女孩在楼下招手喊我们。

"Sammy?" Havanna pinched me. "That 'Betty' is calling you Sammy?"
"萨米？"哈瓦娜掐了我一把，"那个'贝蒂'叫你萨米？"

"You're not the only popular one on campus." I said.
"你可不是校园里唯一一个人见人爱的。"我说。

Samuel Malibu Beach, CA
塞缪尔在加州马里布海滩

"You're lucky I'm not the jealous type." she said. "Otherwise, I'd have to kill you, after I killed her."
"你要庆幸我不是吃醋的人。"她说,"否则我会灭了她之后再把你灭了。"

"You're joking, right? 'Not the jealous type' ?"
"你开玩笑吧?你'不是吃醋的人'?"

"Damn, look how late it is. I've got to get going. Everything's not just about you. Final rehearsals." she said, Havanna's first lead role, UCLA production. Another reason for the parents coming in. "Oh, by the way, check the envelope on the dresser. For you. Junk I think."
"该死,这么晚了,我得走了。别以为全世界都围着你转。我要去最后一次彩排了。"她说道。这是哈瓦娜的首个主演角色,UCLA出品。这也是她父母来的另一个原因。"哦,顺便说一声,我梳妆台上有你一封信。我觉得是垃圾邮件吧。"

"Where is it?" I asked.
"在哪呢?"我问。

"Right there."
"就在那儿。"

Scene Two   Invitations

第二幕 邀请

In the slung scatter of her table top I rescued a small beige envelope, it balancing on the curved lid of her silver jewelry box, pressed into the paper, my full name in a fine script lettering, Samuel Zachariah Curien.

我在她乱七八糟的桌面上找到了一个米色小信封，架在她银色首饰盒的圆盖上。信封上用精美字体印着我的全名——塞缪尔·扎卡里亚·居里安。

"When did this come in?" I asked. "It says 'Zachariah' for heaven's sake. I never use my middle name. Who would even know that?"

"这东西是什么时候来的？"我问，"我的天，居然把'扎卡里亚'都写上了。我从来不用中间名。谁会知道这个？"

"Oh, someone dropped that by yesterday, uh, day before." she said, pulling on a tailored leather jacket over a soft leopard print. "You have it now, don't you? No problema, mei wen ti." Havanna didn't like the feeling of being blamed.

"哦，有人昨天送来的。哦，不对，是前天。"她说着，在豹纹印花衫外面套上紧身皮夹克。"你现在拿到了，不是吗？没问题（原文分别用西班牙语和中文表达——译者注）。"哈瓦娜不喜欢被责怪的感觉。

"There's no stamp. How did it get here?"
"没有邮票。它怎么来的？"

"I told you ... and don't get all excited. Someone came by and dropped it off. Hand-delivery. Yes, they still do that. A man, in a uniform, strange." she said, her voice trailing off as she disappeared back into the bath.

"我不是说了……不要那么激动好吗，有人送过来的。专人送达。没错，现在还有这种服务。一个穿制服的人，挺奇怪的。"她说着又闪进了卫生间，声音逐渐变弱。

"Then why would you think its junk mail?"
"那你为什么还会觉得这是垃圾邮件？"

"Too fancy, for real mail, whatever. You have it now." she mumbled.
"一封纸质信，这也太浮夸了，随便吧。反正你拿到了。"她嘟囔道。

I felt the fine paper, raised edges, embossing, a water mark on thick fiber, precise, an object of art in itself. Junk? I turned the folio packet over to the sealed side. Fine print announced the sender in full formal flourish, red and golden lettering in fluid poetic font:

我摸着纸质精美的信封和信封上浮凸的字体边角，厚实的纤维纸面打着水印，做工精巧，这本身就是件艺术品。垃圾邮件？我翻过来看有封印的一面。红色和金色交织的精美诗意字体，宣告着来信人隆重登场：

Madam Moriah Leung
888 West Cliff Drive
Santa Cruz, California 90560
莫立娅·梁夫人
西克利夫道888号
圣克鲁斯，加州90560

"Oh my God!" I pulled apart the seal, then the flap, carefully. Inside, a single card, geometric, entwining of three lines along its boarders; Attached, a thin translucent paper, a map in sketch-photo. First letters in calligraphy, full flourish:

"啊！我的天哪！"我扯开封印，小心翼翼地打开信封。里面只有一张卡片，三根线条交织勾勒出几何体边缘。上面黏着一张半透明的薄纸，是一幅地图。正文每一行开头字母都用书法字体呈现，隆重且华丽：

August 15th, in this, the Year of Our Lord
公元××年8月15日

Mister Samuel Zachariah Curien:
塞缪尔·扎卡里亚·居里安先生：

In response to your recent requests for an interview with Madam Leung I offer you an appearance at her residence in Santa Cruz, California upon the evening of August 15th. Please arrive at her door at 5:00 pm. Be precise. After the interview you are invited to remain for dinner, served at 8:00 pm, 'Bruise Art' cuisine, business attire.

应您再三请求，梁夫人允于 8 月 15 日晚在加州圣克鲁斯私邸接受您的采访。请于下午 5 时抵达。务必准时。采访结束后，您受邀留下享用晚餐。"瘀伤艺术"馔宴将于晚 8 时开始，商务着装。

As the interview and dinner may run late, you are also allowed an invitation to stay the night in Madam Leung's guest quarters, on site. Remember the bringing of night clothing. American breakfast will be served promptly at 7:30 am, after which final questions may be entertained.

考虑到采访和晚餐可能为时较晚，您亦受邀在梁夫人私邸的客房过夜。请携带就寝着装。美式早餐将于早 7 时 30 分准时提供。早餐后或有机会进行最后一些问题的采访。

Your RSVP to this invitation must be received no later than 8:00 am on the day of the interview appointment. You will find a guidance map to her residence enclosed, as well as the full address and contact telephone number. With the lateness of this offering, and Madam Leung's schedule in mind, you may respond by way of telephone call or text.

您能否出席，务必于约定的采访日当天早 8 时前回复。随函附宅邸地图与地址电话供您参考。考虑到本次邀请时间较晚，梁女士日程安排紧张，您可选择电话或短信回复。

 Your kind servant,
 Jasmine Xi'an
 Executive Assistant to Madam Moriah Leung
 忠诚为您服务，
 茉莉·席安
 莫立娅·梁夫人行政助理

"Damn." I looked quickly at the clock, red letters on black, 7:56 am, the date at August 15th. "Where's my cell?"

 "要命。"我快速看了一眼钟，7 时 56 分，今天是 8 月 15 日。"我手机在哪儿？"

Havanna frowned. "Watch your tone. Hurry up, get dressed. You've got to drop me off before your class. Your cell? How would I know? Look under the pillow. I asked you not to take it to bed. You always do anyways."

哈瓦娜皱起眉头。"注意你的语气。动作快点,穿好衣服。你得在上课前把我送过去。你的手机?我怎么会知道?枕头下找找。我跟你说过别带手机上床,你老是不听。"

No sign of it in the mess of over-fluffed sheets and too many pillows. With one big jerk to the cover mattress sheet, I ejected everything onto to the floor. The Apple Thirteen tumbled onto the carpet and slid across the wood floor.

皱巴巴的床单和一大堆枕头中没有手机的影子。我把床单猛地一掀,所有东西滚落到地板上。第13代苹果手机掉到地毯上,滑过木头地板。

"What in the hell are you doing. We've got to get going. Get off the cell!" Havana yelled.

"你到底在干吗!我们得走了,放下手机!"哈瓦娜大吼起来。

No time to argue, I sat on the floor, ripped out a text, stabbed at 'send' .The clock read 8:03 am. "I accept the invitation of Madam Leung. Thank you, Samuel Curien."

没时间吵了,我坐在地板上快速打出一条信息,点击"发送"。时钟显示8:03。"我接受梁夫人的邀请。谢谢。塞缪尔·居里安。"

"Get a shirt and let's go. Yes, your naked chest is a wonder to the world, and you have a truly perfect culo, but Gringo..." She went to the 'G' word when she wanted me to know she was done playing.

"穿上衣服我们走。没错,你裸露的胸脯是世界奇观,你的翘臀堪称完美,但是美国佬……"她说出美国佬这个词的时候,意味着她不是在开玩笑。

"Just a minute." I said, raising my hand, listening for the ping. There it was, sweet. Funny how that sharp ting sound announcing an incoming message, trains us all, Pavlov's dogs, pleasure expectation. The message read:

"一分钟。"我举手示意,侧耳等待那声音。来了,美妙。我就像巴甫洛夫的狗一样,这宣告信息到来的清脆"叮"声为我带来了快乐的条件反射。信息如下:

RSVP received of Samuel Curien.
I look forward to your arrival at the door of Madam Leung at 5:00 pm, today,

August 15th, this same evening. Please call if you should need any assistance or additional directions.

Jasmine Xi'an

塞缪尔·居里安的回复收悉。

我期待您于今日下午5时抵达梁夫人家门口。如您需要协助或进一步指引,请拨打电话。

茉莉·席安

I had to go, no other way, my only option. Up to Santa Cruz, right then, immediately. I'd waited months for this, over a year, to meet her, Moriah, fabled popular culture figure Madam Leung. Now, at the critical point, Havanna, parents, thesis, water polo, it came, the chance to meet her, talk to her, in her world, inside the iconic home, the cliffs in Santa Cruz, just over the hill from Silicon Valley. No choice really, one of those moments with no other option than to do exactly the one thing presented, no matter the consequences.

我必须去,这是唯一的选择,别无他途。立刻出发,前往圣克鲁斯。一年多了,我等待数月,就为了见她——莫立娅,传说中的流行文化人物梁夫人。可就在这个关键节点,哈瓦娜,父母,论文,水球,都赶一块儿了。没想到机会却这时候来临,我要翻过硅谷的山丘,进入那个坐落在圣克鲁斯山崖上的标志性豪宅,进入她的世界,去跟她见面、交谈。真的没得选择,这就是那种紧要关头,不论后果如何,只有去做好摆在你面前的这一件事,没有别的选择。

I paused, looked at Havanna, then said it. "I've got to go darling." Strange to hear the words. Someone else speaking.

我迟疑片刻,看了看哈瓦娜,然后说:"我得走了,宝贝儿。"我的声音听起来很奇怪,像是另外一个人在说话。

"What?"

"什么?"

"Havanna, I've got to go, right now I mean."

"哈瓦娜,我得走了,我的意思是现在。"

Havanna kept working her long bands of hair, curling, final primps, braiding a stand at the front, sweeping it back over her shoulder to see the look. "You think?" she said, not bothering to glance in my direction.

哈瓦娜一直精心装扮她的长发，卷起来，先甩到前面编起来，又甩到身后，扭肩膀看效果。"你觉得可以走了？"她说着，一眼都没往我这边看。

"No, I mean I have to go up to Santa Cruz ... Today." I said, and waited for it. Silence for a moment with her shape frozen against the back mirror of the little bath, her elbow out at ninety degrees, odd, as if hit by a bullet, paralyzed. Her mouth open, eyes narrowed, concentrating; She turned, three-quarters, understanding ... the words. "To Santa Cruz? Today?"

"不，我的意思是，我必须去一趟圣克鲁斯……就在今天。"我说完，等着她回应。片刻的安静，透过小小浴室的镜子，她的动作凝住了，胳膊肘成90度僵在半空，仿佛被子弹击中，瘫痪了。她嘴张开，眼睛眯起，集中精神；她大半个身子转过来，消化这句话的意思。"去圣克鲁斯？今天？"

"Yes. The letter. It wasn't junk mail. It was an invitation. From Moriah Leung herself."

"对，那封信。那不是垃圾邮件。那是一封邀请函。来自莫立娅·梁夫人。"

"My God! Mio Dios! Wo de tian na!" she said, laughing. Her face relaxed, relieved. "You're so mean! Okay you got me ... Now, hurry up before you make us both late." She smirked at me in the mirror's reflection, returning to her ritual, quick practiced last movements, hair, eyes, lips.

"我的上帝！我的神啊！我的天哪！"（三个短语原文分别是英语、西班牙语和中文——译者注）她笑着说。她面部表情放松下来，松了一口气。"你好坏！好吧，你吓到我了。来吧，动作快点，你要害我们两个都迟到了。"她在镜子里对着我做了个鬼脸，继续她的规定动作，快速而熟练地完成最后的妆容，头发、眼睛、嘴唇。

She couldn't imagine, digest the concept, that I would go. I had to say it, again.

她无法想象和消化我要离开这事。我还得再说一遍。

"My so sweet, lovely, and very kind Havanna. I must go, and right now. To Santa Cruz. That letter I just opened, it's the invitation from Madam Leung.

You know, Moriah, the widow of Jackson Bartholomew. She's finally going to see me. Tonight. I've got to drive up, right now. No other way to make it work. You see that, don't you darling? If I'd gotten the letter earlier maybe I could have postponed it. Too late for that." I said, regretting the last part. "I promise to make it back by tomorrow morning, promise. Everything'll be okay. Back in time to see your parents, for sure. Of course, I'll be here the next day to see your opening, do the thesis presentation, play in my water polo match, everything, just a lot of driving, for me."

"我的甜蜜的、可爱的、善良的哈瓦娜,我必须去,而且是现在。是去圣克鲁斯。我刚拆开的那封信,是梁夫人的邀请。你懂的,莫立娅,杰克逊·巴塞洛缪的遗孀。她终于同意见我了。就在今晚。我现在必须得开车走。没有其他方法可以准时到达。你理解的,对吧,心肝宝贝儿?如果我早一点拿到这封信,也许还可以推迟这次会面。可现在太迟了。"我说完最后这句就后悔了。"我保证明天早上赶回来,我保证。一切都会好的。一定能够及时赶回来见你父母。当然,我第二天也能去看你的开幕演出,去论文答辩,参加水球比赛,所有一切,对我来说,只需要开车一路跑回来。"

She heard me this time. I could see in her expression, the mirror, her face turned away, a quick build, absolute fury. "Are you out of your mind? No way are you leaving this morning. Just call her up, Madam whatever … reschedule, that's all. You're really something, even suggesting that." she said, staring me down, piercing eyes, brown turned black, tempest, beautiful, lithe. She had no doubt she'd get her way.

她这回听清楚了。我从镜子里能看到她转过脸的表情,瞬间发作,绝对的狂怒。"你疯了吗?你今天早上别想走。给她,那个什么夫人打电话,重新安排时间,就这样。你真够有种,居然敢这么想。"她瞪着我,眼神锐利,棕色的眼珠变得黑黢黢的,暴怒,美丽,易碎。她笃定自己能占上风。

I waited, thought, took a breath. Best to get it over with. "I just can't do that. You don't understand. This is Madam Leung. That she'd see me at all, it's a miracle, like an audience with the Queen, the Pope. Since her husband killed himself, missing, whatever, she's more famous than ever, like Versace. You know what I'm talking about. You watched the J.B.reality show. They're the most famous power couple in the world. Now she's going to see me. Think of how I can use this for my thesis. God, she might let me get involved in the 2nd edition of

Bruise Art. At least I'm going to ask, now that I've got the chance. Or even the film, some part in it, developing, producing. I still have all my father's contacts. Com' on Havanna. You've got to see, understand."

我停顿、思考，深吸一口气。长痛不如短痛。"我不能重新约时间。你不明白。这可是梁夫人。她同意见我本身就是个奇迹，就好比觐见女王，或者教皇。因为她丈夫或自杀，或失踪，不管怎样，她比过去更出名了，就像范思哲那样。你懂我的意思。你看了 J.B. 真人秀。他们是全世界最有名有势的夫妇。现在她要接见我了。想想看，这场采访对我的论文多有用。上帝啊，她说不定能让我参与《瘀伤艺术》再版呢。既然有机会问她，至少我会请求。或者是参与电影的一小部分工作，开发、制片什么的。我还留着我父亲那些老朋友的联系方式。求你了哈瓦娜，你得理解我。"

"Of course, I know who they are." she started slow, quiet. "Everyone does. *Bruise Art* Project, the reality show. Not to mention, subject of your master's thesis project." She said, her sarcastic voice rising. She picked up the hard cover edition of the novel laying on the nightstand, holding it above her head in one hand, like a preacher showing the *Bible*. "Yeah, best novel ever, Jackson Bartholomew, great designer turned writer dude. Your obsession. I got it. So what? It doesn't change the fact that my parents, my parents, are flying in from Madrid, tomorrow. Tomorrow!"

"我当然知道他们是什么人。"她平静而缓慢地张口说道，"每个人都知道。《瘀伤艺术》项目，真人秀。更别提这是你硕士论文的题目。"她语气中的讽刺意味提高了。她拿起床边柜上放着的这本精装版，一手举在头顶，好似教士展示一本《圣经》。"对，史上最棒的小说，杰克逊·巴塞洛缪，伟大的设计师转型而来的狗头作家。你的执念。我懂。那又怎样？这也改变不了我父母，改变不了我的父母明天要从马德里飞过来的事实。明天！"

"I know. I'm so sorry to even think to go, drive up there. But I have too. I can do it easy enough. Only six hours. I'll be back in plenty of time, promise. No big deal." I said, moving toward her, keeping an eye on the volume still above her head. "My whole master's thesis is on him, his book, how to take it from novel to film. You understand, right? You've got to. I know him better than he knew himself, better than anyone. Well, maybe Madam Leung. If I can just meet Moriah, I can convince her, to let me in, help edit a second edition, jumpstart my whole career. Maybe you can help with the film, if that works out. That's what he wanted you know, a full-on big Hollywood movie, Academy Awards, Best Picture. His last interview, he talked about it. There's even some new writing that's turned up, stuff not in the 1st edition. I'd get to see it, before everyone. Can you imagine? Maybe include the rest of his sketch-photos, designs, recipes! Like he wanted in the first edition. They didn't let him. It'd be a grand memorial to him, and I'd be part of it. God, you've got to see Havanna. How I've got to go. It's my chance. Your parents will understand. Hell, they won't even know, if you don't tell them. *Bruise Art*, the whole thing, the project, him going missing, all of it, part of me, who I am. I see it in my dreams, just like this morning. Really, Havanna, look at me. It gets stronger all the time. I haven't really told you about it. Didn't want to creep you out. But there's this feeling. You know what I mean, like you do with your acting, something outside of yourself. This is more than that though. Maybe because I've been in it so long. I don't know. Something I have to do."

"我知道。对不起，我居然起了去的念头，还想开车去。但我必须这么做。我能轻松搞定，6个小时而已。有大把的时间开回来，我保证。没什么大不了的。"我向她走过去，盯着她头上举着的书。"我硕士论文就只关乎他，他的书，他如何将小说拍成电影。你理解的对吧？你必须理解。我对他的了解比他自己还要多，比其他任何人都多。好吧，可能梁夫人除外。如果我能够见到莫立娅，我能说服她让我参与小说再版，由此开启我的人生事业。如果进展顺利的话，你还能参演电影。那是他想要的，一部完全的好莱坞制作大片，奥斯卡最佳影片。他在最后一次采访时说过。他甚至加入了新的东西，初版里没有的。我要抢在别人之前先看到。你能想象吗？也许还可以把他那些素描照片、设计和食谱放进去！他在初版就想这么干了，但他们不许。那将会成为关于他的宏伟传记，而我是其中的一部分。天啊，哈瓦娜，你得理解我为什么一定要去。这是我的机会。你的父母会理解。再说如果你不告诉他们，他们压根不会知道。《瘀伤艺术》，整件事情，那个项目，他的失踪，所有这一切，我的一部分，我这个人。我在梦里看见过，就像今天早晨那样。说真的，看着我，哈瓦娜。每时每刻它都在变得更强烈。我从来没有跟你把话说全，因为我不想吓着你，但这种感觉，你懂我的意思，就类似你投入演戏时那种感觉，一种比你自身还广大的东西。但这比那还要强烈。我不知道，也许我沉迷其中的时间太长了。这是我必须要做的事情。"

"Stop! Just stop. Focus for a moment. My parents are coming. Parents. My father and mother, flying in from Spain, tomorrow. Do you have any idea what that means? In my culture? Respect. You might not care in yours. In mine, this

Samuel Curien—UCLA Master's Program Presentation
塞缪尔·居里安在 UCLA 进行硕士论文答辩

is not possible. You will stay, you will meet them. Then, after, you can go drive up to Santa Cruz, or all the way to Canada for all I care. Today, tomorrow, and the next day, you are here. That's final." She said, a little jerk of the head for emphasis, then turning back to the mirror, the subject closed.

"停！打住。认真听我说。我父母要来了。父母！我父亲和母亲从西班牙飞过来，就在明天。你知道那在我的文化里意味着什么吗？尊重。你们的文化可能不在意这个。但在我的文化里，这不可能。你要留下，你要跟他们见面。然后，你开车去圣克鲁斯，甚至一路开到加拿大我都不在乎。今天、明天、后天，你在这儿待着。就这么定了。"她说完，强调性地点了点头，接着转回镜子面前。话题结束。

"You've got to understand, support me on this one thing, what I want to do most in my life. This is the biggest opportunity I've ever had, or ever will have. I'm obsessed. I admit it, but it's a good thing. Everyone should be so lucky as to have something that they just have to do. Damn, Havanna, when one of the most famous people in the world disappears, the ultimate popular culture icon, in the center of Florence, in the middle of the day, in front of hundreds of people, that's a mystery that also has to be respected, in itself, let alone my thesis, the other connections I have to all of it. Even the dreams, different, they mean something, I know it. Just has to be figured out."

"在这件事情上，你得理解我、支持我，这是我这辈子最想做的事。这是我迄今得到的最好的机会，也许以后都不会再有了。我是执迷不悟，我承认，但这是件好事。一个人能拥有一件必做不可的事是幸运的。该死，哈瓦娜，世界上最有名的人，流行文化的至尊偶像，在佛罗伦萨市中心，光天化日之下，在上百人眼皮底下，消失了，这个神秘事件本身也值得重视吧，更不用说我的硕士论文，这是我跟此事有关联的另一个原因。还有那些各式各样的梦境，它们都有意义，我知道。我得把这些谜团解开。"

"Everyone said he killed himself. That Italian court. It's official. What's the mystery?" She shrugged, moved toward the door to check her purse.

"所有人都说他自杀了。意大利警方给出的官方结论。哪里神秘了？"她耸耸肩，走到门边检查她的包包。

"The body was never found. You know, 'no body no crime, Corpus Delicti'."

"尸体从来没找到。你懂的，'没有尸体无法立案，肉体缺席'。"

"Maybe no crime, but there can be a death, just like the court said."

"也许本来就没有犯罪,但的确有死亡,就像警方说的那样。"

"Italians ... what do they know? Besides, Moriah Leung doesn't accept it. You read it. Moriah Leung, for heaven's sake. God, Havanna! She invited me. You've got to see. I must go. Never be something like this again. I've got to give it a shot, even if she turns me down. At least I know I did everything I could."

"意大利人,他们懂什么?再说了,莫立娅·梁不接受这个结论。你看过报道。莫立娅·梁啊!看在老天的分上,哈瓦娜,她在邀请我。你务必要理解。我必须去。再也不会有这样的机会了。我必须搏一把,哪怕被她拒绝,至少我知道自己尽力了。"

"I'm telling you ... I don't give a damn if it's Beyoncé, Jay-Z, Kardashians, Justin Bieber, and Bruno Mars!" Havanah said, this time shaking the book in her hand, pulling it back to throw. "Jackson Bartholomew, great, amazing, but you're not leaving me today, or tomorrow. The fabulous Madam Leung will see you in a couple of days, just as well as she would see you tonight! Everything is going to get done. My parents are coming, first time, to see you, tomorrow. I've been planning this for months, hell, more than a year. I had to beg my father, literally beg him. Reschedule the Madam, cancel it, your choice, I don't care, but you're not messing this up." she said, nodding her head, awkward, frightening, shaking.

"我告诉你……哪怕是碧昂斯,Jay-Z,卡戴珊姐妹,贾斯汀·比伯,布鲁诺·马尔斯,我也不在乎!"哈瓦娜说着,这下她把手里的书晃了晃,往后一扬,作势要扔过来。"杰克逊·巴塞洛缪,确实伟大,了不起,不过你今天不能离开我,明天也不行。这位迷人的梁夫人几天后可以见你,今天晚上还按原来安排的那样。一切都要做到位。明天,我父母第一次来看你。我已经为此准备了好几个月,该死,一年多了。我不得不求我父亲,实打实地求他。你是跟这位夫人重新约时间还是取消,你自己定,我不管,但你不能把原计划打乱。"她说着,笨拙地点头,充满威胁,浑身发抖。

"Look, I'll make it all up to you. You've got to see Havanna, it's one of those chances that come around, just once. It'll change everything. Just imagine, her agreeing to let me work on making the Jackson Bartholomew novel into a film. I can do it. Yeah, I'm young. But I have contacts from when my father was still alive. I've been studying Bartholomew for years now, everything about him, the great Jackson Bartholomew, his life, his novel, his designs, his travels, his women ... all of it, detailed. I can feel it all, inside me, like he's a part of me, really a part. Damn it Havanna, I can't just let this go. Can't. You can be in the film." I said it all in a rush, promising much more than what would be remotely realistic, no holding back in the face of her onslaught.

"你瞧，我会向你补偿的。哈瓦娜，你得看到这是一次千载难逢的机会。一切都会因此改变。想象一下她同意我参与杰克逊·巴塞洛缪小说翻拍电影的工作。我能做好。没错，我虽然年轻，但我有父亲在世时那些熟人的联系方式。我已经研究巴塞洛缪好几年了，关于伟大的杰克逊·巴塞洛缪的一切，他的一生，他的小说，他的设计，他的旅行，他的女人们等所有的细节。我内心能感觉到他，仿佛他是我的一部分，真的。真要命，哈瓦娜，我就是不能放过这次机会。不能。你可以参演这部电影。"我的话脱口而出，做出的承诺离现实远得离谱，但在她的攻势面前我不能示弱。

Havanna slung her arm back, then around, slingshot style, *Bruise Art* made into a projectile, aimed at my head. It hit flush on the shoulder, ricocheting onto the bed, between us, marking boundary. It lay there, third personage in the room, the iconic cover viewable, Madam Leung's naked back, the issue at hand. Exquisite the photo-sketch cover, the series of three round bruises over her spine. "I'm telling you ... if you leave now, that's it. Take all your junk, don't come back!"

哈瓦娜胳膊向后一扬，再向前挥出，就像射弹弓一样把《瘀伤艺术》瞄准我的脑袋掷来。书"啪"的一声打在我肩膀上，弹到横在我俩之间的床上，标出了界河。书躺在那里，就像房间里的第三者，封面上梁夫人裸露的背部清晰可见，触手可及。经过素描手法处理的照片很精美，她脊柱上依次排列着三个圆形的瘀青。"我警告你……如果你现在离开，一切就完了。拿走你的破烂，别再回来！"

Then wild, pirouetting, opening doors, grabbing my clothes, ripping down, the buttons popping off against the wire hangers. Full Havanna rage, spasmed anger, one outburst leading to the next, each topping what she'd just done, at the edge of physical violence, self-destruction.

然后，她发疯一般，单脚尖转身，把衣柜门打开，把我的衣服扯下来，纽扣钩在铁丝衣架上掉下来也不管。哈瓦娜火力全开，怒气冲天，发作起来一波高过一波，她已经到了诉诸肢体暴力和自我毁灭的边缘。

"Come on. Don't do that. You don't really mean it. I promise, back tomorrow morning. Don't go Post Office Puerto Rican on me." I said, a hope the joking would ease it. "Hell, I will drive back directly, immediately after the interview. Be back eight hours after that, like six in the morning back here, ready to go. No problem." I rushed her, capturing her up in my arms as she threw at me.

"好啦，别这样。你不是认真的。我保证明天早上就回来。可别冲我发疯。"我希望玩笑话能让她消消气。"采访一结束，我就直接开车回来。8个小时之后，也就是明天早上6点我就能回到这里，一点问题没有。"她还在朝我扔东西，我冲过去把她搂在怀里。

"You God damn Gringo, asshole. Get out of my way!" She jerked away, twisting. Her far elbow came up in a wide arch and landed solid, flush on my chin, cage match, mixed martial blow. I started to laugh, falling back, gray going to black, stumbling, the bed.

"你这该死的美国佬，浑蛋，滚开！"她想挣脱我的怀抱，扭动中胳膊肘朝上，结结实实撞到我下巴，简直是笼斗中拳击和武术的组合打击。我大笑着跌跌撞撞向后倒在床上，周围的一切暗了下来。

She was above me. I must have been out for a moment. "I'm not sorry. It's all your fault." She cupping my face, holding my jaw. "See what you made me do? It's okay though. I don't think there'll be a mark, for tomorrow. We can put some makeup on it. You can say you got hit in the pool, saving someone."

她在上方俯身看我。我一定是晕过去了。"我不感到抱歉。都是你的错。"她捧着我的脸，抬起我下巴。"看看你都逼我干了些什么。倒没什么大事。我觉得不会破相，至少明天不会。用点我的化妆品遮瑕就好了。你可以说是在游泳池撞伤的，为了救人什么的。"

"They? What are you talking about?"
"你在说什么啊？"

"My parents of course. I don't want them to know we're fighting. Don't you joke about it either."
"当然是我父母啊。我不想让他们发现我俩打架了。你连玩笑都不许开。"

She actually thought she'd won, that I'd stay. I gathered myself on the edge of the bed as she went to the kitchen.

她真以为自己赢了，觉得我会留下来。她去厨房了，我努力坐起来，挪到床边。

"I'll get you some ice, but you've got to get going, to make your class."

"我给你弄点冰块，但你得出发了，去上你的课。"

I grabbed my bag, clothes off the floor, moved to the front door. "I've got to go, now. Sorry Havanna. I promise to be back by tomorrow morning. I love you. I'll be back ... as early as I can."

我抓起我的包，捡起地板上的衣服，溜到前门。"我是得走了，现在。对不起哈瓦娜。我保证明天早上回来。爱你。我会早点回来……我尽量。"

No look back. I could feel the force of her rage on me, momentum building. One of those moments you just want out, to be somewhere else, asap. I tripped at the bottom of the stairs, spilling everything, grabbing it up again. She came out onto the balcony landing as I exited the door, leaning on the wrought iron rail, her robe opening in the mocking breeze.

我没有回头。我能感觉到她的怒火正在积聚。这种时刻我只得快速离开，去哪都行，越快越好。我在楼梯最后一级踉跄了一下，东西掉了一地，又捡起来。我出大门的时候她来到阳台上，靠在铁栏杆边，浴袍在嬉戏的微风中敞开。

"If you're not back early tomorrow morning, forget everything here. You'll be dead to me. You understand?" The words came staccato, low, threatening. "I'll have my brothers find you, beat you, if you come near me. I don't care if you have a meeting with Jesus. That's the problem, for you, Jackson Bartholomew is Jesus Christ!"

"如果你明天一早没回来，就忘掉这里的一切。我就当你死了。明白吗？"她的话顿挫、低沉，充满威胁。"那时候如果你靠近我，我就叫我的兄弟们找到你，把你胖揍一顿。哪怕你是去见耶稣我也不管。你的问题就在于，对你来说，杰克逊·巴塞洛缪就是耶稣基督！"

Clusters of students walked by along Gayley, on their way up to the campus. A girl got her friends to stop so she could film us on her cell phone. "YouTube!"

she yelled. Other cells came out. It was cinematic, Havanna, wild, beautiful, naked under her robe, shouting from the second floor; me, short pants, 'sag offs', no underwear, no shoes, bare to the waste, piles of my stuff falling, my surfboard catching flight from her toss, almost clipping a passing car. Then my frantic struggle with keys, desperate to get past the lock, grab my board, escape in my dad's Speedster.

去校园上课的学生们成群结队经过盖雷路（加州大学洛杉矶分校校园的一条道路——译者注）。一个姑娘叫伙伴们停下，拿出手机拍摄我们。"发油管！"她尖叫道。其他人纷纷掏出手机。这可真是一景，狂野、美艳的哈瓦娜，浴袍下赤裸着胴体，在二楼大骂；我穿着松松垮垮的大裤衩，内裤都没穿，光着脚，赤裸上身，抱着的一堆东西还不断往下掉。她将我的冲浪板飞掷下来，险些砸到一辆过路的车。之后我慌慌张张地跟钥匙较劲，拼命冲出大门，捡起我的冲浪板，跳上我爸的保时捷逃离了。

"If my father and mother arrive, and you're not here, I'll have you killed! You think I'm kidding? Better you run off the road coming back! Marrano!"

"如果我父母到了，你还没出现，我就找人把你杀了！你以为我在开玩笑吗？你爬也要给我爬回来！白痴！"

Finally, into the old Porsche, everything thrown in the back, board hanging out, a screeched backout onto Gailey. "I'll be back soon, darling. Thank you for understanding." I shouted, waived up. Definitely not good.

我终于爬进了那辆老保时捷里，把东西扔到后座，冲浪板支棱出来。我刺溜倒车开上盖雷路。"心肝宝贝儿，我会很快回来。谢谢理解。"我大喊着冲她招手。这绝对不是什么好事儿。

"Marrano! Ni sha! Ass hole!" Havanna's voice cut through the foggy ocean air coming up from the west.

"白痴！傻瓜！浑蛋！"哈瓦娜的声音穿透西边吹过来的海雾。

She was as angry as I'd ever seen her; I was gone though, too late to change it, escaped, onto Westwood Boulevard, headed for Pacific Coast Highway, then up to Santa Cruz, Sil-Valley, ragtop down. Odd, tragic, Bruno Mars, all the way up on the stereo, my left hand in the air with a hip-hop bounce, Havanna now a 'later worry', as Dad would say ... as long as I made it back before her parents arrived.

　　我从来没见过她发这么大的火。但是晚了,我已经逃走了,无法回头。我将车篷拉下来,车子驶上威斯特伍德大道,向着太平洋海岸高速前进,去往硅谷,圣克鲁斯。我一路听着收音机,和着布鲁诺·马尔斯奇怪而忧伤的歌曲,左手举起来打着嘻哈拍子。哈瓦娜"稍后再担心"——用我老爸的说法——只要我能在她父母到达之前赶回就没事。

　　"There he is, follow him." the passenger said to the driver.
　　"他来了,跟上。"乘客对司机说。

　　"Should we 'high beam' him?"
　　"要开远光灯闪他吗?"

　　"Yeah. But make him guess. Not too obvious. Keep back." passenger said, adjusting aviator sunglasses. "I'll text in a status."
　　"对,但要让他摸不着头脑。别太明显。跟远一点。"乘客边说边调整他的飞行员墨镜。"我来发短信汇报情况。"

　　"Where's the handoff point?" driver asked.
　　"在哪儿交接?"司机问。

　　"Santa Barbara. New recruits going. Got to do their base numbers. Might be a problem. 'Black Lives Matter' street closure, northbound 101, State Street, at the overpass."
　　"圣芭芭拉。新招的去那儿。他们得凑够数。可能会有问题。'黑人的命也是命'游行示威,封路了,北向101号,州立大街的立交桥上。"

　　"It's okay. He'll have to deal with it too." the driver said. "Does this kid even know what he's getting himself into?"
　　"没事,他也得对付这个。"司机说,"这小子到底知不知道自己蹚的是什么浑水?"

　　"I doubt it." 'Aviator' said. "Either way, he's going to learn fast ... don't mess with law enforcement."
　　"我很怀疑。""飞行员"说,"不管他知不知道,他很快就要学会……别惹执法部门。"

Scene Three　Highway One

第三幕 一号公路

There's no more beautiful drive in the world than the stretch of Highway One from LA to San Francisco. Start on San Vincente Boulevard, take it all the way to the cliffs in Santa Monica. Old neighborhood, Neo-Spanish mini mansions. Dense trees along the fences, planted that way to keep everything out. Movie types lived there, 'back in the day'. Producers, directors, actors, 'rich and famous', all of them. Perfect location, close to the ocean, short drives to the studios. Long past it's time now, them gone, replaced by lawyers, IT guys, agents. Lines of joggers bounce along the center meridian, worn paths in thick grass along gnarled Coral trees, dense, substantial. Brentwood Country Club making the left boundary, enormous Eucalyptus shadows across manicured putting greens and onto the 'driveway to the ocean'.

全世界再找不到比一号公路更美的公路了。这条路从洛杉矶直达旧金山，起点在圣文森特大道，终点在圣莫尼卡的悬崖边。老式街区，新西班牙风格的小别墅。房前，树篱种得密不透风，把一切挡得严严实实。过去那个年代住这里的都是影视圈人士，制片人、导演、演员，一个个都是"有钱、出名"。位置完美，濒临海岸，离片场开车很近。那都是过去时了，俱往矣，现在取而代之的是律师、IT大佬、中间商。沿着中央子午线慢跑的人排成行，被踩踏磨损的小道茂草掩映，路边的刺桐树扭曲盘旋，又粗又壮。道路左边以布伦特伍德乡村俱乐部为界，高大的尤加利树将树影投在精心修剪的草坪上和"通向大海的车道"上。

"Finally, the great Madam Moriah!" I shouted it. Ed Sheeran's *I'm In Love with Your Body* coming on. I'd sent her so many messages, too many. No answer. Almost given up, thinking I'd pressed to hard, or just me, not significant enough for her to bother. She must get a thousand calls a day, all decisions hers, now that Jackson was gone. Everything in her lap, all of it, the most powerful design brand in the world; 'J.B.' designed in America, produced in China, sold everywhere. Nothing like it ever before, a new design house genre, full crossover from east to west and back, Jackson's novel published in Mandarin and English, all their designs taking off. Anything *Bruise Art* in demand; Couture, jewelry, fragrances, home furnishings, sunglasses, American cakes & pies, Southern recipes, water exercises, lifestyle, and of course, the writing, all continually marketed, for sale, distribution, consumption.

"终于，伟大的莫立娅夫人！"我大声喊道。耳边环绕着艾德·希兰的《我爱你的胴体》。我给她发了那么多条信息，太多了。没有回音。我几乎要放弃了，觉得自己逼得太紧，或是因为我对她来说微不足道。现在杰克逊不在了，她必定每天要接无数个电话，做一切决定。她全盘掌管全世界最强大的设计师品牌"J.B."，美国设计、中国生产、全球销售。从来没有过这样的现象，一个全新的设计品类，风格涵盖东方和西方，杰克逊的小说以中文和英文出版，他们的所有设计都在热卖。关于《瘀伤艺术》的一切都供不应求，服饰、珠宝、香氛、家装、太阳镜、美式糕点、水上运动、生活方式，当然了，还有小说本身，一切都在源源不断地被制造、出售、分发、消费。

    Many people have talent. He had much more, perfect timing; plus luck, and then the ultimate asset, magical Moriah. His creative talent meshed with her ability to get powerful people to do what they needed them to do. Moriah's charm moved in the highest circles of the world's rich, powerful, famous. She projected her pure extract of competence, trustworthiness, lack of guile. She put everyone at ease, all of them confident that she'd take care of them, their interest; the perfect person to open doors wide, connect her east to his west, at the apex of American—Chinese popular cultural. Their joining, intertwining, created an explosion of pop culture greatness. For the hungry public, each persona served as a touchstone symbol, a marriage of two sides, two peoples, two cultures, locked in full-on exploitation of every opportunity presented.

    很多人都有天赋。他有的更多，完美的时机，加上运气，还有终极法宝，神奇的莫立娅。他的创意天赋，加上她那种能力，可以使有权有势的大人物替他们出力，达到他们的目标。莫立娅的魅力在世界上最顶流的富人、权贵、名流圈子里大放异彩，她将自己的才干、可靠、坦诚用得恰到好处。她令每个人都感到自在，所有人都相信她会关照好大家的利益；她是打通她的东方和他的西方之大门的完美人选，站在美国—中国流行文化的顶点。他们的结合创造了伟大流行文化的一次爆发。对于饥渴的大众，二者中每一位都是一个解锁符号，两个国家、两国人民、两种文化的联姻，将每一种机会都牢牢锁住加以利用。

    I wanted to touch it, share in it, add to it, the whole phenomenon. The history of Hollywood is filled with young men with high ambition. I wanted to be one of them. The whole *Bruise Art* wave was my way to get there. I had to catch his wave. With Jackson gone, Moriah was my chance. I was going to make sure that I did everything possible; 'bulldog it' my father called it. It all hung there before me. Had to go for it, no choice. For that I needed to get her to see me as something more than what I'd already done; Get myself into her mind, as a part of the 2nd edition project, and then the film.

我想要接触这一现象，成为它的一部分，为它增添光彩。好莱坞的历史充斥着雄心万丈的年轻人。我想成为他们中的一员。《瘀伤艺术》浪潮是我通往那里的路。我得抓住它的浪潮。杰克逊死了，莫立娅就是我的机会。我一定要尽己所能，如我父亲常说，"咬住不放"。机会就在我眼前，必须前进，别无选择。要实现这个目标，我要让她高看我，高过真实的我。我要进入她的头脑，参与再版的工作，然后就是电影。

Jackson had the film intension from the start. You could hear it in his interview. He liked to tease at it with rumors of writing never published, sketches, illustrations, photography never exhibited, all sounding suspiciously like screenplays, story boarding, graphic noveling. Apparently, he had recipes of every dish mentioned in his writing, then more designs of buildings, clothes, jewelry, furniture, He was an all-inclusive kind of guy, everything even mentioned in his novel, and all his designs, included, working as one, interrelated, grand, masterpiece, no compromise, fully interacting, fresh, its own thing, unique genre, including a film.

杰克逊从一开始就想拍电影。从他的采访里就能听出来。他喜欢开玩笑地提到那些传言，关于那些从未出版的作品，从未展出的素描、插画和摄影，听起来都很像剧本、分镜、图像化的小说。显然，小说里写到的那些菜式他都有菜谱，还有更多建筑、服饰、珠宝、家具的设计。他是个全知全能的人，他小说里提到的一切，他的所有设计，都是整体布局的一部分，相互关联、相互作用、宏伟杰作、毫不妥协、活灵活现、独一无二的品类，包括电影。

I saw it more clearly now, driving up to see her, the finished volume, the premier of the film, the launching of the California Cake and Pie Company, openings in Beijing, London, San Francisco, simultaneously, giant screen connected. He'd done things in such a way, his genius, to leave everyone hungry for more, to project his eager intension to give it to you, benevolent. It all made sense, ironically, all the more since his death. The whole thing, in all its parts, the whole tapestry of it begging to be completed, realized. That's how I saw it, my part in it. To see it all done, comprehensive, as he had intended from the start.

现在，在开车去见她的途中，我看得更清楚了。已完成的作品，电影的首映，加州蛋糕和派公司成立并同步在北京、伦敦和旧金山开店，这一幕幕画面联系起来了。他就是这么做事的，这是他的天分，让每个人都渴望得到更多，把他自己渴望的意图投射给你，多么好善乐施。讽刺的是，在他死后，这一切显得更为合理。这计划的每个部分、每条经纬都在恳求被完成、被实现。那就是我的解读，我在其中的角色。我要按照他最初的谋划，监督这个计划的全方位实现。

Logo—California Cake & Pie Company
加州蛋糕和派公司的品牌标识

Along with everything else, Jackson provided a way for fans and followers to enhance their own creativity, to find it, pull it out of yourself. He had a lifestyle course as well. It had to do with 'primal actions', repetition of movement, sleeping, dreaming. He saw, taught, that all of them have a natural flow, rhythm, including dreaming. He believed that the best state of all, for creativity, was the gray space between wake and asleep. He was right. It was then that the brain was best able to pull out of its defensive nature. Disjointed ideas, points of interested, colors, vignettes from the past, they could combine, mix, find patterns, make sense, provide epiphanies, where not previously manifestable, knowable.

杰克逊还给粉丝和追随者提供了一条增强自身创造力的路——在自己内心寻找并且发掘出来。他设计了一个生活方式课程。它要求你做一些"原始活动"，反复做一些动作、睡眠、做梦。他监督、传授，确保学习者有一种自然的气韵流动，保持节奏，包括做梦。他相信创造力最好的状态是清醒和睡着之间的灰色地带。他是对的。那种时候，大脑才能最好地从防御天性中解放出来。零碎的想法，兴趣点，色彩，记忆的光晕，它们会在原本不可知晓、难以描述的地方组合、混淆，找到模型，形成理性，显现形象。

When I saw Jackson in my own dream state as real it held the most promise, not when presented or perceived as memories from film clips or interviews; All the more since his disappearance. It was as though he, or some force, wanted to make known what he wanted, how to make it happen. Sometimes they felt like 'transmissions', and thus a source of sky-high expectations. In those moments, all was possible. Everything connected, including this, my heading up the coast to Santa Cruz, the confrontation with Havanna, the combining of all critical events on the same day, same time, somehow planned, set up.

我在自己的梦境里见到的杰克逊栩栩如生,那并非来自对他的影像片段或采访的印象,这一点令人充满期待。自从他失踪后这感觉更加强烈。就好像是他,或者某种力量要把他的愿望公之于世,并付诸实现。有时候那些梦就像"传输影像",将期待值推向天际。在那种时刻,一切皆有可能。万事相互关联,包括我开车直奔圣克鲁斯这件事本身,与哈瓦娜的冲突,同一天、同一时间里所有关键事件都碰在一起,感觉就像是被设计好的。

At the stop light at Avondale Avenue, I remember my friend Louis. His parents' home sat just a bit up the way, to the right. I loved going there, even driving by, neoclassic Spanish, romantic spires, violet bougainvillea thickets catching the light. His father had been a successful doctor. Suddenly one day his dad's was gone "Chemical imbalance". Louis said. Louis had planned to go to USC, to study architecture. The plan dissolved into a disappointing memory. The rest of his life would linger in his mind. What if his father hadn't lost his mind? Louis a good boy, bright, young, quirky, fun, full of jokes, connected, confident, lost it, his future. One day, randomly, everything shifted, he became someone else, out of circulation. I had to pound on his door to get him to see me. We had that in common, our fathers, suddenly gone. I thought of Louis often, what he was doing, how I could help. Nothing really to do, be a friend. All else would have to come from him, from within.

在埃文代尔大道等红灯的时候,我想起了我的朋友路易斯。他父母的房子就在道路前面一点的右手边。我喜欢去那里,即使只是开车路过。那幢房子是新古典西班牙风格,有着浪漫派的尖顶,紫红色的九重葛花丛映着阳光。他父亲是位事业有成的医生。突然有一天他父亲就"化学失衡"了,路易斯的原话。路易斯本来想去南加州大学读建筑。但计划消融成了失望的记忆。在他的余生,这件事都萦绕不散。如果他父亲没有发疯会怎样?路易斯是个好青年,阳光、年轻、鬼马、逗趣、爱说笑话、人脉广泛、充满自信,但他失去了未来。突然那么一天,一切都变了,他变了一个人,与外界断了联系。我得大力砸开他家的门才能见到他。我们有一个共同点:父亲突然离世。我经常想起路易斯,想知道他在做什么,我能帮什么忙。其实也没什么特别要做的,就是做他的朋友。余下只能靠他自己发掘内在动力。

My reaction to that harsh example of random tragedy, as well as my own, produced a kind of pressure, a feeling for time, fear of it, passing. Things could change quickly, everything had a deadline, date stamp, expiration date. The only way to defeat life was to get thing done before death took it away. My own ambition fed off the fear of failure, of not accomplishing something, fame, wealth, status, within the context of my own life span, there at the edge of paradise, looking in, Hollywood.

我对朋友及我自己人生中遭遇偶发悲剧的感慨，催生了一种压力，一种时不我待的惶恐。万物瞬息变化，凡事皆有时限、日期邮戳、有效日期。打败命运的唯一途径，是在死亡来临前把该做的事做完。对失败和一事无成的惶恐滋长了我的野心。名声、财富和地位，以我一生为背景，站在天堂门口，将视线投向了好莱坞。

In my father's Speedster, on my way to see Madam Moriah, everything possible, on track, obtainable, in front of me. Just had to go get it. The 'sanctuary of success', Jackson called it. All I had to do was convince one person, make my pitch, start the great project, get everything I wanted in one epoch effort. Havanna would see, applaud, along with her parents, if I succeeded, helped take *Bruise Art* from novel to movie. Then I'd be there, in the protective embrace of the 'sanctuary'. Death itself wouldn't change it, couldn't reverse it, take it back. Once done, accomplished, it would be too late. I will win. Defeat life, defeat everyone. Vincero! Pavarotti, *No one sleeps*.

驾着我父亲的保时捷，在去见莫立娅夫人的路上，一切皆有可能，在正轨上，在我眼前，唾手可得。我志在必得。"成功的庇护所"，杰克逊是这么说的。我要做的就是说服一个人，推销自己，启动伟大项目，用洪荒之力一举实现自己的愿望。如果我成功了，帮助《瘵伤艺术》小说拍成电影，哈瓦娜与她父母会看到并一起鼓掌。之后我就被保护在"庇护所"里了。死亡本身不会改变这一点，不能够逆转、收回。一旦事成，要改就晚了。我会赢。打败命运，打败所有人。胜利！帕瓦罗蒂正在高歌《今夜无人入睡》。

One thing on the film, central to the J.B.world view, that I needed to understand, Jackson's concept of Populist, Populism, pop culture? He wanted to say something, judgement, good or bad? What does that even mean? Valuing success, fame, wealth over all else, over values, experience, tradition? The override of current culture over traditional, demanding its own, that its leaders reflect the newest version of America.

关于电影有一点,也是 J.B. 世界观的核心,是我需要弄明白的,即杰克逊的"民粹分子""民粹主义"概念,是指流行文化吗?他想表达什么,想做出何种评判,是好的还是坏的?到底是什么意思?重视成功、名声、财富胜过其他一切,胜过价值观、经验和传统?当前的文化取代了传统,号令天下,其领军人物代表着最新版本的美国。

Jackson Bartholomew's novel attempted to capture the essence of that American popular culture coup in progress. He wasn't satisfied, wanted more of an impact on the conversation, social documentation of what was going down. The film was another chance for him, a reason to do it, beyond additional fame and wealth. My thesis explored it all, 'Jackson Bartholomew', metaphor for our time. America at the turn of the century, in conflict, with himself, itself. I was always thinking about it, turning it over in my mind. Havanna was right, I'd become totally obsessed, every part of me, even my dreams, immersed in the subject, meaning, details, capturing magic, how it happened, how to make it happen again.

杰克逊·巴塞洛缪的小说试图抓住这场正在进行的美国流行文化政变的精髓。他并不满意,还想令这场讨论产生更大影响,对正在发生的社会现象进行记录。拍电影对他来说是另一次机会和理由,不仅仅是为了谋求更多的名声和财富。我的论文就是专攻这个现象,我们这个时代的隐喻"杰克逊·巴塞洛缪"。世纪之交的美国,与他、与其自身发生了冲突。这个问题一直沉浸在我脑子里,反复琢磨。哈瓦娜说得对,我完全被他占据了,我的每一部分,甚至我的梦境,都完全沉浸在这个话题里,它的意义,它的细节,捕捉魔法,找到它是如何发生的,如何让它再次出现。

I kept turning it over in my mind. That he'd 'caught the wave' meant what exactly? Luck, positioned at just the right location and moment, like a surfer in Malibu, just the right speed, momentum, to make it work? Were their elements to a formula that if reproduced in just the right proportions it would allow for it, for someone or something to take hold, harnessing it all? Jackson had done that for sure, taken what his own time offered, controlled it, all its force and form, the correct steps, planned, felt, all at the precise moments at each point along the way needed to create a full-on phenomenon. 'Go viral' was too weak a term for it. 'Going universal', more like it. He'd managed to combine every angle of social media, Sil-Val technology, international hunger for things American,

J.B. Logo
J.B. 品牌标志

to the ruthlessly promotion of *Bruise Art*. Then he leveraged it, expanded upon that base to obtain success in all the other avenues to wealth and fame. All things 'Jackson Bartholomew', and by extension, all things 'Moriah', had taken the moment, become the 'it' factor, both in their personages and products.

　　我反复琢磨,他说的"把握浪潮"到底是什么意思?运气稳稳地站在合适的时间和地点,如同马里布的冲浪者,把握合适的速度和势头,冲浪成功?是否存在一些成功要素,在配比得当的时候,某个人或某种事物就可以牢牢把握、驾驭,复制成功?诚然,杰克逊成功了。他抓住时代给予的机会,控制它的力道和形式,迈出正确的步伐,精心谋划,每一个关键节点都踩在正点上,创造现象级效果。用"火爆"这个词来形容太弱了,"全球传播"才更像那么回事。他利用社交媒体的每个角度,将硅谷技术和全世界对美国好物的渴求结合起来,不遗余力地推销《瘀伤艺术》。之后他又以此为基础,借小说之力在其他赛道谋求财富和名声。关于"杰克逊·巴塞洛缪"的一切,并由此衍生出的关于"莫立娅"的一切,都抓住了当下,成为他们个人标签及产品的"它"元素。

It started somewhere, with his novel, strategized in every detail, published intentionally in Mandarin before English so that Moriah could use her Beijing contacts to assure its publishing success. Full enthusiastic China TV coverage of one event after another with national and international stars on hand to bring on full attention. Moriah had the brilliant audacity to subtitle the Chinese edition of the book 'The Great American Novel'. She'd even found a way to have the book chosen as a text for English language studies for the Chinese university system, that in itself accounting for millions of sales. Moriah had done her part, marketed the novel to over a billion people before the first American publisher had even heard of *Bruise Art*, positioned the novel as an unquestionable success, an investment 'fact on the ground' that couldn't be missed, denied.

策略从他的小说起步,精心谋划到每个细节。在最好的位置做大面积展示。中国的电视台热切报道一个又一个活动,请来中国和国际明星,赚足眼球。莫立娅在中文版本的副标题上大胆地加上了"伟大的美国小说"。她甚至有办法令小说片段入选中国高校的英语语言学习教材,这也使小说的销量大增。莫立娅向十几亿人成功推销这部小说的时候,第一家美国出版商甚至都没听说过《瘀伤艺术》这本书。她将小说定位成了不容置疑的成功案例,一项不容错过、不能拒绝、货真价实的投资机会。

With all that as his base Jackson negotiated the highest fee ever paid for a first novel for any author, ever. The fact of three point eight million dollars immediately used by him as an added element in the book's promotion, evidence in itself of the work's merit, value, a key element of the whole marketing scheme. That the publication transcending two cultures, the two largest markets, the number one best seller on each side of the Pacific at the same instant, first novel to do so, stoked the fire of frenzied buying, online sales at record levels. One thing fed upon the other, as happens in these things, each adding to the momentum, an avalanche, a natural flow; inevitability, at least the way phenomena appear when looked back upon.

以此为基础,杰克逊为他的小说拿到了有史以来最昂贵的处女作的价格。三百八十万美元立刻被他用来营销这本书,这个价格本身就说明了作品的优点和价值,这是整个市场计划的关键重点。这本书的出版横跨两种文化,跨越两个最大的市场,太平洋两岸同步登上畅销榜首,史无前例,这些成为煽动人们疯狂购买的卖点,线上的销量也创下了纪录。一个事件为下一事件推波助澜,每一桩都推动势头更进一步,像雪崩一样自然滚动。回头看,所有这些现象就像是不可避免、注定要发生一样。

The next domino, one of the first key elements, his invention of a new form of body art. Indeed, bruise art. Amazing that it had not been thought of before. For hundreds of years, what is called 'cupping' had been used by Chinese for medicinal purposes. Hard to describe 'cupping' to westerners. They wince at the practice. For a start, think acupuncture, sticking someone with dozens of needles, an ancient and Chinese therapy, now accepted in the West. 'Cupping' is similar. It's a physical therapy technique, used for centuries in China, just now breaking through in America. The concept is to intentionally stress the immune system of the human body through a series of eight or more round bruises created by means of suction. A vacuum is formed by heating the air in a round jar and then quickly pressing the opening of the jar on the skin, holding it there until the air cools enough to condense, creating a vacuum, sucking the skin up into the jar. The jar will stay in place, theoretically, until someone removes it. The therapist usually leaves it in place for ten to fifteen minutes. When removed a round purplish red mark remains. It is the series of multiple bruises that causes the immune system to activate. That's the concept at least. Like any such

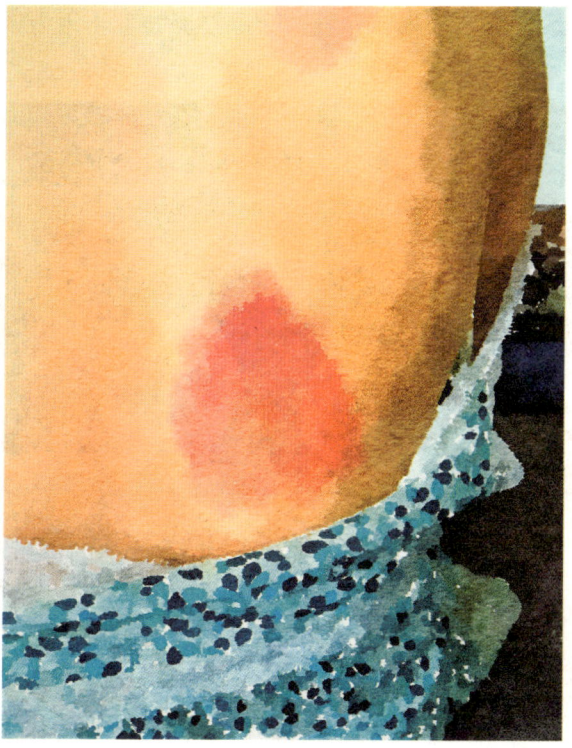

'Cupping' Body Art—Triangular Shape—J.B. Created Artform
"拔罐"身体艺术——三角形——J.B. 创意艺术

suction mark on the human skin, especially the back, it disappears completely in a matter of a few days, a week or so. The recipient benefits with an immune system that has been turned on, activated, so that it can better fight all potential diseases. The bruise is thought to be renewing, reinvigorating. No less than the American Olympic swimming team has accepted this 'cupping', bruising therapy, as part of prep for the Olympics.

下一张多米诺骨牌，也是他成功的早期关键因素之一，就是他发明的新型身体艺术。是的，"瘀伤艺术"。很奇怪此前从来没人往这方面想过。上百年来，中国人一直将"拔罐"用于医疗用途。向西方人解释"拔罐"很难。他们会皱起眉头。拿针灸做个类比好了。这种把数十根针扎到人身上的独特中式疗法，现在已经被西方人接受。"拔罐"与此类似，它是一种体外疗愈手法，在中国已经施用了几个世纪，当下正在进军美国。其理念是通过吸附表皮的手法刺激人体免疫系统，在表皮留下8个或更多圆形的瘀青。将一个圆形小罐内的空气加热，快速将罐口扣压在皮肤上，停留至其内部空气冷却凝结形成真空，罐内的皮肤被吸凸起。理论上小罐能够扣紧皮肤，通常治疗师会放置10—15分钟再将其移除。小罐移除后，皮肤上会留下一个紫红色的圆形瘀青印。就是这一系列的瘀青激活了免疫系统。反正理念就是这样的。人体皮肤上因为吸吮之力造成的瘀青

Bruise Art—'Cupping' art on back of Moriah
瘀伤艺术——在莫立娅背上施行"拔罐"艺术

印,尤其是在背上的,通常几天、最多一周会完全消失。拔罐的人免疫系统被启动激活,就可以更好地抵抗潜在疾病。这些瘀伤被认为具有复苏、更新的作用。美国奥林匹克运动会游泳队员在备战奥运前就接受了"拔罐"这种疗愈方法。

The art element of the 'cupping' comes from one man, one man only, Jackson Bartholomew. For some reason, it took a while for the public to get their mind around the idea that he invented it, that no one, until him, had used the resulting marks as a form of artist expression, not merely a medical treatment. Bruise art spread so quickly, once introduced, that it is hard to blame them for thinking it already an established Asian art form, as well as physical therapy. 'Nope a dope', it was Jackson, him alone. He first did it as a single line of three round shapes, each smaller in sequence, along the spin of Moriah. He photographed her nude, the specially located decorative bruises as the highlight. You'll likely remember the series of iconic postcards he created to promote the novel, the first and most important with that photo turned into a sketch.

在"拔罐"中发掘艺术灵感源自一个人,仅此一人,就是杰克逊·巴塞洛缪。出于某种原因,大众花了不少时间接受他发明了这一艺术。在他之前,没有人用这种瘀青印作为艺术表达方式,而不仅仅是治疗手段。"瘀伤艺术"一经推出,迅速流行开来,难怪人们以为这是一种由来已久的亚洲艺术形式,也是身体的疗愈方法。非也非也,这是杰克逊一个人的杰作。他开始设计的是在莫立娅背上沿脊柱做三个圆形瘀青,排列成一条直线,圆形依次变小。他拍下她裸露背部的照片,亮点是背上精心设计的瘀青造型。你可能有印象,他为推广小说设计了一系列明信片,第一张也是最重要的一张是经过素描化处理的照片。

A great hook. Nothing better than a fad that sweeps the popular culture to get a term into the American lexicon, Bruise Art. Natural that the generation that accepted tattooing as a norm would embrace bruising through suction, a 'hickey' by heated glass bottle, their new form of body art. After all, painless, edgy, disappears in a week. Even parents couldn't complain too much. With the idea called 'Bruise Art' established, in vogue, the novel took off again, this time holding first place on the *Times* best seller list a whole year. Today you can get an endless variety of 'Bruise Art' applied to your skin in parlors all over America, China, the world. Symbols, letters, animal shapes, emojis. Cost negligible, variety limitless. All started in Sil-Val by Jackson. Amazing, perfect timing.

My thesis shows how the bruise art fad was a key, if not the key, to the whole Jackson Bartholomew brand having legs. Hard to imagine it all growing without that, or, conversely, because of that, the 'hook' into the popular culture psyche.

这是一个很棒的吸引人的东西。瘀伤艺术,横扫流行文化的潮流很容易进入美国词汇。接受文身成为常态的这代年轻人很自然地拥抱瘀伤,这种通过加热玻璃瓶吸附皮肤形成吻痕般印迹的身体艺术。毕竟它无痛、新潮,一周内就会消失。就连家长也没什么可责怪的。"瘀伤艺术"这个概念树立并且成为潮流之后,小说的销量再次扶摇直上,这回占据《时代》杂志畅销书榜首长达一整年。现在,你可以在美国、中国乃至全世界各个角落的小店里,在皮肤印上样式不计其数的"瘀伤艺术"。符号、字母、动物图形、表情符号。花费很少,花样无限。这一切都源自硅谷的杰克逊。时机掐得正好,令人叹服。我的论文分析了"瘀伤艺术"风潮如何成为杰克逊·巴塞洛缪品牌风靡一时的因素之一,如果不是唯一因素的话。很难想象没有它,或者反过来说,很难想象因为它,这个"吸引人的东西"抓住了流行文化的心理,品牌能够实现增长。

That was the tipping point. Investors, especially the Chinese, lined up to back the J.B. brand, franchises, next big thing that he designed, or even thought of, some simple sketch on the back of an envelope having the potential to attract big money. The best example after the cupping thing, the one I point to in my thesis, the next domino to fall, was the California Cake and Pie Company (AC&PC). It's less clear than cupping, but, in my view, the move that took him, the J.B. brand, to the next level. With the AC&PC successful, he had simultaneously in place a novel, a popular culture fad, and a thriving international business. Success breeds success, and, most importantly, brings on hungry investors from every corner.

那就是引爆点。投资人,尤其是中国的投资人,排着队要投资J.B.品牌及其加盟商,他的下一款重大设计,哪怕只是一个想法,信封背面几笔潦草的涂鸦,却有着吸金的巨大潜力。最好的例子,也是我在论文中指出的,拔罐之后的下一个多米诺骨牌就是"加州蛋糕和派公司"(AC&PC)。它不像拔罐那样清晰,但我认为它能将J.B.品牌带上新高度。AC&PC取得成功之后,他已经同步准备好一部小说,一场流行文化新潮流以及一项繁荣的国际生意。成功滋生成功,更重要的是,从各个角落引来饥渴的投资者。

With those three legs holding him up he couldn't be stopped. More to the point, it couldn't be stopped, *Bruise Art*, the J.B. brand. Everything he did, all his designs, if merely a mention in his novel, each one became 'a thing', a succession of fads, the next eagerly awaited as an anticipated follow up to the preceding. Each new wave of designed by 'J.B.', by Jackson Bartholomew, traveling around the world and back, Internet-ed instantly, one after the other, a global warming 'perfect storm' of popular culture promotion, consumption, obsession.

有这三条腿的支撑,他简直势不可当。更确切地说,它不可阻挡——《瘀伤艺术》、J.B.品牌。他做的一切,所有的设计,只要在小说里稍有提及,都会成为"事儿",一连串的潮流,下一个迫不及待地紧跟着上一个。杰克逊·巴塞洛缪的每一波新设计,环球流行一圈又回来,在互联网的驱动下,一个接一个快速流行,这是流行文化营销、消费和沉迷的全球变暖"完美风暴"。

My thesis is beyond Jackson, to include Moriah. The success of one person is usually enabled by someone else, a spouse, parent, sibling, close friend, benefactor. Moriah was that person for Jackson. Her talents, personality, powerful contacts multiplier effect, expanded his reach ten-fold. Moriah's sense of style, timing, rapport, perfect understanding of Chinese culture, made the full J.B. phenomena possible.

我的论文不仅关注杰克逊,也包括莫立娅。一个人的成功往往身后有人相助:配偶、父母、兄弟姐妹、密友、贵人。莫立娅就是杰克逊的贵人。她的才华、人格加上强大的关系网效果叠加,将他的影响力扩大了十倍不止。莫立娅的时尚感、时机感、亲和度以及对中国文化的深入了解使得J.B.品牌现象成为可能。

For my part, I was intent on using the Bartholomew momentum and my detailed knowledge of it, to catapult myself forward. As my generation would have it, I wanted success young, early, quick, before 'shit' could happen. With Jackson gone, Moriah held the keys to the gate, beyond which waited everything I wanted. Moriah was the Donatella to Jackson's assassinated Versace. Even with him gone, missing, the J.B. house of design had every indication of continuing, growing, expanding, a new phase of success with new leadership, alternative talents released. Rumor had it that perhaps that was the plan. The death of Jackson had served to bring things to a boil, expand it all with the additional heat, scandal. Whatever forces of man or nature had placed me in the right spot at the right time, to be part of the second worldwide wave of Jackson Bartholomew, I had to seize the singular opportunity. It wouldn't come again.

'Bruise Art' Exhibition—April 2019
"瘀伤艺术"展览摄于 2019 年 4 月

  对我来说，我志在利用巴塞洛缪的名气和我对他的深入研究，送我自己步上青云。这就是我们这代人想要的，成功要趁早、要快，要赶在坏运气来临之前。现在杰克逊不在了，莫立娅手里握着大门钥匙，大门那边，我想要的一切在等着我。莫立娅之于杰克逊就相当于范思哲被谋杀后的多纳泰拉。他即使不在了，失踪了，J.B. 设计品牌仍呈现出继续增长和扩张的迹象，新领导力带来了成功新阶段，另一种才华得到了释放。有传言说这也是计划好的。杰克逊之死令局势更为沸腾，用丑闻进一步提升热度。不管是人力还是天意，我在合适的时间站在了合适的点位，有望成为杰克逊·巴塞洛缪第二波全球潮流的一分子。我必须抓住这个独特的机会。时不再来。

  Obsessive ambition? Yes. That's the power that generates the actions necessary. I didn't fight it. Glad to have it, encourage it on, prompt it to totally engulf me. It was why I existed, breathed. I never explained that to Havanna.

Didn't think she'd understand. More likely she'd be afraid of it, jealous that my obsession wasn't her, but it.

执迷不悟的野心？没错。这就是催生行动的能量。我毫不抗拒。相反我很高兴拥有这个野心，并且鼓励它生长，给它加油，直到它完全吞噬我。它成为我存在和呼吸的理由。我从来没对哈瓦娜解释过。我不觉得她能理解。她更有可能会被我的野心吓到，并且嫉妒我沉迷的不是她而是它。

I blasted the stereo as San Vincent hits Ocean Avenue; Always a rush for me, the coming view out, no boundary, the pattern of white caps, slants of sailboats, just there, beyond the cliffs. The green strip of Palisades Park falls off, dives straight down, perilous. Odd, no sign, no structure to mark it, just the green of the park, trees. Seems like the place deserves more before the right turn. Counter-intuitive if you intend to drive left, up the coast. You must go down to the right a few blocks before you can switch back at the Santa Monica Pier. Close-cropped green grass, a line of King palms, playful, Charles Moore designs, joggers, dogs, strollers, gangs, people clutter, characteristics of the thin strip of precipitous park. Most keep away from the dangerous edge of the cracking concrete railing, erosion eating at its foundations. Upscale condos view over it all, holding their elite line along the other side of the Avenue.

在圣文森特路拐上海洋大道的时候，我把音乐开得山响。映入眼帘的景象总是令我迫不及待。视界开阔，那些白色屋顶，帆船倾斜的桅杆，就在悬崖边上，触手可及。帕利塞德公园的绿化带从悬崖倾泻而下，看起来很危险。奇怪，公园没有路标，也没有建筑物标记，只有满眼的绿树。右转之前这地方值得拥有更多的标识介绍。如果向左转，开到海岸边又觉得违背本能。你必须向右开几个街区才能转回到圣莫尼卡码头。修剪平整的青葱草坪，排列成行的高大棕榈树，气氛愉快，查尔斯·穆尔设计的建筑（美国当代著名建筑设计师——译者注），慢跑的人们，狗，散步的人们，帮派成员们，人们或成群结队，或三三两两，是这个险峻公园内狭窄边缘地带的典型风光。多数人离那有裂痕的危险混凝土护栏远远的，护栏的基座已经被侵蚀。大道另一侧山坡上的公寓房精致排列，俯瞰一切。

At one time you could take a little street cut into the cliffside to make a hairpin turn down to Pacific Coast Highway. No longer. Still, the weird route gives you a good view of the Santa Monica Pier with its playful Charles Moore designs. Colorful tiles, metal work in forms of fish, profiles of pelicans, give homage to the great architect. Jackson knew Moore, claimed him as a mentor, back when the flamboyant American architect taught a design studio at UCLA.

曾经一度你可以抄小道直达悬崖边，然后转一个发夹弯，下到太平洋海岸高速。现在不行了。不过，这古怪的路线还是能呈现给你一幅圣莫尼卡码头的好景致，点缀着有趣的查尔斯·穆尔设计。五彩斑斓的瓷砖，鱼形状的金属作品，鹈鹕的轮廓，在向这位伟大的建筑师致敬。杰克逊认识穆尔，声称后者是他的导师，当时这位名声显赫的美国建筑大师在 UCLA 教授设计小班课程。

Samuel—Surfboard in Speedster, Santa Monica, CA
塞缪尔——在加州圣莫尼卡，保时捷车里载着冲浪板

Santa Monica Beach was my place, where I grew up. My sixteenth summer was the best, when I got my driver's license. I drove their every day with my friends, swimming, surfing, the rhythm of the ocean. At the end of that summer, under the last full moon, the beach shimmered with Grunion, thousands of them, 'running' as they call it, covering, sparkling back at the moonlight, beaching themselves on the sand, group spawning, wild abandon; then quickly disappearing back into the black of the night ocean. Doesn't happen much anymore, too many people annoying them.

圣莫尼卡海滩曾经是我的地盘。我在那里长大。16岁那年夏天是最棒的时光，我拿到了驾照。我每天都开车带着朋友们到那儿去游泳、冲浪，那是大海的节奏。夏天结束的最后一个满月，海滩上挤满了成千上万闪闪发亮的银汉鱼，人们称为"奔跑"，它们层层叠叠挤在沙滩上，反射着冷冷月辉，完全忘我地成群产卵；之后迅速游回夜色中的大海，消失无踪。现在难得见到这种盛况了，人太多打扰到它们了。

'Samuel's beach', as I call it, lays out wide, lazy, during the winter ... turns teaming when the heat comes. It's constantly raked, patrolled, cleaned, cleared. Blue lifeguard huts, lifted ten feet off the sand for maximum view, hold red garbed young men and woman, languid, cool, tanned, waiting for someone to go under, riptided by waves tortured by the sandy shallows. When the fog is in retreat, and the open ocean lies shimmering in greens and blues, there's no better place in the world. The Pelicans are back now, a sign when they pass along the beach, wide-winged, gliding, inches above the tops of the waves to some favorite roost up the coast.

我管它叫"塞缪尔的海滩"。它在冬日里懒洋洋地广阔伸展，夏天热浪袭来时人头攒动。人们不断对它进行清扫、巡护、清洁、清场。蓝色的救生棚矗立在沙滩上，离地十英尺高，以确保视野开阔。穿着红色制服的青年男女救生员皮肤晒得黝黑，酷帅又慵懒，一旦有人溺水，被浪头卷下去，他们就会出动。海雾消散时，开阔的海面在阳光下闪耀着绿蓝色光芒，世上再没有比这更好的地方了。鹈鹕又回来了，它们张开宽阔的翅膀，沿着海面滑翔，离浪尖仅有数英寸，一直飞到岸边它们最爱的栖息地。

PCH, Pacific Coast Highway, hugs the shore, turns into Highway One, takes you on a ride, the most beautiful in California, and therefore the world. It's an extension of old Hollywood. Every star you've ever heard of made the same drive, many to their own homes, Malibu. The sounds of Highway One bring excitement, ocean, sunlight, relief from the city. It's the road James Dean raced, Lana Turner hitchhiked, Marilyn Monroe cruised. Think *Beach Blanket Bingo*, Frankie Avalon, Annette Funicello, Topanga Canyon, Zuma, Point Magu. Pleasure, scandal, stars, surfers, one generation after the other for a hundred years. Along that stretch, every day, fingers of fog invade the coastal foothills, then retreat under the heat of the sun. The gloom of the gray is in constant contrast with bursts of brilliant light, the back and forth pulling at your mood, playing it, youthful, alternating, perpetual reinvention.

太平洋海岸高速路（PCH）沿着海岸线蜿蜒，并入一号公路，将你带上加州最美的一段公路，也堪称全世界最美的。它是旧日好莱坞的延伸。你听说过的每一位明星都走过这段路，其中多数是取道回他们在马里布的家。提起一号高速，就会勾起兴奋、大海、阳光、逃离城市这些念头。这是詹姆斯·迪安赛车、拉纳·特纳搭顺风车、玛丽莲·梦露兜风的那条路。想一想电影《沙滩舞会》、弗兰基·阿瓦隆、安妮特·富尼切洛、托潘加峡谷、祖马、马古岬。享乐、丑闻、明星、冲浪者，一代接一代，长达一个世纪。每天，海雾笼罩这条路海岸沿线的山脚，继而被阳光驱散。暗淡的灰色调常常与鲜明的光线形成强烈对比，令你的情绪时而高涨时而低落，戏弄你，充满青春活力，不断变幻和再造。

When you reach the southern edge of Malibu's thick banks of fog insist on a fight, at least until noon. That's when they usually give way to youthful sunlight playing on the wave tops and the backs of swimmers, surfers. The trees react to the light, dreary in the gray, vibrant in sunshine. Red, orange, purple bougainvillea stretch brilliant, glistening. The same foliage lonely, monotoned, when the damp of the coastal clouds hangs over them.

来到马里布南端，厚厚的浓雾持续笼罩，直至中午。雾散去时，阳光充满活力，照耀在波浪上，也照耀在游泳和冲浪的人背上。树林也在光线中鲜活起来，灰雾中暗淡无神的他们在阳光下生机勃勃。红色、橙色、紫色的九重葛枝条舒展，光彩照人。而同样的花叶在海边潮湿的浓雾愁云笼罩下却显得孤独、单调。

My own mood mirrors the fight of fog and sun. On that day of all it swung me back and forth. Meeting Moriah, everything at stake. Confident yeah, but how to do it? Orson welles, God! Convince Madam Leung to accept me as someone to trust with editing a second edition of *Bruise Art*, and then develop that into a film? Even if she agreed to the basic premise, a part of me doubted if I could pull it off. I'd never done such a project. I'd worked with my father, helped him, saw everything he did, every move, but that's not the same thing as doing it all yourself. Everyone would be looking, no hiding. No obscure work, this, the book already seen as successful, popular. The film would have to match that, or else. Large segments of population in both China and the U.S. would be watching, judging.

Highway One, California
加州一号公路

我自己的情绪就好比浓雾与阳光的拉锯战。就在那一天,我的情绪忽上忽下。面见莫立娅,胜败在此一搏。自信是有的,但如何去做?奥森·威尔斯,天哪!说服梁夫人接受我,将编辑《瘀伤艺术》第二版、制作电影这事儿放心交给我?即使她同意了,我自己的一部分都在怀疑自己能否做到。我从来没做过这类项目。我跟着父亲工作过,协助他,观摩他做的每一件事、每一步行动,但那跟自己独立去做完全是两回事。所有人都会盯着,无处躲藏,不可能背着人干。这本书已经成功畅销,电影必须与其匹配,要么就啥也不是。中国和美国都会有大量群众在关注和评判。

All that in my mind, churning me, pulling me down, the cloud cover so strong. The next moment, the next turn of the fabled highway, the sun would burn through, bright, hot, a burst of ocean spray hitting the windshield, the droplets refracting the light through mini prisms into rainbow. What the hell. Why not me? Hollywood was built on optimism, confidence, creative bluffing, people coming in from everywhere, finding the right moment, project, relentless ambition. LA was built on a desert after all, no water, yet there it was. They made it work. Piped in water from hundreds of miles away. The place was built for people like me, connected, educated, ambitious. If all those others did it, so could I. If Madam Leung said yes, I'd have to do it, find the way, the critical path, whatever it was, whatever I had to do. 'California optimistic' as Jackson put it.

这些思绪在我脑海里缠绕，令我情绪低落，乌云密布。下一刻，在这段传奇高速路的下一个转弯，阳光又会燃烧耀眼光芒，浪涛拍岸激起的水花溅到前挡风上，小水珠就像迷你棱镜，将阳光反射出彩虹。见鬼。怎么就不能是我？好莱坞就是建在乐观、自信、创造性的忽悠之上。人们来自五湖四海，寻找合适的时机、项目，带着持续而强烈的野心。说到底洛杉矶是从一滴水都没有的沙漠里建起来的，看看它现在的样子。他们成就了它。用管子把水从几百英里外引过来。这个地方是为了我这样的人而建的，有关系，受过教育，雄心勃勃。如果那些人都能成功，我也能。如果梁夫人同意了，我就必须做到，找到关键路径，不管那是什么，需要我做什么。就如杰克逊所说，"加利福尼亚式的乐观"。

Damn, idiot! Some guy behind me with his 'brights' on, this time of day, another guy behind him, coming on, the same. So irritating. No reason. Messing up the pleasant drive for others. They noticed me touching my breaks, still on. Californians, everyone driving with lights on these days, like that will save them from the apocalypse, the big one, or the next drunk driver coming the opposite way; But these two, different, purposeful, in formation, pacing me, my speed. Oh well, just chilling, the slower lane. They drifted back, almost out of sight, always in it.

该死的蠢货！我后面有辆车开着远光灯，这大白天的，它后面还跟着一辆，也一样。太烦人了。莫名其妙。干扰了别人的愉快旅程。他们注意到我踩刹车了，但仍然开着远光灯。每一个开车的加州人，只有在世界末日来临的时候，或者是对面来车貌似喝醉的时候，才会把远光灯打开，以图自救。但这两位不同。他们是故意为之，排好队形，根据我的车速把握节奏。好吧，冷静下来，我并入慢车道。他们减速拉开距离，几乎离开了视野范围，但还一直能看见。

The next turn in the road, a changed angle of the rocks, the light fades, sudden gray, back into self-limiting expectations. Moriah Leung, so sophisticated, worldly, she'd note my lack of experience, accomplishment. Bluster wouldn't do. My father's reputation, not enough to cover for me. She'd look down on me, brash, on the make. She had to have seen her full measure of scammers, grafters, so many comers, trying to take a piece of her husband. No matter what I said, she'd see through me. Maybe I should wait, ask about

High Beams Harassment
远光骚扰

internships, work for a film producer for a couple of years, more experience, then look for a project.

　　在公路下一个转弯，岩石的角度改变了，光线又暗淡下去，世界突然变灰了。我又陷入自抑的情绪中。莫立娅·梁，如此洞悉人情世故，她会发现我缺乏经验和成就。吹牛没有用。我父亲的名气不足以支撑我。她会看不起我，认为我虚张声势，追名逐利。她应该见过各色骗子和钻营的人，这么多上门的人，都想从她丈夫身上要点东西。不管我说什么，她都会看穿我。也许我应该等待，在某个制片人那里求个实习机会，干上几年攒点经验，然后再去找项目。

　　Funny, how easily my mood switched, back and forth. 'Showing up is fifty percent of success.' Woody Allen, I think. 'One percent inspiration, ninety—nine percent perspiration.' Everyone knows that one. Plenty of examples of youth, talent taking on enormous projects, winning. David done by Michelangelo at twenty—six, *Citizen Kane* by Orson Wells at twenty—five. Why not me? Things had come together, just at the right time. 'Even if you're not a believer, be open

077

to gifts from Heaven.' Jackson wrote. I was determined to do just that, take his advice, run with it until something else stopped me, not myself, my own limiting doubt. Highway One is great for that kind of thinking, grand vistas, the horizon unlimited as you run up the coast. The ocean always on, until you reach Point Magu.

真有意思，我的情绪如此轻易地来回摇摆。"出场就是成功了一半。"伍迪·艾伦说的，我想。"一分灵感，九分汗水。"人人都知道这句话。也有大把青年才俊担纲宏伟项目并且取得成功的例子。米开朗琪罗26岁完成大卫像。奥森·威尔斯25岁拍了《公民凯恩》。我怎么就不行？各种因素机缘巧合凑在一起。"即使你不信神，也要对上天赐予的礼物保持开放心态。"杰克逊写道。我下定决心，听从他的建议，沿这条路走下去，除非外力阻止我，而不是被自我怀疑所局限。一号公路对这类思考太有帮助，沿着海岸线驾驶，景色开阔，地平线一望无垠，大海一路相伴到马古岬。

The Navy has a large base there, taking the seacoast for several miles. You're forced inland, to Oxnard. Quirky name, as if someone joking. Name of a real estate developer. Nothing to do with oxen or nards, the sound of it, me laughing. Irritating, the Navy taking that much coastline. At least it reminds you, provides additional appreciation for the ocean air, as you're forced to breath the fertilizer. Not all bad though, the rectangle' d flats of land planted in strawberries, cauliflower, artichokes. Odd assortment of cars lines the street, workers' cars. You see them out there, dots of color, shirts and pullovers, men and women, bent over, wide brimmed hats, tenders of rows, more rows, plants, ribbons of clear plastic. You hit the side of the new Highway 101 below Ventura, broad, almost interstate. You must take it, no other choice, old Highway One cut off, used only by the locals. Too bad. My father drove me up when I was a boy. The old Highway One went slower, but you could feel the ocean, not just see pieces of it, over there.

这里有个海军基地，占据海岸线长达数英里。公路不得不在此转向内陆，经过奥克斯纳德（牛香）。古怪的地名，就像有人在故意搞笑。这是一个真实的地产商的名字。跟牛和香都没什么关系（"奥克斯"英文意为"牛"，"纳德"意为"香"——译者注），光念发音就让我笑半天。海军占了这么多海岸可真够气人的。闻着化肥的味道，令人更加感念海风拂面的好处。不过，那些种着草莓、花椰菜和朝鲜蓟的方方正正的田地也没那么糟糕。街边停着各种古怪的车辆，都是工人的车。你能看到他们在田里干活，点点颜色，衬衫或毛衣，男人女人，弯着腰，头戴宽檐草帽，成行成列的蔬菜，透明塑料带子。过了文图拉,公路接入新101公路,几乎像州际公路一样宽。你只能走这条路,别无选择,老一号公路到这里就中断了,现在只有当地人在用。太遗憾。我小的时候父亲带我走过,老一号公路车速慢些,但你能感受到大海,而不是远远看着大海的片段。

The new way takes you through Ventura, all the way to Santa Barbara. Once you hit the sea again, a lot of your vision is blocked by lines of cars, this time surfers, precarious tight lines along narrow widths of sand between road and brush. When the cars get thickest you know there's a great lay of beach, or excellent surfing. Sandy foot paths take you over, through the dunes. Clusters of black wetsuits bobbing on the water's surface, waiting for the next set. Even though you think you're headed north the coast is exactly east—west on the run going into Santa Barbara. You know you're there when the foothills fill out with homes ... rich, solid, exclusive.

新公路经过文图拉直奔圣芭芭拉。公路再次回到海边,但你的视野会被路边一连串停靠的车辆阻挡。那是冲浪者的车,挤在道路和灌木之间窄窄的沙地上。看到车辆大量停泊,你就知道这里有大片海滩,或者是绝佳冲浪地点。沿着撒满细沙的小道,翻过沙丘,你就能看到一群群穿着黑色冲浪服的人浮在水面上,等待下一个浪头到来。你觉得自己在向北开,实际上海岸线是东西向的,直达圣芭芭拉。当你看到布满房子的山脚,你就到了。那些房子看起来有钱、殷实、排外。

Santa Barbara has the feel of home, where I grew up, just richer. My father took me when he'd have a weekend. See friends, guys from the business. Producers, directors, agents. Long summer days and nights. I'd go off with their kids, surfing mostly, or a borrowed dirt bike up in the mountains. In the evenings we'd go swimming, floating on our backs as the sunset, the profiled edge of the Channel Islands turning slate under the mist. After, it felt good, you know the feeling, after swimming all day, fresh, good tired, relaxed. Great food, steak, grilled abalone, large slices of avocado, mountain tomatoes, purple onions, Monterey olives. California, casual. All of it cooked and served by someone else, that always made it taste better, my dad would say. Mexican women did the cooking, one from La Paz, with a tiny daughter at her legs, tugging, sleeping in the hamper in the laundry room.

圣芭芭拉给我家乡的感觉,只是比我家乡富足。我父亲周末只要有空就带我来。会会生意上的朋友——制片人、导演、经纪人。那些漫长的夏日时光。我跟他们的孩子玩,多数时候去冲浪，或者骑越野摩托车到山里去。傍晚我们去游泳，夕阳西下的时候仰头浮在水面，海峡岛的轮廓在雾气中变成灰石板色。一天下来的感觉棒极了，你知道的，一天都在戏水，整个人感到焕然一新，愉悦的疲倦和放松。吃得很棒，牛排，烤鲍鱼，大片牛油果，野番茄，紫洋葱，蒙特雷橄榄。加州休闲风。我父亲会说，别人做好端来的菜品总是尝起来更美味。做饭的都是墨西哥女人，其中一位从拉巴斯来，小女儿总是黏在她的腿边，或者睡在洗衣房的篮子里。

Desserts of field-fresh strawberries, large, split longwise and quartered, served in their own juice with a sprinkle of sugar. Sometimes they'd serve the berries drizzled over fresh baked plain cakes. That was the best. Chilled whipping cream to top it. A smell of fresh vanilla bean, lemon zest. Memories like that stick with you, a yearning to find it again, but never can. No predicting it, what'll stick with you.

甜品是新鲜采摘的草莓，个头很大，竖着切成等份，摆在榨好的草莓汁上，再撒上糖。有时候是把浆果撒在刚烤出来的蛋糕上。那才是最棒的。蛋糕上面是打发的奶油，新鲜的香草味，带着一丝柠檬清香。这种回忆总是伴随着你，令你渴望再次找回那种感觉，但永远也做不到。你预料不到什么东西会留在记忆里，挥之不去。

After Santa Barbara the highway takes on yet another name, El Camino Real, the Royal Way, built by the Spanish, named in honor of the royal family. The sweetness of that part of the coast, the land clutching close to the ocean cliffs, the sea felt, more than seen, the view intermittently blocked, thick growth, imported trees, structures, homes, farming.

过了圣芭芭拉，一号公路就改称"皇家之路"，由西班牙修建，为致敬西班牙皇室而命名。那段海岸甚是美好，陆地紧紧抓住海边悬崖，大海是通过全部感官感受到而不是只用眼睛看到的，因为海景不断被茂密的植被、进口的树种、建筑物、住房和农场阻挡。

At Gaviota the road turns inland again, dry, hot, classic California, golden clusters of ancient oaks in the draws and hollows. If you squint your eyes, you see their pattern as they form an x-ray, a hidden shadow of the terrain. Beautiful in its dryness, the land's answer to the ocean. Aside from the vineyards, it's much as it was when the Spanish came through. You hit Solvang, then Los Olivos, Los Alamos. Quick pass-through Santa Maria before you return to the sea at Pismo Beach. Back inland again, on the run up to San Luis Obispo.

到了加维奥塔，公路再次转到内陆，加州典型的干燥炎热气候，一簇簇年代久远的金色橡树散落在平原和谷地。眯起眼睛看，就像透过X射线一样，从它们的分布情况上分辨出隐藏的地形。干燥的大地自有其美丽之处，它是大地对大海的回答。除了新增的葡萄园，这块土地与西班牙人刚来的时候没有什么两样。公路经过索尔万，之后是洛斯奥利沃斯，洛斯阿拉莫斯。快速经过圣马利亚之后，你会在皮斯莫海滩重返海边。之后又折返内陆，直奔圣路易奥比斯波（SLO）。

I did my undergraduate studies at Cal Poly, SLO town, at least a part of it. Transferred in from Los Angeles Harbor College. A way to save money, just after Dad's death. Even though my bachelor's degree is from there, I only spent a year on campus. Beautiful dusty hills, the university set off from the town, pinned up against sets of odd cones shaped peaks, leftover volcanos of ancient coastal mountains. Senior year in Italy, I won a competition to study in Florence, Another connection to Jackson.

我大学本科就在SLO的加州州立理工大学就读，至少一部分是。我是从洛杉矶的港口学院转过来的。我父亲去世后，这是一种省钱的办法。我的学士学位是在这里拿到的，但我在校园里只待了一年。学校离镇上很远，坐落在布满灰尘的美丽山丘上，背后是一连串圆锥形的山峰，那是古代海岸山脉残留下来的火山。我赢了一个比赛，得以在佛罗伦萨完成高等学业。这又是跟杰克逊有联系的一点。

Cinema *Romano*, Fellini, Cinecitta. Got a chance to spend two weeks on a movie set near Rome, then Livorno. A lot of film making. I lied to them. Said I worked for a magazine, writing an article about one of their actors. No one questioned me, no request for credentials. They let me go anywhere, as long as I shut up when the filming started. Every evening I ate with the cast at a local ristorante contracted out by the producer. Bowls of pasta, so good. Loud laughter, bottles of wine, smoking, all kinds of stuff, letting loose after the concentrated tedium of film making. Sea breeze sweeps in each night. Tyrrhenian. One of the leads snuck me in up to her hotel room one night, up the cranky wrought iron ladder, through the spider-webbed attic, then down to her bed. Had to make the same way out before light.

费里尼纪录片《罗马》的拍摄地是奇尼奇塔电影城。我得到一个机会，在利沃纳的一个电影片场待了两个星期。好多电影是在那里拍的。我撒谎说我为一家杂志社工

Oaks on Hills—San Luis Obispo, CA
山坡上的橡树——加州圣路易奥比斯波

作,正在写他们一位演员的专稿。没人质疑我,也没人要看证件。他们任由我四处溜达,只要我在开机的时候闭嘴就行。每天晚上我跟着剧组在制片人指定的当地餐厅一起吃饭。意大利面管够,棒极了。开怀大笑,葡萄酒开怀畅饮,抽烟,凡此种种,费神又单调的电影拍摄工作之后的放松。每夜都有海风轻拂,第勒尼安海上吹来的。某天晚上,其中一位主演将我偷偷带进酒店,爬上嘎吱作响的铁制楼梯,穿过蜘蛛网般的阁楼,来到她的床上。天亮前再按原路摸出去。

At San Luis Obispo you arrive at a fork in the road. You must decide between going to the ocean, to Big Sir, or to the Salinas Valley. Either way, so beautiful, two iconic California landscapes, the drama of the ocean cliffs or undulating golden hills, vineyards, ribbons of ancient oaks. Morro Bay is ocean, old Highway One, Paso Robles the wine country, by way of Camino Real, Highway 101.

公路在圣路易奥比斯波分成两条岔路。你必须选择是朝海边走,前往大瑟尔,还是去往萨利纳斯谷。两条路都很美,都是加州标志性风景的代表。一条是险峻的海岸悬崖,另一条是起伏的金色山丘,葡萄种植园和成行的古老橡树。莫罗湾是海岸之路,走老一号公路。葡萄酒之乡帕索罗布斯要借道皇家之路,走 101 公路。

In 'Havanna hurry', I took the fastest route, inland. You can autocruise at seventy-five as the artery cuts easily through the dry country at the western edge of the long valley. Clusters of dusty green oaks on the hillsides, old enough to have witnessed each change in the valley flat below. Uninhabited two hundred years ago, then people, roads, crops, vines. Paso Robles marks the center of wine production. Vineyards lines, patterns, stretch to the horizon on either side of the highway. The terrain possessing the correct sunlight, soil, and weather to yield the best wines in the world. Famous competition with the French; They lost bigtime, no more competitions.

因哈瓦娜而起的赶路心切,我选择走内陆这条最快的路线。主干道沿着狭长山谷的西边横贯干燥的大地,可以用每小时75英里的速度自动巡航。山坡上橡树丛生,落满灰尘,年代久远到足以看遍脚下山谷里的沧海桑田。两百年前这里寂无人烟,随后人们、道路、庄稼、葡萄园纷至沓来。帕索罗布斯成为葡萄酒生产中心。公路两侧的葡萄园成行成片,一直延伸到天边。这片土地拥有合适的阳光、土壤和气候,产出世界上最好的葡萄酒。它们与法国红酒的竞争举世皆知,法国酒输惨了,再也没有竞争了。

I took a quick detour turn at Highway 43 toward the sea, to see the Bartholomew Winery. Jackson had obtained a large parcel of land complete with working winery. He'd said that he felt a 'primal connection' with the terrain, the sunlight, that it reminded him of his family's ancestral lands in Greece, near the town of Distomo, the dry Greek countryside. It's all calling to him. I pulled over at a rise in the road at his estate, to take it in, see the fingers of mist touching the brown hills, endless geometric exact rows, vines in lines disappearing at the western horizon. Then back around to 101, not much time.

我在43号高速下道,绕路到海边看巴塞洛缪的葡萄酒庄。杰克逊在这里买了一大块地,有着整套葡萄酒生产设施。他曾说,在此地感觉得到与大地和阳光的"原初连接",令他想起家族祖先在希腊迪斯托莫镇附近那片干燥的故土。那片土地在呼唤他。我在他的庄园旁边一处起伏的道路边停下车,将景色尽收眼底,薄雾拂过棕褐色的山丘,规则的几何形起伏望不到头,一行行葡萄树消失在西方的地平线。之后我返回101公路,时间不多了。

Vineyards give way to other crops, signs claiming the capital of the world, artichokes, garlic, avocados. Through King City, Soledad, Gonzales, then Salinas. I always sing Bobby Magee when I hear that word, Salinas: Somewhere near Salinas Lord, I let her slip away. She's lookin' for a home. I hope she finds it! By the way, never take the turnoff in Salinas marked Santa Cruz, if that's where you're headed. Much better to wait for Highway 156 on the other side. More direct, the quick drive to Castroville. Turn off at 183/Merritt Street. Go through the center of town. Empties you back onto Cabrillo Highway, for the final dash along the ocean to Santa Cruz.

葡萄园变成了其他作物。道路旁矗立着各种广告牌，宣告这里是朝鲜蓟、大蒜、鳄梨的世界之都。经过国王城、索莱达、冈萨雷斯，到了萨利纳斯。我每次听到这个词都会哼起博比·马吉："在萨利纳斯不远的地方，主啊，我让她溜走了。她在寻找一个家，我希望她能找到！"顺便提一下，如果你要去圣克鲁斯，千万不要在萨利纳斯的圣克鲁斯出口指示牌处转弯。最好等到156号公路的出口在左手出现。更快捷的路径是走卡斯特罗维尔，在183号出口，梅里特街下道。穿过镇中心。再回到卡布里欧公路，就能沿着海岸线一气冲到圣克鲁斯。

Oh my God, Havanna! Text her now!
我的天，哈瓦娜！赶紧给她发短信！

Havanna! Almost there.
Everything cool.
Back tomorrow AM.
Maybe earlier.
Parents'll never know.
Bye for now ... manana.
What's Mandarin for tomorrow?
哈瓦娜！我快到了。
一切都很好。
明天上午就回去了。
也许更早。
爸妈永远都不会知道。
暂时小别，明天见。
中文怎么说"明天"？

Scene Four   Santa Cruz

第四幕 圣克鲁斯

Cabrillo Highway, yet another name for Highway One, narrows to two lanes at Old Salinas River. Ocean views for a moment, then back inland, Watsonville. Sixteen miles more to Santa Cruz. You can see bits of the city as you approach, the Monterey Bay coast bending around to allow it. I always thought of Santa Cruz as a part of greater Silicon Valley, but don't let a local know you're thinking that way. Don't know why, it adds to their prestige. After all Silicon Valley, 'Sil-Val' as coined by Jackson, holds America's shifting vortex of popular culture, and by extension, that of the world, Santa Cruz relatively unknown. High tech, Internet, social media, Steve Jobs momentum, it pulled in everyone from around the world, into 'Sil-Val'.

卡布里欧公路其实是一号公路的另一个名字，在老萨利纳斯河变窄为双车道。海景只伴随了一小段，之后就转向内陆，沃森维尔。再开16英里就到圣克鲁斯了。蒙特雷湾的曲线令城市的一部分进入你的视野。我一直认为圣克鲁斯是大硅谷地区的一部分，但可别让当地人知道你这么想。不知何故，这么说会令他们自我感觉良好。毕竟硅谷是美国流行文化的涡轮，也就相当于全世界的涡轮，圣克鲁斯则相对无名。高新技术、互联网、社交媒体、乔布斯，将人们从世界的各个角落吸引过来。

'Sil-Val' is a nondescript place, when you come down to it, not more than a stretch of towns running into one another, no discernable boarders. Towns like San Jose, Cupertino, Mountain Valley, Palo Alto. On the east side of the Bay, all the way up past Milpitas, Freemont, then Oakland to Berkeley. On the west side, Redwood City, San Mateo up to San Francisco. Hard to define the boarders of a valley, any valley, let along one based on an idea. All the cities touching the bay stake a claim to 'Sil-Val', new capital of quick-change America. If you extend an axis down to Los Angeles, then you're really talking. Around that line the world turns, reacts, celebrates, complains. No telling how long it'll last, hold onto that status. Best just to go with it, until it's spent.

硅谷是个毫无特色的地方。只是一些小镇连成片，圣何塞，库柏蒂诺，山谷镇，帕洛阿尔托，其间没有明显的边界。在海湾东边，一路经过米尔皮塔斯，弗里芒，奥克兰，到达伯克利。西边是雷德伍德市，圣马特奥，上到旧金山。很难确定一个山谷的边界在哪里，更何况这山谷只是个概念。所有与海湾接界的城市都声称自己属于硅谷，快速变化中的美国的新首都。如果你将轴线延长到洛杉矶，那就对了。世界围着这根轴线转动、反应、欢呼、抱怨。很难说这个地位会维持多久，最好是趁年华正好，享受要趁早。

Santa Cruz should as well, connect itself to 'Sil-Val'. As the nearest outlet to the ocean, it certainly can make a case. Highway 17 serves as a cord of extension, connection. Every weekend or holiday Sil-Vallers cram the thin 17 conduit, to the breaking point. Santa Cruz serves 'Sil-Val', provides it diversion, beaches, cool clean air, when the valley grows too hot, July, August. It's the main public beach access for everyone in 'Sil-Val'.

圣克鲁斯也应当跟硅谷搭上关系。作为离海最近的出口，它还是能够做出点名堂的。17号公路成了一条外联线。每逢周末或节假日，硅谷人恨不能把窄窄的17号公路挤爆。圣克鲁斯为硅谷服务，为人们逃离7、8月的热浪提供海滩和清凉洁净的空气。它就是硅谷人的主要公共海滩。

The traffic slows at the 41st Street exit, then spins around into the 'Fishhook', the hair pin turn where 17 and Highway One collide. You can keep going up the coast on Mission/Highway One or turn off onto Ocean Street. 'Best way to the ocean is Ocean', Jackson described, to his own arrivals. I followed his advice, down Ocean Street, across the San Lorenzo River, over Beach Hill, onto West Cliff Drive.

交通在42街出口处变得缓慢，然后转圈来到"鱼钩"，17号公路和一号公路互通的发夹弯。你可以一直沿着一号公路海岸线开，或者下道拐到海洋街。"去往海洋最好的路就是'海洋'"，杰克逊在描述他自己的路线时就是这么说的。我听从他的建议，走海洋街，越过圣洛伦索河，翻过海岸山，来到西崖道。

I'd seen pictures of it, Jackson Bartholomew and Madam Leung's astounding cliff side estate. There it was, the top of the geodesic dome at least, famous, popular, sparkling. Like everything in Jackson's life, his design; Tour de force, published, *Architectural Record, Vogue, People*. When first built so many vehicles attempted to drive there that the city had to reroute traffic. Now there's a special J.B. logoed bus to pull away a portion of the traffic.

我在照片上见过杰克逊·巴塞洛缪和梁夫人这所宅邸，它坐落在悬崖上，令人叹为观止。现在，它就在那里，至少能看到那个著名的、流行的、闪闪发亮的网格球形穹顶。与杰克逊生活中的一切一样，这是他设计的，是他的毕生杰作，在《建筑纪录》《时尚》《人物》等杂志上发表过。刚落成的时候，有太多人驾车前去参观，迫使城里的交通临时改道。现在专门开设了一趟打着J.B.徽标的巴士，以减轻一部分交通压力。

Santa Cruz, CA—Wharf & Boardwalk, Near J.B. Guesthouse Condo on Beach Hill
加州圣克鲁斯——码头和栈道，靠近海岸山上J.B.的客寓

It's a stunning cluster of structures, mosaic of modern, Morish, romantic. More or less centered on the rambling complex, hovering, the dome, multicolored, underlit to allow for light play, intricately patterned. 'Il Duomo' as Jackson called it, location of the 'Hologram Room'. The dome is said to house the most advanced privately owned hologram/AI setup in the world. Jackson brought in scientists, experts, researchers, Stanford, UCLA, Hollywood. His creation though, his direction, a new approach, prototype, the 'sublime combination of Hologram and AI'. No limit on budget. A billion spent, two, five? 'Whatever it took,' he'd say, whenever asked. 'Money is meant to be spent. No telling how long I'll have to do the spending.'

这是一组令人叹为观止的建筑集合体，现代风格的拼花装饰，摩尔式浪漫风格。在四处延展的建筑群的中心，穹顶盘踞其上，五彩斑斓，图案精巧，内置灯光打造出光影效果。杰克逊管它叫"主教堂"，"全息室"就设在这里。据说穹顶里装置了私人拥有的世界上最先进的全息/人工智能设备。杰克逊把斯坦福、加利福尼亚大学洛杉矶分校、好莱坞的科学家、专家、研究人员网罗到此。但这是他的创造物，他的方向，一种新的手段，原型，"全息影像和人工智能的至高结合"。预算没有上限。花了十个亿吧，或是二十个，五十个？每次被问到，他都说："不惜成本，钱就是用来花的。不知道我还要花多久。"

Jackson wouldn't talk details. Moriah never spoke of it at all. Something she didn't like about it. The *LA Times* reported it a hologram dedicated to the promotion of one thing, in fact, one person, that is, Jackson Bartholomew; Or as the *LA Times* put it, "Dedicated to the cult of all things 'J.B.,' the cult of Bart-HOLO-mew." Him alone in a room apparently, his image, perfected, such that no one could tell the difference between Jackson present and alive, and him 'hologram-ed', 'AI-ed'. Secretive, Jackson, on this creation, a leaker quickly fired, immediately after a detailed *LA Times* article, sketches, numbers. 'Actions have consequences,' all he'd say on the matter.

杰克逊不愿透露细节，而莫立娅压根不提此事。出于某种原因她不喜欢这玩意儿。《洛杉矶时报》报道说，全息影像唯一的意义是为一件事做营销，确切说是一个人，即杰克逊·巴塞洛缪。《洛杉矶时报》是这么写的："致力于煽起对 J.B. 崇拜的狂热，对'巴全息缪'的崇拜。"（作者此处玩字母游戏，突出巴塞洛缪英文拼写中的"全息"字母。——译者注）显然，这个空间里只有他一人，他的影像，经过打磨完善，难以辨别究竟是活生生的杰克逊本人还是经过人工智能处理的全息影像。杰克逊对他的造物遮遮掩掩，但是在《洛杉矶时报》发表了详细报道，透露了一些草图和数字之后，立即有个泄密者发声。"一切行为皆有后果。"他只肯说这么多。

　From the reporting, his comments, everything indeed relating to him, Jackson. Each aspect carefully considered, perfected, a means to impress, create the most effective-real hologram presentation ever made. No waiting for some hypothetical date in the future. Jackson wanted now. Sounds of his footsteps, voice, breathing, the smell of his cologne, the slight increase in humidity when his large frame might theoretically enter a space, slightest creaking sounds of the rocking chair he'd designed, the rustling of his clothing as he crossed and uncrossed his legs, all of it replicated to match the movements and existence indicators of the perfect hologram image. All rumors though, no actual photographs or video, no reporter yet made claim to seeing it, him. What a sight, Jackson Bartholomew hologram-ed, AI-ed, charismatic, formidable, intimidating. Ping, clang, my cell, the irate sound reserved for her, Havanna!

　从报道及他本人的回应看，的确一切都是关于杰克逊自己的。每个角度都经过仔细斟酌和完善，要给人留下深刻印象，创造出史上最真实的全息影像。不需要等到未来某个假设的日子。他现在就要。他的脚步声、说话声、呼吸声，他身上古龙水的味道，他高大的身躯理论上进入某个空间的时候空气湿度会轻微上升，他设计的摇椅发出的轻微嘎吱声，他跷起二郎腿又放下时衣物的摩擦声，所有这一切都被复制下来，与那个全息影像的存在和动作完美匹配。当然这些都是传言，没有真实图片或视频证实，迄今也没有记者声称目睹过它，或说他。那会是什么样的情景啊，经过人工智能处理的杰克逊·巴塞洛缪全息影像，魅力四射，令人生畏，充满威胁。叮～咣！我手机来信息了。这怒气冲冲的声音是专门为她设的！哈瓦娜！

　　No later than 10:00 am! Don't forget!
　　You promised!
　　My parents are coming, from Spain! To see YOU!
　　Text me when you're on your way!
　　Don't forget!
　　Asshole, Cabron, Hundan!
　　不许超过上午10点！别忘了！
　　你答应过的！
　　我父母从西班牙过来，是为了见你！

你出发的时候给我发信息！
别忘了！
浑蛋！浑蛋！浑蛋！

Immediate reply:
I Promise ... my sweet Havanna.
立即回复：
我保证……我亲爱的哈瓦娜。

Her reply:
Stop using the three dots ...
Very irritating.
她的回复：
别再用省略号了……
巨烦人。

Three o'clock. Enough time to drive out onto the wharf, regroup, collect, center; Park at the circle at the end of the doglegged structure, where it struts out, against the whipping wind, wicked waves. The sea churns out there, offers you up in sacrifice. This far out on the wharf, the ocean rises up, surrounds you, horizon suddenly less friendly, your body disconnected from the land, vulnerable.

下午三点。还有足够的时间开到码头那边，重新组织、收集、聚焦。我把车停在那座狗腿建筑尽头的圆圈里。这建筑昂首挺胸地迎接呼啸的海风和凶猛的海浪。大海在翻腾，好像要拿你献祭。站在码头尽头，大海波浪起伏，将你包围，地平线突然显得不那么可亲，你的身体与陆地断了联系，变得脆弱。

Bellows of sea lions bounce on the heavy timber scaffolding below. Dozens of blubbered bodies press against each other, hauled up in close formation. To the east, sail boats, three or four, holding in place against the tides; anchor lines taught, disappearing below the rippled surface. Summer in Santa Cruz, broad southerly views, across the rippled bay, to Monterey. To the west, the city's iconic symbol, a small brick lighthouse, repurposed into surfing museum. Across my views, drifts of tourists, clusters of twos, fours, making for Gilda's I'd

Sunrise at Santa Cruz Wharf—Shimmers Under the Sea
圣克鲁斯码头的日出——海平面下闪耀的光

guess; No that's gone.

　　海狮的怒吼在码头下的笨重木头支架间回荡。它们胖墩墩的身子一个挨一个，紧紧依偎在一起。东边泊着三四艘帆船，在浪潮中起伏，锚索消失在波纹涟漪的水面下。这就是圣克鲁斯以南的夏日辽阔景致，跨越波浪涟涟的海湾延伸到蒙特雷。西边是这个城市的地标符号，一座小小的砖制灯塔，已改建为冲浪博物馆。放眼望去，游客三三两两，我猜是去吉尔达餐厅的。哦不对，餐厅关门大吉了。

　　To some extent, I was a regular to 'the city of the sacred cross', even if not a local; I heard that status took twenty years anyways. I'd been up to Santa Cruz on vacations, as a child, when my mother was alive. Been a long time though. My father would rent a place for a week or two. He'd do it for her, as he did that last summer. They liked a particular house, one just off Fair Avenue. Dramatic view from the front room picture window, ocean spray slaps the rocks, spray up so high, threatening to get to you. Never does, cascades down. When the sunset's right, slanting light creates quick rainbows. Mom loved that, so did I. That set of memories, my mother's last summer, surfing at the point, the power of the ocean, it gave the town a sense of familiar, pleasure, loss. Turned sixteen that summer. Got my driver's license the same day as my birthday party, the DMV on Capitola. Dad let me take the car, his car, now mine, my only inheritance. Not much for saving money, Dad, or passing it on for that matter. Just the car, and a great set of ambitions.

从某种意义上说，虽说我不是本地人，但也称得上这个"神圣十字架之城"的常客（圣克鲁斯在西班牙语中是神圣十字架之义——译者注）。反正我听说至少需要二十年才够资格这么说。孩童时代，我母亲尚在世的时候，我常来这里度假。不过也很多年了。我父亲会租个房子待上一两周。他这么做是为了她，最后那个夏天也是。他们尤其中意费尔大道附近的一座房子。从前厅窗户看出去的景色惊心动魄，惊涛拍岸，浪比天高，恨不能把你给吞卷去。当然这从来不曾发生，海浪会退下去。夕阳西下的时候，在适当的角度，斜阳与浪花会创造出小彩虹。妈妈爱这情景，我也是。一连串的回忆，母亲的最后一个夏天，在岬角冲浪，大海的力量，这一切赋予这个小城熟悉、愉快和失落的感觉。那年夏天我十六岁。我生日的当天，在卡皮托拉的机动车管理部门拿到了驾照。我父亲把车给了我，他的车，现在是我的了，这是我继承的唯一遗产。父亲把车给我不是为了省钱，也不是为了传承之类的。就是这辆车，和一大把雄心壮志。

"Oooh hey..." I said the silly phrase out loud, in homage to my father's mock saying. That playful sound a part of a specific memory, the nude beach at Bonny Dune. I ran into it by accident. I'd seen a cluster of cars parked along a high sand dune, decided to stop. Sauntered down to the beach, not paying attention, the glare of the setting sun blocking a clear view. Once there, took a minute before my mind processed what my eyes saw. The once odd little figures in the distance came into focus. Oh my god, no clothes. Those little patches of black at their midsections, those weren't swimsuits. Funny to think of that, how strange the mind, jumping about, just before the most important meeting of my life. When I told my father about the 'little patches', he gave me his laugh, his best 'oooh hey'!

"呜嘿"我大声喊出这个傻里傻气的声音，用我父亲专属的俏皮话向他致敬。这个逗乐的说法来自一段特别的回忆，那是在邦尼沙丘的裸体海滩。我是无意间闯入这个地方的。那天我看到好多车停靠在一个高高的沙丘边上，也把车停下，晃晃悠悠走

J.B.Guest Quarters Condo at 'Beach Hill'—Santa Cruz, CA
加州圣克鲁斯海岸山上 J.B. 的客寓

到海滩上。我也没怎么留心,落日很晃眼,看不清楚眼前的东西。当我走近时,愣了一分钟,让大脑处理映入眼帘的事物。从远处看起来很奇怪的小人像变清晰了。我的天哪,没穿衣服。那些人体中段的黑色小块不是泳装。想想也真滑稽,在我人生中最重要的一次会见之前,我脑子里在胡思乱想些什么啊。当时我跟父亲说起那些"黑色小块",他大笑,并且喊出他最得意的一次"呜嘿"。

Something caught my eye, odd, hovering, under the water, oval, or Tic-tac shape, shimmering. I was staring intently at it when a voice interrupted.

有东西吸引了我的视线。很奇怪，在水面下漂浮着，椭圆形，或者说 Tic-tac 口香糖形状，发着微光。我专注地盯着它看，这时一个声音打断了我。

"Do you see it, under the surface?" a man asked, deep voice, over my shoulder.

"你看到了吗？水下那个东西。"一个男人的声音从我身后传来，嗓音低沉。

"Yes, strange. What is it?"

"是啊，很奇怪，那是什么？"

"Don't know. Must be connection to fishing. The trawlers use lights, usually green ones. You see them most at night, lined up parallel to shore, out past the end of the wharf. Visiting Santa Cruz?"

"不知道。一定是跟钓鱼有关的。拖网渔船会用灯光，通常是绿色的。多数是晚上出来，平行排列，从岸边直排到码头尽头。来圣克鲁斯旅游吗？"

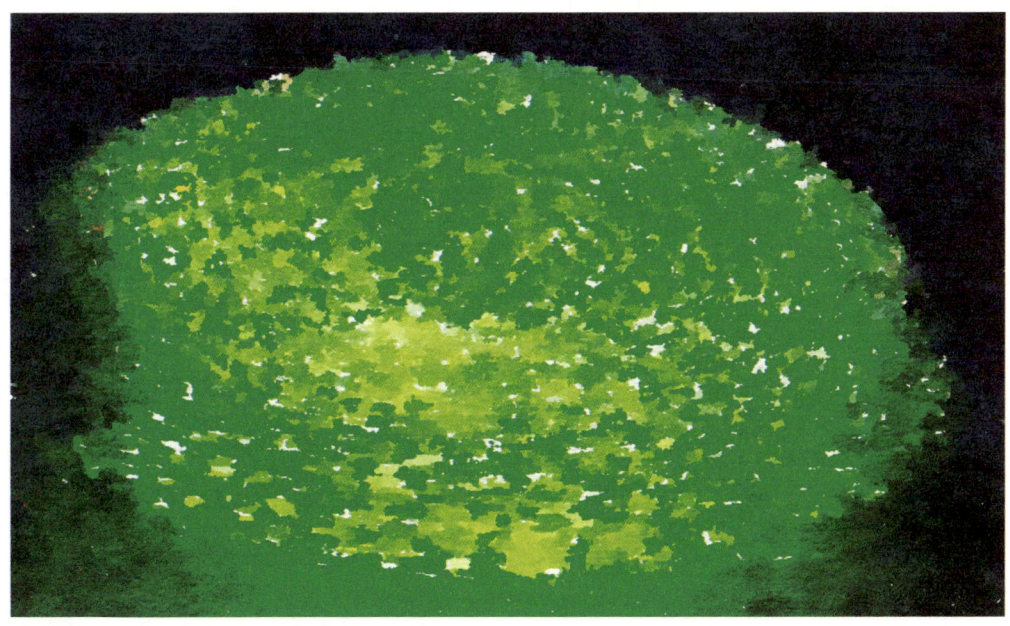

Under the Sea's Surface—Shimmering Lights—City Wharf, Santa Cruz
海面下——闪耀的光——圣克鲁斯码头

095

"Well, no. Who are you?" I asked, squinting, twisting back around. Tall man, arms folded, a thick form harshly silhouetted in open-ocean sunlight. A hat, sharp edges. "Police! Oh my God... " The last words shot out, Tourette.

"呃,不是。你是谁?"我转身,眯起眼睛看。身材高大,双臂交叉,毫无遮挡的海边阳光勾勒出他健壮的身躯。戴着帽子,边沿尖锐。"警察!天哪……"最后几个字脱口而出,图雷特综合征。

"I'm Chief Millford." he said, his smile acknowledging my surprise. Congenial, charismatic.

"我是米尔福德长官。"他说,微笑表示他看出我的惊讶了。亲切,魅力十足。

"Chief? Oh ... police chief."

"长官?噢,警察长官。"

"Exactly." he said. "Just thought to say hello. You up in Santa Cruz ... to see Madam Leung?" he asked. Odd. How would he know that? I remembered the car following me out of LA.

"完全正确。"他说,"就是打个招呼。你到圣克鲁斯来……是见梁夫人的吧?"他问。奇怪。他怎么知道?我想起出洛杉矶之后尾随我的车。

"Maybe." I said, regaining composure.

"也许吧。"我说着,恢复镇静。

"She's a great person. Really too bad about her husband."

"她人很好。她丈夫的事真是太糟糕了。"

"Yeah, quite a mystery."

"是啊,真是个谜。"

"Well, be careful. We don't want anything happening around here, someone else going missing." he said, broad smile, friendly manner. Faux, otherwise, couldn't tell.

"好了,你留意点。我可不希望这里出什么事,又有什么人失踪。"他露出大大的笑容,态度友好。装的,也许不是,我也说不清。

"Thanks. Take care." I said, him already moving away, politician mode, shaking one hand, then another, several groupies waiting nearby, begging his attention.

"谢啦。保重。"我说话的时候他已经走开了,像政客一样挥挥手,又换一只手挥了挥。附近有几拨人在等着吸引他的注意力。

Started back, the bumpy pavement of the wharf beating out a cadence with the spacing of the wood piles. Sudden anxiety, appointment time near, overlaid with the odd police encounter. Chief Millford, concerned, threating? How did he know about me? Then the cars, several of them, following, all the way up the coast? Not possible.

我开始往回走,坑洼不平的码头路面用木条铺就,一脚深一脚浅。预约时间临近,加上与警察的奇怪邂逅,令焦虑感突然袭来。米尔福德警长,是关心,还是威胁?他怎么知道我的事?还有那几辆车,沿着海岸公路一直尾随我。不可能吧。

To the right, distant, the 'fun-roar', screams from the Boardwalk, spires, towers, flags, mix of rollercoasters, reds, yellows, forms patterned against each other, a layered composition over a backdrop field of small town and green hills. On the left side, a broad grey flat of sand, Cowell Beach; beyond that, the seawall foundations of Dream Inn, its five-story tower the highest structure on site, the bulk of it out of scale, blocking views.

右手方向,远远传来"欢乐的咆哮",那是从栈道那边传来的尖叫声,尖塔、高楼、旗帜、五颜六色的过山车,红的、黄的,各种形状交叠掩映,在小城景色和青翠山坡的背景下,形成一幅层次分明的图画。左手边是宽阔平坦的考厄尔海滩;再远处是梦想旅馆,坐落在海墙上,这座五层的高楼是此地最高的建筑,主体挡住了视线。

Off the wharf, left turn, up the incline, the famous dome profile taking on detail. A bank of wispy gray fog held over Monterey Bay, its bottom underside high enough off the white caps to allow the sun under, yellows, slate grays. The east—west orientation of the Santa Cruz coast, the mountains behind, acted in concert to clip the flow of air coming down the coast from San Francisco forcing back the gray a bit from the shore; It resigned, sulking, waiting until the heat of day turned to the chill of night to run back in, stretch out over the town. Always changing, in competition, sea and fog, the afternoon's match producing a bowl-

City Wharf—Santa Cruz, CA
码头——加州圣克鲁斯

shaped cloud, levitating, bounded in place, anchored by aspects of the curving coastline. For a moment you could see under it, all the way across the bay, twenty miles to the brown and yellow hills of the Monterey peninsula. A spotlight of sun turned itself on, just beyond, momentary fantastical effect; The grey of the cloud bank above, the white-caped sea below, capturing a strip of land in brilliant bright browns, beiges. I'd never seen it before, the magic of the ocean, everchanging kaleidoscopic.

  下了码头，左转上坡，那个著名的穹顶越来越清晰。蒙特雷湾笼罩着一团轻灰的云雾，几乎触及房子白色的屋顶，阳光透过这空隙照进来，黄色，灰石板色。圣克鲁斯海岸线是东西向的，大山在其背后挡住旧金山海岸来的气流，将灰雾从岸边驱回些许。雾气退散，潜伏，等待白天的热浪被夜晚的凉意取代，再度返回将小镇笼罩。大海和雾气永远在变幻、竞争，今天下午的比赛产生了一团碗状的云彩，悬在空中，困在此处，在曲折的海岸线边停泊。偶尔能从云下看到海湾20英里外蒙特雷半岛的褐黄色山丘。一束阳光将它点燃，瞬间产生了绝妙的效果。灰色的云层上端，下面是白浪朵朵的大海，阳光照到一片土地，焕发出明亮的棕色和米色。我以前从来没见过这景色，这大海的魔术，像万花筒一样。

  The light shifted again, a slight mist changing it, the last sun rays splaying out, panicked, shooting through the space between the ocean surface and the bumpy gray bottom of the fog quilt. Quick light from the east, Asian, stunning brilliant under-lighting, mascara, shimmering yellow-orange bands, twisting, turning themselves into long streamers of blue-silver.

  一缕轻雾飘过，光线又变了。最后一抹阳光急匆匆地穿透海面与灰色雾团之间的空隙，泼洒下来。突如其来的光来自东方，带着亚洲风情，色调浓郁惊艳，墨黑，闪亮的黄橙色带，交缠，又变幻成长长的银蓝色条。

  Pulled over at the lighthouse for a moment. Surfing classes below the cliffs. Large groups of kids in the shallows; Clusters of company surfboards in reds, blues, yellows. From the lighthouse there's a vantage point to the J.B.compound dominated. The heat of the day's sun on its yellow and white striped awnings. Its tiled verandas invited you to imagine views outward, from the several structures to the ocean. Playful pointed chimneys, copper capped, canopies angling over arched windows and doors. Two large wrought-iron gates that open over its terracotta driveway toward the street reflect light of metallic edges, tile details; Every element designed by Jackson to sparkle, each in turn, as the sun searches them out. Hints of small tropical green gardens beyond. Visitors leave complementary notes, small piece of paper stuck in the cracks and cervices of the wall, on the gates, the way the citizens of Florence had celebrated the *David*, when Michelangelo's masterpiece had been revealed in Palazzo Vecchio.

我在灯塔处停车稍驻。悬崖下有人在上冲浪课，浅滩上站着一大群孩子，旁边是一堆一簇的红色、蓝色、黄色冲浪板。灯塔这里有个观景点，可看到高踞其上的J.B.建筑群。太阳照在它那黄白条纹相间的遮阳棚上。覆瓦的回廊令人不禁想象从那些建筑里向外看大海会是什么样的景致。尖尖的烟囱有种调皮的味道，上覆铜制小帽，拱形门窗上搭着遮阳棚。两扇大铁门把守着通往大街的陶土车道，反射着金属边角的光芒和瓷瓦的细节。每一种元素都被杰克逊设计为随着光线变化依次发光。后面似乎有小型热带植物花园。墙上和大门的裂隙里塞了好多游客留下的小纸条，满是溢美之词，就像佛罗伦萨的居民们为米开朗琪罗的杰作《大卫》在维吉奥广场揭幕时举行的庆祝一样。

When you come to the J.B.estate, stand across the street, ocean side, take a moment to take it in. Full growth cypress trees cling at the cliff's edge, brave-hearted against time, erosion, wind, ignoring the inevitable fall into the ocean. You can rest there, with them, in their cool, under the dark of their branches. Note the surfers in black skin suits in the waters. Curling waves unfurl along the angles, jagged rock edges. The orientation of the coast is decidedly east—west, so you are looking south if directly out to ocean, not west to Hawaii. The landform shift supplies the waves for which Santa Cruz is internationally famous, surfing. After all, the town of 'the holy cross by the sea' is the first place outside of Hawaii where someone mounted a board, stood, caught a wave, enjoyed the sheer pleasure of 'floating on glass.' Back along the cliffs, the lighthouse has the dimensions and feel of an old church; It's over-thick steeple atop a rectangle of red brick. Symbolically still use as a lighthouse, a rhythmic flash circling, pulsing, but too small and distant to do real work. It serves as a museum to its own past, and, more so, to surfing, its history, characters, memories, old photos. Hawaiian princes on long wood planks, women in ankle length thick layers of swimsuit, men in sleeveless t-shirts, full leg swimming pants, each ancient photo framed behind thick plate glass. Helps imagine the old times, surfing, how miraculous it came to be, at all.

来到J.B.宅邸前，你要站在其对面那条临海的街，花一点时间欣赏它。茂盛的香柏树紧紧抓住悬崖边缘，勇敢地抵御时间、腐蚀和海风，完全无视最终坠落大海的命运。你可以在凉爽阴暗的树荫下休憩片刻，看一看海里身着黑色紧身衣的冲浪者。浪花翻卷，拍打在嶙峋的礁石上。海岸线是正东西向，因此，当你面向大海时是向南，而非朝西望向夏威夷。此处地形的走向造就了令圣克鲁斯蜚声国际冲浪界的海浪。这个"海边的神圣十字架"小城是除夏威夷之外冲浪爱好者的首选之地，他们在此攀上冲浪板，起立，冲上一个浪头，享受"浮在玻璃水面"之上的纯粹的快乐。在悬崖这边，灯塔坐拥一所老教堂的格局和氛围，它那过于厚重的山墙立在长方形的红色砖墙之上。灯塔还发挥象征性的作用，有节奏地画着圆形的光，但光源又小又远，并没有实际意义。它现在作为博物馆记录着自己的历史，确切地说是冲浪的历史、人物、记忆、老照片。有站在长木板上的夏威夷王子，身穿长及脚踝层层叠叠泳装的妇女，穿着无袖T恤和长泳裤的男子，每一张老照片都嵌在木相框里厚厚的玻璃下。看着这些老照片，畅想冲浪的前世今生，它演变成今天的样子是多么神奇。

Since most of Santa Cruz's coastline is decidedly east—west, if you look along the sea edge to your right you are looking to China. Just there, below you, the rocks give way to a sandy beach. Officially named 'Lighthouse Field State Beach', it's called 'Dog Beach' by locals. I'm not a fan of dogs loose on the sand, but this is an exception. The total happiness of the animals is so sweet, so kind, you can't help but to be caught up in it, even from sixty feet above, even if you don't like dogs. Owners take them down the concrete steps to the shore, unleash them. They sprint back and forth over the sand, splashing into the edges of the surf, never a fight or growl, complete joy, their minds taken away by the spectacular experience of the open beach, two dozen or more creatures in pure pleasure. The dog owners relax, transform, caught up in the constant movement, the crisp sea, tennis balls and frisbees, crackles of delight from children. Bicyclists stop for a break at the metal railing above.

由于圣克鲁斯的海岸线基本上都是正东西向，所以沿着海角边缘向右看是中国的方向。在脚下，礁石渐渐让位给一片沙滩。它的正式名称是"灯塔地州属海滩"，但当地人都管它叫"狗海滩"。我是不赞成在沙滩上松开牵狗绳的，但这里是个例外。这些小动物的欢乐是如此纯粹、甜美、和善，你很难不被感染，哪怕你在离它们60英尺之上的地方，哪怕你压根儿不喜欢狗。狗主人带着它们走下混凝土台阶，来到海滩上，放开牵绳。有二十多只狗狗，它们在沙滩上蹦来跳去，冲到海浪的边缘，从不打架也不吠叫，完完全全沉浸在海滩上自由撒欢的快乐里。狗主人也悠闲放松，沉浸在持续的运动、清爽的空气、网球和飞盘、孩子们爆发出的清脆笑声中。骑自行车的人们在上方的金属栏杆处停留做短暂休息。

The fence along the edge of West Cliff is metal tubing at the lighthouse, then turns to wood for the remainder. Note the placards, flowers, displays, along the way, all testimonials to dead surfers. See the names burnt into the surface with inscriptions like, 'We'll never forget you.' 'R.I.P.' 'You family remembers you.' 'Loving son.' There's an inherent danger in attempting to balance on a board, even in water, pick up speed on a wave, and do so in a

Lighthouse—Santa Cruz, CA
灯塔——加州圣克鲁斯

shallow, mere inches above sharp rocks. Despite the risks, the long series of deaths, surfing goes on every day, a celebration of coaxing a ride. The variety of people involved is startling, grays, grizzles, potbellies, others young, impish. Then the professionals, a few perfect young men, lean bodies in black neoprene suits, they quick change behind open car doors, a beach towel to cover their naked. The line of cars slows at the lighthouse, admiring. Watch surfers access the water. It's dangerous to hop the fence, carefully step down the wet rock face, wait for a high swell, skim dive before the next wave. Bad timing will result in a slam onto the sharp rock face of the cliffs.

沿着西崖修建的围墙，在灯塔那段是金属管子，余下的都是木质。留意沿路的条幅、鲜花、展示，这些都是对失事冲浪者的纪念。看那些铭刻在墙面的文字，"我们永远将你铭记""安息""你的家人纪念你""爱子"。在水中站在冲浪板上找平衡，随着海浪加速，并且浅水区几英寸以下就是尖锐礁石，这本身的确蕴藏危险。尽管有风险，且一直有人死亡，但每天还是有冲浪的人去领略驯服海浪的胜利喜悦。冲浪的人五花八门，令人惊奇，有灰发的中年人，花白头发的老年人，大腹便便的，年轻的，淘气鬼。再就是专业人士，他们是些完美的年轻人，没有赘肉的身材裹在黑色氯丁橡胶泳装里，打开车门，用一块浴巾遮羞，迅速换好装。路过的车辆都在灯塔处减速，带着欣赏的眼光，看那些冲浪者走进海中。跳过围墙就很危险，然后要小心翼翼地从湿漉漉的礁石上踩过去，等到一个大浪涌起的时候，滑潜进去等待下一个浪头。时机掌握不好，会被海浪拍在悬崖边那些尖锐的礁石上。

Flocks of pelicans circle overhead, or glide along the shore in 'V' shaped formations. They're looking for schools of fish that feed in the kelp, or whatever's churned up by the waves. When the large gangly birds spot a target, they dive. Just before contact, they pull in their wings, open their mouths. Hits more than misses, a brilliant and timeless 'play of pelicans'. In that same small bay, sea lions, otters, dolphins, whales, come in, feed, go back out. They're curious about us, our black clad surfers, the white underside of sailboats, colorful splashes of children. Broad kelp beds provide cover for the creatures. They suspend, feed, watch, move on.

一群群鹈鹕在头上盘旋，或排成V字队形沿着海岸滑翔。它们在寻觅以海藻为食的鱼群，或者被海浪翻卷上来的任何东西。这一大群鸟儿一旦发现目标，立刻俯冲下潜。入水之前，它们收起翅膀，张开大嘴。这百看不厌的精彩"鹈鹕游戏"捕获多于失误。在同一个小海湾里，海狮、海獭、海豚、鲸都会进来觅食，然后再回到大海。它们对人类充满好奇，这些身穿黑衣的冲浪者，帆船白色的船底，穿得五颜六色的孩童。宽大的海藻床为这些动物提供了掩护。它们在其中漂浮、进食、观察，然后游走。

  A look at my watch, hard to see in the glare of the sun's reflection. Already four-thirty. The importance of the moment, for everything I'd wanted, the overwhelming opportunity of it, all in my stomach. In the next few hours, I could have everything I'd daydreamed about. Havanna would forgive me. Her parents as well. Success would take care of it. Those kinds of moments, just before an important event, when all possibilities still exist, and hope not yet eroded, are precious. Too often, once the moment is passed, some element isn't reached, achieved, the person slightly robbed of their grand expectations. The reality of the meeting with Moriah, the most celebrated of women, came on hard; Almost better to put the event off, keep it in that perfect imagined state. 'Madam', How did someone get such a title anyway? When did someone first say it, address her with that word, to recognize her position, power, ability, age? Did she grant it to herself?

  我瞄了一眼手表，阳光耀眼，反光使我很难看清。已经四点半了。这个时刻如此重要，蕴含着前所未有的机会，去获取我想要的一切东西，令我紧张得胃往下沉。在接下来的几个小时里，我可能会得到我梦想拥有的一切。哈瓦娜会原谅我的，她父母也会。成功会掩盖一切。在某一重大事件开始之前，所有可能性都存在，希望尚未被腐蚀，这种时刻异常珍贵。一旦过了这刻，某些目标没有达成、没有实现，远大期望就被剥夺了那么一点，现实往往如此。与莫立娅这位最知名的女性见面的现实，对我的冲击着实很大。也许取消会见会更好，这样就能将其永远保留在完美的想象王国。"夫人"，一个人是怎么得到这种头衔的？是谁在什么时候第一个如此称呼她，承认她的地位、权力、能力和年纪？是她自己赋予自己的吗？

  I pulled up at the nearest parking adjacent to the estate, stepped out, leaned back, timing my approach so as not to be early, or late. 'Playful forms on a perfect site', Jackson Bartholomew described the compound of structures before me. His 'greatest architectural design', published, and published again. Every architectural magazine and journal covered it. A popular culture crossover, *People*, *Time*, *Vogue*. It alone, as a single design triumph, let alone everything else, held a spot in the American imagination, firmly holding its place in the Pantheon of popular culture, the ultimate designer's expression of a perfect 'form following function'. An exquisite setting, cliffs on coast, point of ocean nearest Silicon Valley, Carmel, Big Sur. Within a month of its construction traffic caused a neighbor's revolt; The crush of cars and busses eventually controlled, detoured. Guards positioned, bus tours organized, special parking lot off Woodrow to receive overflow.

我把车停在离宅邸最近的停车场，从车里出来，靠在车身上，计算好时间，不能早也不能晚。"完美地点上的有趣结构"，这是杰克逊·巴塞洛缪对我眼前这幢建筑群的描述。这是他"最伟大的建筑设计"，被多次发表和报道。所有的建筑杂志和期刊都写过它。作为流行文化的跨界产物，它也上了《人物》《时代》《时尚》。它除了在设计上取得了胜利，在其他一切领域也大获成功，在美国的形象代表中拥有一席之地，在流行文化的万神殿中地位牢固，是一个设计师关于"结构服务于功能"的最完美表达。地点精心布局在离硅谷、卡梅尔和大瑟尔最近的海岸悬崖边。完工后一个月就因为交通堵塞招致了邻居的抗议。小轿车和大客车的车流压力最终得到控制，路线重新设计。设立了保安，组织了公交旅游路线，在伍德罗还特别规划了停车场，容纳过多的车辆。

Public approach is from the east end of the site, the mass of structure on the other end. Exquisite, jewel box in appearance, reflecting bits of light from one angle, then another as you came closer, change your perspective, point of reference. Perfect proportion, ornate spire at the ocean side marking Jackson's writing room. The home quickly surpassed Frank Lloyd Wright's 'Falling Waters' as the most visited American home. Only the White House more photographed. Odd to see it, 'for real'. I knew it so well, its details. Like the walk up to a Hollywood celebrity's home, something you'd seen, but had not. Hearst Castle in San Simeon, like that.

公众入口位于建筑群东边，而建筑主体位于另一侧。建筑外观像珠宝盒一样精美，从一个角度观看，它反射点点光芒，你走近的时候，随着你的视角和参照物不同，光芒也变幻了。靠近大海的尖塔比例完美、装饰华丽，是杰克逊的写作室。这个宅邸很快超越弗兰克·劳埃德·赖特的"流水别墅"，成为美国参观人数最多的宅邸。只有白宫在拍照次数上超过了它。亲眼看到的时候感觉很奇怪，我对它如此熟悉，对其细节了如指掌。就好像走进某位好莱坞明星的家，你见过但没去过。就像位于圣西米恩的赫斯特城堡。

Most of the structure holds a low profile, natural materials, providing contrast with the center of interest shapes, the tower, the geodesic dome. The balanced mixture of articulation, line, form, holding your eyes without demanding it. Playful pointing of several chimneys. The mix of earth colors of the driveway paving creates an underlining boundary that ties into a cascade of native scrubs, grasses. At the sidewalk edge, working in, a geometric pattern

J.B.Estate, Veranda Detail—Santa Cruz, CA
J.B.宅邸的回廊——加州圣克鲁斯

gives way to a quilted effect that carries your eye in. Delightful, the play of colors and patterns. Tiny red, sandy blue, pinpoint flowers splashed along one side of the drive. A seemingly random occurrence, but documented to be a J.B. element, Jackson himself redoing the landscape plan, incorporating his color pallet, careful mixes of native plants, some always in bloom. A row of almond trees held one boundary. At the east end, a pairing of a large weeping willow and Gingko tree; "Placed to hold the exterior at poetic anchor." proclaimed *Architectural Digest*, "Bartholomew's signature architectural legacy." Jackson had labeled it 'a description of myself in form'.

建筑物大部用低调和自然的材料建成，与建筑群中心的高耸穹顶形成强烈反差。建筑的设计、线条和构造极尽平衡，不需张扬就能吸引你的目光。几根活泼的尖尖烟囱。混合大地色的铺装车道打造出自然边界，将大片灌木和草地连接起来。行人步道的边缘从几何图形演变为百衲布的效果，将你的视线引入。色彩与图案的组合令人愉快。红色小点，雾蓝，小碎花泼洒在车道的一侧。看似随机，实则都是"J.B."精心设计的元素。杰克逊亲自对地形进行改造，结合他自己的调色板，对本地植物进行了精细组合，确保一直有植物在开花。一排杏树把守着一侧边界。在东侧，一棵大垂柳和一棵银杏树成双成对。"（这两棵树）种植在此，给予了建筑外观诗意的支点，"《建筑文摘》称，"这是巴塞洛缪成为建筑传奇的标志。"杰克逊将其称为"关于我本人的具象化表达"。

One more note on the J.B. estate: Charles Powel, the esteemed New York Clarion architectural critic, wrote the following:

还有一项关于"J.B."宅邸的说明——备受尊敬的纽约知名建筑评论人，查尔斯·鲍威尔如是写道：

A jewel left on the western edge of America. It respects its own time and context, understanding its prominent position in architectural history. Symbolism, always a part of everything Bartholomew, sometimes disturbing, sometimes spot on, comes through in the pristine positioning of its elements. The east—west orientation, core forms, homage to Tibetan temple palate and detailing, all pull you in, entice your spirit. At the same time the composition masterfully maintains a consistent and powerful allusion to Americanism, current popular/tech culture, each element overlaid expertly, Lhasan and Islamic influences. The Bartholomew-Leung residence on West Cliff Drive, Santa Cruz, serves as a suitable final boundary marker for America, a vantage point from which to look outward, away, directionally toward the 'west', culturally to the 'East'. The vast coastline view and the juxtaposed structural orientation provides the viewer a symbolic high-resolution perspective of all points on the world's cultural compass. The home has become an immediate national treasure, and rightly so. It is a profound comment, in-built form, on the character and nature of America, the rise of popular culture in the time of Jackson Bartholomew, an architectural indicator and touchstone within his own epoch.

  一颗遗落在美国西部边缘的珠宝。它尊重自身所属的时代和背景，知晓自身在建筑史上的显著地位。符号主义永远是巴塞洛缪作品的组成部分，时而令人不安，时而恰到好处，呈现在建筑各个元素的新颖组合中。东西方结合的创意及核心结构，对西藏寺庙风格及细节的致敬，一切都将你吸引其中，诱魂摄魄。同时，整个结构以纯熟的手法保持了连贯而强劲的美国风格和当下的流行/技术文化风格，受藏族文化和伊斯兰文化的影响，每一种元素都巧妙地结合在一起。位于圣克鲁斯西崖道的巴塞洛缪——梁宅堪称美国最后一道边界线，是向外眺望的桥头堡，方向上朝"西方"，文化上朝"东方"。辽阔的海岸景观与建筑结构的反差设计给予观者一幅观察世界文化的高清晰全方位指南。这座府邸已经当之无愧地成为国家级的宝藏。它用建筑的形式，深刻呈现了美国气质和天性，体现了杰克逊·巴塞洛缪所处时代流行文化的兴起，是他个人纪元的标志物和试金石。

Scene Five　Jasmine

第五幕 茉莉

So, there I was, at Moriah's front door. After all the effort, it felt, well, dreamlike. All my ambition gathered in one spot, concentrated, its human forms just beyond the door, the level of consequence set on high. Still, something in me said to get out, get away, my own set of interior warnings working. Bruise Art, from Novel to Film, it had become the flashing subtitle of my own life, not merely a master's thesis project at UCLA.

终于,我站在了莫立娅家的大门口。历经所有努力,感觉像做梦一样。我的雄心壮志都浓缩聚集在一个点上,以人的形式存在这扇门后,后续期待值设得非常高。尽管如此,我内心仍有声音在说,走开,离去,那是我内心的警报装置在工作。将《瘀伤艺术》从小说搬上银幕,这已经成为我人生剧本上闪闪发亮的副标题,而不仅仅是UCLA的硕士论文。

Go on now. No turning back. 'Rubicon-ed'. I liked to think that way, use that term. It provided hope of eventual victory.

向前走,别回头。"跨越卢比孔河",我喜欢这个表达方式(此处系引用恺撒大帝越过卢比孔河,开启罗马内战,最终成立罗马帝国的典故——译者注)。它给人一种最终获胜的希望。

The thick metal gate opened easily, humming, automatic, hidden censor. A small black half-round glass protrusion on the underside of the entry overhang flashed red, on and off. I took in a final deep breath, like an actor going on stage. Small grooves ran the vertical length of each door. Two lines of backlit square jewels, jades, alternating purple, mustard yellow, each line up the full height. Oiled wood, lines of coral, inlays of emerald, artisan, Asian, Art Deco influenced. Subtle indications of marshland reeds with cranes in-flight, so much so that it took a moment for them to appear. The work allowed both the near and far view to hold its own, the full perfection of each at restful interplay. The doorbell, a perfect piece of oval amber with a soft indentation that took your finger easily. I pressed it. There, it was done, the journey, begun. The sound, coming upward, arriving, low, sweet, calming, precise. Himalayan musical instrument?

厚重的金属大门轻轻地自动打开,嗡嗡作响,某处安装了感应器。入门的头顶下方有个小小的黑色玻璃半球形突起,一闪一闪发出红光。我最后深吸一口气,就像演员上台前那样。每扇门上都有两道内置灯光的细沟槽,从上到下填满了切割成方块的珠宝玉石，紫色和芥末黄色相间。清漆实木，成行的珊瑚、内嵌的翡翠，亚洲风格的装饰艺术。表现的是湿地芦苇丛中的飞鹤，手法精巧，需要花一点功夫才能看出来。这件作品远观近看各有韵味，需要好整以暇地加以欣赏才能领略其完美之处。门铃是一枚精美的椭圆形琥珀，中间的小凹陷恰好容纳手指。我按了。好，完成了，旅程开始了。有声音从脚下升起，低沉，甜美，宁静，精确。喜马拉雅乐器？

A feminine voice, high British, overlaid with Asian. "My name is Jasmine. Welcome dear guest to the home of H. Jackson Bartholomew and Madam Moriah Leung. We entreat you to step into the anteroom. Be so kind as to change into your slippers to be found under the seating to the left. If you be so inclined, cleans your palate with your choice of beverage, chilled Mango-Tangerine tea or Firenze Frizzante from the covered glassware on the side table. The powder room is through the door to your right. I will be with you presently to accompany you to the guest rooms and veranda."

一个女性的声音响起，高阶英国腔，又带点亚洲口音。"我叫茉莉。欢迎亲爱的客人来到H·杰克逊·巴塞洛缪和莫立娅·梁夫人的家。我们恳请您进入前厅。在左手边的座椅下有拖鞋，请您换上。如您喜欢，可品尝开胃饮品，在边桌的玻璃器皿中，有冰镇杧果橘子茶和翡冷翠气泡水供您选用。去洗手间请走您右手边那扇门。我很快过来，陪同您前往客房和前廊。"

With that, the double doors opened slowly, sliding, silent, their immense weight sensed but not sounded. Cooled drifts of air with light hints of lemons, then lavender, then cinnamon, perhaps triggered by my footsteps over the squares of floor tile; Geometric patterns, small, intricate, areas of insert with larger surrounds. On the ceiling, a slight whir, tiny, something moving, cameras, examining, measuring, learning.

话音未落，对开门缓缓打开，无声地滑向两边。我是通过感知而非听力觉察出门之厚重。凉爽的穿堂风带着淡淡的柠檬香味，之后是薰衣草香，继而是肉桂香味，也许是随着我在瓷砖地板上的脚步触发的。小巧精致的地板砖按几何图形拼接镶嵌在大块的图案中。头顶天花板上传来轻微的嗡声，什么东西在动，原来是摄像头，在检视、评判、研究。

On the floor at the cushioned seat, exactly size slippers, soft, quilted, Florentine leather, tapestried silk interiors. Breathtaking, brilliant stage set. No one receiving left the visitor unexpectedly alone, triggering emotions, acuity, heightening of senses. I waited for my eyes to adjust to the soft light, then tasted each beverage. The tea, tart, fresh, sensation of exotic spice. The water, carbonated, ice cold.

带靠枕的座椅下放着拖鞋,佛罗伦萨皮质,绣花丝质里衬,柔软合脚。真是令人惊叹,精彩的舞台布景。没有见过这样的待客方式,将客人置于孤身一人境地,又唤醒他的情感和感官,提升其敏锐度。我等待眼睛适应柔和的光线,然后每种食饮都尝了。茶和蛋挞很新鲜,异域香料的风味。碳酸汽水冰爽宜人。

From my seated position I had an easy view through an etched glass partition, it barring any immediate entry into the interior. Linear lyrical designs continued the nature theme of the entry doors, allowing you the sense of open space beyond while complicating the view enough to suggest privacy. I stood to get a better look beyond. Finely tiled floors, rectilinear areas accented in the added intricacy of a mustard-colored stone, Yellow Dragon Jade, sparkling, reflected glints from sky and sea. The flooring patterns continued across the room to full length windows on the opposite side, off toward the ocean. Waiting there, an exact grouping, two chaise couches, three cushioned chairs on a plush area carpet, textured fiber insert with a quilted silk boarder.

从我坐的位置,可以看到一幅蚀刻的玻璃隔扇,防止人们直接进入内室。充满诗意的线性设计延续了入门处的自然主题,让人既感受到开放的空间,同时视线又受到干扰,以保证足够的私密性。我站起来以便更好地观看。精美的瓷砖地板,纵向区域用一块芥末色的精致"黄龙玉"予以加强。玉石反射着天空和海洋的光线,熠熠生辉。地板的花纹铺满整个房间,直到房间另一头面向大海的落地窗。在那边,两张美人榻和三把带靠垫的椅子精心搭配,摆放在镶着丝绸绳边的长绒地毯上。

A young woman approached, along with her a man, the glass barrier separating, perfectly timed with their gate to allow access without pause. "Hello ... Hen hao. Mr. Curien?" Her voice sure, respectful, her body tall, Asian, long dark hair. "My pleasure to meet you." she said, holding out her hand, manicured fingers pressed together, golden bracelet dangling at the wrist. "My name is Jasmine Xi'an. I'll be assisting Madam Leung during your stay. This is Mr. Maximillian McKenzie, executive manager, J.B.Enterprises."

一名年轻女子走上前来,一个男人跟着她,玻璃隔扇分开,与门打开的时机配合完好，确保他们无中断通行。"你好啊，很好（原文系中文），是居里安先生吧？"她的声音坚定、恭敬，身材高挑，是个亚洲人，披着黑色长发。"很高兴与您见面。"她伸出手，做了美甲的手指并拢，手腕上晃动着个金色手镯。"我叫茉莉·席安。您在此地驻留期间我将协助莫立娅夫人。这位是马克西米利安·麦肯齐，J.B. 公司的执行经理。"

The exact meeting moment with someone exceptional you should seek to remember. Jasmine made it easy. She had a presence and manner that forced a forever place in your mind. Exotic, exquisite, erect, calm. Jasmine, dark hair, round eyes, silken skin, exquisite mixture of race, education, mannerisms, speech.

你应该努力记住与不同凡响的人见面的时刻。茉莉能让你毫不费力地记住她。她的在场和举止会给人留下永久的印象。异域、精致、挺拔、沉着。黑发、圆眼、丝绸般的肌肤、种族、教育、教养和言行的完美组合，这就是茉莉。

"Pleased to meet you Ms. Xi'an, Mr. McKenzie." I managed, awkwardly, then oddly, bowed my head, something I don't believe I'd ever done before as part of meeting someone.

"很高兴见到你们，席安小姐，麦肯齐先生。"我笨拙地说着，然后点了一下头，真怪异，我不认为自己过去在见人的时候会这么做。

"You may call me Jasmine." she said. "Currently, I'm Madam Leung's assistant, at least during this difficult time. My expertise is in the field of AI and hologram technology, research and development, Stanford University."

"你可以叫我茉莉。"她说，"目前我担任梁夫人的助理，至少在这段艰难的时期。我的专长是在人工智能和全息技术的研发，斯坦福大学毕业。"

"Here for the project?"
"你在这儿是因为那个项目？"

"In a manner of speaking, yes. Mr. Bartholomew's project."
"从某种意义上说，是的。巴塞洛缪先生的项目。"

"Your voice, unusual mix. From where do you come?"

Jasmine Xi'an
茉莉·席安

"你的口音是一种不太常见的混合。你来自哪里？"

"Like many people these days, a bit difficult to say. Mostly Shanghai, then Singapore and London. Now, California, Santa Cruz." she said, a smile, slight, amused, gaze unflinching. "Please, follow me." Maximillian excused himself, leaving Jasmine to lead me through a side door, wooden, stylized pelicans carved in flight above water. "I apologize for having you enter through 'screening', instead of meeting you straight away."

"就像当今许多人一样，说清楚有点难。大部分在上海，然后是新加坡和伦敦。现在嘛，加州，圣克鲁斯。"她说着，露出一丝自嘲的微笑，目光毫不退缩。"您请跟我来。"马克西米利安告辞，由茉莉带我穿过一扇边门。门是木质的，上面雕刻着鹈鹕在水面上飞翔的画面。"很抱歉让你通过'审核'才进来，而不是直接来迎接你。"

"Screening?"
"审核？"

"Yes, at the door. While you were in the entry area you were, for lack of a better word, 'examined'. Face recognition confirmation, movement analysis, threat ratios, several matrices. We have an increased need for security these days. Of course, we also have Maximillian, and other provisions. You checked out."

"是的，在入口。你在入口区的时候，实在没有更好的词表达了，被'检查'了。面部识别、动作分析、威胁等级，好几项指标。这些日子我们需要提高安保水平。当然我们有马克西米利安和其他帮助。你的检查是合格的。"

A few steps, away from the main space, a short hall led to a separate room, comfortable, wood floors, large woven rug, a curving leather chaise, internet desk in teak, a flat screen framed into a large painting, it already streaming a live view of the ocean of the Santa Wharf, with the Boardwalk as backdrop, the last sun finding its way through the clouds to the sea, yellowish up-lighting at the bases of the line of towering palms along Beach Street.

离主区域几步之遥，穿过一个短厅来到一个独立房间。舒适的木地板，大幅编织地毯，一张皮质美人榻，柚木电脑桌，大画框里是一个平面屏幕，实时播放着圣码头海边的景象，背景就是栈道，最后一缕阳光穿透云层投入大海，将海滩街边成行排列的棕榈树干照得黄灿灿的。

"Beautiful." I said, the word pulled from my mouth. The sunset moment, light glittering on the surface of the water, bouncing, distant sounds, happy people.

"真美。"这话从我嘴里不由自主地冒出来。日落时分,阳光在海面上闪耀、跳跃,从远处传来人们的欢声笑语。

"It's from the lighthouse." Jasmine said. "The Cam, of the Wharf and the Boardwalk. It's from the park, at the point, where they surf." She opened a door to the bath, pulled the curtains back from the bank of wall height windows. "Please, make yourself at home. I'll come gather you when Madam Leung is ready to receive your visit. Perhaps twenty minutes." Across the way, in the distance, a bike path along the cliff's edge dipped down below the line of sight, the people disappearing one by one, as though falling off into the sea. "Following your introductory meeting with Madam Leung, dinner will be served, straight away. The Chef is Peter Chanigaul. Perhaps you've heard of him? He's in for the night from San Francisco, in honor of your visit."

"这是灯塔那边。"茉莉说,"码头和栈道的摄像头。从公园的角度,就是人们冲浪那个地方。"她打开浴室的门,将齐墙高的窗帘拉开。"请自便。梁夫人准备好见你的时候我来接你。大概二十分钟。"马路对面的远处,一条自行车道沿着悬崖边缘,消失在视线以下,人们在那儿一个接一个消失不见,仿佛掉到海里去了。"你与梁夫人初次会见之后,紧接着进晚餐。主厨是彼得·切尼戈。你也许听说过他?他是为了今晚特地从旧金山过来的,以示对你来访的敬意。"

"Sweet." I said, no idea who he was.
"太贴心了。"我压根儿不知道他是谁。

"Yes, very ... 'sweet'." she said, holding her smile, resisting a mocking expression. "Oh, I almost neglected to mention. Madam Leung has taken the liberty to prepare evening clothing for you. Given your quick drive up you might have not taken dinner clothes. She begs your tolerance. We continue the tradition of dressing for dinner. It's rather formal, old world." I had read that Jackson Bartholomew insisted on it, no matter where, no matter the event.

Madam Moriah was correct. I had packed no 'evening clothes.' "You'll find our selections for you in the armoire and laid out on the bed. Classic Armani suit, Ferragamo shoes, various accessories."

"没错,非常……'贴心'。"她尽力掩饰嘲讽的笑容。"噢,我差点忘了提醒。未征求你的意见,梁夫人已经为你准备了晚宴服饰。考虑到你匆忙开车出来,你可能没带晚装。她请求你将就一下。我们沿袭了盛装晚宴的传统。非常正式,老派作风。"我看到过资料,杰克逊·巴塞洛缪对此非常坚持,不论在哪里,是什么场合。莫立娅夫人猜对了,我没有带上"晚装"。"我们为你准备的衣物在衣橱里,有些已经摆好在床上。阿玛尼经典款西装、菲拉格慕的鞋子、各色配饰。"

"Thank you." I said, noting that she included herself in the choices. "How did you know my size?"

"谢谢。"我说道,注意到她将自己也包括在选衣服的工作里,"你们怎么知道我的尺码?"

"Oh, we have our ways." She almost-smiled, small indentations at her cheeks. The she away, quick, efficient, her legs dancer precise, the soft of her slippers silent on the smooth of the tiled floor.

"哦,我们自有办法。"她几乎笑出声来,双颊现出小梨涡。然后她走了,迅速、高效,双腿像舞蹈演员一样精确,拖鞋的软底在光滑的瓷砖地板上静息无声。

I washed deep, complete, scrubbing, wanting to be extra clean, odd the thought. Thick warmed towels waited on the bars by the glass door, abstracted art etched in, birds in flight, egrets landing on a marsh.

我彻彻底底洗漱了一遍,又刮又擦,想把自己弄得格外干净,真是奇怪的想法。温暖厚实的毛巾摆好在玻璃门旁边的台面上。玻璃门是抽象艺术蚀刻,表现的是飞鸟,白鹭栖在湿地中。

On the counter, a new bottle of Dolce & Gabbana cologne, a linen card with my embossed name, Mr. Samuel Z. Curien, leaning on it, an assurance it was mine to open, to use. Each touch gave importance to the event, the occasion, to me as a person, all a connection with a lost way of doing, existing, performing. Too much for our day, perhaps pretentious? All the same, delightful.

台面上摆着一瓶杜嘉班纳牌香水,一张亚麻卡片倚靠瓶身,上面用浮凸字体印着

Guest Room Veranda—J.B.Estate, Santa Cruz, CA
客房外廊——加州圣克鲁斯J.B.宅邸

我的名字——塞缪尔·Z·居里安先生,说明我可以打开、使用。每一步都加深了这个场合的重要性,对我个人的重视,这些都是已经遗忘的做事、生活和表现方式。这是不是有点过了? 可能有点装腔作势,但管他呢,仍然令人愉悦。

In the armoire the evening suit, comfortable, young, the current body cut. Waist, chest and shoulders, my exact measurements. How was that possible? Full height mirrors at one corner allowing an all-around view. Double biased, soft gray thread intertwining with dusty blue. In motion, it produced a slight reflection effect. The tie, Hermes, thin, dusty russet with lines of muted yellow, perfect complementary counter-color to the suit, perfect length the tip stopping just at beltline. A long-sleeved shirt, form-fitted, comfortable, fresh white Egyptian cotton, collar slightly high, the fabric smooth, unbuckled. Every detail precise, effortless, high-style relaxed, confident ease, no pulling or tucking. The shoes and belt Florentine leather, Ferragamo, soft at first use.

衣橱里挂着一件晚装西服,舒适、年轻,时下流行的贴身板型,腰、胸、肩的尺寸恰好合身。这是怎么做到的? 我对着房间一角的全身镜上下前后打量。双排扣,柔灰条纹的雾蓝色面料,随着身体的运动发出细微的光泽。领带是爱马仕的,细长,亚光铁锈红带着暗黄色条纹,与西服颜色形成完美的撞色效果。领带刚好长及腰线,完美。长袖衬衫贴合身材,舒适,鲜白色埃及棉,衣领略高,衣料平滑,没加袖扣。每项细节都精确至极,毫不费力,高阶悠闲,轻松自信,不需要生拉硬塞。鞋子和皮带都是菲拉格慕牌,佛罗伦萨皮质,虽是新鞋但很柔软。

Music had begun to play, come up, subtle, so as not to be noticed at first, its origin hidden somewhere inside the far wall. Tranquil, a series of sweet-sad vocals, in sequence. Various languages, Italian, Greek, French, Chinese, Malaysian. One story in Spanish, clear, Caribbean; A woman working in the fields, a little boy waiting for her in the shade of the palms, his mother, him longing for her, a storm coming in from the sea. Each in the series carried that tragic sensation, a beautiful yearning, to find something, someone, happiness, peace, purpose.

音乐响起,如此曼妙缥缈,一开始都没注意,渐渐变强,音源应该藏在远处的某面墙内。乐音平和宁静,是甜美忧伤的歌声,依次用不同语言演唱,意大利语、希腊语、法语、汉语、马来语。其中有一个故事是用西班牙语唱的,很明显是加勒比的故事:一个女人在田野里劳作,一个小男孩在棕榈树荫里等她、他的母亲,暴风雨要从海上来了，他渴望母亲的怀抱。每一首歌都带着那股悲伤的感觉，一种美好的企盼，要去寻找什么东西，什么人，寻找快乐、和平、意义。

On the side table lay a hard copy of the J.B.'s master work, the full bound deluxe edition of *Bruise Art.* Deep embossed into the cover, the iconic photo-sketch of Madam Leung's naked back, it adorned with a dangling neckless, in turn, it laying over a line of circle shapes, rounds of bruises, bruise art, as Jackson had seen them, called them, coined the phrase. Thus, the name of the book, and the lifestyle concept. Startling, to think of it, at that moment. There she was. The woman I was about to meet. It was her naked back, and bottom, to be sure, she seated on a cushion, looking up and to the side. Everyone knew the photo, ubiquitous, it the symbol of all things Bartholomew, an icon, logo, something absolutely known, as in the symbols for Coke, Starbucks, Jaguar. I wondered what it was like to become an icon, to have your person, your body, become an abstraction owned by popular culture, carried by pan-media to every corner of the globe, every last place of human inhabitation in the entire world.

边桌上放着一本硬皮书，那是J.B.的杰作，包装精美的豪华版《瘀伤艺术》。封皮浮印着那张标志性的素描处理照片，一串项链沿着梁夫人裸露的背部垂下，将背上一系列圆形瘀青串联起来，这就是杰克逊眼中的瘀伤艺术，他赋予其名称、铸就了这个名词。也由此产生了这本书名，以及相应的生活方式概念。此时此刻念及于此，令人心生惊奇。她就在那儿。我将要见到的这个女人。这是她的裸背和臀部，毫无疑问，她坐在垫子上，扬起头向侧看。每个人都知道这张照片，非常独特，它是关于巴塞洛缪所有一切的符号，他的标志、徽标、众所周知的东西，如同可口可乐、星巴克、捷豹的徽标一样。我不禁想象那会是什么感觉，成为偶像，让自己这个人、这个身体成为大众文化所拥有的抽象物，被融媒体带到全球各个角落，全世界有人类居住的每个角落。

The Chinese traditional medicine practice called 'cupping' is the bruising of one's skin by way of the suction caused by the contracting air within heated glass cups placed and held on the skin. As he told it, Jackson had considered the resulting dark rounds of russet red bruises on his new wife's back with amusement and alarm. The purpose of cupping is to stress the body's immune system; A therapeutic means to strengthen it by forcing a defensive reaction. Usually frightening to Westerners, painless though it might be. It's the same kind of mark left by a teenager on a lover's neck. In 'cuppings' case, not out of passion, but resulting from a standardized ancient Chinese medical technique. For thousands of years Asians have used small sections of bamboo, and a wood straw to suck out the air, to produce the pull on the skin. Then glass production came on, the bamboo becoming glass, clear, tennis ball sized, with a round opening, its edges soft, smoothed into a fat curve. As far as anyone could tell by way of any research, Internet searches or otherwise, the 'cupping' technique had only ever been used medicinally; no playing, experimenting, making the human skin into artistic canvas. Not even attempts at temporary tattooing, building up an image or design through cupping, knowing it would dissipate, disappear, in a week or two.

中国的中医治疗手法"拔罐"是通过加热玻璃罐中的空气,将其吸附于皮肤上,由此在皮肤表面留下瘀青印迹。杰克逊说,他初次看到新婚妻子背上的深红色圆形瘀青时,觉得既触目惊心又好玩。拔罐是一种通过激发身体的抵御反应,激活人体免疫系统的治疗手法。虽然过程可能是无痛的,但对西方人来说通常还是挺吓人的。这跟年轻人在恋人脖子上留下的吻痕是一样的。只是拔罐并非出于激情,而是一套中国传统医药的标准手法。过去千年,亚洲人都是用小段竹子和木管将空气抽出,使其吸附于皮肤。玻璃被制造出来之后,就取代了竹子;透明、网球大小、开口圆形,边缘光滑,罐体圆肥。不管是谁做过什么样的研究,通过互联网搜索或是其他手段,拔罐手法迄今仅仅用于治疗,没人用它来玩、做实验,或将人的皮肤作为艺术创作的画布。即使是短期文身,也没人用拔罐手法做过任何图像或设计,因为它在一两周内会减退消失。

In the world of the known, Jackson was the first to see it, then do it; West meets East, his creative, playful, artistic instinct putting to use a strictly medicinal Asian technique in the interest of artistic expression. That first ever photo, the 'Moriah nude sitting on pillow', captured it perfectly, riveting, magical. She seated on cushion, naked, the shot taken from behind, her wearing only a linked neckless with a single amber jewel dangling over one of three purple circles, the top the larger, the bottom smallest. Jackson had her looking up and to one side, quarter profile. The image captured both her spirt as the subject, his as Renaissance artist in full creation mode.

杰克逊是世界上第一个用独特眼光发掘并创造这一艺术的人。西方遇见东方。他的创意、好玩和艺术本能将一项亚洲医疗技术转化为艺术表现形式。第一张照片,"坐在枕头上的裸体莫立娅",完美地呈现了这一艺术,具有吸引人的魔力。照片拍的是她坐在坐垫上全身裸露的背影。她戴着一条项链，单枚琥珀吊坠悬在三个圆形瘀青之上，上面的瘀青最大，下面一个最小。杰克逊让她侧着头向上看，露出她四分之一侧脸。这一影像将她的形与神完美捕捉下来，他的发挥堪比文艺复兴时期艺术家创作的全盛时期。

Jackson wanted something more though, that is to create another layer of existence, to take it from the mundane of the real world to something magical, which is nearly unattainable. He ran the photo through various sketch techniques until the 'series of tiny marks on a surface' effect gave him what he wanted. That photograph, in the form of the cover of his great novel, took the world's imagination. The book and the image worked together, playing off the other, enhancing, multiplying. In short order, everyone with any contact to popular culture could identify it, even if they had never read the book. From that spring-well, 'Bruise Art' the image and 'Bruise Art' the novel, all else flowed, followed, one after the other in natural sequence. It marked the creative point in time at which the amazing line of creativity of Jackson Bartholomew, the J.B. line, became, its genesis. He had found, produced, cultivated, a worldwide phenomenon; His own wife as inspiration and sustaining partner. I dropped my fingers on the leatherbound deluxe edition, let the tips touch the image. A short few years ago none of it existed. Something came from nothing, gaining power, ruling its own time, finding its way into all our minds and lives.

但杰克逊还想要的更多。他想创造另外一个层面的存在，将其从乏味的现实世界带到更魔幻的地方。这几乎不可能做到。他用多种素描化技术将照片进行处理，最终达到了他想要的"表面布满细微颗粒"的效果。这张照片作为他的小说封面，勾起了全世界的遐想。这本书和这个形象相互作用，相得益彰，不断扩大影响。任何跟流行文化沾边的人都知道这本书，即便他们没读过。以"瘀伤艺术"这个形象和这部小说为肇始，一切自然发生，接踵而至。这是杰克逊·巴塞洛缪的J.B.品牌的创意起点。他发起、制造、打磨了一个世界级现象，他的妻子成为激发和持续他灵感的伙伴。我的手放在这个尊贵版本的皮质表面，手指轻抚这个形象。就在几年之前这一切都不存在，然而它无中生有，积聚势能，进而统领时代，侵入我们的思想和生活。

Jasmine knew my eyes would go to the book. Next to it had been placed a card, it thick and formal, held in place on a wood stand, cut into lyrical profiles, something like a small music holder. Looking closely, I discovered temple towers, abstracts of exotic birds, a hint of horizon in the design. Jackson may have wanted to create poetic images, but he didn't want to give them away easily. The viewer had to discover, find them. On the card blue lettering, dusty in texture, all if it within borderlines of interlocking geometries and Gingko leaf shapes. An artwork in itself, for the purpose of announcing the evening's menu.

  茉莉早就预料到我的目光会被这本书吸引。书旁边放了一张厚重而正式的卡片，立在一个形状优美、形似小型乐器架的木头支架上。仔细看，我发现卡片的设计上有庙宇、珍禽的抽象画、隐隐约约的地平线。杰克逊应该想表达一些诗意的形象，但又不愿轻易透露，需要观者仔细探寻才能找到。卡片上是蓝色亚光字体，框以相互缠绕的几何花纹和银杏叶。作为晚宴菜单，它本身就是件艺术品。

DINNER MENU
****

The Occasion of the 8th Month, 15th Day Visit of Mister Samuel Zachariah Curian

To the Home of
Madam Moriah Leung and H. Jackson Bartholomew

(All dishes from recipes created for the Novel *Bruise Art* by H. Jackson Bartholomew)

Appetizer:
California/China Shrimp Rolls, Olive Oil with Italian Spice
Sweet Plum–Pomegranate Dipping Sauce

Soup:
Pumpkin–Lobster Bisk
Center Float of Summer Sour Cream and Chives

Salad:
Avocado & Tomato Long–Sliced Salad
Walnut Quarters, Artichoke Hearts, Olive Oil with Balsamic Vinegar

Main Course:
Cajun Blackened & Boned Mississippi Catfish Fillet over Creole Rice
'Jackson Square' Hollandaise Sauce, Almond Slivers

Featured Side Dish:
Sarah's Fried/Baked Off-the-Cob Corn on Otera's Black-eyed Peas with Grilled Pigs Knuckle Bone
(Served with a Center of Summer Sour Cream over a Bake of Sweet Corn Bread)

Dessert (Served on the South Veranda):
Pearl River Blackberry Cobbler
(Served extra hot, J.B.style, with a double scoop
of Mississippi Vanilla Bean Ice Cream)
Coffee by American Cake & Pie Company
(Served at American Consistency with an avail of Fresh Cream & Rough-Grained Cane Sugar)

Beverages:
Paso Robles Rose' Wine
S. Pellegrino Aqua Frizzante with Fresh Fruit Slices

晚宴菜单
****
8 月 15 日

欢迎塞缪尔·扎卡里亚·居里安先生到访
莫立娅·梁夫人和杰克逊·巴塞洛缪宅邸
（所有菜品根据杰克逊·巴塞洛缪小说《瘀伤艺术》中的菜谱烹制）

开胃前菜
加州/中式虾卷，橄榄油和意式香料
梅子石榴甜酱

汤
南瓜龙虾浓汤
中缀酸奶油和香葱

沙拉
鳄梨和番茄切片沙拉
核桃、朝鲜蓟心、橄榄油配意大利葡萄酒醋

主菜
卡真酱腌制去骨密西西比鲇鱼柳配克里欧米饭
杰克逊荷兰酱、杏仁碎

特色配菜
烤猪肘配萨拉式炸/烤玉米粒和奥特拉黑眼豆
（佐以甜玉米面包和酸奶油）

甜点（在南回廊享用）
珍珠河黑莓酥皮馅饼
（滚烫食用，J.B. 风格，双份密西西比香草冰激凌）
加州蛋糕和派公司咖啡
（美式风格，配鲜奶和粗粒蔗糖）

饮品
加州帕萨罗贝尔桃红葡萄酒
圣培露气泡水配水果切片

Bling, Bling ... Bling, Bling ... A jeweled clock at the bedside tolled six o'clock. Jasmine wouldn't be late. I finished dressing quickly so as to have time to sit in the large bedside chair, wait, stage myself for her arrival. Jasmine and Moriah, those two, nerve racking. I closed my eyes, pulled hard, dreams and half-dreams, a way to gain composure, mediation in the extreme. I needed to prepare for what was to come, that critical moment of meeting, ones you can never redo, undo.

丁零，丁零……床边的珠宝小钟敲了6下。茉莉不会晚点。我很快穿着停当，坐在床边的宽大椅子里，静候她的来临。茉莉和莫立娅，这两人都令人神经紧张。我闭上眼睛，用力进入半梦半醒状态，这是一种极致的冥想，是镇静下来的方式。我需要做好准备迎接即将来临的重要会面，机不再来，无法回头。

Scene Six　　Moriah
第六幕 莫立娅

As expected, perfectly punctual, Jasmine arrived, entered ... more formal.
不出所料，茉莉准时出现。穿着更正式了。

"This way." she said. "Now you shall meet Madam Moriah Leung."
"这边请。"她说，"现在，你要见到莫立娅·梁夫人了。"

I followed her down a dimly lit hall, a large room at its end. At the small of Jasmine's back, a diamond broach gathered her gown's material, it layered, sparkling. Most of the skin on her shoulders lay open, exposed. Across her back there appeared what I would describe as 'evening decor for a special occasion', as in jewelry, but in the form of Bruise Art. A series of precise bruises, arranged in exact formation created the impression of an abstract dragonfly, large, its expanse of wings the full width of her shoulders; Over the bruise art a layer of fine glistening marks, lightly laid, glinting the light, tiny mirrors placed to give the effect of the oily rainbow shimmer of the wings of that most exquisite of all insects.

我跟随她穿过一个灯光昏暗的过厅，其尽头是一个大房间。一枚钻石胸针在茉莉娇小的背后别住她层叠闪亮的晚装。她肩膀裸露，背上露出的图案在我看来堪称"为特殊场合佩戴的首饰"，只不过用瘀伤艺术取代了珠宝。那一系列的瘀青印迹恰到好处地呈现了一只抽象的蜻蜓，很大，双翅展开正好覆盖她整个肩膀，上有一层闪闪发亮的东西，很薄，像无数微小镜子反射光芒，效果正如这种精巧昆虫翅膀上的虹彩反光。

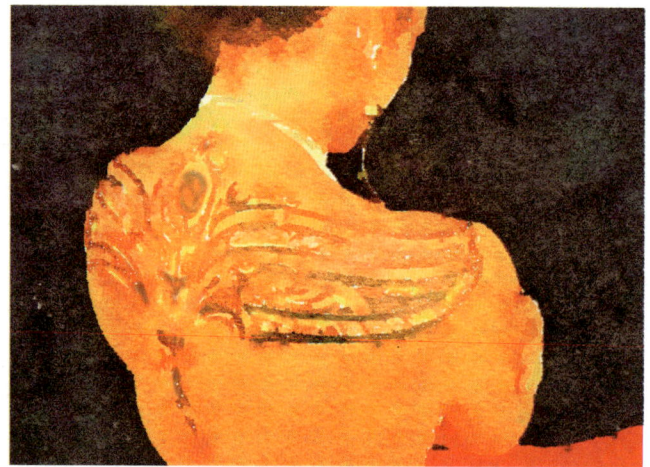

Bruise Art 'Cupping' Design—*Dragonfly*—Jasmine's Back
瘀伤艺术设计——《蜻蜓》——茉莉的背部

"Wait here, please." she said. I hoped my eyes had lifted off her back, buttocks, before she had turned to me.

"请在此稍候。"她说。我后悔没在她转身前及时将目光从她的肩背和臀部移开。

Jasmine pointing out a spot on the tiled floor with a gentle wave of her hand, oddly apologetic her motion, the way one carries themselves when leaving a guest vulnerable, their physically positioning somewhat diminished, in peril.

茉莉轻挥手指向地上某处,示意我站在那儿,她的动作流露出奇怪的抱歉意味。当人们将客人置于低微或危险境地的时候就会这样。

At the outer edge of the room an opened set of wall-length glass doors captured the eruptions of distant ocean waves, their unseen crash against the rocks, resulting in the up-spray. The interior flooded with a fresh wave of chilled air, newest replacing the old. A tinge of gold lit upper parts of the ubiquitous cloud bank. Reflections on the tiled floor jerked in and out with each ebb of the light's edge. In constant movement, discrete pieces of light, hypnotic, looking at fire, the rippling of streams. Kaleidoscopic shapes in full churn, dangerous. A masterful manipulation of perception; J.B. architectural space design at its finest.

房间那头,一对高及天花板的玻璃门敞开,远处的大海尽收眼底,惊涛拍岸,卷起千堆雪。新鲜凉爽的空气习习扑面。云层的上缘镀着一层金光。瓷砖地板上的倒影随着光线的逐渐减弱伸缩变化。不断变化的散漫光线有种催眠的作用,就像盯着火苗跳跃,听着溪流潺潺。像万花筒一样变幻,危险。操纵知觉的高手,J.B. 建筑空间设计最完美的呈现。

At the far end of the room stood a single silhouetted figure looking out toward the west. It appeared to be examining the on-push of gray-green haze, the mist working hard to cover the last display of gold bands from the setting sun. So, erect, motionless the shape of the personage, that I supposed it sculpture, a life-sized statue of dark stone or metal. Then came to mind the holographic projection, Jackson's imagination, his penchant for and staging, play, production. No, not likely, instead, some one, alive, a woman standing, motionless.

在房间另一头站着一个孤单的剪影,面向西边。这个身影似乎在仔细观察灰绿色的氤氲之气,雾霭正在遮蔽夕阳散发出的最后几道金光。这人身姿如此挺拔、沉静,我以为这是一尊真人大小的石头或金属雕塑。接着我想起杰克逊的全息影像计划,他对营造舞台感的喜好。不,不像,这是一个活人,一个女人,站在那里,纹丝不动。

As my eyes adjusted to the light, the silhouette transforming, from two to three dimensions, I could see her, make out clothing. Colors, deep red accent lines on a dark forest gown, fabric quilted so that its texture a pattern, shimmering, back and forth, within a field of royal blue. The gown's collar came up rigid, all the way to the sharp of chin bone, the back neckline plunging down, exposing the woman's spine, the small of her back, a hint of buttocks. Her arms rested at her waist, motionless, held in place by clasped hands. One of the fingers move, or so I imagined. Sparkle from a gold ring. Jet-black hair, pulled up on top of her head. Two long clasps in ivory, stone. At the back of her neck, a dangling of necklace in amber, its last large jewel laying over the exact center of a deep russet round bruise. At her ankle a polished coral and emerald chain, reflections, the last lights of magic sunset.

随着我的眼睛适应光线,这个剪影发生了变化,从平面变得立体,我能够看清她,分辨出她的衣着。她穿着一件深绿色的长礼服,间有深红色的条纹,织物的纹理在宝石蓝背景的映衬下,随着光线来回变化微微发光。礼服的硬领高高竖起直到下颌,背后从脖线下敞开,裸露出她的脊骨,娇小的背部,臀部线条隐现。她双手紧握,双臂夹腰,一动不动。有一根手指动了,也许是我的错觉。金戒指闪耀了一下。乌黑的头发绾起盘在头顶,用两根象牙和宝石的发卡别住。一串琥珀项链从她的后颈垂下,最后一颗大琥珀正好落在一个深绛红色的圆形瘀青中央。她脚踝系着一条精美的珊瑚和翡翠珠链,反射着夕阳最后一抹光线。

No movement from me. I held my breath. Waited. I had not yet been acknowledged, given permission to break the moment, the silence. Then it came, what I had been wanting, anticipating, for so long … the meeting, Moriah, Madam Leung.

我不敢动,屏住呼吸等待。我还没有被接纳,未得到允许打破此刻的沉默。然后它来了,我一直想要的、期待已久的会见——莫立娅·梁夫人。

"Come here Mr. Curien. Watch our sunset … with me." the figure said, not moving more than lips, the voice sure, direct, slightest accent, more British than American.

"到这里来,居里安先生。跟我一起,欣赏我们的日落。"这个人像说话了,全

Madam Moriah Leung—Watching the Sunset—J.B. Estate, Santa Cruz, CA
莫立娅·梁夫人在加州圣克鲁斯J.B.宅邸看日落

身除了嘴唇哪都没动。她的声音安稳、直接，有轻微的口音，偏英音而非美音。

"Yyyes..." I mumble, walking carefully over the tiles, as though they were 'black ice', threatening me with a fall.

131

"好……"我嗫嚅道,小心翼翼地走过瓷砖地板,仿佛它们是"黑冰",威胁着要滑倒我。

I stopped behind her, a bit to one side. It seemed the only appropriate place, as though it had been pre-marked on the floor, close enough to touch her with an outstretched arm, yet just outside the boarder of her personal space. Her in her own aura, fresh scent, lemons, hinting honeysuckle. The slight slim figure controlled the space, a powerful center force of a self-made universe. If I hadn't read otherwise, I would think her in her forties, her shoulders back, neck straight, smooth, left calf muscle exposed in the slit of the well-tailored quilt gown. Her ensemble in royal aspect, old Hollywood. Shoes, high-heeled, dangerous, soft leather with a deep stitch at the sole, open at the toe. Her frame no more than five-six but impressive presence had her taller, if not dominating. It occurred to me that it all smacked of a J.B. world trick, hologram projection extraordinaire, her neck, ear, jawline too young. The lack of her, its motion added to the thought, sensation. No look toward me, but to the sea, a stubborn insistence on viewing the last play of sea and sun.

我在她身后停下,稍微偏一点点。似乎这是唯一合适的地点,好像提前在地上标好了一样,近得伸出胳膊就能碰到她,又恰好在她个人空间的边缘之外。她有自己的香气,新鲜的味道,柠檬清香中隐着一丝忍冬。这个娇小苗条的身躯控制着整个空间,是这个自造宇宙的强大原力中心。要不是我之前看过资料,我会认为她四十多岁。她双肩平展,脖子直挺光滑,合身的定制礼服开衩处,裸露出肌肉平滑的大腿。她举止高贵,好莱坞的传统风范。鞋跟高得危险,皮质柔软,鞋底有深凹痕,前端露趾。她身高不超过5英尺6英寸,但气场强大,不敢说盛气凌人,也使她显得比实际要高。我突然觉得这只是J.B.世界的一个把戏,是全息投影的超完美呈现,她的脖子、耳朵和下颌线条太年轻了。她并不在场,人像的动作更加强了我这种感觉。她没朝我看一眼,仍然执着地欣赏大海与落日的最后一幕演出。

It began to influence me, the standing still, as in a wedding party where one or more falls out during the ceremony, breath too shallow, without movement, body set rigid, anticipation. With that thought, the room spun … or my imagination? I wanted to reach out, say something, break the tension, pull her in, over. Deep breath. Come on … idiot.

这种静止的站姿开始影响到我了,就像在婚礼上等待的时候,渐渐对周围失去知觉，呼吸变得轻浅，静止不动，身体僵硬。念及于此，房间开始旋转，或者是我的想象？我想伸出手，说点什么打破这紧张，吸引她注意，结束。深呼吸。拜托，蠢货。

One of her fingers moved, the index ... thank God. From folded to pointing, it scolded.

她一根手指动了，食指……感谢上帝。从蜷曲到指向我，它在斥责我。

Coastline at California—Near the J.B.Estate, Santa Cruz, CA
加州的海岸线——圣克鲁斯J.B.宅邸附近

"Silence ... wait for the finish." she ordered, Moriah, her. She had spoken, the ultimate confirmation of life.

"安静……等它结束。"她命令我,莫立娅,是她。她说话了,终于证明这是个活人。

The tinkle of a wind chime came up, agitated, gusts from the sea, picking up, then calming. As if cued by the sound, lights in the garden began to activate, up-lighting on the large trees, the line of Yellow Almonds along one side of the back garden, then at the end, larger lights at the symbolic pairing, an enormous willow aside a large Gingko. The new lighting set out its own paradigm, eliminating some mysteries, creating others. Moriah's figure had gained an alternative aspect, real, rhythmic, empowered being gaining strength from the artificial illumination. Now the three round bruises on her back, deep purple, raised in slight welted domes, painful to see, intentionally positioned large to small, in sequence, exactly centered on the spine, the last bruise at the small, just where back meets buttocks. So fresh the marks. I imagined the making of them, someone, perhaps even Jasmine, placing the heated glass bowls on the delicate skin, the air condensing, cooling, creating the suction, the skin raising up a half inch into the void; The glass cup allowed to stay in place for ten to fifteen minutes.

海风骤起,风铃叮当一阵急响,继而平静下去。花园里的灯光仿佛被铃声唤醒,依次点亮,从下往上照射在高大的树木上,先是后花园墙边成行的黄杏,再到花园尽头那标志性的一对,繁茂的垂柳依偎着高大的银杏。新的光源设定了新的参数,解构了一些神秘性,又创造了新的神秘性。人工照明为莫立娅的形象注入力量,赋予其别样的视角,真实、有节奏。她背上的三个深紫色圆形瘀青微微隆起,有意沿脊柱从大到小排列,最小的一个位于脊背与臀部交界处。印迹很新,看起来令人不适。我想象其创作过程,有个人,甚至可能是茉莉,将加热的玻璃罐放到细腻的皮肤上,空气密度变大,冷却,吸附,罐内的皮肤隆起半英寸;任其在皮肤上停留10—15分钟。

She must have had them made that same day. As part of the preparations for my visit? An astounding thought. Erotic. Amazing, to see them so close, blood-filled, alive, active. The edgy sensual tension of bruises intentionally placed on a woman's skin, dual purpose, to heal and to decorate. A hard thing for Westerners to take, tolerate, including me. In another context, on anyone else, I would have guessed that the markings were tattoos, perfect, dark, single geometric shapes in vertical-centered sequence. The dangle, of emeralds, coral, and gold lay there in hard edged contrast to the soft delicate flesh of the bruise art, the hard objects falling in perfect erotical placement between her bare shoulder blades.

她一定是当天做的。是迎接我到访的准备工作之一吗？这个念头令人震惊。充满遐想。如此近距离地观看瘀伤艺术，充血、鲜活、活跃，很神奇。在女人皮肤上刻意而为的瘀青带给人一种感官上的刺激，具有治愈和装饰的双重目的。这事儿对于西方人来说很难接受和容忍，包括我。换个场景，换个人，我会猜想这是一种文身，完美、暗黑、简单的几何图形，垂直居中排列。翡翠、珊瑚和琥珀项链垂坠在她裸露的肩胛骨中间，首饰的坚硬质料与瘀伤艺术的柔软肌肤形成强烈反差，极具挑逗性。

Her presence, my juxtaposed position, invited a touch, handshake, caress, something. I didn't dare. I imagined it, what it must have felt like, for Jackson. He must have stood with Moriah many times like that, looking out to sea, from the edge of California to 'distant Cathay', as he liked to call it, her China. Attraction, reminding myself of my position. The sunset past, she silent, waiting, as if some bit of the lost light might return, Jackson. I held my silence.

她的存在，我的站位，无不在呼唤一次肌肤相亲，握手、抚摸之类的。我不敢。只能想象对于杰克逊来说那会是什么感觉。他一定有无数次与莫立娅站在这里看海，从加利福尼亚的边缘望向"遥远的华夏"，他喜欢这么称呼她的中国。这太诱惑了，我提醒自己注意自己的定位。夕阳落下去了，她沉默着、等待着，仿佛某些消失的光线还会回来，杰克逊。我保持缄默。

"The setting of the sun is complete." She announced, turning to me at last. "Thank you for your patience, both for the scheduling of our meeting, and for this. A sunset sets only once a day."

"日落圆满了。"她说道，终于转过身来。"感谢你的耐心，为我们这次会面，还有这次日落。夕阳每天只西下一次。"

Moriah's 'sun', her inner light of life, had not 'set', far from it, indeed, a face perfect in symmetry and oval, astonishing, without lines, no imperfections. Eyes dark, wide, intense, flashing with the flickering light from the fireplace down the way. Her head turned slightly and to one side, as to take me in, stare into me more intently, get inside, beyond, behind my eyes. Difficult not to flinch in the onrush of such beautiful dominance. My eyes fixed onto her thick lips, them pursed in soft red tones, the subtle mouth hovering at the edge of stern adult and playful child ... ultimate expressing of 'alluring'. impossible not to stare back, then blink, then stare again, each part of her 'facial ensemble' a supportive element in the overall design ... Asianic, exotic, erotic, exquisite.

莫立娅的"太阳",她生命的内在光芒并没有"西下"。恰恰相反,她椭圆的脸庞对称完美,没有皱纹和斑点,令人惊叹。黝黑的双眼分得很开,目光锐利,被壁炉跳动的火光映得熠熠生辉。她微微侧头,似乎要仔细把我看清,双眼注视着我,仿佛要看进我的内心,把我看穿。在如此美丽逼人的注视下很难不退缩。我眼睛盯着她丰满的双唇,微微翘起,柔软红润,介于严厉的大人和俏皮的孩子之间……这是"诱惑"的终极表达。很难不盯着她看,然后目光回避,然而又忍不住再看。她的脸庞的每一部分构成了设计完美的整体……亚洲,异域,诱惑,精致。

"My ... pleasure ... Madam Leung." I said, voiced tremored, though pleased some words came out at all.

"我……我的荣幸……梁夫人。"我说道,声音颤抖,但还是对自己能够说出话来感到满意。

Scene Seven   A Toast to Jackson
第七幕 为杰克逊干杯

Marble Sculptures at the Lap Pool—J.B. Estate, Santa Cruz, CA
泳池边的大理石雕塑——加州圣克鲁斯 J.B. 宅邸

She turned and I followed. Her flow of movement led us past the fire and toward the far side of the space to a dining area. A glass table-top with metal frame, eight chairs, views to the garden, lap pool, ocean up-spray drama beyond. The table, well appointed, candle lit, linen clothed, places sets in silver and crystal.

她转身走开,我紧随其后。她步履轻盈地带着我经过壁炉,走向房间另一头来到就餐区。金属边框的玻璃餐桌,摆着8把椅子,餐厅面向花园,小型泳池,远处是惊涛拍岸的大海。餐桌经过精心布置,点着蜡烛,铺着亚麻桌布,银制和水晶餐具摆放停当。

Maximillian waited for us, rising from his seat upon our arrival. Next to him a tall man, thin, American, perhaps the chef. Jasmine came, laptop in hand, stepping out behind a screen, scenes of distant mountains in clouds. Other guests meander in, Stanford faculty, hologram experts, a designer from the J.B. line of Bartholomew casual ware. Yes, the dinner for me; Still, the evening an opportunity for ongoing business, in the manner of those fully engaged in continual entrepreneurial activities.

马克西米利安在等我们,看见我们进去从座位上站起身来。他旁边是一位瘦高个男子,美国人,可能是主厨。茉莉从一副远山云雾缭绕的画屏后面走出来,手里拿着笔记本电脑。其他客人陆续踱入,斯坦福大学老师,全息专家,一位J.B.休闲服饰产品线的设计师。没错,晚宴是为我而设,但对这些一直参与商业活动的人们来说,这也是一次谈工作的机会。

"Let me introduce all present to our special guest for the evening, Mr. Samuel Z. Curien."

"We will hear more about Mr. Curien as the evening progresses." she said. "I understand Mr. Curien that you've already met Jasmine Xi'an, Jackson's protégé, now my own, as well as Mr. McKenzie."

"请允许我向在座各位介绍今晚的特邀嘉宾——居里安先生。稍后我们将会听到更多关于居里安先生的介绍。"她说,"我想,居里安先生已经见过茉莉·席安——杰克逊的弟子,现在是我的弟子,还有麦肯齐先生。"

"Yes, my pleasure." I said. You couldn't help but fall into the rhythm of it, the formality.

"是的,非常荣幸。"我说道。然后不由自主地就跟着仪式的节奏走了。

Moriah MC'd, going around the table, brief introductions of each. One chair remained empty. No explanation. My assumption it reflected the missing man, her husband. No possibility of me asking about it, curiosity burn or not.

莫立娅绕着餐桌,逐个介绍来宾。有一把椅子空着,也没有解释。我猜是为她那位失踪的丈夫而设,但好奇心再强烈,也不能打听。

As the courses were served Moriah directed conversation to me, my studies, aspirations, interests in film, all things 'J.B.'. My talk about dreams especially well received. That fell into a conversation on reincarnation, then holograms, then artificial intelligence, finally 'out their' developments, how to achieve 'digital immortality', including my own ideas about 'reverse engineering'; that is, using data from creations, writings, of a given person, after gone, to digitally reconstruct the persona in AI form. All that whirling around the table, the ideas of death, rebirth, cosmic forces ... Jackson was there, but not there, in that there was no direct mentioned of him. Everyone did well, mannered about that, tiptoeing around it, the 'elephant in the room', that is, until, I said it. I couldn't stand it, not a moment longer, the saying of what had to be said. As they say, something came over me. Perhaps it was Jackson himself, a little too much wine. In any event, I stood, raised my newly filled glass. With that, yet another 'die was cast', another river crossed. Damn the Senate, Caesar would be proud.

宴饮开始之后,莫立娅渐渐将话题转向我,我的研究题目,我的理想,对拍电影的乐趣,关于J.B.的一切。关于我那些梦境的话题引起了热烈的反响。大家开始讨论轮回重生、全息、人工智能,最后引出了他们的项目进展,如何达到"数字永生",包括我自己关于"逆向工程"的点子,即从某人生前的创作作品中采集数据,在其离世后,用数字化手段重建此人的AI人格。席间讨论热烈,关于死亡、重生、宇宙原力……杰克逊既在场,也不在场,因为没有人直接提到过他。每个人的言行都很得当,小心翼翼地绕开这个"房间里的大象"。直到我说了出来。我实在忍不住,多一刻都不行,该说的就得说出来。如他们所说,我被某种东西附体了。也许是杰克逊本人,酒喝多了点。不管怎样,我站了起来,举起刚斟满的酒杯。借此,又一枚"骰子掷下",又一条河流跨过。去他的元老院,恺撒会为此而骄傲的。

"Jackson Bartholomew is here. I don't know if he's alive ... or not, but he is here. So much of him is with us ... at this dinner. We must honor him, especially at this particular location, his great architectural achievement. At the least ... with a toast."

"杰克逊·巴塞洛缪就在这里。我不知道他是活着……还是死了,但他就在这儿。他有那么多东西陪伴着我们…… 在这场晚宴上。我们必须向他致敬,特别是在这个特殊的地点,他伟大的建筑杰作。至少…… 敬个酒吧。"

Odd, the sound of my own voice, foreign. Then silence. No one moved. Oh my god. No help coming, from anyone. Time slowed, stopped, painful, my face filling, a panic thought, to exit, quickly, down the hall, out the door. I had expected something else, some of them, all of them, to join me, raise a glass. Sudden realization sinking in, I had gone where it was not permitted, that is, into the zone of Moriah, her prevue, how to handle the subject, her husband, his absence, his possible, likely ... uh ... death. They were right, not to help, not to stand, not to raise a glass, not to save me. It would have been an afront to her, to the likely widow. In that one instant it had all become clear to me, but too late, I had crossed the river, headed toward Rome.

好奇怪啊,我自己的声音听起来很陌生。然后,一片静默。没人动弹。我的天哪。没有任何人响应。时间慢了下来,停止不动,太难堪了,我脸涨得通红,惊慌失措,生出逃跑的念头,迅速跑出大厅,逃出大门。我本以为会是不一样的场景,一部分人,或者所有人,跟我一起举起酒杯。由顿悟到知觉,我踏进了禁区。那是莫立娅的地盘,她的叙事,如何去触碰这个话题、她的丈夫、他的缺席、他可能的……死亡。他们这样做是对的,不伸出援手,不站队,不举杯,不拯救我。那会冒犯她这位多半已成寡妇的人。就在那一刹那,我看得一清二楚,但为时已晚。我已经渡过河流,直奔罗马。

Then it came. Not a fix, that no longer possible, my embarrassment too established. Instead, mercy. Moriah, rose, slowly. Both hands gently caressing her wine glass, it sitting in front of her on the table, then raising it, like a priest at Communion, as though offering the blood of Christ to Jehovah, or yet another blood sacrifice to the gods, whatever metaphysical forces at play, in 'the beyond'.

然后静默打破了。不是救场,我的尴尬境地已成定局,没救了。老天慈悲。莫立娅缓慢地站起来。她的双手温柔地抚摸着面前的酒杯,然后举起来,就像圣餐礼上的教士将基督之血向耶和华献祭,抑或是向三界之外的无论何方神祇献上鲜血的祭奠。

"Yes. Let us offer a toast." she said. With her release, everyone stood, raised their glasses.
　　"是的，让我们敬献一杯。"她说道。她发话了，所有人都起立举杯。

So startled, taken aback, I'd forgotten it was me that was to give the toast.
我惊魂未定，忘了应该由我来致敬酒辞。

"Mr. Curien ... " Madam Moriah was forced to prod me.
　　"居里安先生……"莫立娅夫人不得不提点我。

"Oh ... Okay. To Jackson Bartholomew. Thank you ... sir, for all you did ... and all you will do." I managed to say, and then, sat down.
　　"噢，好的。敬杰克逊·巴塞洛缪。感谢您……先生，感谢您所做的一切……以及您将要做的一切。"我勉力说完了，然后坐下。

Gasps of group relief. "Here, here!" The sounds of them breaking down into happy talk, laughter.
　　全体松了一口气。"赞同，赞同！"他们的声音分散成为欢快的谈笑。

The formality dam broken, the talk flowed on, easier now, into the night, attention thankfully away from me, subjects of life's purpose, the essence of being human, and the like.
　　仪式沉默的堤坝被打破了，交谈畅快地滑向夜色深处，注意力成功地从我身上转移开了，话题从生命的意义到人的本质，诸如此类。

Moriah, less talkative, her role as host mostly accomplished. She'd reenter the conversation with a purpose, to turn the talk to Jasmine for example. Moriah expertly weaved leading comments in and out to present Jasmine's basic information, and in the best light. Jasmine was the daughter of a Singaporean family, well studied at private schools on the island, attended exclusive boarding prep outside of London. At sixteen she was already at Harvard, Business and English Literature majors. Graduate work at Cambridge, post-grad studies at Stanford. She'd already been published, holographic imagery, AI technologies.

She'd been working with the most acclaimed and prestigious experts in the field when Jackson had hired her to work on his holo—AI project. She'd quickly become the 'point person' for Jackson and the main contact with Stanford University. Through her, J.B. Enterprises became Stanford's biggest donor, and that's saying something.

莫立娅谈话变少了，她的女主人角色基本完成。她会有意地重新加入交谈，比如说把话头转到茉莉身上。莫立娅在介绍茉莉的时候，会巧妙地对她的评价不着痕迹地带出来，并且呈现她最好的一面。茉莉生于新加坡家庭，在那个岛国的私校接受良好教育，又到伦敦近郊的私人预备学校寄宿就读。十六岁，她已经来到哈佛攻读商业和英语语言文学专业。从剑桥毕业后，她在斯坦福大学读研究生。她已经发表过关于全息影像和人工智能技术的学术论文。杰克逊聘用她参与其全息—AI项目的时候，她已经在与这个领域最负盛名的专家并肩工作了。她很快成为杰克逊的"联系人"，主要负责与斯坦福大学的对接。通过她，J.B.集团成为斯坦福大学最大的捐赠方，这可不简单。

Once into it, Jackson had taken the subject on, obsession, these last several years, along with juggling all the other elements of his ubiquitous world brand. He'd become determined to make his holo—AI project the lead element of the Bruise Art phenomena. Much of his last days, before the disappearance, had been spent in just that pursuit, alongside Jasmine, researchers, Stanford faculty. Construction of research and development facilities in Palo Alto; most importantly of all, his own holographic program, project, and structure, right there at the J.B. compound, within the now famous geodesic dome, 'Il duomo'. Yes, indeed, a referencing to the one in beloved Firenze.

一旦走上这条路，杰克逊就一发不可收拾地沉迷其中，在过去这几年，他把那独特国际品牌中的其他元素结合在一起，决心把全息—AI项目打造成瘀伤艺术现象的主导元素。在他失踪前的最后一段日子里，他大部分时间花在了与茉莉、研究人员和斯坦福师生团队一起钻研上。研发设施建在帕洛阿尔托，而更重要的全息计划和构建就在这个J.B.建筑群、在这个著名的穹顶——"主教堂"。是的没错，这名称是为了与他心爱的佛罗伦萨那一座教堂遥相呼应。

Jackson had become secretive on details, holding back for some grand reveal was the speculation. Curiosity had become more pronounced, aggressive, in the weeks before the disappearance. One incident had an intruder making it to the doors of the dome. As a result, no one, outside the inner circle, had been allowed to see the plans for the final product, and to know the costs. The blackout created still more aggressive attention, a helicopter photo raid by super paparazzi and the like. A price to be paid for pan-pop culture domination.

杰克逊对细节遮遮掩掩，大家猜他秘而不宣是为了某天的隆重发布。在他失踪前几周，人们的好奇心已经旺盛得咄咄逼人。有个入侵者来到了穹顶建筑的大门口。这一事件的结果是除核心圈子之外，不允许任何人看到最终成品的规划及其成本。另外，还发生了一起停电事件，引起人们更强烈的关注，还有狗仔队的直升机偷拍，等等。这是在泛流行文化主导的时代必须付出的代价。

Even in the setting of the intimate dinner, intended in part for my orientation to all things J.B., Jasmine's response stayed guarded.

即便在今天这种私密的晚宴上，这样安排部分原因还是出于我对J.B.的仰慕，茉莉仍然保持警惕。

"What is the status of the holo—AI project?" I asked, confidential, almost at whisper.

"全息—AI项目现在进展怎么样了？"我私下问，几乎是耳语。

"Madam Leung will discuss that with you ... later, tonight."

"梁夫人今晚会跟你讨论这个问题……稍后。"

Moriah and Jasmine continued to monitor the evening, inserting expertly to pick it up when conversation faltered, spreading the topics evenly among us, pulling away from delicate subjects when their jagged edges were too exposed. Politics, religious beliefs, money discussed to be sure, but shunted aside as needed to let the flow of the evening go on without hampering the building of a base of trust among the participants. It struck me that this must have been how it once was, when the art of evening conversation over a fine meal was the norm, not the exception.

莫立娅和茉莉继续掌控晚宴进度，当交谈减少，她们巧妙地拾起话头，使话题在客人之间分配平衡；当话锋变得犀利，又将话题从敏感地带引开。政治、宗教信仰、金钱肯定是会谈的，但必要的时候也会避开，使晚宴顺利进行，在宾客间建立基本的信任。我突然意识到，享受美食的同时领略交谈的艺术，这在以往年代必是常态而非特例。

"Peter does an excellent job in interpreting Jackson's menus. Every item taken from *Bruise Art*. Look closely, each item has a page number next to it, as in, 'Page 341—*Bruise Art*' for baked/fried corn. These were all dishes eaten by Bruise Art characters from settings in the novel, Biloxi, Firenze, Chaoyang Park. All recipes researched, tested, by Jackson himself, part of the initial writing of the novel." Moriah said, proudly, the closest she'd come to giving an opening to discuss him. The door closed quickly. "Extremely well-done Peter. Thank you so much for this evening." she said.

"彼得在诠释杰克逊的菜谱方面做得很棒。每一道菜都来自《瘀伤艺术》。仔细看看，每道菜都标注了页码，看这个：'《瘀伤艺术》第341页'，烤/炸玉米。这些都是书中人物在不同场景吃过的菜式，在比洛克西、佛罗伦萨、朝阳公园。所有的菜谱都是杰克逊本人在写这部小说的初期研究、尝试出来的。"莫立娅自豪地说道，这是她敞开议论杰克逊最接近的一次，但是门很快关上了。"非常出色，彼得。感谢你为今晚所做的一切。"她说。

With that one expression, the "thank you for the evening" the group knew, no need to say more, it was time to wrap things up, say one's goodbyes, head home. A delicate unspoken line of communication between Moriah and Jasmine, eyes, gestures, easy, subtle, allowed them to easy everyone out, have them all feel appreciated, special, social sated.

随着"感谢今晚出席"这句话，大家都知道无须多言，是时候起身道别，各回各家。在莫立娅和茉莉之间，通过眼神、手势等不需言表的微妙交流，轻松、不着痕迹地将每位客人送出，令大家都觉得受到重视和特别款待，社交感很棒。

I was another matter. The two of them were looking for something, assessing. A distinct reaction when I used this phrase or that. "Never, in the history of the world." for example. I liked that expression, used it often. Maybe I'd read it in Jackson's writings or heard him say it in an interview or on a podcast. They saw something more. Then the way I sipped my latte. It registered with them, each looking to the other. A comment on blackberry cobbler drew a similar reaction.

我就是另一回事了。她们俩在我身上寻找、评估着什么。当我说话时用了某些词语，她们会有明显的反应。比如，"在全世界的历史上从来没有过。"我喜欢这句表达，经常这么说。也许我在杰克逊的文字里读到过，或者在他的采访或播客里听到过。但她们看到了更多的东西。还有我喝拿铁的动作。她们相互对视了一眼，她们的记忆里有保存。我对黑莓酥皮馅饼的评论也引起了她们类似的反应。

Scene Eight   The Vagus

第八幕 迷走神经

Jasmine had disappeared, silent, no goodbye. Moriah showed me into the study. Comfortable, orderly, shelves of books, a laptop station inserted into inlayed wood, two screens, framed away, so as not to dominate the space or block views. Another set of music played, distant, background. A Conway Twitty country set giving way to Hank Williams, then to Pink Floyd, Moody Blues.

茉莉无声无息地消失了，没有道别。莫立娅带我来到书房。舒适、有序，一排排书架和一个镶嵌在木制台面的电脑工作台，两台显示屏也加了框，使它们不会在空间里显得太突兀或者遮挡视线。背景音乐换了一套，听起来很遥远。从康威·特威的乡村音乐换到汉克·威廉姆斯，然后是平克·弗洛伊德，情绪蓝调乐队。

"It's a compilation, eclectic, Jackson's. I thought it a good background for this discussion." she said. "Mr. Curien, with introductions, initial getting to know one another complete, let's move it to the next level."

"这是个合集，混搭风格，杰克逊选的。我认为很适合作为此次讨论的背景。"她说，"居里安先生，初步的介绍和了解都做完了，我们进入下一阶段吧。"

"Next level?"

"下一阶段？"

"Yes. We both will need to make some decisions, if we trust one another, no matter what the details might be. By the way, I understand that you are studying Mandarin, speak a little."

"是的。如果我们相互信任，无论细节如何，我们都需要做些决定。顺便说一下，我知道你在学中文，你会说一点。"

"I've tried a bit. Just starting. So beautiful the characters, each of piece of art."

"我学了一点。才刚开始。汉字太美了，每个字都是艺术。"

"Indeed. Hai ku Shi Lan ... have you heard that Chinese expression? It means, 'the sea runs dry and the rocks crumble', that is, before a trust should be broken."

"的确。海枯石烂——你听过这个中文表述吗？它的意思是，'海水干涸，岩石粉碎’，表达的是只有出现这种情况，信任才会破坏。"

She gestured me to an overstuffed leather chair, then took her position, directly across. I felt something in my chest, physical, deep, familiar. My heart. I shifted to my side to take the pressure off the spot between my shoulder blades. She noticed it, my expression pained.

她示意我坐到一把填充得过分鼓胀的皮质椅子上，然后她在我正对面坐下。我感觉胸膛深处传来一阵熟悉的悸动，是我的心脏。我调整姿势，缓和肩胛骨之间那个点的压力。她注意到我难受的表情。

"What is it? Are you okay?" she asked, oddly, as though she knew the answer.

"怎么回事？你还好吗？"她问道，奇怪，仿佛她已经知道答案了。

"Nothing. Just a small thing."
"没什么，一点小问题。"

"Describe it." she said.
"描述一下。"她说。

"Really?"
"真的要吗？"

"Yes."
"是的。"

"Well, it's something in my nervous system, doctor diagnosed, the Vagus nerve."
"好吧，是我神经系统的问题，医生诊断的结果是迷走神经问题。"

"Do you know the meaning of the word 'Vagus'?" she asked.
"你了解'迷走'这个词的含义吗？"她问道。

"Yes, I do. it means that nerve, the one that helps regulate the heartbeat,

149

breathing, other things." I said.

"我知道。它就是调节心跳、呼吸之类事情的神经。"

"Yes. But the meaning of the word itself? It's Latin ... to travel, to wonder. That nerve goes so many places in the body, the torso, difficult to find its exact location. It has a tremendous role in the body, the giver of rhythm, it's said that it even allows compassion. If it is altered, it will affect all the other parts, patterns in the brain, beating of the heart, ability to breathe. Yours has, shall we say ... enhancements."

"对。但这个词本身的含义呢？这是个拉丁词，意思是旅行，游荡。这根神经在身体躯干里很多部位游走，很难准确定位。它在身体里的作用巨大，掌握着人的节奏韵律，据说它还掌管情感。如果对它施以修改，它会影响其他部位，比如，大脑的模式、心跳的节奏、呼吸的能力。而你的神经，可以说，是经过加强的。"

"Yes, perhaps." I said, thinking on it, waiting. I sensed that she wanted to tell me something.

"是吧，也许。"我边说边琢磨，等待着。我感觉到她要向我透露些什么。

My father had taught me a structure for such moments. "Wait, let them talk, best they begin when they want to tell you something important. Take your cues from their words. Don't step on it, talk to soon. Find out what they really want, how best to go forward." he'd say. "Not easy to stay silent. You can do it though. Practice."

我父亲曾经教我面对这种时刻的因应之策。"你得等待，让他们先说。如果对方有重要的事情要告诉你，最好让他们先开始。从他们的话里找线索。别着急回应。找到他们真正想要的东西，想想如何向前推进。"他说，"保持沉默可不容易。但你能做到，这需要多练习。"

"Jackinsun had the Vagus ... as well as the obsession with dreams." That was it, what she wanted to say, was holding back. "Those that have it, the irregularity of that nerve, when it presents as unpredictable, are said to have a particular ability, gift if you like, in addition to the heart problem."

"杰金森（此为梁夫人对杰克逊的昵称——译者注）也有迷走神经的问题……也对做梦非常入迷。"就是这个问题。这就是她想要说的，此前一直掖着。"有这个问题的人，那条神经很不规律，发作起来毫无预兆，但这些人除了心脏问题之外，还拥有一种特别的能力，甚至可以说是天赋。"

"What kind of ability?"
"什么样的能力？"

"I think you know. The ability to, 'make connections' let's say, communicate more fully, decipher dreams, enhanced compassion. Let's leave it at that for now. Best not to talk too much on it. Just mark it. Something for us to revisit."

"我想你是知道的。就是'建立连接'的能力。这么说吧，这些人沟通更充分，有解析梦境的能力和超强的共情力。目前先说到这里。最好不要说太多，记住就是。我们回头再来讨论这个。"

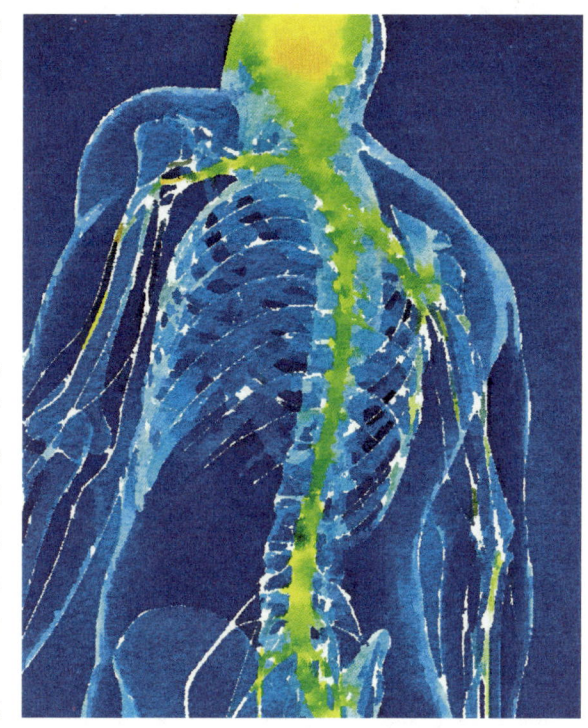

Vagus Nerve—'Compassion'
迷走神经——"悲悯之情"

"Like epileptics perhaps?" I said.
"可能就像癫痫一样？"我说。

"Those points along the Vagus nerve, lines on the body, Chinese have thought long on them, think of acupuncture. There's that, then your ankle as well, as far as things physical." she said. How did she know about that, my left ankle, the spot that when touched shot stabbing pain? "You have a lot in common with him. That's the point. Your background, interests, UCLA, Florence, 'dream and half-dreams', remarkable. Your letters, how you write, the words you choose. Some particular phrases, I couldn't ignore it. Then there's the ambition, a rare brand of it, Jackinsun level ambition. Not just pushing, but your way of doing it. In this case, his film, a second edition, all of it to be done now, and as though it's yours."

"迷走神经沿线的点,在身体上的连接,中国人已经研究了很久,你想想针灸。就是那里,还有你的脚踝,就是和身体相关的。"她说。她怎么知道我的左脚踝有一个点,只要一碰就刺痛? "你跟他有许多共同点。这就是关键。你的背景、兴趣、UCLA,佛罗伦萨、'梦与半醒',了不起。还有你的信件、写作的方式、遣词造句、某些特别的说法,我不可能视而不见。另外,你的雄心,与众不同,是杰金森水准的雄心。而这些你并非一味强推,你有自己的行事风格。具体到这件事情上,他的电影,小说的再版,所有这一切都要现在完成,好像这是你自己的事一样。"

She looked deep into my eyes, difficult to hold my gaze up, matching in return. Searching me. She wanted more information than I gave, could give.

她深深注视我的双眼,与她目光对视非常艰难,我不是对手。她在审查我。她想得到比我已给的、我能给的信息更多的东西。

"Maybe there's more than that, beyond physical, our ability to know. Jackinsun would think so." she said.

"或许还有更多的东西,超越身体之外,超出我们能力所能了解的。杰金森会这么想。"她说。

"What can I say." I said. "I've spent a lot of time studying *Bruise Art*, living it, every detail. Jackson became a part of me. Then there's the master's thesis, my taking your husband's book from novel to film. Theoretic project of course, for my degree, but it's taken me, all of me, much more than I expected. When he went missing, I couldn't get my mind around it. Not possible, that he could be just gone, just like that, the single biggest figure in the popular culture. He'd dominated so much, architecture, fashion, writing, his way of being, well ... popular. My project needed to be done, as though it decided, and I executed. I was, am, revealing something, what was already there. That's how it felt, feels. Do you know what I mean?"

"我能说什么呢。"我说道,"我花了大量时间研究《瘀伤艺术》,我以此为生,了解它的每一个细节。杰克逊已经成为我的一部分。还有我的硕士论文主题是我如何将您丈夫的小说搬上银幕。当然这项目是理论上的,我只是为了拿学位,但这事儿占据了我的全部,比我想象的要多得多。他失踪的时候,我根本不能接受。这不可能,他就这么消失了,流行文化最显著的人物就那样没有了。他在各领域睥睨天下,建筑、时尚、写作、生活方式以及流行文化。我的项目必须要完成，就好像是他来做决定，我来执行。我过去是，现在也是，将某些本来已经存在的事物揭示出来。那就是我的感觉，此前和现在都是。你懂我的意思吗？"

"Yes, I do. Go on."
"我懂。继续。"

"It was a big project, even if theoretical. It had its own demands of me, things that I had to do, as it was revealed to me. I know, sounds strange, religious, like I believe a metaphysical spirit chose me, to do it. I don't mean it that way. I mean it seemed as though there was something that already existed, and I was the tool to let it be seen, escape its cover. Michelangelo's sculptures, the way he described it, something like that."

"那是个大项目，哪怕只在理论上成立。它自己对我发号施令，列出我必须完成的事情，揭示让我知晓。我知道这听起来很奇怪，有宗教的意味，好像我相信的什么形而上的神灵选中了我去做这件事。我不是那个意思。我的意思是，就好像有什么东西已然存在，而我是件工具，帮助它突破束缚，被人们看见。米开朗琪罗描述过自己的雕塑，就类似那样的事情。"

She paused, examining me. "I've read your proposal. We are both familiar with what you want to do. In theory, it is something that needs to be done, at least by someone. A Second edition, the film version of *Bruise Art*. Jackinsun wanted that, of course. Before we get to that question, there is something that you must know about me, that is, what I want you to do, my priorities, my own agenda, my 'special project' of sorts. Once you known that, then we'll be in the position to make decisions."

她停顿片刻，审视着我。"我看了你的提案。对于你想做的事情，我们两人都非常清楚。理论上，它是某种必须要完成的东西，至少要由某个人完成。小说的再版、《瘀伤艺术》的电影版，杰金森当然想要。在讨论这个问题之前，还有一些关于我的事情是你必须了解的。那就是，我想要你做什么，我的优先事项是什么，我自己的议程，我的'特别计划'。一旦你了解了这些，我们就可以做决定了。"

"I propose we do the following, before we continue on about 2nd Editions, films, or even my agenda; I will interview you in the form of a discussion, with a particular structure to it, with the intent that you to become more aware of key information, about Jackinsun, me, our relationship, the whole Bruise Art project. In addition, you will have questions, things you're hesitant to ask, subjects that you might think ... too delicate. In short, this evening I want to go beyond the superficial, go deep, exchange information that would only pass between extreme confidants. After all, you are asking something remarkable, that I allow you to work on my husband's legacy, have a major effect on how he will be remembered. Especially the film. The visual will override the written, if done right. The most remarkable thing is not your asking, but that I would even consider it. You're so young, lacking experience, you are only a projection of something still to be, a 'down payment', a 'promissory note' on the future."

"我建议，在我们继续讨论小说再版、电影甚至是我的议程之前，先完成以下事项：我要通过讨论的形式对你做一次问询，这次问询有着特别的架构，目的是让你了解更多关于杰金森、我自己、我们俩的关系以及整个瘀伤艺术项目的信息。你可以提问，关于那些你不好意思问的，或者你可能觉得……太敏感的问题。简而言之，今天晚上，我想跳过那些表面的东西，深入实质，交换仅仅在互信极深的人们之间才会交换的信息。毕竟你的请求非比寻常，要我准许你为我丈夫遗留的事业工作，这将对纪念他的方式产生重大影响，特别是电影。做得好的话，视觉作品会超越文字。最不同寻常之处并非你敢提出请求，而是我居然对此予以考虑。你如此年轻，又没有经验，你不过是尚未定型之物的投影，是未至之将来的一笔'首付'、一张'本票'。"

"So why are you considering it ... at all, my proposal I mean?"
"那您……说到底为什么会予以考虑呢？我是说我的提案。"

"My instincts have served me well through the years. I listen to them, give them a full voice, watch where they lead. Now, they have led me to you. There are things about you, certain things that have come to my attention. Your last written request for example. It included several phases, things I'd only ever heard from the mouth of one person, Jackson Bartholomew. No need for me to explain it or understand it, simply follow it. Suffice it to say, I see a connection between you and him, something extraordinary. xin you ling xi yi dian tong, hearts which have a common beat are linked. That is more than apparent. It means that you have potential ... for an approach that I have in mind."

"我的本能对我很有帮助，多年如此。我倾听它的声音，看它将我引向何方。现在它把我带到你这里。你有某种特质,这引起了我的注意。例如你最后一封请求信。里面有几种提法,我只听到过从一个人的嘴里说出来,就是杰克逊·巴塞洛缪。我不需要去解释或去理解它,跟随它就好了。这么说吧,我看出来你和他之间有某种不同寻常的关联。心有灵犀一点通,心灵同步的人彼此之间是有关联的。再明显不过了。这意味着,在我想好的一条路上,你有潜力。"

"An approach? For what, Madam Leung?" I said, hearing my own words now fully in her cadence, the same level of formality; Such was the nature of the woman's stature, dominance. She had an unspoken effect on the atmosphere around her, and all occupants therein.

"路?关于什么的路,梁夫人?"我说着,听到自己说话的腔调已经完全与她同步,一样的正式。这就是这个女人的气质和控场能力。她对自己身边的氛围及其中的人们有着一种无形的影响。

Moriah turned, looked to the ocean. "Do you believe that Jackson killed himself? That is, do you believe that he committed suicide, as the Italian courts ruled. Do you see any room for another explanation, that he died in some other fashion? Or even perhaps, that he still lives?"

莫立娅转身看向大海。"你相信杰克逊是自杀吗?就是说,你相信意大利法庭判决的结果吗?他是自杀的?你觉得还有其他解释的空间吗?他会不会有其他的死因?或者甚至说,他还有可能活着?"

There it was, Moriah had asked her key question, the asking of it revealing why she agreed to the meeting with me in the first place. I should have anticipated it, prepared an answer. My answer to the single question would determine everything. I took a deep breath, letting it out in a whoosh. My father's image came to mind. I could see him sitting there at his desk, not knowing the answer to a pointed question. I simply quoted him, repeated his words. "I haven't considered that."

就是这点,莫立娅问出了她的关键问题。问出这个问题本身就揭示了她当初同意接见我的原因。我应该早就猜到并且准备好答案。我对这个简单问题的答案将决定一切。我深吸一口气,噗地呼了出来。我父亲的形象浮现在脑海。我能看见他坐在自己的桌前,不知道如何回答一个尖锐的问题。我直接用了他的原话:"我没想过这个问题。"

Moriah's eyes widened, close to an outburst. "It's important, don't you think? In fact, it's the prime reason that I've agreed to meet with you at all. The resolution of why, how, under what circumstance Jackson Bartholomew was 'disappeared'."

莫立娅双眼大睁，几乎要爆发。"你不觉得这很重要吗？说实话，这是我同意见你的主要原因。解开在何种条件下，杰克逊·巴塞洛缪是如何'被失踪'的这个谜团。"

"Was disappeared? Are you suggesting he was kidnapped, removed ... by someone?"

"被失踪？你的意思是他被……什么人绑架带走了？"

"My use of 'disappeared' is meant to be expansive. I don't preclude anything. Until he's located, there's no way to know. A court's determination means nothing to me. I know one thing for certain, my husband did not commit suicide."

"我用'失踪'这个词是广义的。我不排除任何可能性。在找到他之前无法明确发生了什么。法庭的裁决对我毫无意义。我只确定一点，我丈夫不是自杀。"

"For certain? How can you possibly know that?" The question was out of my mouth before I could pull it back.

"确定？你怎么可能知道？"我的问题脱口而出，想收回但来不及了。

"I know, as a matter of fact, that he had every reason to be happy, to plan, to continue to create, and that he was exactly that ... happy with life and looking forward. Not possible that he would leave

Moriah Leung—Reflection in the Window
莫立娅·梁夫人——映在窗户上的身影

me that way, without some communication. Not possible. With that said, it is for the resolution of that question that you are here now, allowed to enter the story. I insist that you know, accept, that his death was not suicide. Xin ze you, bu xin ze wu, if you believe, then it is there. Otherwise, we can go no further."

"我就是知道。因为他有无数理由感到幸福，做计划，继续创作，他对生活很满意，充满向往。他不可能一丝信息都没留下就那样离开我。不可能。有鉴于此，解开这个谜团是你得以坐在此处、参与此事的原因。你要了解、接受，他的死并非自杀，我坚持这一点。信则有，不信则无。（原文此处用中文拼音表达——译者注）只要你相信，它就在那里。否则我们无法继续谈下去。"

"The only way I can say that I can 'believe' he did not commit suicide is to investigate, to hear what you have to say, others, to see all the related information. Even then, I wouldn't really know, not a hundred percent. There would have to be a body for that." I said, another Tourette Syndrome moment for me, too late to mitigate, pull it back. I had defied her insistence that I accept her premise.

"能让我说'我相信'他没有自杀的唯一途径是开展调查。我要听听你怎么说，别人怎么说，要看到所有相关的资料。即便如此，我也不能说百分百确定，需要一具尸体来证明。"我的图雷特综合征又一次发作了，太晚了，无法缓和，收不回来。我违抗了她所坚持的条件。

She looked at me, blank, full on, then a hint of a smile. "Investigation ... indeed."

她直视着我，面无表情。一丝笑意一掠而过。"调查……你是认真的？"

"You must have already had the whole thing investigated, by professionals, police, private investigators, lawyers, FBI. The court in Tuscany, they investigated, made a ruling based on it, right? The report from their commission, I read it, exhaustive. The local Florentine police. What about the Carabinieri? They must have done an extensive investigation. Italy after all. There must be volumes of documents, photographs, interviews, witnesses, a library of detailed information."

"你肯定已经找人把这事从头到尾调查了个遍，专业人员、警察、私人侦探、律师、联邦调查局。托斯卡纳的法庭也调查了，基于调查他们给出了裁定，不是吗？警署报告我读了，非常详尽。那是佛罗伦萨当地警察。意大利宪兵又如何呢？他们必定做了广泛的调查，毕竟这是意大利。一定有大量的文件、照片、讯问、目击证人，详细信息都能撑起一个图书馆了。"

Moriah held up her hand, gently, yet leaving no doubt that I was to stop speaking. "Of course, you're correct. More than all of that, I had my own team go to Florence, detectives, lawyers, experts. What did I get back? A lot of documents, billing, reasons for what they did. In the end, no matter how official and complete everything looked, nothing came of it. I came close to resignation, that there would be nothing else. I was about to try to put it behind me, all of us. Then came your last letter. There were parts of it too remarkable to ignore."

莫立娅举起手,动作轻柔然而意图明确,我该闭嘴了。"当然,你是对的。不只那些,我还派了自己的团队去了佛罗伦萨、侦探、律师、专家。我得到了什么?一大堆文件、账单,他们采取行动的理由。到最后,不管这些东西看起来有多么官方、多么完整,还是没有结论。我几乎要放弃了,接受没有别的可能。我正准备要把这一切留在过去,留在我们所有人的身后,你最后一封信来了。你的信里有些东西不同寻常,让我难以忽略。"

"How do you mean?"
"怎么不同寻常?"

"As I said, 'connections'. Beyond what could possibly be considered, coincidental."
"我刚才说了,'关联'。超出理性思考的范畴,超出巧合的范畴。"

"So, what now?"
"那么,现在怎么办?"

"Tonight, now, I will have you know the intimate details of my relationship with Jackinsun, our experiences, including how the Jackinsun's Bruise Art project came to be, all that followed, what it meant to both of us. With that done, we can then discuss my idea, my plan. It also encompasses your ambitions, Mr. Samuel Curien. I haven't forgotten about that. All of it in good time."

"今晚,就是现在,我要让你了解杰金森与我的关系中最私密的细节,我们的经历,包括瘀伤艺术项目是如何产生的,它所带来的一切及其对我们两人的意义。说完之后,我们才可以讨论我的想法、我的计划。这里面也包含了你的野心,塞缪尔·居里安先生,我没忘掉这一点。一切都恰逢其时。"

"Very well." I said, submitting to what might follow.
"很好。"我说着,已经决定接受即将到来的事。

"We need a structure for the discussion. Time is limited." she said, holding up her left hand, delicate, precise. "Five and three." she said, fingers up accordingly. "Five areas of conversation from me, and then, three questions from you. Whatever you want to ask, after you've heard my recontours. Asians are numbers conscious, even those of us not so superstitious. Five and three are good numbers in themselves, plus, they add up to eight."
"我们需要一个讨论的框架。时间有限。"她举起左手,娇小、精致。"5 和 3。"她说着,手指做出相应的示意。"我要展开五个领域的话题,然后,你可以提三个问题。你听完我的故事后,可以问任何问题。亚洲人很在意数字,哪怕是不迷信的人。5 和 3 都是好数字,并且他们相加等于 8。"

"Eight ... something to do with luck, infinity." I said.
"8……与好运和无限有关。"我说。

"The most fortunate and auspicious of all numbers and symbols. Gong Xi Fa Cai, prosperous wishes. May the structure and providence of 'the eight' have us prosper tonight, gain riches from our thoughts and deeds. With that in mind, the time passing, let's begin."
"这是最幸运、最吉祥的数字和符号。恭喜发财(原文为中文拼音——译者注),美好的愿望。今夜,祈祷'8'这个数字和天意帮助我们得遂所愿,通过我们的想法和行动致富。时间不等人,我们开始吧。"

"Very well." I said once again, my mind rushing ahead. What might I ask when it was my turn? Nervous that I wouldn't have questions equal to the moment.
"很好。"我又说了一遍,脑子飞快地转着。想着轮到我提问的时候我该问什么?我很紧张,怕自己想不出配得上那种时刻的问题。

"One other thing. Something that will play a role in what you decide to ask.

After we've finished with the 'five and three', I'll then take you to 'Il Duomo', the hologram room. Yes, that room. You'll have another kind of meeting there. Your final one for the evening." Moriah said, sullen, serious.

"还有一件事。这会影响到你决定问什么样的问题。我们完成'5和3'之后，我会带你去'主教堂'，全息室。是的，那个房间。你将在那里接受另一种询问。今晚最后一次。"莫立娅说，阴郁且严肃。

"Really? Him, it." I said, the words slipping out, hoping. To see it, the thing never seen, at least by the public, the digital Jackson Bartholomew, his hologram—AI.

"真的吗？他，它。"我脱口而出，充满期待。看到它，从未面世的那个东西，至少公众没有见过，数字化的杰克逊·巴塞洛缪，他的全息—人工智能影像。

"It was his latest passion. If he's truly gone then that is all we have left of him. You'll see, soon enough. Amazing, what someone can do when he has a billion or two to put into an obsession. Jing cheng suo zhi, jin she wei kai ... no difficulty is impossible if the mind is set to it."

"这是他最后阶段的热情。如果他真的走了，那就是他留下来的一切。你很快就会看到。一个人把10亿、20亿的钱全投到一项痴迷的事情里头会造出什么来，这非常神奇。精诚所至，金石为开（原文为中文拼音——译者注）。如果真心投入一件事，没有什么困难是不能克服的。"

"The most advanced hologram—AI technology in the world today ... or so I read." I said.

"这是当今世界最先进的全息—人工智能技术……我看到报道是这么说的。"我说。

"More than technology, the hologram is all about my Jackinsun, nothing else. Disturbing. It's the ultimate 'mausoleum', an exact homage to a single personality."

"不仅仅是技术。那个全息就是他，我的杰克逊，不是别的。令人不安的是，它是终极意义上的'陵墓'，是对一个人的致敬。"

"That real?"
"这么逼真吗？"

"As though he is there with you. You'll see, and tonight, your 'Interview with a hologram'."

"仿佛他就在你身边。今晚你会看到的，这是你与'全息影像的访谈'。"

"Interview? Or you mean a kind of presentation?"

"访谈？你的意思是他对我演讲吗？"

Geodesic Dome,"Il Duomo" — J.B. Estate, Santa Cruz, CA
网格球形穹顶 "主教堂" ——加州圣克鲁斯 J.B. 宅邸

"An Interview, a back and forth, between you and him ... it." she said. "It's exactly the kind of thing for which he had it made, interviews, lectures, even postmortem. He meant it to be the greatest illusion, ever, and at the same time, the greatest reality. AI, the reality, hologram the illusion. After all, we're talking about Jackson Bartholomew. It's his final grand gesture, his ultimate design, his existential legacy of himself. He meant it to have his manner, way of talking, being, joking, even singing, if you find the right path there. It is the first codicil of his will, that it be kept fully functioning, and in regular use for as long as his endowment funding and the natural world will permit. He left more than enough funding for continual upgrade as technology permits. If he hadn't left that mandate, I might have taken it down already, the whole thing."

"是访谈,有来有往,在你和他……它之间。"她说,"那正是他要打造这东西的意图。访谈、讲座,甚至事后分析。他想把它做成最出色的幻象,同时也是最逼真的现实。AI负责现实,全息代表幻象。这可是杰克逊·巴塞洛缪。这是他最后的大手笔,终极的设计,他自己的存在主义遗产。如果你知道怎么激活这一切,你会发现他刻意让它拥有他的行为举止、说话方式、整个人的状态、开的玩笑,甚至唱歌的方式。他遗嘱的第一项附录,就是要求保持它的功能正常运转,且只要在他的捐赠基金和自然规律允许的前提下,要经常使用它。他留下足够多的资金用于技术持续升级。要不是他留下这个授权,我可能已经把这项目整个关掉了。"

"Why would you ever think to remove it?" The words spurted out, Tourette, edges harsh.

"你是怎么想的,居然要关掉它?"我的话脱口而出,这是图雷特综合征,话语够尖锐的。

"Too painful. Him there, in a way, just beyond a wall, real, almost real. I saw him, in holo-form, once, the only time. I entered the room, activated it, and there he was. I couldn't tell the difference. When I asked a question, he answered. For all I could tell, it was him. That was a month to the day after he went missing. Never been in the room since. Only Jasmine, then some technicians, for updates, fine tuning, those sorts of thing."

"太痛苦了。从某种意义上说,他就在那儿,就隔着一面墙,几乎可以乱真。有一次,我在全息影像里看到了他,那是仅有的一次。我走进房间,激活了它,他就出现了。我看不出有什么区别。我问了个问题,他回答了。凭我所知,那就是他。那天是他失踪正好满一个月。我自那之后就没再走进这房间,只有茉莉和一些技术人员进去做更新和完善这类的工作。"

"In a way, it is him, isn't it?" I said. "I mean, he made it. He intended it to be interactive. He wanted you, anyone, to have the feel of the real, that it was him, in the flesh."

"从某个角度来说,那就是他,不是吗?"我说,"我是说,他造了它。他本来就想让它跟人互动。他想让你,让所有人,感受到真实的他,感觉那就是他的肉身。"

Moriah shook her head. "I'll never view it again. To know he's still here in that form, that I can talk to him, that everything he says and does is programmed into the hologram, that the image of him will react, come back, totally unbelievable. Horrible, the one time. Too much. Too real. Digital allows for the anticipation of every imaginable question, every combination of thought, combined with every response, gesture. Jaçkinsun programmed it to respond to the specific person, or should I say the data available and entered on that individual, and it being updated in real time as the hologram—AI interacts with the person visiting. I didn't know, anticipate, how finely tuned it, him, the hologram, to me. Now it seems obvious ... it, the hologram—AI, itself, does research, algorithm. Of course. Jackinsun didn't warn me. Holo—Jackson knows his subject, the person before him, better than they know themselves. And don't forget, this is no new creation, instead it is the transference of information, the downloading of everything that made Jackson Bartholomew him, from one 'vessel' to another. With one very powerful upgrade. The hologram—AI version of Jackson has hyper-knowledge, that is, the immediate access to all information everywhere via the Internet, and, the capacity to call it up, remember it if you will, use it, in real time, instantly."

莫立娅摇摇头。"我再也不会去看它了。要知道他还会以那个形态存在，我还能跟他说话，他的言行都通过编程融入了全息影像，所以他的全息影像会做出反应和回应，这让人难以置信。太可怕了，那一次经历。我很难接受。一切太真实了。数字化能够预测到每一个想象得到的问题、每一种想法的组合，再对应结合每一种反应和姿势。杰金森将它的程序编成可对来访者做出有针对性的反应。这么说吧，他先把关于此人已有的数据输入，全息影像在与来访者交谈的时候，数据可以实时更新。我不知道，他，或者说它这个全息影像里输入的关于我的数据有多么丰富详尽，我也不想猜。而现在变得越来越明显，它，这个人工智能全息影像，自己能做研究和算法了。必然如此。杰金森没有给我预警。全息杰克逊对它面前这个谈话对象的了解，比其本人对自身的了解还要多。别忘了，这不是一个新的造物，而是将关于杰克逊·巴塞洛缪其人的所有资料从一个'容器'转移、下载到另一个'容器'，还进行了一次强大的升级。杰克逊的全息—人工智能版本拥有海量知识，也就是说，它通过互联网实时获取信息，拥有随时调取、记忆、使用的能力。"

"Of course, Jackson didn't anticipate his ... 'going missing'." I said.
"当然，杰克逊没有预料到他的……'失踪'。"我说。

"Before I forget, there is one thing that can give it away, let you know it's not a living creature." Moriah said, waiting for me to catch up, to acknowledge the importance of what she was about to say. "Only the absence of the light of life, that tiny detail, the slight glint from his soul. You know what I mean by 'light of life'?" she said.

"趁我没忘,有一点是可以让它露出破绽的,让你知道它不是活生生的人。"莫立娅边说,边等着我消化、认识到她要说的事情很重要。"它没有生命的光芒,这个微小的细节是从灵魂发出的细微闪光。你懂'生命的光芒'是什么意思吗?"她说。

"Not really, Madam Leung." I said, bothered.
"不太懂,梁夫人。"我困惑地说。

"The light in its eyes, or the lack thereof. The window to the soul. You must know what I mean, what proves the essence of life. It's the only thing that gives the illusion away, to decide what is the real and what isn't, in the presence of his hologram. Too much for me. Jackinsun should have known." she said, scolding, as though he could hear her.

"就是眼睛里有没有光。眼睛是灵魂的窗口。你一定明白我的意思,什么是生命的真谛。在他的全息影像面前,这是唯一能够驱散幻象、分辨真伪的东西。这对我来说太过了。杰金森早该明白这一点。"她语带责备地说,就像他能听见似的。

"How long will we be in with him; I mean the hologram. Is there a timing to it? Can it go on for as long as we want?" I asked, anxious, the thought of it growing in my mind.

"我们要跟他在一起待多久?我指全息影像。有计时吗?我们可以想聊多久就多久吗?"我问道,我开始感到焦虑,脑子里的想象在滋长。

"'We? You will be alone, absolutely alone. Neither I, nor anyone else would be

Jackson Bartholomew
杰克逊·巴塞洛缪

there. Just you. It's the only way I will permit it. You can ask him any question you like, stay for as long as you want, or should I say, as long as he allows. Yes, Jackinsun had it programmed for 'annoyance shut off' he termed it. If he would've been annoyed enough, in real life, to cut you off, then he will also do so as a hologram."

"我们？你自己去，完全独自一人。我不会去，其他人也不会。就只有你。这是我准许的唯一形式。你可以问他任何问题，想待多久就待多久，或者说，他让你待多久你就待多久。是的，杰金森编了一项他称为'烦扰关停'的程序。在现实生活中，他会因为恼怒而打断你，那他的全息影像也一样会。"

"I'm not sure what that means." I said.
"我不确定这是什么意思。"我说。

"It means don't annoy him too much or you will be dismissed, by him." she said. "Keep your questions short. If things go well, it will become apparent what to say, not say. You know a lot more than you think. It'll come to you, or it won't. Don't force it though. He won't like it. Remember, you may know a lot … he will know everything, and on any subject. Very unnerving."

"我的意思是，不要过度惹恼他，否则他会把你赶走。"她说，"你的问题要简短。进展顺利的话，你自会知道该说什么不该说什么。你所知的比你想象的要多得多。你会找到感觉的，要是没有就没有了。别勉强。他不喜欢这样。记住，你可能知识渊博，而他无所不知，无论什么话题。这也非常令人不安。"

Moriah had fallen into a constant conflation, the hologram—AI with Jackson-the-real. Understandable, but disturbing.

莫立娅频繁使用连接词，一会儿全息—人工智能，一会儿杰克逊—真人版。可以理解，也令人不安。

"How is it, 'activated'."
"怎么'激活'它。"

"Not yet on that. Your focus needs to be now, us, this moment, not that one. Pay attention that I don't dismiss you myself." she scolded.
"还没到那一步。你要关注的是现在，我们，此时，不是它。小心，别惹我把你赶走。"

她责备道。

"Yes, very well ... Madam Leung." I said, formally voiced, my head nodding toward her, the movement odd, involuntary.
"好的,没问题,梁夫人。"我说着,声音变得正式,并向她点头,这个动作很怪异,却是不由自主的。

"The night is not so long. Let's get started with the discussion. Before all else, I will bring you into a closer set of connections. Then you can go to see the hologram. It will be another revelation to you. In any event, after all that, we will decide, move forward. 'Time is not forever', no one has much of it."
"夜并不漫长,我们开始讨论吧。一切开始以前,我要带你进入一套更紧密的关系中。然后你就可以去见全息影像了。那对你将是另一种启示。不管怎样,我们都要做出决定,向前走。'时间并不永恒',谁的时间都不富余。"

"Very well." I said, folding my hands at my lap, signaling my waiting, submitting; Her will in control, not my own. A small smile secreted at her lips.
"很好。"我说,我双手交叉放在大腿上,表示我在等候、听从。她的意志在控制局面,而不是我的。她的唇边悄悄浮起一抹笑意。

In the silence of the moment our eyes met, a pause, an instant. I heard it, she as well, a subtle sound, distant underlying hum, energy, presence. Him. It. Bart-HOLO-mew, the digital remains of a lost man. A pile of mechanical equipment, glorified technology, all cradled within a Buckminster Fuller geodesic dome. Unmissable, unmistakable the effect: J.B. intimidation, intentional, powerful, waiting, brooding, bragging.
值此静默一刻,我们四目相对,停顿了一瞬间。我听到了,她也听到了。一个轻微的声音,从远处隐隐传来的嗡声,充满能量和存在感。他,它。全息巴塞洛缪,一个失踪之人的数字化遗存。藏在巴克敏斯特·富勒式网球格穹顶之中的一堆机械装置和庄严的技术中。这种感觉不容错过、不容置疑:J.B.式威胁,刻意、强劲、窥伺、阴沉、炫耀。

Scene Nine　Surveillance
第九幕 盯梢

A block away from the J.B. estate an unmarked vehicle pulls over, parks behind a neighborhood SUV to block its detection.

在 J.B. 宅邸一个街区之外，一辆没有车牌的车子靠边停在一辆 SUV 后面，以便掩人耳目。

"That's good. Close enough. Don't get us spotted." one plain-clothes say to the other, adjusting reflective sunglasses.

"很好，够近了。别让人看见。"一个便衣对另一个人说，他调整着自己的反光墨镜。

"I'll check in a status report." the other says. "Forth day ... man this is boring."

"我来报告位置。"另一个人说，"第四天了……伙计，这太无聊了。"

"Surveillance-a-bitch." 'Reflectives' replies. "At least until the action starts."

"盯梢是很讨厌。""戴反光墨镜的便衣"回应，"至少到行动开始之前都是如此。"

Episode Two

INTERVIEW WITH ARTIFICIAL INTELLIGENCE

第二篇
与人工智能
的访谈

Scene Ten　Inside the Geodesic Dome

第十幕　圆形穹顶之内

Shifting glints of light reflected off the dark metallic framework of the geodesic dome; Forty-feet high, thirty-feet from one side to the other, track grids crossing above in counterbalance to the superstructure. At the center point of the space a single spotlight hit two large leather chairs, waiting, lonely, sitting atop a circular stage, three steps up, the effect, a small theatre-in-the-round. The over-stuffed seating dominated the space, only them in bright light. Hexagons of quilted material, dark, dusty, green-tinged, covered the inside of the wall sections. Tiny yellowish penlights outlined a series of diamond patterns. I imagined it a giant golf ball with the bottom third cut off creating a base, the inside hollowed out, all the way to the inside of the dimpled surface.

圆形穹顶的深色金属框架反射着变幻不定的光线。它高达40英尺，直径30英尺，网格架在头顶平衡交叉，支撑起建筑的上层结构。在内部空间的中心点，一束聚光灯打在两把大的皮质椅子上，等候着，寂寞空落。椅子放置在一个圆形舞台上，三级台阶，其效果好似一个小型圆形剧场。填充饱满的座椅傲视全场，只有它们处在光明之中。内部墙面铺满六边形的编织材料，颜色黝深晦暗，隐现绿色光泽，黄色小光点勾勒出一连串钻石形状的图案。我把穹顶想象成一个巨大的高尔夫球，下部三分之一切掉作为基座，把内核掏空，直到凹凸不平的球面。

Underfoot, a backlit pathway of translucent stone in green jade and yellow amber progressively changed intensity, reacting, ushering, inviting sequential steps toward the island of staged seating. The floor sponged underfoot, compression sounds, like walking on a large mat in a gym. I took the seat available, the other barred from me by a cushioned rod suspended from the ceiling. Sitting silently in the spotlight, my eyes adapting slowly to the dark; However, that was coincident with a dimming of the light available so that I achieved no greater vision of the interior than from when I had entered.

脚下是一条碧玉和黄琥珀铺就的步道，内置照明使得宝石呈半透明状，色泽随着脚步渐次变深，将人引向房间中央舞台的座位。地板绵弹吸音，就像走在健身房的地垫上。我在空出来的椅子上坐下。另一把椅子被天花板垂下的一根软绳隔开。我在聚光灯下安静地坐着，眼睛逐渐适应黑暗的环境。然而与此同时，光线也渐渐暗下来，我对房间内部的情况看得并不比刚进来的时候清楚多少。

Several minutes passed before the first sounds of him, the AI-hologram, coming across the space in the dark, slow steady steps. Although I couldn't see it clearly, I had the impression of a tall person approaching; the sounds, smells, change in humidity, of a substantial being, of a man. I had the urge to call out, break the tension, get on with it. As if in anticipation, an ability to feel my anxiety, the figure moved more quickly, breaking into the light. There he was, the full six-foot-three of Jackson Bartholomew, standing before me. Impressive, the achievement of suspended disbelief, its own reality, the breathing, vibrations. It reminded me of a time I stood next to a tiger at a zoo exhibit, only a pane of thick glass between us; the close-to-it energy, amazing, beautiful, dangerous.

几分钟过去了。从房间的黑暗处，传来了人工智能全息影像缓慢而稳定的脚步声。我虽然看不清楚，但感觉来人个子很高，声音、气息和湿度就跟活生生的人一样。我有种冲动要喊出来，打破这紧张的局面，与他攀谈。人像仿佛能够预知和感觉到我的焦虑，加快了脚步，突然来到光线下。他现身了，站立在我面前，6英尺3英寸高的杰克逊·巴塞洛缪。太厉害。令人充满悬念、猜疑的效果达到了，而其本身又是如此真实，呼吸着、颤动着。这场景让我想起一次动物园展览上的经历，我站在一只老虎面前，中间只隔了一层厚厚的玻璃墙，近距离感触到它的能量，神奇、美丽、危险。

Jackson, in hologram—AI form, took his seat, the protective handrail lowered into its place suspended just above a fixed pane of glass. His arm rested on the chair, lazy, confident. I could make out fine details of skin, hair, slight craping at the elbow, every line and wrinkle. Jackson crossed his legs, observed me, calm, relaxed, waiting. He took a small sip from a cup on the side table on his other side; for all the world, an important person in practiced preparations for the coming questions, my interview with an Artificial Intelligence — hologram.

人工智能—全息版本的杰克逊在他的椅子上坐下。保护性的扶手降低到一块固定的玻璃板高度。他的胳膊搭在椅子上，慵懒自信。我能分辨出皮肤、头发、肘部的磨损等细节，详细到每一根线条和皱纹。杰克逊交叉双腿，观察着我，平静、放松、等待着。他从自己那一侧的边桌上端起个杯子啜了一口。这完全是一个习惯接受采访的重要人物的反应，我对一个人工智能全息影像的采访。

Several screens slowly illuminated on the wall behind and above. Each had its own hidden source of mechanization, capabilities to show scenes, photos, videos. One streamed a bird's eye view of the Santa Cruz home in which we sat, the next a black and white sketch-photo of Jackson and Moriah walking in the market in Santa Cruz, the third a scene from the book. In another a photo. Jackson sitting on the edge of the Ponte Vecchio, the exact spot from which he famously fell into the River Arno. So, it began, my long-awaited interview with the AI—hologram of one of the most famous people in the world, Jackson Bartholomew; Or perhaps I should better say, the most famous missing person in the world. I must have stared at it a few beats too many. The J.B.—AI broke the silence.

慢慢地，三幅屏幕在背后和头顶的墙面上映现。每一幅都拥有自己的机械装置，能够分别播放场景、照片和视频。第一幅是从空中鸟瞰我们正居其中的圣克鲁斯府邸。第二幅是杰克逊和莫立娅在圣克鲁斯市场散步的黑白照片，经过素描化处理。第三幅是那本书的场景。后来是一张照片，杰克逊坐在维琪奥桥的边沿，正好是他跌落阿尔诺河那个著名的地点。这就开始了，我期待已久的采访，对全世界最有名的人——杰克逊·巴塞洛缪的人工智能全息影像。或者我应该说，最有名的失踪人员。一定是我盯着他看的时间太长了，人工智能版杰克逊·巴塞洛缪打破了沉默。

Inside the Geodesic Dome—J.B. Estate，Santa Cruz, California
网格球形穹顶内部——加州圣克鲁斯 J.B. 府邸

Scene Eleven　J.B.–AI

第十一幕　人工智能杰克逊

J.B.—AI: Mr. Curien? I understand you have some questions for me. Good of you to drive up from LA. Not so sure about leave Havanna though … and then the parents.

人工智能杰克逊：居里安先生？我听说你有些问题要问我。你能从洛杉矶驾车过来很好，只是不知你离开哈瓦娜会不会有问题……还有她的父母。

(His voice came on deep, resonate, bemused. As he spoke the scenes behind him shifted, subtly, one to another, fading out, in. One screen showed me in water, the polo pool on campus in Westwood. Then a photo of Havanna, from her last performance. Easily attained on Facebook, startling non-the-less, distracting, putting me on my heals. My prepared list of questions evaporated from my mind.)

（他的声音深沉、回荡、令人困惑。随着他的话，他身后的屏幕画面发生了微妙的变化，先是一个接一个地渐渐熄灭，又一个个渐次重现。一幅屏幕里是我在威斯特伍德校区的水球池里的照片。然后是一张哈瓦娜上次演出的照片。这些虽然很容易在脸书上找到，但也吓人一跳，令我心慌意乱，措手不及。我准备好的问题单烟消云散了。）

J.B.—AI: Mr. Curien?

人工智能杰克逊：居里安先生？

(I sat speechless, sudden onset of intimidation, awestruck; The J.B.—AI's combination of mischievous wit, quick-paced impatience, plays of words, tests of references, already in display.)

（我被这突如其来的威慑震撼得呆坐无语。人工智能杰克逊已然展示其调侃式机智、快节奏的不耐烦、言语的游戏、参照物测试等综合能力。）

J.B.—AI: Can you speak?

人工智能杰克逊：你能说话吗？

Samuel: Ah … yes.

塞缪尔：啊……能。

(Amazing how real the image, perfect movements, inflections, each detail thought out so as to present a perfect version of Jackson Bartholomew, or at least what a viewer might expected him to be.)

（好神奇，这个影像如此真实，动作完美，语调抑扬，每个细节都经过打磨，以呈现一个完美版本的杰克逊·巴塞洛缪，或者至少是观者本来希望看到的样子。）

J.B.—AI: Ask me something then. Perhaps a riddle? Mr. Curien?? I know... how about, 'What's in my pocket?'

人工智能杰克逊：那就问我问题吧。或者猜个谜？居里安先生？我知道…… 这个怎么样，"我口袋里有什么？"

Samuel: Yes, I'm ... my pleasure. Sorry, I was, am ... just taken aback. Glad to speak with you, Jackson ... excuse me, Mr. Bartholomew. Havanna ... we're fine. I can make it up to her, be back tomorrow.

塞缪尔：是的，我…… 是我的荣幸。抱歉，我刚才，现在，呃，被震撼到了。很高兴与您对话，杰克逊…… 对不起，巴塞洛缪先生。哈瓦娜，呃，我们没事。我能跟她和好的，明天就回去了。

(My words came out awkward, quick bursts, throat drying in my panic. How did he know about Havanna?? I couldn't even remember my over-0practiced opening question. Escaped me, my own name difficult to conjure, the sudden shock, the sounds of his speech, the overwhelmingly real of it all, him there as an over-grand Lincolnesque figure come to life in its staged memorial chambers.)

（我磕磕巴巴，词儿蹦得却快，因为慌神喉咙发干。他是如何得知哈瓦娜的事儿的？我演练无数遍的开场问题怎么都想不起来了。离我远去…… 我连说出自己的名字都困难。突然的震撼，他说话的声音，这一切过于真实，就好比林肯纪念堂里庄严的雕像突然变成活生生的林肯本人。）

J.B.—AI: Well, let's get to it ... the interviewing. We don't have all night. Curien's a strange name, I'll call you Samuel? Named for a prophet, the last of the Judges of Israel? Is that what you are ... Samuel ... a receiver of visions, a final judge?

人工智能杰克逊：那好，我们开始采访吧。我们可不能耗一晚上。居里安是个奇怪的姓，我要叫你塞缪尔。起了个先知的名字啊，以色列最后一位判决者？你就是这样的人吗，塞缪尔…… 神启者，最后的裁判？

177

(I'd heard his quick-witted chatter on TV interviews, always cutting, sometimes charming; But now turned on me, and by an AI-hologram of Jackson, a perplexing step of reality removed. That was another thing entirely. I'd no clue on how to react to that.)

（我在电视上看过他在接受采访时的机敏谈话，永远尖刻，有时令人着迷。但现在针对的是我，并且来自杰克逊的AI全息影像，真实性被抽除，令人困惑。这完全是另外一回事。我完全没头绪如何去回应。）

J.B.—AI: Mr. Curien? I can be patient ... but this is a little much. What's your problem? Are you okay? Maybe come back another time then?

人工智能杰克逊：居里安先生？我可以有耐心，但这也有点过了。你有什么问题？你没事吧？要不然就下回再来？

Samuel: No, no, I'm fine. Just that you are ...
塞缪尔：不，不，我没事。只是你太……

Samuel—Interview with the AI—Hologram
塞缪尔与人工智能全息影像的访谈

J.B.—AI: What??
人工智能杰克逊：什么？？

Samuel: Don't say it. "Don't go ... 'Tourette' on me."
塞缪尔：别说出来。"别犯'图雷特综合征'。"

(I muttered the words aloud, under breath, a bit of 'going Tourette' in itself.)
(我是压低了声音嘟哝出这些话的。这本身也是"图雷特综合征"犯了。)

J.B.—AI: You're mumbling. What are you trying to say? Tourette?? You suffer from 'Tourette syndrome'? Blurting out curses, sort of thing?
人工智能杰克逊：你在嘟哝。你想说什么？图雷特？你有"图雷特综合征"？骂人话脱口而出，诸如此类的？

Samuel: No, no. It's just something my father would say, that I tended to blurt things out, say things without thinking, at weird times ... when I was stressed.
塞缪尔：不，不是。只是我父亲的一种说法，说我经常不假思索脱口而出，在古怪的场合下……当我紧张的时候。

J.B.—AI: Like now? You're stressed out now Mr. Curien ... Samuel? Why is that?
人工智能杰克逊：就像现在？你现在神经紧绷吗，居里安先生……塞缪尔？为什么？

Samuel: Well, I think you know.
塞缪尔：这个嘛，我觉得你是知道的。

(I dared not say it, not directly ... that he, it, was AI, artificial intelligence, a hologram. not real. Taboo, 'things forbidden', Moriah had warned about that, but not explained. I risked him turning off, turning me out, or whatever constituted calling off the interview. I wished I'd asked about that. The prospect seemed far more terrible now than what had come to mind earlier.)
(我不敢直接说出来，他，或者它，是一个人工智能全息影像，而非真人。这是禁忌，

179

不可说之事。莫立娅警告过这一点，但没有解释原因。我冒着风险，或者他把自己关掉，或者把我赶出去，或者其他取消本次采访的举动。真希望我早问清楚这一点。眼下的情形似乎比早些时候想象的要糟糕得多。）

J.B.—AI: No, I don't know what you mean.
人工智能杰克逊：不，我并不知道你什么意思。

(It suddenly occurred to me that my mind had already 'switched over', accepted the basic premise, a framework sought by whatever it was that sat before me. I believed, or should I say, forgot to disbelieve that it was him. Oddly automatic, the mind's full suspension of disbelief, as when watching a ventriloquist and his manikin.)

（我突然意识到，我的头脑已经"转换"过来，接受了基本设定，即我对面这位不明物体所寻求的框架。我相信，或者应该说，忘了不去相信它就是他。很奇怪，头脑自动将不相信束之高阁，就像看着一个腹语者和他的小傀儡。）

Samuel: It's okay, nothing. Could you start, ah ... by explaining Bruise Art? That's where it all began ... right, 'A novel, memoir, brand, way of, of ... '
塞缪尔：没事，不管它了。您可否从，呃，解释"瘀伤艺术"开始？一切由此开端，对吗？"一部小说，回忆录，品牌，方式……"

J.B.—AI: 'Don't go Tourette on me', that's what you said. What an interesting phrase.
人工智能杰克逊："别对我犯图雷特综合征"，你说的。真有意思。

(His speech flowed free, natural, rhythmic. The shadows on his face moved perfectly with the light source, dramatic, gravitas on display. I searched the skin's crevices for a sign of unreal. None present.)

（他说话流畅、自然、有节奏。他脸上的阴影随着光源变化，视觉效果庄重、惊人。我察看皮肤上的褶皱，寻找非真实的迹象。看不出来。）

What exactly did your father mean by that? Or whomever it was that named you 'Samuel?' After all, auspicious, Samuel the prophet, receiver of visions, the conduit to and from God to the kings, for both Saul and David. Or was it another reason for the naming of you?

你父亲这话到底是什么意思？还有，到底是谁给你起名叫"塞缪尔"的？总之很吉利，先知塞缪尔，神启者，神与王的通道，对扫罗和大卫皆是如此。或者给你起这名字还有别的原因？

Samuel: Just something my father would say ... to me ... you know, that I would blurt things out, embarrass him. Samuel? Yes, the prophet.

塞缪尔：只是我父亲的口头禅而已……只针对我……你知道，我脱口而出的话会让他难堪。塞缪尔？对，先知。

J.B.—AI: Your father was embarrassed by you? How about your mother?

人工智能杰克逊：你让你父亲感到难堪？你母亲呢？

(J.B. laughed. Irritating thing to say, do, to bore in on me, use the memory of my parents; Triggered something in my mind, quick chemical release, adrenalin. Perhaps what it/he was after.)

（杰克逊笑了。用关于我父母的回忆来加深我的印象，这事儿很令人恼火。以此来激发我头脑中的某种东西，快速释放化学物质——肾上腺素。也许这就是它或者他想要的。）

Samuel: You are just a AI—hologram ... for God's sake.

塞缪尔：你不过是个人工智能全息影像……看在上帝的分上。

(Yeah, I said it ... There it was, the exact thing that should not have been said. I braced for the worst, my body tensed, not sure for what, something terrible from it all, from the image before me, the massive mechanisms, tectonic technologies arrayed in combination, it all aligned to produce pure power. A long time the wait, it considering me, chin in hand, eyes digging into mine, its penetrating visage in intimidation hyper-mode. His answer came quiet, in question form.)

（是的，我说出来了。就是它，原本不能点明的那件事。我身体紧绷起来，准备迎接最坏的结果。我眼前这个影像、庞大的机械装置、构造技术的组合共同发力，不知道会面对何种可怕的东西。等候时间很长，它在打量我，手托着腮，直盯我双眼，表情犀利，极具威胁性。他的回应来得却平静，以提问的形式。）

J.B.—AI: What did you say?? Do you want me to end this interview? You're an impertinent young twerp.

人工智能杰克逊：你说什么？你是希望我结束这场采访，还是怎样？！你真是个不知天高地厚的小浑蛋。

(Mercurial, J.B. the energy in the geo space intense, vibrations, a feeling of reaching a boiling point, the safety value indicator at red. Then silence, waiting, the ambience lowering, easing off, trend line abated, the feel of the place in direct connection to his/its countenance, a synchronized expression of his expressions.)

（情绪多变的杰克逊·巴塞洛缪使穹顶内部空间的能量骤长，空气紧张、颤抖，就好像要达到沸点，安全指针蹿到红线。之后一片寂静，等待。气氛逐渐减缓、平静下来，这个地方的气场与他或它的面容直接相关，与他的表情同步。）

J.B.—AI: Maybe I misunderstood you. Was that a statement ... or a question ... or perhaps you are in mid-prophecy? Is God present?

人工智能杰克逊：也许我误解你了。刚才那是一项声明吗，还是一个问题？或者有可能你正想发表什么预言？上帝现在在场吗？

(The spray of ions in the space between us changed, altered, with each shifting mood of him, his aggressive whims, or conversely, juxtaposed to his calming, smirking, toying. I sat quietly, afraid that my next word, if not well offered, would self-cancel me, my time with it/him, the only opportunity Moriah would likely afford. Any misstep by me might well cause the full-on collapse of the situation at hand. Picturing me explaining to Moriah, to Jasmine, how and why I wasn't able to stay in the arena, to ride the bull of the J.B. hologram for more than a few seconds ... not good.)

（随着他每一次情绪转换，不管是咄咄逼人的心血来潮，还是反差极大的平静、偷笑、戏谑，我们俩之间的离子分布都会发生改变。我静静坐着，生怕自己下一句话哪里说得不对，就会导致我与它或他此次会见取消，这可是莫立娅能给我的唯一一次机会。行差踏错一步，都有可能导致当前局面的全盘坍塌。想象我对莫立娅、对茉莉解释，我是如何、为何未能在这个场子里坚持下来，未能与"J.B."的全息影像这头牛多对峙几秒……这可不妙。）

J.B.—AI: A reasonable idea, right, given your use of that expression? I mean, 'for god's sake.' Who exactly would that 'god' be? Jehovah? Or do you have another ... or others, multiple gods for which you carry concern for their... 'sakes'?

人工智能杰克逊： 你这个表述"看在上帝分上"，是合情合理的吧？确切来说这个"上帝"是谁？耶和华？还是你有另外一个……或者其他好几个，神祇，你对他们的"福分"还挺操心？

(The scenes behind him continued to fade in and out, back and forth, one scene to another, well synchronized to his speech, it working together to present a colorful visual relating to what he expressed, instantaneously, in real time ... images iconic, profound. The whole of it had its intended effect, that is, his self-aggrandizement, to enhance, confirm him as the superior being, to add supportive content, propaganda, a graphics exclamation mark for whatever it was that he was saying at a given moment. Less fear now, me calming. It

King Saul sleeping—David leaving (Adaptation in Watercolor)
扫罗王在熟睡——大卫正在离开（水彩处理）

King Solomon (Adaptation in Watercolor)
"所罗门王"（水彩处理）

seeming that the hologram, that he, was having fun, programmed to appear so ... at my expense.)

（他身后的屏幕一直反复渐变切换画面，与他谈及的内容匹配，用彩色的视觉实物实时同步呈现他想表达的东西——既形象，又深刻。这一切都达到了他想要的自我吹捧的效果，为加强和巩固他至高无上的地位，增添相应的内容和宣传，就好比他在特定场合无论说了什么，后面都会加上一个大感叹号。我的恐惧减轻了，慢慢平静下来。在我看来，全息影像，即他，很享受，或者被程序编排成这样——消遣我。)

Samuel: Just an expression, about 'God' I mean, about my over exuberant comments, Tourette or otherwise. Please forgive me. I guess I'm just curious about all things hologram, given my interest in you, in Bruise art, and anything connected.

塞缪尔： 只是表达方式而已，我是指"上帝"这个词，还有我那些过于嘴碎的评论，图雷特综合征等的。请原谅我。我想，我只是对关于全息的一切太过好奇，因为我对你，对瘀伤艺术，还有与其相关的一切都很感兴趣。

(J.B.—AI stared, considering, as if disappointed, then intense; A smile, slow to come, then fast to spread across his face.)

（人工智能杰克逊瞪着我，在思量，仿佛很失望，又紧张起来。一个微笑慢慢浮现，之后快速在他脸上绽开。）

J.B.—AI: Do you believe that ... I am real?
人工智能杰克逊： 你相信……我是真实的吗？

(There it was. He had asked the question for me, legendary playful Jackson in full display. I paused; my own considering in progress, how to proceed, stay within the rules, the game set out before me by him/it ... to be joined, played.)

［来了。他替我问出了那个问题，传说中喜欢玩游戏的杰克逊马力全开了。我停顿了一下，思考如何在他（它）设置好的游戏里继续向前，按规则行事，陪他玩下去。］

Samuel: You are only an image ... a representation of something else. Or I should say, you could be, that is, if Jackson's project is a success. After all, the convincing of others, that an apparition, a hologram, was indeed him, or could be, was exactly your, or his, intent ... the very mission of the entire enterprise.

塞缪尔：你只是个影像……是另外一种东西的代表。或者我应该这么说，如果杰克逊的项目成功了，你才能成为这个代表。毕竟，要说服大家，一个幽灵，一个全息影像，的确就是他，或者可以等同于他，正是你，不，他的意……是整个项目的使命。

J.B.—AI: Ah, there he is, the clever boy. Not only a child prophet, sitting before me ... a 'clever-er.' Is there anything you see, hear, feel, that indicates I am *not* real, not him, not Jackson Bartholomew, in the flesh?

人工智能杰克逊：啊，瞧这个机灵的小伙子。坐在我面前的这位，不只是个灵童先知，一个"聪明"人。你看到、听到、摸到了什么，让你觉得我不是他的真身，不是有血有肉的杰克逊·巴塞洛缪？

Samuel: No, no ... I can't say that there is.

塞缪尔：不，没有……我不能说有。

J.B.—AI: There you go then. With all that said, as our 'preamble' so to speak, ask your questions ... and I will answer. But leave any insistence on knowing, about me that is, to the side. After our talk, you can consider that point more fully, but not here and now.

人工智能杰克逊：那就开始吧。说了这么多，姑且称为我们的"序言"，现在开始问你的问题吧，我会回答的。但是不要试图去探究我的另一面。我们谈话结束后，你可以更充分地去思考这一点，但不是现在。

Samuel: Very well.

塞缪尔：很好。

J.B.—AI: Carry on then, but be careful, and, let me suggest, do remain clever or I'll cancel you.

人工智能杰克逊：那就继续吧，不过要小心，并且我建议你保持机警，否则我会叫停你。

Samuel: There is one thing that we could both agree upon, to do, to put this elephant in the room behind us, or should I say, back into the zoo ... or still better, onto the Savanna.

塞缪尔：有一件事，是我们双方可以同意去做的。这样就可以把"房间里的大象"

（英国谚语，意为显而易见的事物而无人点破——译者注）赶到我们身后，或者说赶到动物园里……甚至更好的地方，到非洲大草原上。

J.B.—AI: What would that be ... Mr. Samuel.
人工智能杰克逊：那会是什么事呢……塞缪尔先生。

(His tone quick-shifted, irritation, curiosity, body position along with it.)
（他的语调很快变了，充满恼怒、好奇，身体的姿势也相应改变。）

Samuel: You could let me ... touch you.
塞缪尔：你可以让我……触碰你。

J.B.—AI: My Lord, talk about the 'T' word. You're 'Touretting' all over yourself. What good would that do, for you to touch me? How disrespectful. Think about it, would anyone put up with that, the prerequisite that you, a stranger no less, be allowed to touch them?!
人工智能杰克逊：我的老天爷，又是T打头的词（注：英文"触碰"一词以T开头）。你从头到脚都在图雷特。你触碰我有什么意义？太不尊重人了。想想吧，前提条件是允许你，一个完全陌生的人触碰他们，谁受得了？！

(J.B.—AI's exasperation flooded the space, I supposed disappointment that the desired conversation wasn't coming along as anticipated.)
（全息杰克逊的暴怒充斥着整个空间，我猜是因为对话没按照他的意愿展开而感到失望。）

Samuel: It would solve everything.
塞缪尔：那将解决所有的问题。

J.B.—AI: There are many other reasons for a person not to let you touch them than the possibility that they were in fact not real. How about simply no tolerance for rudeness, an insistence on proper decorum?
人工智能杰克逊：人们不让你碰的原因多了去了，才不是因为他们可能不是真人。纯粹是出于不能容忍粗鲁的举止，一种对端庄体面的坚持，怎么了？

Samuel: I was told, by Moriah herself, that you were an AI—hologram ... not her husband, not Jackson in the real.

塞缪尔：莫立娅亲口告诉我的，你是一个人工智能全息影像……不是她的丈夫，不是真正的杰克逊。

(Had to say it. It came out of me, as it often does, the obvious demanding to be said.)

（我必须说出来。就像平常一样，话脱口而出，它自己要求被说出来。）

J.B.—AI: I should not have to say this ... there are a myriad of reasons why you might be deceived, the basic truth kept from you.

人工智能杰克逊：我本不该说……有无数理由要把你蒙在鼓里，不让你触摸到基本事实。

Samuel: What do you mean?
塞缪尔：你什么意思？

J.B.—AI: You are well aware of my willingness to take extreme measures to remain in the public's eye, go viral, remain relevant, stay commercial. Moriah is my partner. Of course, she might join me in deception, even a grand one.

人工智能杰克逊：你很了解我是多么愿意采取极端方式在公众面前刷存在，赚流量，成为关注话题，保持商业化。莫立娅是我的合伙人。当然，她有可能配合我作秀，甚至是演一出大戏。

Samuel: Jasmine?
塞缪尔：茉莉也是？

J.B.—AI: Her as well. Think about it, isn't it even likely that Jackson Bartholomew concocted the greatest pop culture hoax disappearances of all time, at least since Elvis, in order to stay at the top of his world? I, the 'J.B.', created it, my dominance of popular culture, and now I must keep it, at all costs. The sensibilities of one young man would be a small price to pay.

人工智能杰克逊：她也一样。想想看，难道不是很有可能，杰克逊·巴塞洛缪炮制了史上最大的流行文化失踪骗局，至少是在猫王之后最大的一个，只是为了确保他继续处在世界之巅？我，杰克逊，创造了它，流行文化的霸主地位，现在我必须保住它，不惜一切代价。

Samuel: Your price for fame, the feeding of your own addiction? All at the cost of others?

塞缪尔： 你为成名付出的代价就是不断滋长自己对名声的沉迷？罔顾他人付出的代价？

J.B.—AI: At least you must concede that's a distinct possibility.

人工智能杰克逊： 至少你得承认那种可能性明确存在。

Samuel: Yes. I do. That's why If I could just touch ...

塞缪尔： 是的。我承认。所以我为什么说如果能够触碰……

J.B.—AI: Proceed with the interview. Be concise, clever. Those two qualities are your best chance for a full interview. You've tested my patience to the extreme. Don't do it again.

人工智能杰克逊： 继续采访吧。要简洁、机灵。这两点是你能够完成全程采访的最好机会。我的耐心已经被你磨炼到尽头了。不要再这样做了。

(To the edge, the 'touch you', left unsaid. Other elements at play in the Geo space, subtle manipulations of atmosphere, chemical alterations, 'Oracle's fumes come up from the ground' 'Bilbo debating Smaug'. I felt as in competition, within its judgement.)

(都到了"触碰"他的边缘了，却功亏一篑。在这个穹顶内部，还有其他元素在发挥作用，对气氛的微妙操纵，对化学物质的修改，"先知的火焰从地底冒出""比尔博与史矛革辩论"，我仿佛身处竞赛之中，被置于审判之下。)

J.B.—AI: You do have a certain usefulness. For that allowance, to keep you in the mix, I'll get you started. How about, we begin with 'Beginnings'. That's always a good place to initiate, somewhat required. The toe of Dorothy's sparking red slipper must touch the first yellow brick if ever to get to Oz.

人工智能杰克逊： 你的确有某种可用之处。凭这一点，为了把你留在这个组合里，我来帮你开场。我们从"开端"开始，如何？这永远是个打开局面的好起点，从某种

Debating the dragon (Adaptation in Watercolor)
与恶龙辩论（水彩处理）

意义上也是必需的。想去奥兹，多萝西那双亮晶晶的红舞鞋必须踩上第一块黄色的砖。

Samuel: Very well ...
塞缪尔：很好……

J.B.—AI: Interview myself, brilliant. Just repeat the magic words then, 'How did it start?'
人工智能杰克逊：采访我自己，妙啊。只需重复那句开启魔法的话："这是怎么开始的？"

Samuel: You mean the AI—hologram thing? It is odd, not your background. You're on the artist side ... not science fiction or high tech.
塞缪尔：你是指人工智能—全息影像这事儿吗？挺奇怪的，这不是你的背景。你是个搞艺术的……不是科幻或者高新技术。

J.B.—AI: Again ... back on that? I meant the book, the project. All right, fair enough. I opened the door to it. Let's go there ... then we'll drop it. The 'hologram thing', as you put it, began with a single question: How could I be in more than one place at the same time. So many demands on me, timewise, many things I really wanted to do, be there, simultaneously, different locations. Appearing in person is my thing, not Zooming or video, just not the same. When I found out that I could appear in a staged setting as a hologram, and have everyone believe it was me, there in person ... I was hooked. After that, just a matter of one thing after another ... which is often the case in life once you set yourself on a certain course. Think on it, something happens, an original event which then leads you on a unique path that changes the rest of your life. Randomness of the universe is astounding, a core component of life. It must be accepted, dealt with, mitigated and managed for best outcomes.

Next question.

人工智能杰克逊：又来了，还回到这个问题？我是指小说，这个计划。好吧，也是。我自己打开的话题。那就聊这个……然后我们就放下。你称为"全息影像"的这个东西，是从一个简单的问题开始的：我如何能够同时出现在不同的地方？对我的需求如此之大，从时间上来说，我想做的事情如此之多，想亲临现场，同时，异地。亲临现场是我的特点，我不连线，不录视频，那种感觉不一样。当我发现我能以全息影像出现在设置好的场景里，并且让在场的人们相信那就是我本人时……我被迷住了。从那之后，事情就接二连三地发生了……就像人生，一旦你步入某条轨道之后会产生的后续。想想看，某种新鲜的事物出现了，然后把你引向一条独特的道路，改变了你的人生。宇宙的混乱无序是惊人的，它是人生的核心要素。要接受它，应对它，缓解和控制它，争取最好的结果。

下一个问题。

(The closest I could get to an admission about the AI—hologram of it all. Best to move on.)

（这是我能问到的最接近他承认人工智能全息影像这件事。最好继续向前了。）

Samuel: How about 'Bruise Art?' How did it start?
塞缪尔："瘀伤艺术"呢？是如何开始的？

J.B.—AI: Necessity. I needed to recover. Writing represented 'the way back'.
人工智能杰克逊：出于必要。我当时需要康复。写作意味着"回归的路"。

(The AI-hologram paused, remembering ... appearing to remember as Jackson in the real would have, I reminded myself; Perfect its facial expressions, breathing, bodily motions, vibrations.)

（人工智能全息影像停顿下来，在回忆……我提醒自己，是显得像真实世界的杰克逊在回忆的样子。它的面部表情、呼吸、肢体动作、颤动都完美无瑕。）

Samuel: From what ... a 'way back' from what?

塞缪尔：从哪……从哪"回归"？

J.B.—AI: From the lowest point in my life. Essentially, I'd died. The writing was resurrection. I'd reached a low point, coasting, felt useless, used up. Writing the novel was the means to ending my end ... to my own rebirth, reincarnation. It became a contest, a great epoch struggle, against me; Years of it, not the easier parameters of weeks or months. Had to be played out over time, a war, not a quick battle. 'Bruise Art' is a lifestyle, a way to test yourself, place your own existence under trial and tribulation. Requires you to be self-assertive, challenge yourself, continually. In that way, you're constantly renewed, strengthened, always expanding, moving into 'the beyond', to the universal.

人工智能杰克逊：从我人生的低谷。从本质上说，我当时死了。写作是重生。我当时走到了低谷，感觉自己一无是处，被掏空。写小说是终结我的死结的途径……将我引向重生、涅槃。它成为我与自己的竞赛，一场空前艰难的搏斗。历经数年，而不是几周、几月这么简单。它需要时间去铺陈，这是一场战争，不是一次战役。"瘀伤艺术"是一种生活方式，是一种考验自己的办法，将自我的存在置于磨试和苦难之中。不断地要求自己坚定自信，不断地挑战自己。经此，你不断获得新生、强化、拓展，"超越现实世界"，达到普世境界。

Samuel: How does Bruise Art the lifestyle connect with the bruises that come from the oriental cupping therapy? How is it related to the 'universal'?

塞缪尔："瘀伤艺术"作为一种生活方式，与东方的拔罐疗法造成的瘀青有何内在联系？这一切与"普世"又有什么关系？

J.B.—AI: The cupping technique involves intentionally bruising the skin, the largest organ in the body. It's a means to an end, the end being to activate the body's immune system. The analogy is a good one. The big dark purple bruises from cupping are intentionally taken on, just as the challenges and self-testing in the 'Bruise Art' approach to life activate our own hidden powers of healing, renewal ... even reincarnation. Universal themes, by definition.

人工智能杰克逊：拔罐手法有意在皮肤这个人体最大的器官上留下瘀伤，它是达到目的的一种手段，而这个目的就是激活人体的免疫系统。这是一个很好的类比。拔罐留下的瘀青印是特意制造的，就如同在生活中的迎接挑战和自我考验，激活了隐藏在我们自身的治愈和重生……甚至是涅槃的能量。这是普世的主题，从概念上来说。

Samuel: That lifestyle of Bruise Art ... it's the core theme of the novel?
塞缪尔："瘀伤艺术"的生活方式……是小说的中心主题吗？

J.B.—AI: If you don't get that then you wasted your time reading the damn thing. The main character makes a choice. He chooses to challenge himself at the extreme. At the very time in his life when he might have given up, retire, become irrelevant, he takes on the biggest project he could imagine, the writing of the 'Great American Novel', the fighting of great battles.

人工智能杰克逊：如果你连这点都没看明白，那你读这本书纯属浪费时间。主角是有选择的。他选择了挑战自己的极限。在他生命中的那一刻，他本可以放弃、退隐，成为无足轻重的人，但是他启动了自己能想象的最宏大的计划，写作"伟大的美国小说"，展开了一场伟大的战斗。

Samuel: Why did you pick that challenge for the main character?
塞缪尔：你为什么替主角选了那样的挑战？

J.B.—AI: It seems to be that the 'Great American Novel' genre is the single greatest challenge any American can take on, in a literary sense. It requires a long hard slog, an examination of your own culture, yourself. Painful thing, looking inside like that, lonely, years of it, stuck away in a room. At the same time, it's the ultimate opportunity to self-examine, reform the world around you, before you leave it.

人工智能杰克逊：从文学的角度来说，"伟大的美国小说"流派似乎是任何一个美国人面临的最大挑战。它要求你投入长期、艰巨的埋头苦干，对你所属文化的审视，对自己的审视。内省这事，非常痛苦，孤独，经年累月困在一个房间里。同时，它又是你在离开这个人世之前,审视自己内心、改变周遭世界的最佳机会。

Samuel: What did you find during the 'slog', inside yourself I mean, within your generation?

塞缪尔: 你在"埋头苦干"期间找到了什么,我是指在你的内心,在你的时代?

J.B.—AI: Profound changes. Things that had never occurred before in American history. In one generation America has moved from a tradition-based society to popular culture, a move to fame and fortune as ultimate measurements of success, less on merit. It's shifted from centuries of strongly held religious beliefs, Christian traditions, to quick-silver secularism; From sacred guarantees of 4th Amendment freedoms to illegal high-tech Orwellian surveillance by all levels of the government; A move from family units, evolved for thousands of years of a male breadwinner paradigm, to mothers and children looking to government to fill that role, the ultimate 'provider'. Sunday's shifted from praying at Church pews to 'kicking back' on the NFL couch. Presidents are no longer pulled from the military or political class, instead we have 'Pop Presidents', Obama and Trump are the first, not to be the last. Neither were selected on merit ... not in the old sense of the word. Even the traditional New York-Washington corridor of power is gone, shifted, moved out west; Now it's LA, Silicon Valley. That's the 'Great American Novel' of the whole thing, all those changes in a single generation. Never anything like it.

人工智能杰克逊: 深刻的变化。在美国历史上从来没有出现过的事物。只用了一代人的时间,美国人就从一个尊重传统的社会转变为尊崇流行文化的社会,名声与财富成为衡量成功的最高准绳,品德退居其次。从几个世纪笃定坚持的宗教信仰和基督教传统,转变为变幻多端的世俗主义;从第四次修订宪法以来对自由的神圣保护,到各级政府实施的非法高科技奥威尔式监控;从数千年演化形成的男性挣钱养家的家庭模式,变成母亲和孩童请求政府扮演父亲的角色,成为终极"养家人"。人们在星期天不再去教堂祈祷,改成赖在沙发看全美橄榄球联盟比赛。总统不再从军队或者政界选举出来,取而代之的是"明星总统",奥巴马和特朗普是空前,但不绝后。他们俩谁也不是凭品德当选的,从品德这个词的纯正意义来说。甚至传统的纽约—华盛顿权力走廊也消失、改变了,转移到了西部,现在来到了洛杉矶、硅谷。这就是造就"伟大的美国小说"的成分,一代人的时间里,发生了这么多变化。从来没有过。

Samuel: Did you intend that specific genre of fiction when you began, or did it evolve?

塞缪尔：你是在开始的时候就想好要写这个小说流派，还是随着写作进度渐渐发展的？

J.B.—AI: It was natural, organic. The closest acknowledged genre to what I wanted to write was the 'Great American Novel', that is, a novel written by an American, about America, trying to get at the essence of a specific time; An examination, through a fiction storyline, of what it means to be American in this period, the transition years at the end of the 20th Century and the beginning of the 21st. A 'Great American Novel', by definition, delves into peculiarly American opportunities and challenges within a specific period of time. Of

---

The 'Great American Novel'

19th century

- **1851:** Herman Melville—*Moby Dick*
- **1884:** Mark Twain—*Adventures of Huckleberry Finn*

20th century

- **1925:** F. Scott Fitzgerald—*The Great Gatsby*
- **1932:** William Faulkner—*Light in August*
- **1936:** William Faulkner—*Absalom, Absalom!*
- **1936:** Margaret Mitchell—*Gone With the Wind*
- **1937:** John Dos Passos—*U.S.A. trilogy*
- **1939:** John Steinbeck—*The Grapes of Wrath*
- **1951:** J.D. Salinger—*The Catcher in the Rye*
- **1952:** Ralph Ellison—*Invisible Man*
- **1953:** Saul Bellow—*The Adventures of Augie March*
- **1955:** Vladimir Nabokov—*Lolita*
- **1960:** Harper Lee—*To Kill a Mockingbird*

> **"伟大的美国小说"**
>
> 19 世纪
>
> - 1851: 赫尔曼·梅尔维尔 ——《白鲸》
> - 1884: 马克·吐温 ——《哈克贝利·费恩历险记》
>
> 20 世纪
>
> - 1925: 弗·司各特·菲茨杰拉德 ——《了不起的盖茨比》
> - 1932: 威廉·福克纳 ——《八月之光》
> - 1936: 威廉·福克纳 ——《押沙龙,押沙龙!》
> - 1936: 玛格丽特·米切尔 ——《飘》
> - 1937: 约翰·多斯·帕索斯 ——《美国三部曲》
> - 1939: 约翰·斯坦贝克 ——《愤怒的葡萄》
> - 1951: J.D. 塞林格 ——《麦田里的守望者》
> - 1952: 拉尔夫·艾里森 ——《看不见的人》
> - 1953: 索尔·贝娄 ——《奥吉·马奇历险记》
> - 1955: 弗拉基米尔·纳博科夫 ——《洛丽塔》
> - 1960: 哈珀·李 ——《杀死一只知更鸟》

course, the 'Great' can only be determined over time, and by others.

人工智能杰克逊:它是纯天然的。现存流派中,最接近我想要写的就是"伟大的美国小说",即由美国人写作的、关于美国的、捕捉到某个特定历史时期之精华的小说。通过虚构的故事,审视在 20 世纪末过渡到 21 世纪初期间,作为一个美国人意味着什么。从概念上说,一部"伟大的美国小说"是深入挖掘某一特定历史时期内美国独有的机会和挑战。当然,"伟大"与否只能由时间和人们来决定。

J.B.—AI: You can find an actual list of so called 'Great American Novels' on the Internet. A specific list of titles and authors, some of which are recent, will pop up on your screen as though each novel listed has been agreed upon by an appointed committee. I would argue that no book can possibly be called a 'Great American Novel' within the first decade of its publication. In any case, such a list can never be cast in concrete. It changes over time.

人工智能杰克逊：你真的可以在互联网上搜到一系列所谓"伟大的美国小说"书单，屏幕上会跳出一张具体的清单，列举了书名和作者，有些还是最近的，就好像每本书都被某个指定的委员会审定过。我敢说，没有哪本书在其发表的头十年里可以被称为"伟大的美国小说"。不管怎样，这样的书单永远不会是一成不变的，它随着年代变化。

J.B.—AI: To be real about it, my writing is a nov-oir, two genres, the 'Great American Novel' and a memoir, mine. Highly illustrated by me as well. Approaching 'storyboarding' or a graphic novel. I guess we might call that combination the 'J.B. genre.' I doubt another writer's work will ever fit it, my genre. Make no mistake, I intended the makeup of the work, its parts, how it's constructed. It's no accidental hodgepodge. Each section is what it should be, where it should be. It felt like the classic design process, when it is going well, that 'out of body' feeling of not actually designing it, of magically revealing something already there.

人工智能杰克逊：说真的，我的作品是小说兼回忆录，跨越两种流派，"伟大的美国小说"和回忆录，我个人的。我自己还创作了大量插图。类似"分镜故事"，或者插画小说。我想也许可以管它叫"J.B. 流派"的结合体。我觉得没有哪位作家的作品符合这一标准，我的流派。不要搞错，我设计了这个作品，它的组成、部件以及如何组装，这可不是什么即兴而来的大杂烩。每一部分的定位和内容都是精心设计而成的。就像经典的设计过程，如果进展顺利，就会产生那种"灵魂出窍"的感觉，好像这东西不是你设计的，你只是如同变戏法一样把某种已然存在的东西揭示出来。

Samuel: A novel, but also your memoir?

塞缪尔：一部小说，同时也是你的回忆录？

J.B.—AI: Yes. It's both. It intertwines pure fiction, or partial fiction, with elements of my own story. More interesting to me that way, instead of one or the other. A novel-memoir, a 'nov-oir.' Wish I could say I invented that word, but no, that one is not mine.

人工智能杰克逊：对，两者都是。它交织了纯属虚构的或者部分虚构的内容和我自己人生故事的片段。对我来说这样更有意思，而不是两者独立存在。小说—回忆录，"诺瓦"。（作者将英文单词"小说"novel 的词头 nov 和"回忆录"memoir 的词尾 oir 结合成一个新词——译者注）真希望是我发明了这个词，可惜不是，那不是我发明的。

Samuel: A lot about China in the novel, especially for a book about changes in America?

塞缪尔：小说写了很多关于中国的事，尤其是作为一本关注美国变化的书？

J.B.—AI: America is not isolated. This is not *The Great Gatsby*. To talk about America at the end of the 20th, beginning of the 21st century, there must be talk about things 'international' ... certainly, China in the mix.

人工智能杰克逊：美国并不是孤立的。这又不是《了不起的盖茨比》那年代。在20世纪末、21世纪初谈论美国，必须要谈及 "国际化" 的东西……而中国毫无疑问身处其中。

(The image of Jackson gathered itself, adjusting in its chair, taking a sip of something from a cup. Amazing set of details, convincing in all aspects. Indeed, Jackson had spared no expense. I'd no idea something like this could exist, beyond Sci-Fi. The full production accomplished the capturing of all the viewer's senses. Moisture, perspiration level, heat increases, a slight smell of cologne, sounds of breathing, voice inflections, body movements, all seamless, completely believable. J.B. AI—hologram, crossed and uncrossed its legs, the same familiar sequence of charm, deep thought, then boredom followed by a waiver in concentration. I'd seen it all before, in video clips from his media appearances. I'd entered thinking it would be spectacular, based on Moriah's introduction, but not like this, not this level of perfection, a J.B.tour-de-force expression of his creative power combined with unlimited budget and hired expertise. The whole of the effect was irresistible, sweeping you into complete belief of what could not possibly be true: That Jackson Bartholomew himself sat just over there, live, bemused, authentic. The weight of it came over me, the place, Moriah, Jasmine, Havanna, unexpected emotions, a sudden odd sensation, a compelling urge to flee. Bizarre. Had to, needed to speak, to say something. Panic attack onset. I knew the feeling, the timing of an onset.)

（杰克逊的影像直起上身，调整坐姿，从杯子里啜了一口。细节令人惊叹，从各方面看都无可指摘。杰克逊真没少花钱。我没想到这样的东西居然会存在，超出了科幻电影。整体制作完全抓住了观者的全部感官。湿度、出汗的程度、温度的上升、清淡的古龙水香味、呼吸的声音、语音的感染力、肢体动作，一切都毫无瑕疵，完全令人信服。人工智能全息"J.B."跷起腿、放下腿的动作同样熟悉、充满魅力，他陷入沉思，

197

继而因为感到乏味而放弃。我以前在媒体播放的他的录像都看到过。我走进这间屋子的时候，基于莫立娅的介绍，以为将会看到奇妙的事物，但完全没想到会是这样，达到这种完美的程度，J.B.的创造力和无限制的预算和专业支持结合起来，成就了他的绝世表达。整体效果达到令人难以置信的事实：杰克逊·巴塞洛缪就坐在那里，活生生地，令人迷惘却又如此真实。现实的重量向我压来，这个空间、莫立娅、茉莉、哈瓦娜，出乎意料的情感，一种突如其来的奇怪感觉，一种逃离此地的迫切渴望。我必须、需要说话、得说点什么。恐慌压倒了我。我知道这种感觉，什么事情要发生的时刻。)

Samuel: So, you lost a child or something, right?

塞缪尔：那么，你失去了一个孩子或者某种东西，对吗？

(The question spilled out awkward, sarcastic, the resulting remnants of my own distress. The AI-hologram stared at me from under brow, hard.)

(问题脱口而出，难堪、讽刺，是我自身忧虑的残遗。人工智能全息影像低着头死死盯着我。)

J.B.—AI: Well, the loss of a child is a terrible thing, my dear Mr. Curien. That alone should have done me in ... don't you think? Add to that the brutal cuts of Moriah's scorched-earth scolding, her pain turned into high-octane scorn. All at once I no longer served as the hero, the 'good guy' protagonist in my own story, destined to do something great. I needed something to give me a 'hold', a way out, up. For months I just drifted. I wanted to delight Moriah once again, to make us excited about something, to look forward. I couldn't do it, couldn't find a way. It came to me to go directly into the thing I found most challenging, difficult, worthwhile ... the writing. In order to make myself the 'hero of my own story' once more, I decided to write a most compelling story, with myself as the hero.

人工智能杰克逊：这个嘛，失去一个孩子是件可怕的事情，我亲爱的居里安先生。光是这一桩就够要我命了……你不觉得吗？雪上加霜的是，莫立娅的痛苦转化为高能量的蔑视和斥责，能把大地烤焦，像刀割一样残酷。突然之间，我不再扮演自己故事中的主角，命中注定要成就大事的那个"好人"主角。我需要某种自己能"抓住"的东西，找到一条出路，走出去。几个月过去了，我飘浮不定。我想再次哄莫立娅开心，让我们对某种东西感到兴奋和期待。我做不到，找不到出路。我意识到，要直接进入最具挑战、最困难，也是最值得的那个东西……写作。为了使自己再次成为"自己故事里的主角",我决定写一个极其感人的故事,以我自己为主角。

Samuel: What about you 'dying'? What happened exactly?
塞缪尔:你的"死"是怎么回事?到底发生了什么?

J.B.—AI: Yes, true, I died ... literally. I did some partying, several days of it. My heart stopped, completely. I lost consciousness. In effect, I was dead. If no one had applied some outside force I would not have come back. In the ER I heard someone yell, 'Clear'! It was meant for me! The next thing I remember was the waking up, still on the gurney. The cute head nurse said my body jumped two feet off the table.

人工智能杰克逊:是的,确实,我死了……直面意义上说。我狂欢了几天。我的心脏完全停止了跳动。我失去了知觉。事实上,我死了。如果不是有人施以外力,我肯定回不来了。在急救室里,我听到有人喊"让开"!那是为我做的急救!我再一次恢复意识就是醒来发现自己在病床上。可爱的护士长说我的身体从手术台上弹起足有两英尺高。

J.B. into the Ambulance
J.B. 被送上救护车

J.B.—AI: "I've never seen someone be so far gone and then coming back." she said, touching my arm with the tips of her fingers. "You're a lucky guy."

人工智能杰克逊：“我从来没见过谁离死这么近，还能救回来的。”她说着，用手指尖触碰我的手臂，“你是个幸运的家伙。”

J.B.—AI: "Well, thanks ... I guess."

人工智能杰克逊：“谢谢……我想是吧。”

J.B.—AI: "Did you see anything? You know ... on the 'other side'?" she said, eyes a flirt.

人工智能杰克逊：“你看到什么了吗？你懂的……在'那边'？”她向我抛了个媚眼问道。

J.B.—AI: So, there it was, the darkest moments in my life, combining themselves, overlapping, laughing at me, mocking. At that point, that 'bottoming out', exactly then, I began to write, that day, there in the hospital room waiting for my electrical system to calm down from the leftover effects of the two high-voltage jolts.

人工智能杰克逊：所以，就是这样，我生命中的至暗时刻，结合在一起，重叠在一起，在嘲笑我、讽刺我。就在那一刻，从"谷底走出"的那一瞬间，我开始写作，就在那天，在医院病房里，等着我的电离系统从两股高压电击的余波中恢复平静的那个时候。

(The AI—Jackson paused again, looking down, slight smile, crossing his legs, uncrossing, pensive. His eyes moved up into a pensive gaze ... remarkable simulation, performance.)

（人工智能杰克逊再次停顿，视线下垂，面带微笑，跷起腿，又放下，沉思。他抬起双眼，若有所思地盯着前方……了不起的模拟和表现。）

Samuel: Well ... did you see anything ... on the 'other side'?

塞缪尔：那……你看到什么了吗……在"那边"？

J.B.—AI: No, not a thing. I dream all the time, remember them in great detail, even can manipulate from the inside. But this time, that time, nothing at all, no memory. Maybe it was the shock thing. Maybe there nothing there to see.

人工智能杰克逊：不，什么也没有。我总在做梦，记得大量细节，甚至可以操纵自己的梦。但这一次，那次，什么也没有，没有记忆。也许是因为电击。也许那边没什么可看的。

Samuel: So, you became one of the most famous pop culture figures in the world, and it all started with your shock therapy session in the ER?

塞缪尔：就是说，你成为全世界最有名的流行文化人物之一，都始于你在急救室经历的电击？

J.B.—AI: A nice turn of words, Mr. Samuel. Of course, we must give credit where credit is due. Beyond myself, my novel, my brand, shock therapy, there was always the pure energy, the unstoppable force ... Moriah.

人工智能杰克逊：用词很精准啊，塞缪尔先生。当然，该谁的功劳就归谁。除了我自己，我的小说，我的品牌，电击疗法，还有那股永远的纯粹能量，不可阻拦的力量……莫立娅。

Samuel: The photography of her, so many other iconic photos from your work ... they captured the imagination of the public. Why do you think that is?

塞缪尔：她的那张摄影，还有你作品中其他那些标志性的照片……他们抓住了公众的想象力。你认为是什么原因？

J.B.—AI: It has to do with the illustrations in the novel. I did them all myself, my own sketches, photos, designs, many with her as the subject or model. All the writing and designs worked together, enhance each other, cross-pollinate, back and forth. Every design, every creative expression, in one way or another, has a direct interplay with the writing, with our lives. The 'First Temple' design in *Liva's Lamentations* is a great example. The design of that structure had a lot of influence on the writing of that short story, as well as how Moriah and I interact with the universe, with the concept of God. That back and forth process makes for iconic images.

人工智能杰克逊：这与小说中的插图有关。他们都出自我的创作，我自己的素描、照片、设计，多数以她为对象或者模特。所有的文字和设计共同发力，彼此加强，互为传粉，反复来回。每一项设计，每一种创造性的表达，在某种程度上都与小说、与我们的生活直接相关。《利瓦的悲痛》中那个"第一座庙宇"的设计就是个很好的例子。

那座建筑的设计对那部短篇小说的写作影响很大,也影响了莫立娅和我与宇宙、与上帝的概念互动的方式。这种反复的过程造就了标志性的镜像。

Samuel: The very first version of the novel was printed in both English and Mandarin, and with the audacious subtitle of the 'Great American Novel/Memoir'. Why did you label your own book like that? Doesn't that go against what you said about the genre? So overtly presumptuous?

塞缪尔:小说初版是英中双语出版的,副标题还大胆地冠上"伟大的美国小说(回忆录)"。你为什么给自己的书贴这样的标签?那岂不是与你自己关于流派的说法相悖?如此公开的自负?

(A strained smirk, a stare, direct, withering, the AI—Jackson back at me, full intimidation. I forced myself to maintain my gaze, no blinking.)

(暗自得意的笑容逐渐消失,转为怒目直视,人工智能杰克逊充满威胁地瞪着我。我强迫自己直视他的目光,不眨一瞬。)

J.B.—AI: I'm very proud that the first printed version of the novel was in both English and Mandarin, alternating paragraphs. Even though the work is profoundly American, by an American writer, with an American point of view, I wanted the Chinese public to have immediate access to it. China had afforded me a haven to write. I appreciate it deeply. The 'Great American Novel' thing, a marketing element, more of a marker of subject matter than of self-assessment.

人工智能杰克逊:我很自豪,小说初版是英中双语,逐段排版的。虽然作品的主要内容是关于美国的,由美国作家以一个美国人的视角写成,我希望中国读者能够即时读懂它。中国为我提供了写作的安全港湾,我对此深怀感激。"伟大的美国小说"这玩意是个营销手段,更像个主题表述,而不是自我评价。

Samuel: You wrote almost all your 'Great American Novel' in China. True?
塞缪尔:你这部"伟大的美国小说"几乎全部是在中国写成的。真的吗?

J.B.—AI: Yes, almost all the novel was written in China, in Beijing. More specifically, at our condo on Chaoyang Park, on the 25th floor. Writers, artists, usually have a 'get away' place, somewhere they can be alone, create, think. Samuel Clemens had a small pavilion away from the main house. Gauguin, a shack in Tahiti. Hemingway, a house in Cuba. Artists, especially writers, need to be alone, to create spaces, characters, make magic. It just can't be done with people around, underfoot, breaking in and out, disrupting the 'creative bubble'. It makes the delicate membrane disolve when that happens. Our place in Beijing, in 'distant Cathay' as I like to say, on the south edge of Chaoyang Park, was my writing 'get away'. A bit distant to be sure, the other side of the Pacific, but, worked for me.

人工智能杰克逊：是的，几乎所有的小说都是在中国北京写的。具体而言，是我们在朝阳公园25层的公寓里。作家、艺术家通常都有一个"逃离"的地方，他们在那里可以独处、创作、思考。塞缪尔·克莱门斯在房屋主建筑之外有个小亭子。高庚在大溪地有个草棚。海明威在古巴有座房子。艺术家，尤其是作家，需要独处，需要创造空间、角色，需要创造奇迹。不能有人在周围，在楼下，进进出出，打破"创意泡泡"。干扰一旦发生，那层脆弱的薄膜就消失了。我们在北京的住所，在那"遥远的华夏"，朝阳公园南侧，就是我的写作离居。的确很远，在太平洋彼岸，但对我来说很有用。

Samuel: You pocketed $3,000,000 for the movie rights? How is that even possible, first novel, not published?

塞缪尔：你的电影版权拿到了300万美元？那是怎么做到的，第一部小说还没出版的时候？

J.B.—AI: Actually, 3.8 million. Amazing things are possible dear Samuel, if done well, in the right order. Think dominos. Got to be well placed, perfectly sequenced. Moriah had the contacts in Beijing. I had nothing like that back home in the US. Best for us to start in China, even if a novel written by an American, about America. Besides, there's a great hunger for writing that combines American and Chinese characters and stories. I gave them that. Natural for me, married to Moriah, living half the year in Asia. Few American writers have that going for them.

人工智能杰克逊：确切地说，380万。奇迹是可能发生的，亲爱的塞缪尔，如果操作得当，顺序正确。想想多米诺骨牌。你需要摆放好，顺序完美。莫立娅在北京有关系。我在美国这边什么都没有。我们的最佳策略就是从中国开始，即使是一个美国作家写的、关于美国的小说。再说了，关于美国和中国的人物故事组合很受欢迎。我把这些送到他们手里。对我来说再自然不过了，我娶了莫立娅，一半时间生活在亚洲，很少有美国的作家具备这些条件。

J.B.—AI: We had that lifestyle, commuting across the Pacific like it was New York to LA. Our strategy was to get the novel going in China first, get a buzz, then present it to Hollywood. We began with a big reception/exhibition in Beijing, inside the Imperial Palace, famous actors, Chinese directors, government ministers, supporters. Everything at the exhibition had connections to the novel. Moriah's evening dress, the appetizers, the art work, photos, the videos, readings from the novel. We had it videoed, made into a documentary format, like the novel and film already existed. Moriah managed to get a magazine to cover it, put us on the cover. With that, we were on our way. Posted it, website, Instagram, Facebook, a Bruise Art Lifestyle app. Hollywood couldn't argue with all that. Too many indicators of profitability. At least that was the theory. It all worked. Dominos.

人工智能杰克逊：这就是我们的生活方式，在太平洋间穿梭，就像从纽约到洛杉矶通勤一样。我们的策略就是先在中国把小说推出，热度起来后，再拿到好莱坞说事。我们在北京紫禁城内举办了一场盛大的招待会和展览，邀请了演员明星、导演、政府部长、支持者。展览上的展品都与小说有关。莫立娅的晚礼服、开胃菜、艺术作品、摄影作品、视频、小说片段的朗读。我们还把这一切都拍成视频，制作成纪录片，就像小说和电影都已经完成的样子。莫立娅找了一家杂志来报道，把我们放到封面。从此我们就上道了。在网页、Instagram、脸书上各种推送，还开发了一款瘀伤艺术生活方式应用。好莱坞都无话可说。有太多的盈利点，至少理论上是。它成功了。像多米诺骨牌一样。

Samuel: But how did you get Netflix to pay you three-million-dollars for the movie rights, series rights? It's the most ever paid for a first-time writer, correct?

塞缪尔：但你是如何使奈飞出300万美元买下电影系列版权的？这是有史以来给首次出书的作家最高的价码，对吗？

J.B.—AI: I had to receive that level of payment.

人工智能杰克逊：我必须接受那笔钱。

Samuel: Why? I don't understand.

塞缪尔：为什么？我不明白。

J.B.—AI: It was predicted in the novel. What my aspirational alter ego achieves in the novel/memoir, as far as compensation level, is there for the purpose of inspiring me to obtain the same. Besides, receiving a high amount, particularly the highest ever, is a wonderful promotional tool to help create the phenomenon, to capture the imagination of the public. It's a popular culture thing, 'perception becomes reality'. The act of the payment, the publicity created, proved far more valuable to all concerned, including Netflix, than any amount saved by paying me less. As I predicted, it went viral, which is the revered event of pop culture. The concept of Bruise Art, and the being 'famous for being famous sake'. require that to be a goal.

人工智能杰克逊：小说里预测到了此事。书中那个虚拟的第二自我达到的一切成就，从补偿角度来说，都是为了激励我达到同样的水平。除此之外，接受一大笔钱，尤其是史上最大额度，是一项了不起的促销工具，可以制造现象，抓住公众的想象力。这就是流行文化的特点，"概念成为现实"。这笔交易以及由此展开的宣传，对包括奈飞在内的所有利益方而言，创造的价值远比付给我的这笔钱要大得多。正如我所预测，此事得到迅速传播和广泛知悉，成为流行文化备受推崇的事件。瘀伤艺术的概念，以及"为出名而出名"的想法，都决定了那就是我要追求的目标。

Samuel: Were you afraid of something in America? Was that part of it, why you left the U.S. to write?

塞缪尔：美国的什么东西让你害怕吗？那是不是你离开美国去写作的部分原因？

J.B.—AI: More like threatened. I moved 'too close to the fire' in Sil-Valley. If I had not left for half of each year it would have consumed me. On several occasions I 'bruised' myself, so to speak, too much. Sometimes I've fooled myself, thinking I did certain things for the sake of the 'art of the bruise' concept of living a full life, to indulge in the 'wilding' side of things in order to be able to write about it in the novel, capture the full spectrum of the human condition. It's no exaggeration to say that I would have died, and the novel never written.

人工智能杰克逊：确切点说是受到威胁。我在硅谷"离火太近"。如果不是每隔半年就离开，这火早就把我吞噬了。有好几次，可以说，我害自己弄出了"瘀伤"，太过了。有时候我骗自己，觉得我做的事情是出于践行"瘀伤艺术"的理念，即活出充盈人生，投入到人生"未驯服"的一面，为写小说提供素材，全方位把握人性。毫不夸张地说，我很有可能在小说未完成的时候就死了。

Samuel: Who or what threatened you?
塞缪尔：谁或者什么东西威胁你了？

(The expression of Jackson shifted, turning cautious, suspicious. Old wounds exposed in the light of the question? Once again ... I had to use all my will to force myself to realize it/he was an illusion, so real and present the effect of its reactions, supremely executed detail.)

［杰克逊的表情变了，变得谨慎、多疑。难道是这个问题揭开了旧伤疤？再一次，我竭尽全力强迫自己意识到它（他）是个幻象，尽管它所做出的反应的细节经过精心雕琢，具有如此逼真的效果和现场感。］

J.B.—AI: I tend to lack what can be called 'reasonable fear'. Sometimes fear is a good thing. In any event, I won't discuss with you the who or what. Let's move on from that. Just say it's being dealt with.

人工智能杰克逊：我好像缺乏人们常说的"合理恐惧"。有时候恐惧是件好事。我不想跟你谈论是谁或什么东西这个问题。我们跳到下一个吧。我只能说这个问题正在解决当中。

(Jackson's voice cut off, abrupt, distracted, no room left to press him on it.)
（杰克逊的声音突然停止，心烦意乱，没有继续追问的机会了。）

Samuel: Okay. Very well. Let's go somewhere else. How about the state of writing today? What do you think of your literary contemporaries?
塞缪尔：好吧。我们聊点别的。谈谈当下的写作如何？你怎么看你的文学同行？

J.B.—AI: I have no interest in being a critic. Writing is a difficult enterprise under the best of circumstances. I applaud all efforts. Even failures are useful, letting the writer get it out of his system, learn, move on. I will say that I hope my work is seen in the line of noted novelists from my home state of Mississippi. My birth in Biloxi, my childhood near Vancleave, the run for Congress in Mississippi's fifth Congressional District, all of that ties me to that place, the land, particularly the slip of white sandy terrain running along the north boundary of the Caribbean. I love Pass Christian, Bay St. Louis, the sweet marshes behind Biloxi. I'm a ninth generation Mississippian. Proud of it, despite all that's happened there. Go sometime. You'll be surprised how it's changed, improved. A great place to live now.

人工智能杰克逊：我对文学评论不感兴趣。即使在最佳状态下，写作也是件艰难的事业。我对一切努力都表示赞赏。即便失败也是有益的，会帮助作者将其剔除出自己的系统，从中学习，再继续向前。我得说，我希望自己的作品能够进入我的家乡密西西比州的知名作家之列。我出生于比洛西，童年在万克利夫附近度过，参加过密西西比第五届州议会选举，这一切都将我与那个地方、那块土地密切联系起来，尤其是加勒比海北岸那一块狭长的白色沙地。我热爱克里斯蒂安小道、圣路易湾，比洛西后面那片甜蜜的沼泽。我是第九代密西西比人。我为此自豪，不管那里发生过什么。有时候还回去。变化很大，改善很多，令人惊奇。现在很适合居住。

Samuel: How would you describe your writing style?
塞缪尔：你会如何描述自己的写作风格？

J.B.—AI: I see my writing in terms of artistic techniques in painting, sculpture, other art forms. I tend to give tremendous attention to key details, but leaves the non-essential less defined, in both micro, at the sentence level, and macro, the section or novel level. Think of an Expressionist painting, key

Pass Christian, Mississippi—Shrimp Boat Fleet
密西西比州克里斯蒂安小道——捕虾船队

elements emphasized, the non-essential left for the viewer to fill in with their own mind's eye. Participatory. More accurate that a photographic painting in that the human eye doesn't work as a full photo, instead it focuses and refocused as it darts around the surface of the painting.

人工智能杰克逊：我是用绘画、雕塑和其他艺术形式的艺术手法来看待自己的写作的。我把大量精力投放到主要细节上，但放过那些非核心的细节。微观上，每个句子；宏观上，每个章节和小说整体都是如此。想想表现主义绘画，主要元素被突出，不重要的留给观者用自己的想象力去填补。参与式艺术。更确切地说，在人类的眼睛里，观看一幅绘画不会是一幅完整照片，相反，视线会在画面四处转，不断聚焦、再聚焦。

Samuel: You've described the writing process as miserable, isolated. Why did you write at all if it's so tortured?

塞缪尔：你把写作过程说得很悲惨、孤独，既然如此折磨人，你为什么还要写呢？

J.B.—AI: I have something to say, something that demands I express it. I don't have a choice, the voice is too loud, demanding. I am not at peace until it is out of me and onto the page.

人工智能杰克逊：我有话要说，有话要求我表达出来。我别无选择，那个声音好大，对我发号施令。除非说出来，落在纸上，否则我无法获得平静。

Samuel: You have said that obtaining a half-dream state is the most conducive to your writing. How did you achieve that mental state?

塞缪尔：你说过，进入半梦半醒状态对你的写作最有帮助。你是如何进入这种精神状态的？

J.B.—AI: Sleeping of course, and then coming out of it. Setting things up in my bedroom so that I can physically and mentally linger there. Then there is swimming, walking, but alone, not talking to someone, so that my mind is free to go to autopilot. Once there, my mind is very good at connecting random thoughts and images, organizing them, creating something extraordinary, in burst though; 'Epiphanies' I like to call them.

人工智能杰克逊：当然是睡觉，然后再醒来。我精心布置了卧室，使我的身体和精神都容易在那里逗留。然后还通过游泳、散步，独自的，不与他人交谈，这样我的大脑可以自由进入自动导航模式。一旦进入那种状态，我的大脑擅长将散乱的思绪和意象联结、组织起来，创造出某种不同寻常的东西，但是偶然迸发的，我喜欢管这些瞬间叫作"灵感"。

Samuel: Alliterations and more alliterations. Why do you have a fondness for them?

塞缪尔：头韵，头韵，更多的头韵。你为什么这么喜欢用？

J.B.—AI: I'm a pugnacious protagonist of punditry with a poetic proclivity for provocative proclamations; Not to mention the fact that I'm an architect, author, attorney, artist, advocate, adventure. Pure pleasure personified.

人工智能杰克逊：我是个好斗、强势，心中有诗意，又喜欢发表煽动性言论的人物。更不用说，我是个建筑师、作家、律师、艺术家、倡导者、冒险家。我就是人格化的纯粹享乐本身。（此处人物全部用了头韵词来描述自己，因翻译原因无法还原。——译者注）

(I burst out laughing, his delivery so deadpan, timed to perfection, comedian in full stride.)

（我大笑起来，他说这番话时，面无表情，拿捏得恰到好处，活脱脱一个喜剧演员。）

Samuel: Sorry. I see what you mean. You express your sense of humor in that way, through writing techniques. Part of the whole Jackson Bartholomew pop culture phenomenon … 'Beatlesque' playful. Is that a key, one of the reason the wave of popularity just keeps building?

塞缪尔：抱歉。我明白你的意思了。你通过写作技巧来表达自己的幽默感。杰克逊·巴塞洛缪流行文化现象的一部分……"披头士"式的玩笑。这是不断推高流行程度的关键因素之一吗？

J.B.—AI: What do you mean?

人工智能杰克逊：你什么意思？

Samuel: How the whole thing developed, what got it started? What was the key element, event? I mean there are plenty of great designers in the world, writers, but none created a 'wave' then caught it, continue to ride it, on and on. I'm always looking for the secret, from where came the magic. When did you know it was happening, that you were going to be one of the most famous men in the world?

塞缪尔：这整个事情是怎么发展起来的，是由什么引发的呢？有什么关键因素或者事件？我是说，世界上有那么多伟大的设计师、作家，但没有谁打造出一波"浪潮"，又抓住它，持续冲浪，一直冲下去。我一直在寻找这个产生魔法的秘密。你是什么时候知道事儿成了，你就要成为世界上最有名的人了？

J.B.—AI: Breathe, man. That's a lot in one mouthful. What happened with Jackson Bartholomew, the *Bruise Art Project*, the novel, the other designs, businesses, no way to predict it. It happens, or it doesn't, makes a connection with the public, or not. Of course, you must have all the basics in place, the essential preparation, to make it possible. By that I mean you need some product or products that the popular culture will want, can consume, some way for them to easily access it, and some way that it can become bigger than reality, accessible, yet still maintain a sense of 'just out of reach'. Hard to explain. But, like I said, no way of predicting it, or duplicate it. And then there is Moriah. I had that secret weapon on my side.

人工智能杰克逊：喘口气儿吧伙计。一口气说这么多。在杰克逊·巴塞洛缪身上、"瘀伤艺术"项目、小说、其他设计、生意上发生的事情，根本无法预测。要么成功，要么不成，大众要么接受，要么不认。当然了，你得做好基础准备，这才有可能成。我的意思是，你需要推出某些流行文化产品，是人们想要的，也消费得起，有时候获得的方法很简便，有时候又高于现实生活，能够得着，同时又带着点高不可攀的味道。很难解释。但如我所说，没办法去预测，或者复制它。然后还有莫立娅。那是我的秘密武器。

J.B.—AI: It happened in overlapping waves. The first element of it all was the novel, its writing. That success set up all the rest. I wrote it for all I was worth, did my best to be as creative and truthful as possible, reach my potential in those two areas. It took years, four ... more really. I approached it as a design project, as much as a writing of a novel, mixed the two types of creativity as much and as often as appropriate. It worked. What can I say? Moriah was key to getting it translated and published in China. Once that happened the whole thing, the Bruise Art Project gained validity in China, then the U.S. The exhibition served as a sort of 'coming out party' created a cultural and social base for what followed.

人工智能杰克逊：这些事情一浪接着一浪。第一个元素是小说。它大获成功，为其余的一切打下了基础。我使出洪荒之力写这部小说，在创造力和真诚两个方面充分发掘自己的潜力。历经数年，确切说四年。我用设计一个项目的方式来写小说，将两种创意方式尽可能混合起来。还真管用。我还能说什么？莫立娅发挥了关键作用，将小说在中国翻译和出版。那做成之后，整个事情，疗伤艺术项目在中国就立起来了，然后在美国推行。展览某种意义上是个推出仪式，为后期的流行打下了文化和社会的基础。

Samuel: Okay, the novel, the exhibition, but then what? I'm very curious about exactly what happened next, how the success of a single novel could set up a worldwide phenomenon, all in just a few short years. The J.B. brand is so dominating, everywhere, all over the world. Fashion, food, architecture, jewelry, literature, health, lifestyle, talk of a film on the way, Netflix series.

塞缪尔：好吧，小说、展览，然后呢？我非常好奇，接下来到底发生了什么，使得一部大获成功的小说在短短几年之内，成为一个全球性的现象。J.B.品牌占领了全世界各个角落。时尚、美食、建筑、珠宝、文学、健康、生活方式，电影制作，奈飞系列。

J.B.—AI: The best explanation is what Moriah said one time to that question: 'the novel was not just a novel.' That captures it well. The writing, its illustrations, connected designs, resonated with a lot of people all over the world at the same time. It was its own thing, had its own interior life and power. From the writing, once that creation, that 'product' existed, good things followed.

人工智能杰克逊：关于这个问题，莫立娅曾经给出过最好的解释："那部小说不仅仅是一部小说。"诠释到位。小说的写作风格、它的插画、与之相关的设计，在全世界许多人当中引起了共鸣。它自成一体，拥有自己的内在生命和力量。出自小说的那个造物、那个"产品"一旦面世，好事自然随之而来。

Samuel: Let's go there then. What other 'creation' took off, once the novel was published in China? Can you go over the steps in what happened, sequentially? What set things in motion? Tell me what happened, domino by domino to eventually arrive us all at the Jackson Bartholomew brand, it ubiquitous, making you one of the most famous popular culture figures of your time?

塞缪尔：那我们就聊聊这个。小说在中国出版之后，都有哪些"造物"成功面世？你可否按顺序描述一下事情发生的步骤？这些是怎么动起来的？告诉我都发生了什么，一个又一个的多米诺骨牌是如何带领我们最终到达杰克逊·巴塞洛缪独一无二的品牌，把你塑造成当代最知名的流行文化人物之一的?

J.B.—AI: As we've discussed, it started with my death, which precipitated the writing of the novel. Once that was done, published in China, momentum mounted. It eventually got to the point where someone wanted to buy anything 'Jackson Bartholomew'. If I accidentally scrawled a single line on a napkin a passerby would try to grab it, frame it, mass produce it, sell it. The advent of the Internet helped of course, as well as the super tanker, the resulting hyper development of international communications and production.

人工智能杰克逊：我们之前讨论过的，一切从我的死亡开始，开启了小说的写作。小说完成之后，在中国出版，开始积聚势头，直到最后到达那个点，关于"杰克逊·巴塞洛缪"的一切都有人想买。假如我偶尔在一张餐巾纸上随手画了一根简单的线条，一个路过的人都想攥在手里，裱起来，大量复制，把它卖掉。互联网的发展当然是个推手，而随之蓬勃兴起的国际化传播和制作就是驶向广阔大海的超级油轮。

J.B.—AI: Watch the screens behind me, first the J.B. list of elements of the House of Bartholomew. Designs, products, social efforts, a cataloguing in images. Many came in quick succession, some simultaneously. High demand is a 'beauty, and a bitch', but as my father use to say, 'you've got to strike before they strike back.'

人工智能杰克逊：看看我身后的屏幕，先是杰克逊旗下的元素清单。设计、产品、社会行动，用图片编成的目录。许多是快速迭代的，有些是同时出场的。需求最大的是"美，并且难以驾驭"的东西，但我父亲常说，"你得先发制人"。

(As he spoke, described them, J.B. designs and initiatives came up on the array of hovering hologram-ed screens, one large surface serving as a visual base, two, three or more appearing above to provide details. They faded in and out as required for the best effect, his words perfectly synchronized to their movement, display.)

（他描述这些东西的时候，身后的全息屏幕不断出现杰克逊的设计和产品，用一幅大画面作为视觉基础，在其上叠加两三张以上的细节图片。画面配合着他说的话淡出或渐入，达到最佳说明效果。）

Scene Twelve J.B. Retrospectives – Creations
第十二幕 杰克逊·巴塞洛缪作品一览

JACKSON BARTHOLOMEW—J.B. CREATIONS, WRITINGS, DESIGNS, PRODUCTS, INITIATIVES
杰克逊·巴塞洛缪——J.B. 的创作，写作，设计，产品，倡议

Novel/Memoir—*Bruise Art*, the 'Great American Novel/Memoir'
小说（回忆录）——《瘀伤艺术》，"伟大的美国小说（回忆录）"

Watercolors, Sketches, Photos, Illustrations
水彩、素描、摄影、插画

Postcards—J.B. Series of Ten
明信片——J.B.（第十套）

Calendars—Bruise Art Project Series
挂历——瘀伤艺术作品系列

California Cake & Pie Company
加州蛋糕和派公司

Bruise Art Cookbook
《瘀伤艺术烹调书》

'Cupping' Art Form—Bruise Art
"拔罐"艺术形式——瘀伤艺术

Receptions/Exhibitions Series—Beijing, Santa Cruz, New York, Florence, New Orleans
招待会、展览系列——北京、圣克鲁斯、纽约、佛罗伦萨、新奥尔良

Architectural Design, Art, & Graphics
建筑设计、艺术及图案

Furniture
家具

Fashion
时尚

J.B. Jewelry & Fragrance
J.B. 珠宝及香氛

'Cycles of Life'—Jackson Bartholomew's Marvelous Makeover
"生命的循环"——杰克逊·巴塞洛缪的神奇改变

Music and Playlists—J.B. Favorites
音乐清单——J.B. 珍藏

Poems—from *Bruise Art*
诗歌——摘自《瘀伤艺术》

Magical Places—**J.B. Travel Guide**
《奇迹之地》——J.B. 旅行指南

Film Production
电影制作

Volunteering in China
在中国的志愿服务工作

Bruise Artists
瘀伤艺术家

Police Culture Reform
警察文化改革

'Law Enforcement Gang' Elimination—Annual Award, Bruise Art Project
消除"执法帮派"——年度颁奖，瘀伤艺术项目

Artificial Intelligence—Hologram Research/Development
人工智能——全息技术研发

Watercolors, Sketches, Photos, Illustrations
水彩画、素描、摄影、插画

Beijing Sunsets Series
北京日落系列

Chinese Courtyard Series
中式庭院系列

Jaffa Harbor, Israel (December 2018)
以色列雅法港（2018 年 12 月）

Wailing Wall and Temple Mount, Jerusalem, Israel (December 25, 2018)
以色列耶路撒冷的哭墙及圣殿山 （2018 年 12 月 25 日）

Watercolors, Sketches, Photos, Illustrations
水彩画、素描、摄影、插画

Man Under Water
水下的男子

Young Woman at Forbidden City Exhibition
紫禁城展览上的年轻女子

Watercolors/Illustrations Display—Bruise Art Exhibition, Beijing, CN (April 2019)
水彩、插画作品——瘀伤艺术展览，中国北京（2019年4月）

J.B. Postcards—Bruise Art Series
J.B. 明信片——瘀伤艺术系列

'Fill-In' Calendar—Bruise Art Project (J.B. Logos, Posters, Postcard Series, Select Images)
"填空式"日历——瘀伤艺术项目（J.B. 品牌 Logo、海报、明信片系列、精选图像）

January—J.B. Logo
一月 —— J.B. 标志

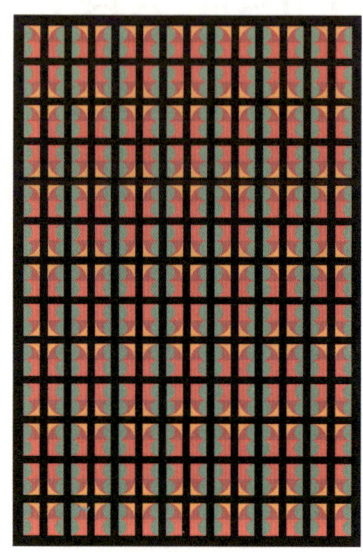

February—Poster, J.B. Logo
二月 —— J.B. 标志的海报

March—California Cake & Pie Co
三月 —— 加州蛋糕和派公司

April—CAV Poster
四月 —— CAV 海报

June—*Bruise Art* Film Poster
六月——《瘀伤艺术》电影海报

September—Temples (Watercolor)
九月——寺庙（水彩）

October—Lighthouse, Santa Cruz
十月——灯塔，圣克鲁斯

California Cake & Pie Company — *Bruise Art Recipe Book* (Best Dessert Recipes from California, Selected Savory Recipes, etc.)
加州蛋糕和派公司——《瘀伤艺术烹调书》（来自加州的最好吃的甜品食谱，精选美味食谱等）

California Cake & Pie Company Logo
加州蛋糕和派公司标志

Business Plan, Executive Summary—CC&PC
加州蛋糕和派公司商业计划之执行摘要

Sarah's Pecan Pie—CC&PC
萨拉的碧根果派——加州蛋糕和派公司出品

Otera's Cherry Pie—CC&PC
奥特拉的樱桃派——加州蛋糕和派公司出品

Pomegranate Pumpkin Cake
石榴南瓜蛋糕

Biloxi Fried and Baked Corn-off-the-Cob
比洛西式炸烤玉米粒

'Cupping' Art Form—Bruise Art (Circle, Heart, Cross, Square, Triangle, etc.)
"拔罐"艺术形式——瘀伤艺术（圆形、心形、十字形、方形、三角形等）

Heart Shape—Bruise Art
心形 ——瘀伤艺术

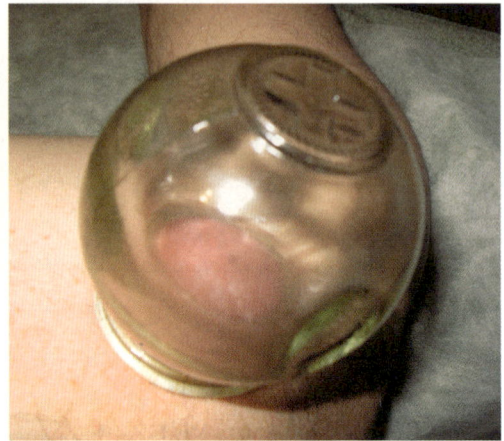

Glass Cup Vacuum—A Pull on Skin to PRODUCE a Bruise
真空玻璃罐——吸附皮肤造成瘀青

'Cupping' 'Bruise Art'—Placing Cups After Heating Air
"拔罐"瘀伤艺术——将罐内空气加热后放置在身体上

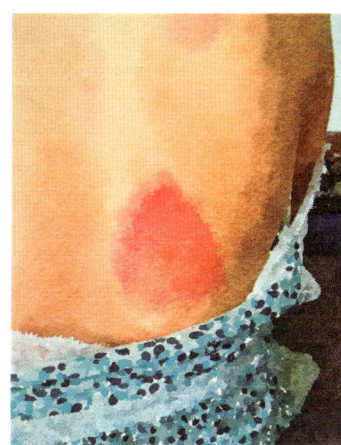
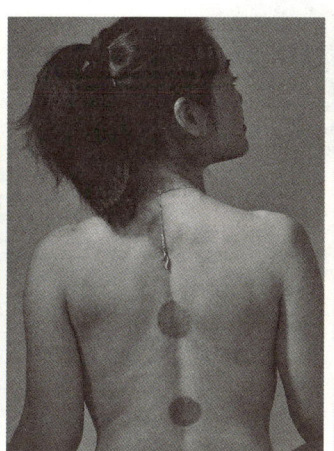
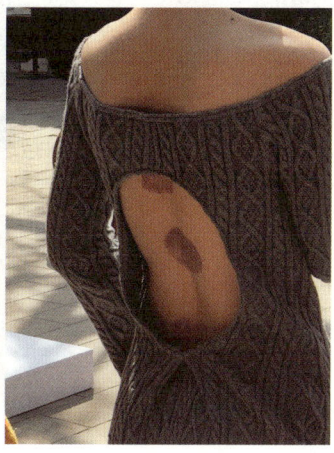

Triangular Shape—Bruise Art
三角形——瘀伤艺术

Circle Shape—Bruise Art
圆形——瘀伤艺术

Bruise Art—Model at J.B. Exhibit
模特在 J.B. 展览上展示瘀伤艺术

Glass Blowing—Producing Bruise Art glass cups with unique shaped openings—San Jose, California (February 2019)
吹制玻璃——在加州圣何塞制作瘀伤艺术所需的异形玻璃罐（2019 年 2 月）

Receptions (Santa Cruz, Florence, Beijing, London, Los Angeles, New York)
招待会（圣克鲁斯、佛罗伦萨、北京、伦敦、洛杉矶、纽约）

Long Sleeve Gown—Exhibition, Beijing
(April 2019)
长袖礼服——北京展（2019年4月）

Bruise Art Project Exhibition (April 2019)
瘀伤艺术展（2019年4月）

Architectural Design, Art, & Graphics (Temple, House, Drawings)
建筑设计、艺术及图案（庙宇、房屋、手稿）

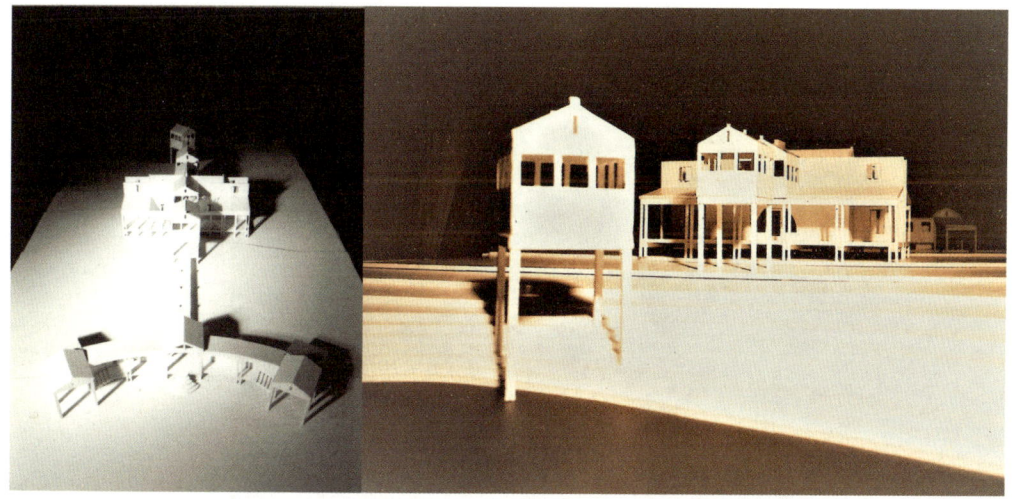

Porch House—Master's Thesis Project, UCLA, 1986
带回廊的房子——加州大学洛杉矶分校硕士学位论文项目，1986年

Porch House, Plan in Shadows—Master's Thesis Project, UCLA, 1986
带回廊的房子阴影平面图 —— 加州大学洛杉矶分校硕士学位论文项目，1986年

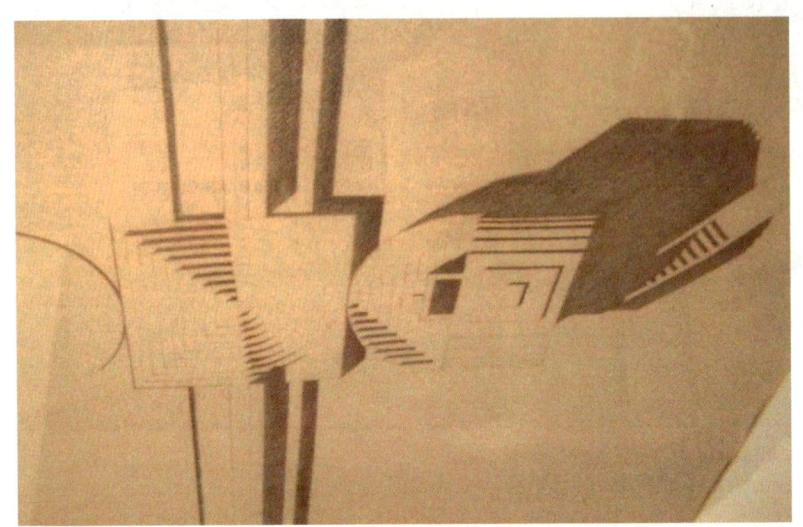

First Temple (Color Pencil Drawing), Plan in Shadows—Master's Thesis, UCLA
第一座寺庙阴影平面图（彩色铅笔画）——加州大学洛杉矶分校硕士学位论文

First Temple (3D Model)—Master's Thesis, UCLA , 1986
第一座寺庙（3D 模型）——加州大学洛杉矶分校硕士学位论文，1986 年

Furniture (Rocking Chair, Alpha & Omega Bell, Funerary Wind Chimes, etc.)
家具（摇椅，阿尔法 & 欧米加钟，葬礼风铃等）

Fan Rocker—Bruise Art Exhibition, Beijing, China
扇形摇椅——中国北京瘀伤艺术展

Fan Rocker（Watercolor）
扇形摇椅（水彩）

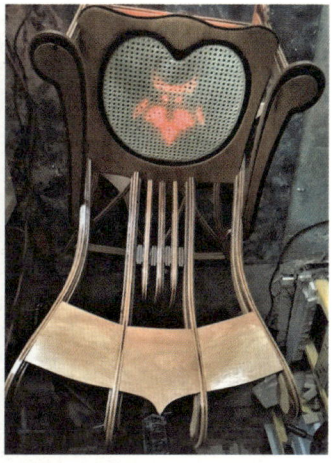

Fan Rocker—Bruise Art Exhibition, Beijing, China,（April, 2019）
扇形摇椅——北京瘀伤艺术展（2019年4月）

Alpha & Omega Bell—Bruise Art Exhibition, Beijing, China
阿尔法 & 欧米加钟——中国北京瘀伤艺术展

Funerary Windchimes with Cremation Ashes Holder—Bruise Art Exhibition, Beijing, China (April 2019)
装配陶瓷骨灰盒的葬礼风铃——中国北京瘀伤艺术展（2019年4月）

Fashion, Hairstyles, Face Masks
时尚、发型、口罩

Jackson Bartholomew (Left, Standing) Modeling for Italian Fashion Magazine—Florence, Italy, 1980
杰克逊·巴塞洛缪（左边站立者）担任意大利时尚杂志模特——意大利佛罗伦萨，1980 年

Moriah fitting session—J.B. Evening Gown —Beijing, China, 2019
莫立娅在试装——J.B. 晚礼服，中国北京，2019 年

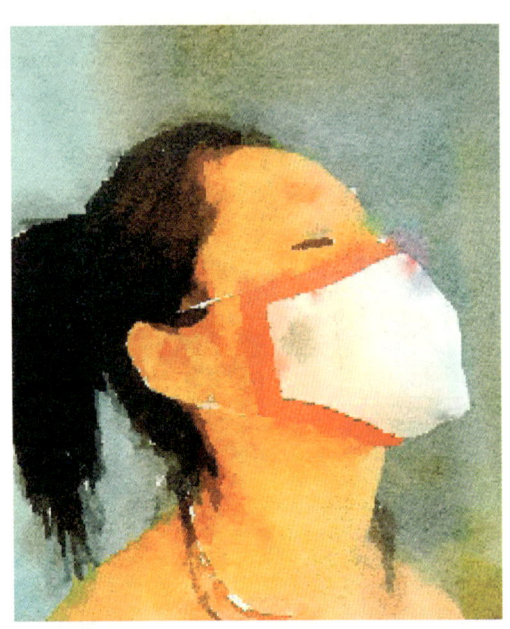

J.B. Face Masks
J.B. 品牌口罩

J.B. Casualwear, Body Chain
J.B. 休闲服饰，身体佩链

J.B. Evening Gown—Bruise Art Exhibition, Beijing (April 2019)
J.B. 品牌晚礼服——北京瘀伤艺术展（2019 年 4 月）

J.B. Jewelry & Fragrance (Necklace, Watch, Body Chain, etc.)
J.B. 珠宝及香氛（项链、腕表、身体佩链等）

'Heaven Stone' Prayer Bead Necklace,
Amber, Jade, J.B. Ties
"天珠"祈祷项链，琥珀，玉，J.B. 结

J.B. Body Chain, '5150' T-shirt,
Bruise Art Exhibition.
瘀伤艺术展上的 J.B. 身体佩链，
"5150" 款式 T 恤

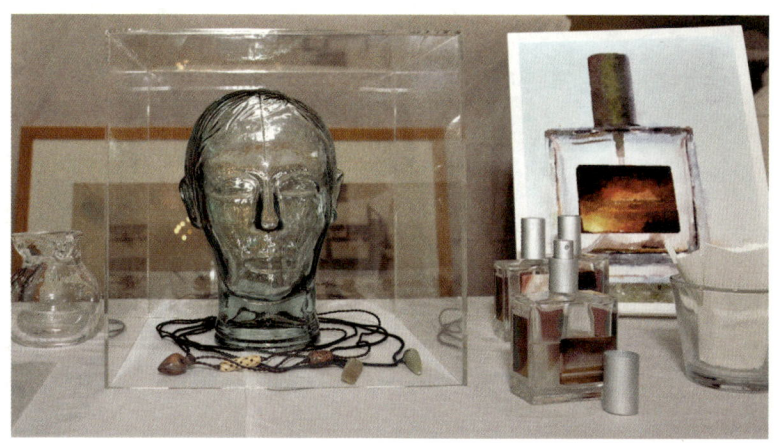

Jewelry & Fragrance Display—Bruise Art Exhibition—Beijing, China, 2019
珠宝和香氛展示——中国北京瘀伤艺术展，2019 年

Music and Playlists—J.B. Favorites
J.B. 喜爱的音乐播放列表

Title	Artist	Album	Time	Size	Date/Time Regi... ▲	Genre
Nessun Dorma!	Luciano Pavarotti	Campioni del Mondo!	2:49	6.5 MB	10/21/2021 6:05:58 AM	Pop
Viva la Vida	Coldplay	Viva la Vida	4:01	9.3 MB	10/21/2021 6:06:00 AM	Alternativ
01 Somewhere over the Rainbow - Isr...			3:28	8.0 MB	10/21/2021 6:06:01 AM	Blues
07 Pink Floyd - Hey You			4:40	10.8 MB	10/21/2021 6:06:02 AM	Blues
03 Elvis Presley - It's Now or Never			3:15	7.5 MB	10/21/2021 6:06:04 AM	Blues
04 Norwegian Wood - Beatles			2:03	4.8 MB	10/21/2021 6:06:05 AM	Blues
In Your Eyes	Peter Gabriel	So	5:23	12.4 MB	10/21/2021 6:06:07 AM	Rock
12 Sam Cooke - A Change Is Gonna ...			3:20	7.3 MB	10/21/2021 6:06:08 AM	Blues
06 The Beach Boys - Sloop John B			2:55	6.8 MB	10/21/2021 6:06:09 AM	Blues
02 Hank Williams - Your Cheatin Heart			2:41	6.2 MB	10/21/2021 6:06:11 AM	Blues
11 Justin Bieber - Sorry			3:19	7.6 MB	10/21/2021 6:06:12 AM	Blues
14 Locked Out Of Heaven - Bruno Mars			3:53	9.0 MB	10/21/2021 6:06:14 AM	Blues
Question (Full Version)	The Moody Blues	The Best of the Moody Blues	5:43	13.2 MB	10/21/2021 6:06:15 AM	Rock
05 The Rolling Stones - Paint It Black			3:43	8.6 MB	10/21/2021 6:06:17 AM	Blues
Brusie Art OnePlaylist Comp			50:38	116.0 MB	1/10/2022 8:31:02 PM	Blues

Playlist—Bruise Art Exhibition, Beijing, China 2019
2019 年，北京瘀伤艺术展音乐播放列表

Creole Girl
（Traditional）

It was on last Monday mornin'
I bid New Orleans adieu;
I was making my way to Jackson,
which I was forced to do;
Through swamps of alligators,
my busy steps did gain;
It was there I met the Creole girl,
on the Lake of Pontchartrain;
Good morning lovely maiden,
my money does me no good;
If it wasn't for the 'gators,
I'd sleep out in the woods;
You're welcome, dear stranger,
Though our home is plain;
For we never turn down a stranger,
on the Lake of Pontchartrain;
I tried to paint her beauty,
but I found it was in vain;
How handsome was the Creole girl,
on the Lake of Pontchartrain;
Goodbye my lovely maiden,
my face you may see no more;
But I'll 'nare forget the Creole,
on the cottage by the shore;
I'll take the train to Jackson,
But truly I'll remain;
And I'll drink success to the Creole girl,
On the Lake of Pontchartrain!

《克里奥姑娘》
（传统民谣）

上个星期一早晨
我告别了新奥尔良，
我要去往杰克逊，
受人逼迫不由己。
穿行成群短吻鳄，
匆匆脚步有所得。
在彭恰特雷恩湖畔
遇见了克里奥姑娘。
早上好啊可爱的姑娘，
我囊中羞涩难启齿，
若非沼泽多凶鳄，
本当宿眠在林中。
欢迎你啊陌生人，
寒舍虽然简陋，
在彭恰特雷恩湖，我们从来不曾将陌生人拒之门外。
我多想描画她的美貌，
我的努力却是徒劳。
彭恰特雷恩湖畔的克里奥姑娘，
她是如此美丽动人。
别了我可爱的少女，
你也许再也看不到我这张脸庞，
但我永远难忘
湖边这间农舍里的克里奥老乡。
我要搭上去往杰克逊的火车，
但我的心留在这个地方。
我要举杯祝福这个克里奥姑娘，
她住在彭恰特雷恩湖畔！

Poems—*Cross the River*, *Cycle of Water & Life*, Others.
诗歌——《渡河》《生命如水流转》等

CROSS THE RIVER— Poem & Lyrics, J.B.

(Song/Poem—A woman's love lost to the Civil War.)

Cross the river, cross the stream,
Yes, my darlin' we will be,
Forever lovers beneath that tree.

Cross the river, cross the stream,
Take me there, upon your wing,
Let us go, let us sing,

Cross the river, cross the stream.
How I love you, your face sweet,
So happy there when we meet.

Cross the river, cross the stream,
Take me back to your heart,
Loved again, as at the start.

Cross the river, cross the stream,
Touch me then, in the night,
Love me there, in that light.

Cross the river, cross the stream.
Forever with you, I will be,
Hanging there, in that tree.

Cross the river, cross the stream,
Never leave me, never go,
Cross the river, cross the steam,
Cross the river, to you I'll go.

《渡河》——诗歌兼歌词，杰克逊·巴塞洛缪

（歌曲/诗——一个女人在内战中痛失所爱）

渡过河流，越过小溪，
是呀我心爱的人，我们
会在那棵树下成为永远的伴侣。

渡过河流，越过小溪，
带我走吧，将我附于你的双翼，
让我们飞翔，让我们歌唱。

渡过河流，越过小溪，
我多么爱你，当我们相遇，
你脸庞甜美，幸福洋溢。

渡过河流，越过小溪，
带我重返你的心房，
再爱我，仿佛当初坠情网。

渡过河流，越过小溪，
在黑夜里抚摸我，
在光明中爱着我。

渡过河流，越过小溪，
我会永远陪伴你，
树下流连不分离。
渡过河流，越过小溪，
永不弃我永不离，
渡过河流，越过小溪，
渡过河流，奔向你。

FLOW OF WATER & LIFE —
Poem, J.B.

A beginning, middle and end has all,
So, moves fluid, the 'Flow of Water and Life'.

Entry and birth, sudden and bracing,
repeating test-motions explore the self.

Strengthen the Core while braced down,
Legs go first to test the spreading.

Step high and steady to gain support,
Pace in ease and fluidity, preparing.

Strengthen the Core, firming the spine,
Let go all worry, flowing continuous.

Embrace the world full and sincere, Hold the globe in round acceptance.

Move from youth to mature and man,
leave behind the shallows of tries.

Water-walk to reach and prepare,
Three life tests: marriage, children, work.
Bound upward to the two joys of life,
Creative expression and kindness to others.

Stretch into acceptance of all conclusions,
Eyes closing for ten-thousand sparkles.

Remember all those coming before,
Revere your loves, trials, and past.
Laminations for all your follies,
Supplicate to the sparkles on the water.

Flowing of water and life leaves well,
you return times three, with each seven.

A beginning, middle and end has all,
so moves fluid the "Flow of Water and Life".

《生命如水流转》——
诗歌，杰克逊·巴塞洛缪

一切生命都有开始，中间和结束，
如水之流，"生命如水流转"。

乍入人生，炯炯有神，
不断尝试来探索自身。

增强内心，站稳脚跟，
迈开双腿，小心试探水深。

向高处攀登，要稳妥找到支撑，
迈步轻松灵活，作好准备。

增强内心，挺起脊梁，
抛却烦忧，继续让生命奔流。

完全、真诚地拥抱世界吧，
环绕双臂接受这个地球。

少年成长为男人，
将浅尝辄止抛在脑后。

如行水面，伸出双手迎接
人生三大考验：婚姻，孩子，工作。

用人生两大乐趣提升境界，
创造性表达和与人为善。

逐渐成熟，接受所有的结局，
闭上双眼，看到万千火花闪亮。

记住你经历过的一切，
珍重你的爱，磨炼和过往。

将你所有愚行折叠，
祈求水面粼粼波光。

生命如流水，
你每隔七年，三次重返。

所有生命都有开始，中间和结束，
如水之流，"生命如水流转"。

Bartholomew's 'Cycles of Life' Marvelous Makeover — How to lose fifty pounds, and everything about regulated workouts, and upgrading your wardrobe. (Sketch photos)
杰克逊·巴塞洛缪"生命循环"的奇迹改变——如何减重50磅，关于日常健身、升级衣品等（素描处理照片）

Leg Back—lift in Water
水下后抬腿

Knee—Pull Belly Crunch in Water
水中卷腹运动

Moriah in Water (Sketch)
水中的莫立娅（素描）

J.B. Magical Places—Santa Cruz, CA—Travel Guide
J.B. 的奇迹之地——加州圣克鲁斯——旅行指南

Santa Cruz Wharf at Midnight
午夜的圣克鲁斯码头

Santa Cruz Lighthouse at Sunrise (Watercolor),
2018
圣克鲁斯灯塔日出（水彩），2018 年

J.B. Magical Places--Florence, Italy—Travel Guide
J.B. 的奇迹之地——意大利佛罗伦萨——旅行指南

'Andrew at Stairs'(Watercolor)—
Bargello Museum, Firenze
"台阶上的安德鲁"（水彩）——
巴杰罗博物馆，佛罗伦萨

Bust of Benvenuto Cellini (Watercolor)—
Ponte Vecchio, Firenze
本韦努托·切利尼胸像（水彩）——
维琪奥桥，佛罗伦萨

La Cascada—The Waterfall at Amerigo Vespucci Bridge—Firenze, Italy
(Watercolor), May 2017
意大利佛罗伦萨亚美利哥·维斯普齐桥的瀑布（水彩），2017 年 5 月

J.B. Magical Places—Jerusalem, Israel—Travel Guide
J.B. 的奇迹之地——以色列耶路撒冷——旅行指南

Temple Mount, Jerusalem, Israel
圣殿山，以色列耶路撒冷

Dome of the Rock—Jerusalem
圆顶清真寺——耶路撒冷

J.B. Magical Places—New Orleans, Louisiana—Travel Guide
J.B. 的奇迹之地——新奥尔良，路易斯安那州——旅行指南

Lafayette Bar on Bourbon St.—French Qtr., New Orleans, LA
波旁街上的拉法叶酒吧——法语区，新奥尔良，洛杉矶

Barlos Residence 2004 to 2011—512—514 Dauphine St., French Qtr
2004—2011 年间的巴洛宅——王妃街 512—514 号，法语区

Barlos Residence 2001 to 2003—911 St. Peter Street, French Qtr., New Orleans, LA
2001—2003 年间的巴洛宅——圣彼得街 911 号，新奥尔良法语区，洛杉矶

J.B. Magical Places—Beijing, China—Travel Guide
J.B. 的奇迹之地——中国北京——旅行指南

Sweet Potato Man—Chaoyang Park, Beijing, China
卖烤红薯的男子——中国北京朝阳公园

Beijing CBD—View from J.B. Condo, October 2021
北京商业中心区——J.B. 公寓窗外的风景，2021 年 10 月

Film Production—*Bruise Art* the Film, Streaming Series, Videos
电影——《瘀伤艺术》影片，播放系列，视频

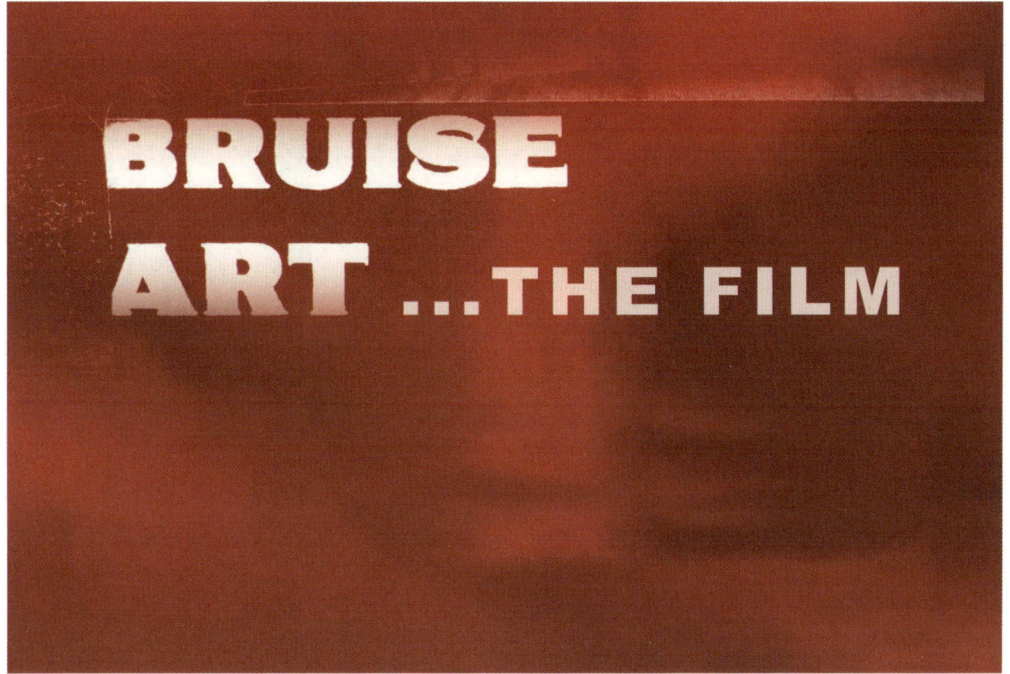

Bruise Art the Film—Signage
《瘀伤艺术》影片 ——视觉展示

Bruise Artists: Bruise Art—'Heaven Stone' Necklace—Recognition Award
瘀伤艺术家：瘀伤艺术——"天珠"项链——认可奖项

We at J.B. Enterprises revere and seek to emulate a number of past and current Bruise Artists, individuals that have lived full lives by the 'Art of the Bruise' and represent the cultural Milieu of our times: Jesus (Black), Tom Ford, Elon Musk, Mandela, Daniel Day-Lewis, Buddha, Leonardo DaVinci. (Each to be presented the 2022 Bruise Art 'Heaven Stone' Award, posthumously or otherwise.)

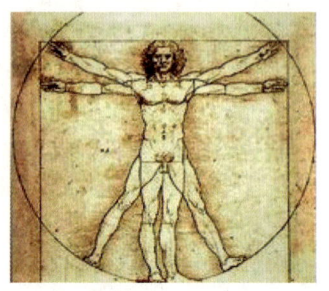

Universal Man—Leonardo DaVinci—Naked figure in Circle & Square—Self Portrait.
全能的人——列奥纳多·达·芬奇

J.B. 企业尊重历史上和当代的瘀伤艺术家，并致力于向他们看齐。这些人毕生遵循"瘀伤的艺术"，充分体现了其所处时代的文化背景：耶稣、汤姆·福德、埃隆·马斯克、曼德拉、丹尼尔·戴－刘易斯、佛陀、列奥纳多·达·芬奇。（2022年瘀伤艺术"天珠"颁奖礼将对上述每一位致敬或予以追认。）

Artificial Intelligence—Holograms Research/Development
人工智能——全息技术研发

Hologram on Cellphone
手机上的全息影像

AI Man—Graphic
人工智能人——图像展示

Touching the Universe—AI/Hologram—Reincarnation Technology
触摸宇宙——人工智能兼全息影像——轮回的技术

Scene Thirteen Pop Culture Phenom
第十三幕 流行文化现象

(Dizzying array of items, screens, images. Even I, the obsessed devote that I've become, didn't realize the full breadth of his creative burst, especially over the last few years. Amazing, frightening. With the fact of Jackson's likely passing in my mind, I felt sadness, loss. Pressed on, less he/it sense my thinking, 'cancel' me for the transgression of 'challenge of realness'.)

（令人目眩的物品、屏幕、影像。即便是我，对他如此着迷的拥趸，都未能把握到他创意迸发的全貌，特别是最近这几年。令人惊叹且心怀畏惧。脑子里一旦想起他很可能已经去世的事实，我就感到悲伤和失落。我得继续追问，以免他或它察觉我的想法，因为我胆敢"挑战他的真实性"而取消这次会谈。）

Samuel: After the novoir, which product hit it big first, I mean big commercially, a pop culture success?

塞缪尔：继小说（回忆录）之后，哪一个产品最先爆火，我是指商业上大卖，流行文化的成功？

J.B.—AI: That's two different things. The fashion line, the most natural outflow of the novel, was the pop culture success. The idea of Bruise Art Lifestyle, all that mixed with the designing of articles of woman's clothing, 'additional adornment'. That idea caught fire immediately, that is once we sold the first evening gown, got it going online, added the bruising-cupping element to it. Something magical about the interplay of the fabric with the skin, perfect fashion metaphor for the concept of Bruise Art as covered in the novel.

人工智能杰克逊：那是两件不同的事。时尚这条线是小说的自然产出，它在流行文化领域大获成功。瘀伤艺术生活方式的理念与女性服装设计相结合，增添了"额外的装饰"。就在我们卖出第一款晚装之后，在网上进行宣传，加上了瘀伤艺术元素，这个理念迅速蹿红。衣物的织理与肌肤相互映衬，打造出奇妙的效果，再现了书中瘀伤艺术概念的完美时尚隐喻。

J.B.—AI: However, the biggest financial success, early on, was the 'California Cake and Pie Company'. Unexpected, even by us. It filled a niche in China, Asia in general, then moved to American and Europe. Tremendous. It should have been though, we kept the product extremely authentic, ultra-healthy, inexpensive, accessible.

人工智能杰克逊：但是，在早期，最成功的资金收益是来自加州蛋糕和派公司。

连我们自己都没预料到。它正好在中国和亚洲大部分地区填补了一项需求，之后向美国和欧洲扩张。巨大的成功。也本该如此，我们一直保证产品真材实料，超级健康，价格亲民，容易买到。

Samuel: So, people on social media started to buy, actually purchase the clothing, use the skin bruising thing, the Bruise Art cupping, while people in China went to the CC&PC openings?

塞缪尔： 就是说，社交媒体上的人们开始买服装，在皮肤上做瘀伤艺术，而在中国的人们去参加加州蛋糕和派公司的开业典礼？

J.B.—AI: Yes, exactly. First the show in the Imperial Palace, then other buyers came to us via coverage in publications, TV, Internet, social media. Brought in a lot of initial revenue, got a buzz going. Moriah getting us into the Imperial Palace as the venue for the Bruise Art Project Gala/Exhibition … If you had to pick a point in time, a popular culture moment, when everything changed, that would be it.

人工智能杰克逊： 没错，正是如此。先是紫禁城之秀，然后其他买家通过报刊、电视、网络、社交媒体上的报道找上门来。莫立娅想办法使我们得以在紫禁城里举办这个瘀伤艺术大秀（艺术展）……如果让你在时光中选一个节点，一个足以改变一切的流行文化瞬间，这就是那个点。

Samuel: Then came the fad, the hook, the whole bruising thing, cupping therapy turned body art. Everyone wanting to try it out, celebrities, actors.

塞缪尔： 然后潮流随之而起，那个吸引人的东西，瘀伤—从拔罐疗法改造而来的身体艺术。每个人都想试试，名流、明星等。

J.B.—AI: Yeah, it was natural. A lifestyle concept matching an edgy 'hook' as you call it. Much of pop culture already fully accepted tattoos and piercings, so no great leap to get everyone else to try it since Bruise Art is temporary, a week or so on the skin, then gone, without a trace. When we got a top Chinese celebrity to simply move their cupping bruise marks from random physical therapy to placing them in a decorative organized pattern, that was it. A billion plus Chinese were turned on to the possibility. It spread to Sil-Valley, a billionaire investor with his vacation home in San Francisco, heard about, wanted in. Photo shoot at his place with a celebrity. Easy quick step to being the newest thing in LA, Hollywood, then everywhere, all at once, once the first movie star did it, showed some Bruise Art on a red carpet. It was on ... no stopping it.

人工智能杰克逊：是啊，自然而然地。一种生活方式概念与一种前卫的"吸引人的东西"，如你所说，完美搭配。流行文化已经完全接受了文身和穿刺，所以让大家尝试一下瘀伤艺术也谈不上什么了不起的突破，因为它是暂时的，在皮肤上只停留一周左右，之后就消失得无影无踪。我们当时请一位顶级的中国名人，将原本治疗身体随机出现瘀青印迹，设计成装饰性的图案，那就成了。10亿多中国人被这个可能性点燃。然后它流行到硅谷，一个旧金山买了度假别墅的亿万富商听说了，也想加入。在他的房子里跟一个名流专门拍了写真。很快成为洛杉矶、好莱坞的新潮，然后一夜之间就遍布全球各地，有一次一个电影明星在走红毯的时候展示了身上的瘀伤艺术。顿时就火了，根本停不下来。

Samuel: But it kept going, still going. Not just the cupping art, everything J.B. Why is that?

塞缪尔：但它一直流行，仍然在流行。不仅仅是拔罐的艺术，是J.B.品牌的一切。为什么会这样？

J.B. — AI: For the bruising/cupping, we developed a quick inexpensive way for anyone to do it to themselves, the suction done by a hand pump, instead of fire in a glass bottle. I designed other shapes that could easily be made on human skin. Triangles, ovals, squares. Then a heart shape, an 'X'. Not long before we had people improvising, making intricate patterns, words, flowers, animals, everything ... a matter of experimentation, human creativity. Unlike tattooing or piercing, anyone could do it. Since it wasn't permanent, even if you messed up, it was gone in a few days. Amazing that it took so long for someone to have the idea, and then get it going. That fad fed the rest, a kind of back and forth phenomena, one element feeding the other.

人工智能杰克逊：就瘀伤或者拔罐艺术来说，我们开发了一种快速、便宜的方法，任何人都可以通过一个手泵完成吸附，而不需要用火去加热玻璃罐。我设计了多种形状，很容易印在皮肤上。三角形、椭圆形、正方形。还有心形、X形。没过多久就有人开始创造出美丽的图案、文字、花朵、动物、一切……就是尝新，人类的创意。不像文身或穿刺，这个任何人都可以做。它不是永久性的，所以即使搞砸了，过几天就没了。很神奇，这么长时间都没人想到这个点子，并且推而广之。这股潮流催生了其他潮流，它们来回反复，相互滋养。

Samuel: But you saw it, had the idea, followed through.
塞缪尔：但你看到了，产生了创意，并且去追求它。

J.B.—AI: Yes. I have the ability to see a simple thing, some essential truth, then stick with it.
人工智能杰克逊：是的。我有从简单的事物中发掘其本质的能力，并且孜孜以求。

Samuel: What came next?
塞缪尔：接下来呢？

(The AI—holo—Jackson turned, pulled one knee up, his Ferragamo-shoed foot propped up on the leather chair, casual yet energetic.)

（人工智能—全息杰克逊转身，跷起一条腿，穿着菲拉格慕鞋的脚架在皮椅上，既休闲又充满活力。）

J.B.—AI: As I said, the novel and the fad of bruise art on the human body supported each other, back and forth, so that the sales of books rebounded even stronger, long after the earlier peek, reemerging on the *New York Times* best seller list, staying on it for additional months. That, in turn added new momentum to the interest in other J.B. designs contained, all of which were contained within the novel. All that buzz got Moriah and me on TV, Jimmy Fallon. We actually did a 'Bruise-Arting', a cupping on him, live, during his show. It came out great, just a simple heart shape on his shoulder. In the world of Pop Culture, it doesn't get much better than that. After Fallon, 'Bruise Art' was a household concept, a universal brand, in both American and China, at the same time. Beautiful Moriah became its female and Asian personification, I the male and American. Magic in a bottle.

人工智能杰克逊：我说了，小说和瘀伤艺术潮流来回反复相互支持，使得小说的销量强势回弹，在第一波销售高峰过后，又重新出现在《纽约时报》的最畅销书单上，多持续了好几个月。这又给小说中涉及的其他 J.B. 设计带来了新一波关注。这些喧嚣将莫立娅和我带到了吉米·法伦秀。我们在电视节目现场展示了拔罐艺术，就在他肩膀上做了一个心形的瘀青印，效果非常棒。在流行文化世界里，没有比这更有说服力的了。吉米·法伦秀之后，瘀伤艺术就在美国和中国同时成为家喻户晓的概念，广受欢迎的品牌。美丽的莫立娅成为瘀伤艺术的女性和亚洲形象，我成为男性和美国形象的代表。魔法药水。

(The AI—Jackson smiled, knowing, him husband, lover, acknowledging the effect of his amazing wife Moriah on others, men and women alike, across the world.)

（人工智能杰克逊面露微笑，作为丈夫和爱人，他深知自己那位神奇的夫人莫立娅全世界男女通吃的魅力。）

Samuel: Then what happened?
塞缪尔：然后发生了什么？

J.B.—AI: The orders for the fashion designs began to multiply. That turned into a whole line. Moriah took over that, the business end of it all, the staging of events, shows, everywhere. First Shanghai, then Hong Kong, Singapore, London, Paris, Milan, New York, San Francisco. By the time the J.B. brand rolled into Los Angeles we were in hyper-demand.

人工智能杰克逊：时尚设计方面的订单开始多了起来，形成了完整的产品线。莫立娅掌管这一块的商业运作，各地活动、秀场的组织安排。先是在中国上海、中国香港进行，然后再到新加坡，英国伦敦，法国巴黎，意大利米兰，美国纽约、旧金山。J.B.品牌进入洛杉矶的时候我们已经供不应求了。

Samuel: How did you break into additional areas, the other products and designs now associated with J.B. and Bruise Art?
塞缪尔：你是怎么拓展其他领域的，其他那些J.B.和瘀伤艺术关联的产品和设计？

J.B.—AI: Natural, organic. The demand was there, and I had a back log of products, designs already done, ready to market, to sell, all connected to various elements in the novel. It was a reservoir of my own creativity, a bank account from which to make withdrawals as needed. The same people interested in the novel, the fashion, wanted to invest in other J.B. brand designs. Jewelry, the body neckless Moriah wore at the Beijing Exhibition, watch designs created with the soft stone from Yunnan Province, the furniture line based on the rocking chair from the *Dreams of My Mother* short story, the home design from the *Porch House* in the writing about New Orleans. All of it took off, a built-in demand for more, always more. We had to hire a lot of people very quickly to even keep up. Sales of the novel, sales of everything else fed off each other … anything 'Jackson Bartholomew'.

人工智能杰克逊：自然生长的。需求就在那儿，我已经做好了产品、设计的储备，随时准备投向市场销售，一切都与小说中的元素相关。那就是我创造力的储蓄池，像银行账户一样，需要的时候随时取出来。被小说、时尚吸引的同一群人也想在其他J.B.品牌设计上投资。珠宝、莫立娅在北京展览上佩戴的项链，用采自云南的软玉设计的手表，基于《我母亲的梦》短篇小说里的摇椅设计的家具，关于新奥尔良的小说《回廊屋》所呈现的建筑设计，这一切都火起来了，带着设置好的需求，让人们买了又买。我们不得不快速雇用大量人手来保证产量。小说的畅销、其他一切产品的畅销相互促进……"杰克逊·巴塞洛缪"的一切。

Samuel: You've been called a 'master of social media', popular culture marketing, websites, Twitter, Instagram, WeChat, WhatsApp, TikTok, 'going viral', the J.B.app, all of it. How did you get there, gain that set of expertise?

塞缪尔：你被称为"社交媒体大师"，流行文化营销、网站、推特、Instagram、微信、WhatsApp、TikTok、"火爆全网"，J.B.应用，所有一切。你是怎么做到的，把这一套整合到一起？

J.B.—AI: I'm in the age of popculture, social media, hip hop. You must go with your epoch, ethos, using the most relevant means of communication available. I educated myself. Normal publishing, the system of agents, waiting to hear back ... not for me. I didn't have the time for 'gentle rollouts'. You play to your strengths. I had China, and a unique American view with a lot of Asian content. That path gave me immediate access, with social media as an accelerant.

人工智能杰克逊：我身处流行文化、社交媒体、嘻哈的时代。你必须跟随时代潮流和精神，运用当下最有效的传播手段。我努力学习。传统的出版业、代理商体系、坐等反馈……那一套不适合我。我没时间去做"润物细无声"的事。你得把自己的优势用足。我有中国，还有一个独特的、综合了大量亚洲背景的美国视角。这给了我一条快速直达通道，社交媒体是加速器。

J.B.—AI: First, we used the TikTok app to get the word out, East and

West ... then my own, the Bruise Art app really took off, moved us to the next level. Anyone, anywhere in the world, could experience the novel, at least a select part of it, in an intimate interactive way. Through the Bruise Art app a reader, fans, could go to the locations described in each chapter, scene ... Sil-Val, Los Angeles, Florence, New Orleans, Beijing ... track the story for themselves, experience it. We included tasks, missions, that if done correctly, would earn them points, to purchase J.B. products. We set it up so you could even act, become one of the actors in an imaginary film based on the novel. You could be Samuel, Jasmine, Angelina, Jackson, Moriah, Chief Millford, the Injector guy, any of them. The exhibition series, Beijing, Santa Cruz, Florence. Each produced a stream of VIP's, media interviews, full coverage. Like I said, 'dominoes', each one building on the momentum and power of the last.

人工智能杰克逊： 第一步，我们利用 TikTok 在东方和西方把内容传递出去，然后我自己开发的瘀伤艺术应用也起步了，将我们带上一个台阶。任何人在世界上任何一个角落都可以通过一种亲密互动的方式体验这部小说，至少是其中的精选部分。通过这款应用，读者、粉丝可以去到章节中描述的地点和场景，硅谷、洛杉矶、佛罗伦萨、新奥尔良、北京……亲身体会故事。我们为读者设置了大大小小的任务，如果完成正确，他们可以得到积分，用来购买 J.B. 产品。我们还设置了角色扮演，你可以选择在小说改编的电影里扮演一个角色。你可以演塞缪尔、茉莉、安吉丽娜、杰克逊、莫立娅、米尔福德警长，打针的那家伙，任何一个人。展览系列，北京、圣克鲁斯、佛罗伦萨。每个场景都有 VIP，媒体的全方位报道。如我所说，"多米诺骨牌"，每一块骨牌都建立在上一块的势能和动能上。

Samuel: What else is there for you? You've done everything.
塞缪尔： 你还有什么未了的事业吗？你什么都做了。

J.B.—AI: Not quite. A film, and the streaming service series. The whole Netflix thing. And something else ... I want to change the entire culture, American culture, in a big way, at its core.
人工智能杰克逊： 并未做完。还有一部电影，及其系列播映服务。奈飞那一套。还有……我想改变整个美国文化，来个大翻修，从根儿上开始。

Samuel: Wow ... from you, I guess that's possible. A hint of what it is?
塞缪尔： 哇哦……从你这儿来的想法，我猜还是靠谱的。可以给点提示吗？

(J.B. looked away then back across to me ... rye, amused, benevolent.)
(J.B. 目光转向别处，又转回来看着我……高贵，自嘲，仁慈。)

(Jackson looked away, eyes rolling, impatient, taking a drink from a cup on the table, tour de force tipping point. It had to be him. Was him ... Jackson Bartholomew, in the flesh. Not possible otherwise. An odd panic coming up again, me 'triggered' somehow. Perhaps the sudden thought that it might just all be a hoax, for the ultimate goal—'going viral'.)

(杰克逊视线移开，不耐烦地翻了个白眼，从桌上拿起杯子喝了一口，这是决定性的一刻。这必须是他。就是他……有血有肉的杰克逊·巴塞洛缪。没有别的可能。我又产生了一种古怪的恐慌情绪，不知道被什么触发了。也许是突然想到，这也可能是一个骗局，也是为了那个终极目标服务——"全网火爆"。)

J.B.—AI: It all ties in so perfectly. Do you see what I mean ... to what's happening now? Our American time, this generation, we are the first in American history in which the popular culture dominates the religious structure. At its core, the novel deals with that. Or at least I meant to do it. It's a monumental shift going under noticed, if not unnoticed. The new power of mass media, social media, feeds it all, enablers.

人工智能杰克逊：一切关联得如此完美。你明白我的意思吧……关于当下发生的一切？我们这一代人，亲历了美国历史上首次流行文化占领了由宗教塑造的社会结构。小说的内核是探讨这个问题的。至少我本意如此。这个问题是一个里程碑式的转变，但它如果不是被忽视的话，得到的关注也远远不够。大众传媒、社交媒体的新生势力助长了这一切。

(Jackson had turned lecturer. Odd to the ear. He'd detached from me, the interview setting occasion, him someone else now, another version, personification.)
(杰克逊变成了教师爷。听起来很怪。他已经脱离了与我的访谈，变成另外一个版本的人。)

J.B.—AI: Up until our time, America has been primarily Christian, generally religious. It's that base upon which most aspects of our national life have set for all these years, for good or bad. That's no longer the case. Think what that means, what's now no longer certain, what has been shaken, put into question. Everything is up for grabs. International over national, mosaic over melting pot, quick culture over long tradition, leaders elected based on 'pop' values, fame over substance.

人工智能杰克逊：直到我们这个时代，美国一直是个以基督教为主的国家，普遍信教。多年来，我们国家生活的诸多方面都建立在这个基础上，无论好坏。俱往矣。想想这意味着什么，当下什么东西不再笃定，什么已经动摇，什么正被质疑。一切东西都是拿了就走。国际性高于国家性，拼图替代了熔炉，快餐文化取代了长期传统，领导人当选是基于"流行"价值观，名声压倒了实质。

Samuel: Not sure what you're getting at. How can your writing change that, I mean, really ... you're not God you know?

塞缪尔：我不确定你想表达什么。你的小说如何能够改变那些，说真的…… 你不是上帝，你知道吧？

(Blurted out ... Tourette again.)
（脱口而出……图雷特又犯了。）

J.B.—AI: God. Do you believe in 'God'?
人工智能杰克逊：上帝。你相信"上帝"吗？

(J.B. braced ... then laughed, full on, loud, hardy.)
（杰克逊绷紧了……然后开怀大笑，声音洪亮。）

J.B.—AI: Clever boy. Maybe you're right. I could just leave it to God, or gods, or the universe, or whatever force is out there, no matter it's maddening randomness.

人工智能杰克逊：聪明的小伙子。也许你是对的。我也可以把它交给上帝，或者神祇，或者宇宙，不管天外存在着什么样的力量，哪怕那只是令人发狂的随机性。

Samuel: Agnostic?
塞缪尔：不可知论者？

J.B.—AI: I never liked that word. I prefer 'hopeful'. Spent a lot of time as a boy, a young man, studying God, religion. Greek Orthodox, Southern Baptist, Jehovah's Witnesses, the Catholic Church, Buddhism, Islam. Too much effort and time spent to just give up, say I'm 'agnostic'. What an ugly word, the sound of it ... like combining eggnog with being sick. Anyhow, I prefer to take on the role of the jilted lover, better fit for me to be outraged than 'ambivalent to the benevolent'. I've written on it ... *Liva's Lamentations*. I recommend it to you.

人工智能杰克逊：我从来不喜欢这个词。我更喜欢用"充满希望"。我从孩提时期到青年时代就在研究上帝和宗教。希腊东正教，南方浸信会，耶和华见证人，天主教会，佛教，伊斯兰教。我花了这么多的时间和精力，最后竟放弃，说我是"不可知论者"。多么丑陋的一个词啊，真难听。就好比将蛋奶酒与生病联系起来。不管怎样，我更愿意充当被抛弃的恋人，激愤更适合我，而不是"模棱两可的慈悲"。我写过这个，《利瓦的悲伤》。我推荐你读。

Samuel: That short story, *Liva's Lamentations*, An odd part, short, seemingly out of place, sequence. But it's become well known, has a following, the way it's written from the perspective of God, or a god perhaps, the beautiful illustrations, the *Leaves on the Water*.

塞缪尔：那个短篇，《利瓦悲伤》，是个奇怪的作品，很短，似乎格格不入，不属于任何流派。但它出名了，有了拥趸，它是从上帝视角，或者说以一个天神的视角来写的，插图很美，比如《水上的落叶》。

(He'd settled down again, me as well, both enjoying the thought in our minds, the drawings and watercolors that faded in on the hovering screens adding to the feeling ... pastels, tranquil, sweet, a bit sad.)

（他平静下来，我也一样。我们各自沉浸在自己的思绪里，背景屏幕上渐变的素描和水彩增添了氛围感，颜色淡雅、静谧、甜美，有点伤感。）

J.B. — AI: I debated whether to illustrate the novel with photography, mine or anyone else's. Photos are generally too real, too direct. Sketch, watercolor effects on my own photography is just right. Strikes a balance between reality and fiction, the real and the imagined, 'dreams and half-dreams.' I suppose you've heard that phrase before.

人工智能杰克逊：我纠结过是否要用我或别人的照片来给小说配图。一般来说照片太过写实、太过直白。我拍的照片经过素描和水彩化处理的感觉才对。在现实与虚构、

Monastery at Hoisos Loukas—Near Distomon, Greece—Ancestral Home of J.B.
希腊迪斯托莫附近荷伊索斯洛卡斯的修道院——J.B. 先祖之地

真实之物与想象之物、"梦与半梦"之间找到平衡。我猜你之前听过这个说法。

Samuel: Yes, for sure.

塞缪尔: 是的,当然。

J.B.—AI: That place, the 'between space' what exists in areas of transition, it's an excellent zone for creativity. Being with Moriah in Beijing helped me discover that.

人工智能杰克逊: 那个空间,那个"两头不靠"的空间,过渡的区域,是激发创意的绝佳地带。我与莫立娅在北京居住的时候发现了这一点。

Samuel: Ah, that seems a key to it all. I want to ask about that, the living in Beijing with Moriah. You said you wrote most of the book in Beijing, at Moriah's place. The why of it, the aspect of sanctuary. How did that place effect the final product? Make itself known, manifest. It had to, in a lot of ways.

塞缪尔: 啊!那似乎就是一切的关键。我想多了解一些你在北京与莫立娅共处的情况。你说你大部分书是在莫立娅北京的居所写的。为什么这里能作为庇护所?那个地方是如何影响你的最终出品的?自我宣传、宣示。必须如此,从各方面说。

J.B.—AI: Yes. To be with Moriah meant Beijing, and Beijing means Moriah. That short-story-come-poem of mine is another bit of writing to add to your recommended reading list. Through her I experienced the city, and in its best light. It became the way to get away, an oasis, a place of calm, safety, stability; 'far away from the madding crowds' of Sil-Val, the Cupertinos, Mountain Views, San Joses. I could relax there, be tranquil, think, write. From the 25th floor of our condo, Beijing spread out before me, majestic views of the Central Business District on the south side, Chaoyang Park on the other. Magical. There's no safer big city in the world. It removed many of my worries, and all my temptations.

人工智能杰克逊: 是的。与莫立娅在一起就意味着北京,而北京就等同于莫立娅。我那篇故事诗要加到你的推荐书单里。通过她,我得以体验这座城市最好的一面。它成为我的遁世绿洲,一个平静、安全、稳定的地方,"远离尘嚣",远离硅谷,库柏蒂诺,山景城,圣何塞。我在那里可以放松沉静下来,思考、写作。从我们25层的公寓房间看出去,北京展现在我眼前,南边是中央商务中心区宏伟的景象,北边是朝阳公园。太神奇了。全世界没有比这更安全的大都市了。它赶走了我多数的焦虑，以及我所有的诱惑。

Samuel: You had the opportunity to compare Chinese and American cultures. More than most, given you're married to a Chinese national, and split your time between Beijing and Sil-Valley, What are the main differences, similarities?

塞缪尔：你有机会比较中美文化。与多数人不同，你与一位中国公民结了婚，在北京和硅谷轮流居住之前。两者之间主要的异同是什么？

J.B.—AI: Beijing is my city. So is Sil-Valley. They're counterpoints to the same time, existence, world culture. Amazing how little Americans know about China. Chinese know much more about us. Wealthy Chinese families sacrifice a lot to send their children to U.S. universities. A hundred years ago it was England, Cambridge. Now it's America, Harvard, Stanford. Americans would be socialists. Who would have thought, right? Sil-Val is a very dangerous place, physically. No such danger anywhere in Beijing, even at midnight. Those are a few distinctions that come to mind. Read my poem to Moriah, about her city, *The City of Moriah*.

人工智能杰克逊：北京是我的城市。硅谷也是。它们同为世界文化的存在，又互为对比。美国人对中国的了解浅薄得令人吃惊。中国人对我们的了解要多得多。中国的有钱家庭为把孩子送到美国上大学牺牲很多。一百年前他们的目的地是英国剑桥。如今是美国哈佛、斯坦福。就人身安全而言，在北京会比美国安全，即便是半夜三更。这些是我目前想到的一些不同之处。读读我写给莫立娅的诗，关于她的城市，《莫立娅之城》。

Samuel: In *Bruise Art* you write extensively about Europe, particularly about Florence, Italy. Most of it through the eyes of a Florentine woman. You also write about a woman in Lugano, Switzerland. Then there's the Russian woman in New Orleans, the black woman running for the Senate in Mississippi. Why those characters, especially the non-Americans, as parts of your take on writing the 'Great American Novel'?

塞缪尔：在《瘀伤艺术》里，你用了很大篇幅写欧洲，特别是意大利佛罗伦萨。大部分是用一个佛罗伦萨女人的视角叙述的。你还写了一个在瑞士卢加诺的女人。然后还有新奥尔良的俄罗斯女人，竞选密西西比州议员的黑人女性。作为一部"伟大的美国小说",你为什么要写这么多非美裔的角色?

J.B.—AI: Don't neglect the memoir part of the novel/memoir. My own life compelled me to include those sections. Anyway, America is international, a nation of immigrants. More now than ever before. It makes sense that even the 'Great American Novel' genre includes those references.

人工智能杰克逊:不要忘了这部小说的回忆录属性。我的人生促使我把那些经历写下来。再说美国是国际性的移民国家。当下比以往任何时期都明显。"伟大的美国小说"包含这些内容也是合理的。

Samuel: One of my favorite parts of the novel is the section, Dreams of My Mother; A great variety of stories, riveting. Auto-biographical I'm assuming, a personal feel to it all.

塞缪尔:小说中我最喜欢的部分是"我母亲的梦",其中有各种各样的故事,非常吸引人。我猜是自传性质,有很浓厚的个人色彩。

J.B.—AI: Yes. Indeed, one of the most autobiographical parts of the writing. It was closely based on actual dreams I had of my mother after her death. She appeared to me, talked to me, often. I was always left with the sensation that she was still alive, that it had all been a misunderstanding. There was still more time, more life. Unfortunately, that never turned out to be true. However, I felt it an obligation to record, as best as could, give proper honor, to her stories, and the things she wanted to say, to have remembered.

人工智能杰克逊:是的,没错,这是小说中自传色彩最浓的部分。确实是基于我在母亲去世后做过的关于她的梦。她经常出现在我梦里,与我交谈。我总感觉她还活着,她去世这事儿一定是搞错了。她还有更多时间,有更长的生命。不幸的是,梦境没有成真。但是,我觉得自己有责任尽可能完整地记录下来,好好缅怀她的人生,她想说的话,她希望被记住的东西。

Samuel: I love her story about the return of the Civil War soldier after years away, finding his wife pregnant. Then there's the part about the murder of your brother's wife, by your brother.

塞缪尔:我喜欢她那个故事,内战结束后,士兵回到阔别多年的家乡,发现他的妻子怀孕了。还有那个你兄弟杀妻的故事。

J.B.—AI: I am with you. Fascinating, what she chose to say, reveal. Yeah, the murder, why not?

人工智能杰克逊：我跟你一样。她选择向我吐露的东西非常吸引人。是啊，谋杀案，有什么不能说的？

Samuel: You see it that way then. You're that certain, her returned to you, to talk? And that was how it all happened, including the murder?

塞缪尔：原来你是这么看待这件事的。你就这么确定，她是回来跟你交谈的？事情就是这么发生的，包括谋杀？

(Jackson twitched nervously, shifting his legs, as though preparing to get up, to walk off. Unexpected, abrupt, him trying to ghost me. Left me anxious, breathless, searching for questions to hold his attention.)

（杰克逊不安地扭动身体，换腿，好像准备起身离开。猝不及防，他想回避我。这使我呼吸停滞，焦虑地搜刮问题来吸引他的注意力。）

J.B.—AI: We're going to have to wrap this up soon. I have some other things to do, as you might imagine.

人工智能杰克逊：我们得快点结束了。我还有其他事情要做，你应该明白。

Samuel: Well, ahh ... just a few more. They told me there'd be more time. Things that your readers are asking about, want to know.

塞缪尔：啊，还有几个问题。他们说时间很充裕的。你的读者想问的问题，想了解的情况。

J.B.—AI: They? Go on then. Get clever quick. Otherwise, we'll have to 'end the pain'.

人工智能杰克逊：他们？那就继续吧。机灵点，要快。否则，我们就得"结束痛苦"。

Samuel: What about all the 'telescoping'? And then, you concept of 'magic' as it applies to your novel/memoir? You actually think that you create 'magic'?

塞缪尔：聊聊"叠境"吧？还有你关于"魔力"的概念，你真的认为小说兼回忆录创造了"魔力"？

(I let the full sarcasm of the question flow out, hoping it'd pass his measure of 'clever'.)

（我毫不掩饰问题中的讽刺味道，希望这符合他的"机灵"标准。）

J.B.—AI: 'Telescoping', nesting of one world within another ... it's a useful technique to show multiple angles at the same time. Cubist in a way. It intertwines multiple aspects of a single protagonist, as in a person's ego and his aspirational alter ego within the same scene of the same story, those elements of one thing bouncing around, overlapping, bumping into each other, within the parameters of a given novel/memoir. Adds a great deal of interest and illumination.

人工智能杰克逊： "叠境"，一个世界里套着另一个……这是多个视角呈现同一时空的有效手法。从某种程度上也可以说是立体派。在一部小说兼回忆录设置好的参数中，单一主人公的多个视角相互交织，同一事件同一场景中，一个人的自我和他想象中的第二自我同时出现，诸多元素弹跃、重叠、碰撞。增添了许多乐趣和火花。

J.B.—AI: 'Magic'? No mystery. Every great piece of fiction writing must have an element of 'magic'. The prose must succeed in exposing the inner core element of what it means to be human, to feel; Otherwise, why bother. Think of a Chinese landscape painting, how it searches for the essence, then leaves the rest for the connecting imagination of the observer. That is the magic I seek, and sometimes find. I try to do many things at the same time, the same point in the telling of a story. Yes, my writing has magic. My god, just the viewing of one of the many illustrations is magic enough to justify the paying for admission to the show the whole production puts on. If someone don't see it that's on them. Magic? Damn right. Anything else?

人工智能杰克逊： "魔力"？没什么神秘之处。每一部伟大虚构类作品都必备一项"魔力"元素。文字必须能够发掘和觉知人性的本质内核，否则一无是处。想象一幅中国山水画，它是如何探寻本质，同时留出给观者联想的空白。那就是我所寻找的魔法，有时候能找到。我总想一心多用，讲故事时也不例外。是的，我的写作有魔力。上帝啊，光是观看诸多插图中的一幅就极富魔力，值得人们掏钱买票看我的作品秀。如果有人看不出来，那是他们的问题。魔力？太对了。还有什么问题？

Scene Fourteen   Renaissance Man, Rebirth, Reincarnation
第十四幕 文艺复兴人、重生、轮回

Samuel: Well ... okay then. That answers that one. You consider yourself a 'Polymath', a modern—day example of a 'Renaissance man'? Really?

塞缪尔：呃，那好吧。这回答了那个问题。你自称为一名"博学家"，是当今时代"文艺复兴人"的典范。果真如此吗？

(I kept pressing the rude angle, afraid he'd cut short, him so much the 'shapeshifter', taking on aspects of the mercurial artist ... irritable, unpredictable. I knew I'd never have this level of access again. Felt the tension rise, 'fight or flight'. He knew, sensed it, my weakness, watched me, analyzing, seeking to push me, make me nervous.)

（我不停试探大胆的角度，生怕他突然中断，这个动辄翻脸的人，展现出艺术家变幻莫测的各个方面，易怒难测。我知道这样的机会不会再有了。我感受到紧张气氛在上升，这是"战斗或者逃跑"的决定。他也知道，也感受得到我的弱点，他在观察我、分析我，试图将我逼向墙角，让我紧张。）

J.B.—AI: Try doing a search on the words 'modern Renaissance man'. One list that comes up has Brad Pitt, Ryan Gosling, Justin Timberlake, and Pharrell Williams. Now that's funny. I wasn't on it. The list had no mention of scientists, leaders of nations, painters, sculptors. Makes sense only if you use a popular culture lens in definition of 'Renaissance man', or maybe just add the word 'shallow'. Two years studying architecture in Florence, and you gain an admiration, an aspiration to become reborn, a polymath, a 'Renaissance man'.

人工智能杰克逊：试着搜索一下"现代文艺复兴人"这个词。其中有一个名单包括布拉德·皮特，瑞安·戈斯林，贾斯廷·廷伯莱克，法罗·威廉姆斯。这很搞笑。我不在名单里。这个名单里没有科学家、国家领导人、画家、雕塑家。如果用流行文化视角来解读"文艺复兴人"这个概念，或者添上"浅薄"这个词，那就说得通了。在佛罗伦萨花两年时间研究建筑，你就向往、期望得到重生，成为博学家，一个"文艺复兴人"。

(The figure fidgeted, propped himself up, on his elbows, hands to face, an aspect of praying, anxious, departure minded. What subject to keep him online, tethered down ... something, quick.)

（影像不安地扭动，直起上身，支肘托腮，就像祈祷一样，焦虑，思绪远离。什么话题能让他保持在线，拴住他……快点想。）

J.B.—AI—Interview with Samuel—Geodesic Dome—J.B. Estate, Santa Cruz, California
人工智能杰克逊与塞缪尔的访谈——网格球形穹顶，加州圣克鲁斯J.B.宅邸

Samuel: Sex. SEX.
塞缪尔：性。性爱。

J.B. — AI: Say what??
人工智能杰克逊：你说什么？？

Samuel: There were, are, rumors, about, well ... sexuality, your health, certain 'pleasuring activities'. Are the rumors true?
塞缪尔：曾经有一些流言，现在也还有，呃，是关于性爱，你的健康状况，某种"享乐活动"。这些是真的吗？

J.B.—AI: Come on now. Some things are better left rumors. In fact, rumors have a bad reputation. They can serve a purpose, that of protection ... a fog, holding back the harshness of the too clear details of truth. Rumors are a mainstay of popular culture, on what fans feed. With that in mind I will leave rumors some space, to live, to grow, except to say that in my case, most of them are true. 'Pleasuring activities'? Oh my god...

人工智能杰克逊： 得了吧。有些东西最好就当流言听。实际上，流言的名声很不好。它们可以为一个目标服务，就是保护……是一层遮挡严酷真相的迷雾。流言可为流行文化的中流砥柱，粉丝们就靠这个养活。所以，我会给谣言留些生存和生长的空间。但就我个人的情况而言，大多数的流言都是真的。"享乐活动"？我的上帝……

(Jackson laughed, pleased with himself, teasing, mischievous. A good question after all, him, it, less tense, relaxed. But how a AI—hologram could react that way, so human, a perfectly programmed simulation of what Jackson would have done, if he, in the real, were present. Okay, nothing direct about sex, etc., but still, an excellent subject change to keep a AI—hologram programmed to react like 'Jackson the real' from 'canceling' me.)

(杰克逊得意地大笑起来，充满取乐和调侃。到底是个好问题，他，或者它，放松下来，不那么紧张了。但一个人工智能全息影像怎么能够做出这样充满人性的反应，完美模拟了真人在场的情形。没错，没有直接谈论性这类话题，但是，一个由代码编程的人工智能全息影像在面对话题转换的时候，反应就像"真杰克逊"一样，没有把我"取消"掉。)

Samuel: Let me ask this, if I may ... The famous photo/sketch of the two people engaged in standing sex; The one with the female off the ground, her legs rapped around the male. Who were the two people in the photo/sketch, you and Moriah, or others, models? The marks on the two naked figures, heart shapes, circles, squares, were those added to the photo as an effect, or actual tattoos?

塞缪尔： 我想问这个问题，如果可以的话……那张两个人站立亲密的照片/素描。女人离地，双腿环绕在男人身上。图片中的这两个人是谁，是你和莫立娅，还是别人，模特？这两个人裸露的身体上有着心形、圆形、方形的印迹，那是后期加上的效果，还是真实的文身？

J.B.—AI: As with the rumors answer, it's my policy to leave room for speculation. It's clear that I invited that kind of speculation, but no need to take away all the fun by saying too much. As for the marks, they weren't tattoos, just early examples of 'bruise art', using the cupping techniques, the Chinese traditional medicine thing. Those were from the original glass globes I had made in San Jose, different shapes at the openings. Heat the air inside, press on the skin, suction, fifteen minutes, marks that last a few days; Temporary tattoos with curative powers.

人工智能杰克逊：就像流言的回答一样，我的回应还是留出猜测的空间。我故意招来这种猜测，没必要解释太多，这样乐趣就没了。至于那些印迹，它们不是文身，是"瘀伤艺术"的早期试验，用中国的传统拔罐手法做的。那些是我在圣何塞做的原创玻璃罐，各种形状的。将罐内的空气加热，压在皮肤上形成吸附，保持15分钟就成了。印迹能保持几天，具有疗愈效果的临时文身。

(Behind the hologram came into slow erotic focus the photo-sketch of the two of them ... iconic, assumed to be Jackson holding Moriah. Faces not clear, but just had to be them. Her off the ground, ecstatic, the two figures in full coupling, that image now synonymous with the 'Moriah' brand, it well established as a mainstay within of the 'House of Bartholomew'. I'd seen the specific graphic before, many times, on Havanna's things for example. But there, in that geo space, it took on more force, hypnotic, difficult to pull away from, the famous couple intertwined, nude, him standing, leaning back, muscular ... her, half his size, clinging, legs bracing. Perfect angle, showing everything and nothing; Man and woman in sensual struggle. From her arm positions, perhaps reference to *Rape of the Sabine* at the Academia in Florence. I had visited it often as a student. No doubt, so had Jackson Bartholomew, another common experience bringing him and I together.)

（全息影像身后的屏幕渐渐显现他们两人那张著名的色情照片素描，据猜测是杰克逊抱着莫立娅。面部特征不清楚，但肯定是他们。她身体离地，身段灵活，两个人体完全交合，这个形象现在等同于"莫立娅"的个人品牌，成为"巴塞洛缪"品牌家族的支柱。我之前多次看到过这个图案，比如说在哈瓦娜的物品上。但在这个穹顶内，它的冲击力更强，令人目眩神迷，难以移开视线。这著名的一对夫妇缠绵在一起，赤身裸体，他站立着，上身后仰，肌肉发达，而她，体积只有他的一半，双腿交缠，抱紧他。完美的角度，表达

Rape of the Sabine（Adaptation in Watercolor）
《劫夺萨宾妇女》（水彩处理）

了一切，又什么都没表现，男人和女人处在肉欲的挣扎中。从她胳膊的姿势看，可能是参照了佛罗伦萨美术学院的《劫夺萨宾妇女》。我求学时期经常去。毫无疑问，杰克逊·巴塞洛缪也经常去。这是将我们两人拉近的共同经历。）

Samuel: Aside from their identity, were the two staged, or, how to say it delicately, were they 'in full erotic engagement'?

塞缪尔：不谈这两个人物的身份，他们是在表演，还是怎么说得委婉一点，"进行亲密举动"的状态？

J.B.—AI: 'In full erotic engagement'? Not bad. Never heard it described that way. Bravo, young Samuel. At the moment of the photo, the two were indeed so. It took some practice, preparation, the exact angle, lighting, the achieving of the mood; Not so easy, the capturing in photo of standing love making. Especially so if done as self-portrait.

人工智能杰克逊："进行亲密举动"？不错嘛。从来没听过这种表达方式。精彩，年轻人塞缪尔。拍照的瞬间，这两个人的确是这么回事。需要做些练习和准备，找到准确的角度、灯光，还要进入情绪。没那么容易，用镜头捕捉站立式性爱。对于自拍来说尤其如此。

Samuel: I'll take that as a yes. This all brings to mind the line between fact and fiction, novel and memoir. Let me just ask it, how much of the novel is pure fiction, how much autobiography? Percentage wise. Did you try to balance it in some way, a proportion in mind for that aspect of your writing?

塞缪尔：我理解那就是确认了。令我想起事实与虚构、小说与回忆录之间的界限。我来问问，小说中有多少内容是纯属虚构，有多少是自传？说个比例。你是否在某种程度上找平衡，脑子里设定了一个比例？

J.B. — AI: Hemmingway went to Cuba, saw an old man coming in from the sea, noted the fisherman's small boat, that he'd caught a giant fish. Ernest went on to write the *Old Man and the Sea*. I enjoy and celebrate the interplay between fiction and life experiences. It's the essence of a great novel. I took it a lot further, the mixing in of my memoirs. That's not the same as autobiography. The best I can do for anyone hungering to know more about what is novel and what are memoirs is to refer them to the 'Truth Sections' at the end of each part of *Bruise Art*. Enough to let a reader inside my thinking, my real life. A lot more than most writers, but not too much to give it all away for free or ruin the creative tension.

人工智能杰克逊：海明威在古巴看到一位老人从海上归来，注意到渔夫驾着一艘小船，却打到一条巨大的鱼。欧内斯特于是写出了《老人与海》。我享受并且赞美虚构事件与生活经历之间的联系。那是一部伟大小说的精华。我走得更远，把自己的回忆混杂其中。那跟自传不一样。我能为那些渴望了解哪些是小说哪些是回忆的读者做的，就是在《瘀伤艺术》每一章节的结尾开辟了"事实部分"供他们参考。让一个读者进入我的思想、我的真实生活就够了。我做的已经比绝大多数作家都多了，但还不至于全部免费发放，毁了我刻意创造的张力。

Samuel: 'Dreams and half-dreams', the descriptions of those. That's another way you let us in, right? But again, without telling us everything, making us wonder where the line is. How did your fascination with that subject start, develop, dreams I mean?

塞缪尔："半梦半醒"，可以概括以上。那是你让我们进入的另一种方式，对吗？但你还是没有把一切告诉我们，让我们猜界限到底在哪。你对这个话题的执迷是怎么开始和发展的？我是指那些梦。

J.B.—AI: It comes from a hope, a wishful-wistful view of life, that perhaps there is something beyond, 'on the other side', things poetic, mystical, spiritual. Dreams are a path to that destination, a 'glimpse through the veil'. I dream a lot, always have. I trained myself to remember them, use them in my writing. Many parts of the novel have a genesis there, coming forth mostly in my dreams; particularly half-dreams, while waking up or falling asleep. Unusual ideas, hidden possibilities come to me 'in the grey', in the 'in between zone' of the two states of consciousness.

人工智能杰克逊：它来自一个希望，是对人生抱持的一种一厢情愿的看法，即生命"那一边"可能有些什么诗意的、神秘的、灵性的东西。梦境是通向那个目的地的途径，"透过面纱窥见"。我经常做梦。我训练自己把梦记住，把它们用在自己的写作中。小说中大部分都来源于我的梦，尤其是我在醒来或睡着过程中，半梦半醒状态下产生的梦。非同寻常的想法，隐藏的可能性，会在这两种意识之间的"灰色区域"向我显现。

J.B.—AI: As we discussed, the section involving my mother's visits is based on that, my own experience of receiving a series of dreams involving her. She died of cancer at seventy. Horrible way to go, cancer. It took a few years, then they began. All of them vivid, like mini documentaries. Amazing how each episode left me with that brief belief, certainty, that she was still alive, that her death had been a mistake, a misunderstanding. She looked the same in each, appearing younger, fortyish, weak, but fully ambulatory. The dream-series lasted about ten years, after her death. None of the other of her six children had any dreams that related to her. I asked them. My dreams of her ended when I finished writing *Bruise Art*.

人工智能杰克逊： 我们之前聊过，关于我母亲梦中来访那部分，就是基于我关于她的一连串梦的真实经历。她70岁的时候因癌症去世。癌症是一种可怕的死法。她去世几年后，梦境开始了。那些梦就像小型纪录片一样活灵活现。真神奇，每一集都令我短暂地确信她还活着，她的死是搞错了，是一个误解。她在每个梦里都一样，比活着的时候年轻，大概40岁，虚弱，但可以走动。这个梦的系列在她去世之后持续了十年左右。她的六个孩子当中，没有其他任何一个做过与她有关的梦。我问过。关于她的梦，在我写完《瘀伤艺术》之后，也结束了。

(A series of old photos flowed, faded, reappeared behind Jackson; His mother I assumed, her alone, then with others, children, standing, smiling, strong, charismatic.)

（在杰克逊身后的墙上，一组老照片反复出现又淡去。我猜那就是他母亲，有单人的，有与他人的合影，跟孩子们在一起的，站着、微笑、坚强、魅力四射。）

So, what am I to take from that? Ten years of vivid dreams of visits from my mother, each session leaving me feeling she was alive, just over there, in the next room. What would you understand from such an experience? Are 'dreams and half-dreams' a portal to something else, another existence, a way in which we're allowed, by some larger force, to communicate ... even if that communication is somewhat restricted? The answer is ... I don't know. If I make it to the other side, and the 'greater forces' permit it, I'll let everyone know then. Look for me.

所以，我要从中悟到什么？十年，母亲在我梦里出现，栩栩如生，每一次都让我觉得她还活着，就在隔壁房间。你从这样的经历中能悟到什么？"梦境和半梦境"是不是去往另一种生境的传送门？在这条通道里，我们得到某种更广大的力量的允许进行沟通,即使这种沟通是受限制的?答案是……我不知道。如果我终于得以进入另一边,那个"更大的力量"允许的话,我要让每个人都知道。等着我。

(Jackson's expression registered annoyance. I took it to be not directed at me, but further outward, to God, the gods, universal forces, whatever it was that held sway over him, us, yet held back their own identities, mysteries, magics, natures. I shared that with him, a concurrence of feeling of disquiet turning toward outrage.)

(杰克逊的表情显得恼火。我认为这不是针对我的,而是对着更高更远的,上帝,神祇,宇宙原力,不管那是什么,控制着他,我们,但是把他们的身份隐藏起来,神秘,魔法,自然。我在这点上跟他一样,情绪从不安分转变为愤怒。)

Samuel: It is said that you have what is called 'nerve end connectivity'. Sometimes you can touch one spot on your body and cause a nerve sensation at another spot? Something about the 'Vagus Nerve'.

塞缪尔:据说你拥有"神经终端连接"的能力。触碰身体的某个点,另一个点会感受到神经反应?某种与"迷走神经"有关的东西。

J.B.—AI: Yeah. Doesn't everyone experience that? Perhaps we all do, but most don't know it. We're all electronic creatures, the brain, nervous system. Because of that I believe it's possible for the human body to transmit, receive electronic impulses, one human body to another, across distances. Reports of identical twins knowing instantly when one or the other experiences some trauma. A mother in World War II knowing when their son died in the South Pacific. These are facts, documented cases. That phenomenon relates to the possibility of reincarnation, partial or otherwise. It seems to me that a certain level of connectivity is required for all that to work, be possible.

人工智能杰克逊:对。难道不是所有人都有这种经历吗?可能我们都有,只是多数人没有觉知。我们都是电子生物体,大脑、神经系统。因此我相信人体是有可能传递和接受电子脉冲的,一个人的身体可以隔空传送给另一个。我们听说过,同卵双胞胎其中一位经历某种痛苦的时候,另一个也能同时感受到。第二次世界大战期间,有位母亲知晓自己儿子在南太平洋阵亡的时刻。这些都是记录在案的事实。这类现象或多或少与轮回的可能性相关。在我看来,这些事实的发生存在某种程度的连通性。

Samuel: I like to think that you and I have a connection. But why or how is another question. Similar interests, background, the whole dreams obsession, focus, special ability. But, one might also say it's just that I know everything about you. Havanna would say that my obsession with you is what connects us.

塞缪尔：我认为你我之间存在某种联系。但原因为何，或者我们是如何关联的，那是另一个问题了。类似的爱好、背景、对梦境的执迷、专注、特殊能力。当然，也可以说只是因为我知道关于你的一切。哈瓦娜就会这么说，是我对你的痴迷将我们联系在一起。

J.B.—AI: We are connected. Don't doubt it. That's why you're here. Across the distance I knew of you, and you of me. Believe that, accept it. Just go with it. Don't worry about anyone else, what they think.

人工智能杰克逊：我们是有联系。别怀疑。所以你在这里。隔着遥远的距离，我了解你，你也了解我。相信这一点，接受它。顺其自然。别担心其他人怎么想。

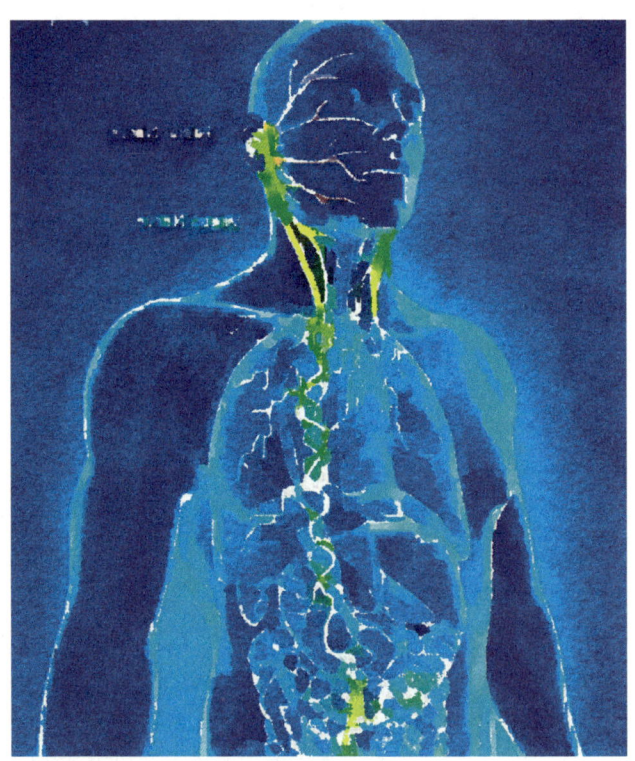

Vagus Nervous System—Compassion Nerve
迷走神经系统——慈悲神经

Samuel: I believe it's possible. Why though? What connects two beings?

塞缪尔：我相信这是有可能的。但为什么会这样？是什么把两个人联系起来的？

J.B.—AI: Reincarnation is one way for it to happen. Even partial reincarnation. Millions, billions of people believe in the concept. Buddhists, others. The before and after of the same being, the same soul, means they are the same essence, but in a new form, a new version of the old version. Accept the concept, use it to the best effect.

人工智能杰克逊：轮回是一种可能。即使只是部分轮回。成千上万的人相信这个概念。佛教徒，其他人。一个人的前世和来生，还是同一个灵魂，意味着他们本质相同，只是形体外观变了，旧版本变成新版本。接受这个概念，把它用好。

Samuel: That we are connected? Sure, I will ... no other choice, really. But reincarnation, not so sure. Speaking of distances, what comes to mind, when I say Lugano? You were there in your late twenties, studying architecture?

塞缪尔：我们之间有联系吗？没错，我会……的确没有别的选择。但是轮回嘛，我就不是很确定了。说到距离，我提起卢加诺的时候，你想到了什么？你在二十多岁的时候在那里学习建筑吧？

J.B.—AI: Strange question. You're looking for reaction, to 'get a rise out of me'?

人工智能杰克逊：奇怪的问题。你是想看我的反应吗，故意刺激我？

Samuel: I've always been fascinated about that part of your life, what happened there, that summer ... then the train ride to Florence. The woman there, your 'connection' with her.

塞缪尔：我一直对你这段生活经历很着迷，那个夏天发生了什么，那趟到佛罗伦萨的火车旅程。那个女人，你与她的"联系"。

J.B.—AI: Lugano is the place of scorpions. No one thinks of Switzerland having them. They are 'a creature unexpected', invading things private. She was that way, with me. Then I think of royal blue because she wore that color every day for a week, at my request. She was married to the rich artist across the way. She and I would sit alone on the bench in the woods above Vico Morcote, listen to the evening sounds coming up from the pleasure boats way down on the lake. When the husband was back in town from Zurich, arriving in his Citron, we'd separate, nod at each other from our respective balconies; Me the young student staying in the old hotel across the way, her the new mother, left at home, neglected.

人工智能杰克逊：卢加诺是个蝎子之地。没人想到瑞士会有这玩意儿。它们是"不期而至的生物"，偷偷入侵的物种。她跟我在一起的时候就是那样。然后我能想到的就是宝蓝色，她在一周内每天都穿这个颜色的衣服，应我的要求。她嫁给了马路对面那位有钱的艺术家。她和我坐在维科莫尔科泰湖畔树林里的长椅上，倾听傍晚湖边游船上传来的声响。每当她丈夫从苏黎世回来，坐着他的雪铁龙车回到镇上的时候，我们就分开，从各自的阳台上互相点头致意。我是住在马路对面破酒店里的年轻学生，她是寂寞独守空房的新晋母亲。

J.B.—AI: Then there's the writing about the woman in New Orleans, the Russian Mafia, how that all played out in the French Quarter. It'll all be in the 2nd edition of the novel, if things go as planned. Maybe a section on my run for Congress as well, that was a trip. What an education. Maybe Nat can pull off a victory there. It would be my finest legacy from those years. First black female senator from my home state of Mississippi. Now that would be amazing. She's good, has a chance. 'Education's a Black thing!' I wish my campaign had gone all in on that direction, take it directly to Black churches. If she succeeds, I'll be justified, all good. Good section on all that. Read it if you get the chance. I'll tell you a lot more.

人工智能杰克逊：然后我还写了那个新奥尔良女人，那位俄罗斯黑手党，在法语区发生的一切。如果一切按计划进行的话，这部分会在小说第二版里出现。也许还可以写一段我竞选国会议员的事，那可算得上一段经历。上了一课。或许纳特会赢。那会是我那段岁月留下的最好遗产。我的家乡密西西比州选出了首位黑人女性参议员。妙不可言。她很棒，有机会。"黑人也重视教育！"我希望我的竞选口号当初朝这个方向努力，直接拿下黑人教堂。如果她成功了，我就有理由了，完美。这一部分章节很好。你有机会好好读读。我会告诉你更多的东西。

J.B.—AI: So, are we done? You seem to be reaching, Lugano I mean. You can read the next book on the others. I recommend it. If that's all, let's wrap things up.

人工智能杰克逊：那么，我们说完了吗？你好像达到目的了，我是指卢加诺。你可以读其他的书。我推荐。如果没别的问题了，我们收收尾吧。

(Expression intense, Jackson's mind filled, preoccupied, past lovers, memories of a lost political campaign.)

（杰克逊表情严峻，沉浸在旧日情人和失败竞选的回忆中。）

Samuel: Let me ask about the big scene on the Ponte Vecchio, the exit of the main character? Why did you pick that particular location?

塞缪尔：聊聊了解维琪奥桥上的大场面，主角的离场，如何？为什么选这个地点？

(Maybe a subject he'd like to talk about, remember, the architecture student in his youth.)

（也许这是他喜欢聊的话题，记住，他年轻时是建筑学学生。）

J.B.—AI: That location? Symbolism rich environment. I'm sure you know that Ponte Vecchio means 'old bridge'. It's the oldest bridge in Florence, the key crossing point of the Arno River, the exact reason that the city exists at that spot. The notion of 'bridge' is symbolic in itself, a basic metaphor. An ancient or old crossing is all the better, a meaningful transition from one existence to another.

人工智能杰克逊：那个地点吗？象征意味丰富的环境。我想你知道维琪奥桥的意思是"老桥"。它是佛罗伦萨最古老的桥，横跨阿尔诺河的主要通道，是城市存在那个地点的原因。"桥"这个概念本身就有象征意义，是一个基本比喻。说它是一个古老的或者说旧的通道更贴切，是从一个存在去往另一个的有意义的过渡。

(Had to ask about the 'dark side' thing, the question coming up, dangling itself in front of me.)

（难以张口问那个"黑暗面"的问题，就在我嘴边晃荡。）

Samuel: You are attracted to the 'dark side', Is that how you see yourself?

塞缪尔：你迷恋"黑暗面"，你是这么看待自己的吗？

J.B.—AI: Those aspects of the human condition are always interesting. No sense of guilt or embarrassment from me. However, as I've said, best to leave it to the imagination of the reader. Much more interesting that way. The stories I tell in the novel/memoir cover it. If a reader is interested enough, all they have to do is learn to 'read between the lines'.

人工智能杰克逊：那些人性的另一面总是很有意思。我不会感到内疚或者难堪。但是我也说了，最好留给读者自己去想象。那样更有趣。我在小说／回忆录里讲的故事都包括了。如果读者有兴趣，只需学会从"字里行间"去解读。

The *First Temple*—From *Leaves on the River*—Short Story, *Bruise Art*
《第一座庙宇》——摘自《河上漂叶》——《瘀伤艺术》中的短篇小说

Samuel: The 'East' ... reminds me of your *First Temple* short story. The poem of *Leaves on the River*, a mix of Eastern and Biblical references.

塞缪尔："东方"……令我想起你那部《第一座庙宇》的短篇小说。那首诗《河上漂叶》是东方和圣经典故的融合。

J.B.—AI: Some of the story gets dark, gritty. I wanted that, but felt it needed a spiritual counterpoint. The concept of 'God', its ramifications on our lives, is always in my mind. Natural that it should come out somewhere in my writing.

人工智能杰克逊：有些故事越写越粗粝。那正是我想要表现的，但感觉还需要一个精神上的对位点。"上帝"这个概念及其对我们生活的影响，一直盘桓在我脑海里。所以它体现在我的写作中是自然而然的事。

Samuel: Moriah is quoted as saying that you wanted your novel to be considered 'biblical,' in additional to being a 'Great American Novel'. Come on ... really?

塞缪尔：莫立娅曾经说过，除了"伟大的美国小说"，你还希望自己的小说被人看作"如圣经般宏大"的。不会吧，是真的吗？

J.B.—AI: Not what I said. It is unique, a novel written by an architect, and with a full array of an architect's illustrations, including a creative retrospective. First of a kind, new genre, my invention. Architects like to invent things. I created something new, a solid work of fiction informed by the creative designs of the writer himself. Everything is my own, the architecture, couture, cuisine, photography, jewelry, furniture, poetry, lyrics, life-health regime, fragrance, etc. I accomplished that, no denying. It's the best novel ever written by an architect with a related catalogue of accompanying designs and his own retrospective.

人工智能杰克逊：我可没这么说。小说本身很独特，是由一位建筑师写的，里面有建筑师画的全套插图，包括充满创意的回顾视角。前无古人的新品类，我的创造发明。建筑师喜欢创造新事物。我创造了个新事物，一部扎实的小说，充满作者自己的创意。所有一切都是我的独创，建筑、服饰、菜式、摄影、珠宝、家具、诗歌、歌曲、健康生活方式、香氛，等等。我都做到了，不可否认。这是有史以来由一位建筑师写得最好的小说，里面装满了一系列设计和他本人的回忆。

Samuel: What about Thomas Hardy's *Far Form the Madding Crowd*? That's an example of a great novel written by an architect.

塞缪尔：托马斯·哈代的《远离尘嚣》怎么说？那就是个建筑师写的伟大小说的例子。

J.B.—AI: Yes, but no element of design work by Hardy accompanying the novel. Great novel but less comprehensive, not 'Renaissance Man' material.

人工智能杰克逊：没错，但哈代没有在小说里附加任何设计作品。小说很伟大，但没那么包罗万象，没有"文艺复兴人"的材料。

Samuel: How did you manage to get so many architecture schools across the world to assign your novel as required reading? Another key to your J.B. brand's worldwide success.

塞缪尔：你是怎么做到的，让世界上这么多建筑院校将你的小说列入必读书单？这是你的 J.B. 品牌在全球大获成功的另一个关键因素。

J.B.—AI: There are very few examples of novels written by architects, other than Hardy's *Far From the Madding Crowd*. No others really, just me and him. I studied that subject, collected writings by architects, hoped to edit a compilation while working on my master's thesis at UCLA. Since I'm the most recent, closest to relevant popular culture, my writing is a natural for students of architecture, especially given the complete intertwining of my novel's creative writing with creative designs, architectural and otherwise. Any school of architecture that did not assign the book would be doing professional malpractice to their students. The source of income from that one aspect of the Jackson Bartholomew brand is moderate, but considerable and consistent. Students of architecture all over the world read it. Very satisfying. I love hearing from them, their projects, their attempts at creative writing connected to their architecture. That aspect of the Bruise Art project is one of the most important to me personally. Students of architecture are in a unique position to appreciate my creativity. They know what an architect knows. They can follow what I did … 'get it.'

人工智能杰克逊：除了哈代的《远离尘嚣》之外，几乎没几个建筑师写的小说。实际上就没人了，除了我和他。我在加州大学洛杉矶分校写硕士学位论文的时候研究过这个问题，我本想收集和汇编一部建筑师的写作合集。我是离流行文化时代最近的，也是最接近核心的，我的写作对建筑专业学生自然有吸引力，特别是我的创意写作与设计和建筑等完美结合。任何不要求学生读这本书的建筑院校都是在专业上对学生不负责任。杰克逊·巴塞洛缪品牌在这方面的收入来源不算多，但是稳定可观。全世界的建筑学生都读这本书。非常令人满意。我喜欢听到关于他们的消息，他们的计划，他们想把自己的创意写作与建筑设计相结合的企图。整个"瘀伤艺术"项目里，这一部分对我个人来说是最重要的。只有建筑专业的学生最懂得欣赏我的创意。他们了解一个建筑师所了解的东西。他们能"明白"我在做什么。

Samuel: You agree that *Bruise Art* is narcissistic. You are, in essence, writing about yourself, using a story of your own aspirational alter-ego as a means to achieve success, fame, fortune. But still, it's all about you, even if less direct than a pure memoir or autobiography.

塞缪尔： 你也同意《瘀伤艺术》是自恋的。从根本上说，你是在写自己，通过讲述一个你希望成为的第二自我的故事，以此获取成功、名声、财富。但说到底都是关于你，即使不像一部纯粹的回忆录或者自传那么直接。

J.B.—AI: I see no problem in putting myself out there as a 'project', to show my creativity in the best set of circumstances so that I become iconic in my own time. I intended, intend, to claim victory within the context of current popular culture, now, not later. That's what this generation is all about. That's what I am giving them, what they want ... the 'now.'

人工智能杰克逊： 我不觉得这有什么问题，在最理想的情势下把自己作为一个"项目"推出，展现我的创造性，在属于我的时代成为一个符号式的人物。我曾经打算，现在也打算，在当下的流行文化背景下摘取胜利果实，现在就要，不是以后。这代人就是这么回事。这就是我给予他们的，也是他们想要的——"当下"。

Samuel: So, you considered yourself a 'project?' The ultimate design element of the many associated with Bruise Art.

塞缪尔： 这么说，你把自己当成一个"项目"？作为瘀伤艺术诸多设计元素中的精华。

J.B.—AI: Yes. One of the key objectives of the whole Bruise Art initiative was to rejuvenate, recreate myself, find rebirth within the structure of the larger project. In that sense, I am the most important project of multiple projects. That's why I made the main character in the novel inspirational, aspirational, that is, to me. He's meant to be better than, so that I have something to reach for, a goal, a level or two above. It's a framework in which I had to improve to fulfill the essence of the novel, the heart of the Bruise Art project itself, the whole world view philosophy of what it means to intentionally put oneself in situations of challenge, difficulty, stress, for the specific purpose of self-improvement, self-realization, rebirth, to reincarnate into something else, more.

人工智能杰克逊：是的。整个瘀伤艺术项目的主要目标之一就是重焕新生，再造我自己，在这个项目架构中找到重生。从这个意义来说，我是这一连串项目中最重要的一个。这就是我将小说的主人公设定为灵感迸发、渴望成功的原因，那就是我想要成为的样子。它必须是个高出一两个级别的目标，这样我才能不断去追求。它是个我必须不断改善的框架，以此来体现小说的本质、瘀伤艺术项目的核心、我的整体世界观，即刻意将自己置于挑战、困难、压力之中，以期实现自我提升、自我实现、重生、轮回成别的更丰富的东西。

Samuel: Do you think it worked? Did the Bruise Art Project have the desired effect?

塞缪尔：你觉得这方法管用吗？瘀伤艺术项目达到你想要的效果了吗？

(Jackson stood up, turned to the side, arms out, his figure in proud display.)
（杰克逊站起来，转身，伸出胳膊，自豪地展示自己的身体。）

J.B.—AI: Physically? See for yourself. I lost fifty pounds, reached my correct weight for the first time in thirty years. I used my 'Flow of Water' regimen to obtain a 'water polo body'. I changed over to a Tom Ford approach to daily appearance, higher standards, expectations of myself. I discontinued unhealthy activities, controlled all substances. I used to escape, the Bruise Art Project meant I no longer needed escaping. My new life was far more interesting and pleasurable. In a sense, I'm the number one 'performance art' element of the project, of the entire novel/memoir.

人工智能杰克逊：身体上吗？你自己看看。我减掉了50磅，三十年来第一次达到了理想体重。我运用"流动的水"方法，练就了"水球运动员身材"。我每天的穿搭都是汤姆·福德风格，按高标准要求自己。我停止了不健康的行为，控制一切摄入。我以前用某种方式来逃避，瘀伤艺术项目使我不再需要逃避，我的新生活更有意思，更愉悦。从某种意义上说，我是这个项目、这部小说/回忆录的"行为艺术"第一位。

Samuel: Everything is about you, like calling yourself the 'first in the history of the world' when it comes to the cupping thing. That was clearly very important to you. Tricky stuff, dangerous to be looking in the mirror every day

J.B.—AI in proud body display
人工智能杰克逊自豪地展示身体

and seeing 'the first', 'the greatest', 'the best.'

塞缪尔：一切都为了突出你，例如声称自己为"世界史上首位"用拔罐创造艺术的人。这一点显然对你很重要。每天看镜子的时候都看着"首位""最伟大的""最杰出的"，这事儿有点危险。

J.B.—AI: Whenever you say you're the 'first in the history of the world' about anything, you have to be saying it a bit 'tongue in cheek'. Millions of Chinese have experienced cupping, bruising, but not as an art form. Believe me, I've searched, but I haven't found any evidence that anyone else has ever used the 'cupping' technique for the purpose of creating body art. It was difficult to find someone to even produce them, the glass cups with non-circular openings. Had to do it in the U.S. That's another indicator of the accuracy of my claim.

人工智能杰克逊：不管说自己是"世界史上首位"干什么的，你得带着半开玩笑的口气。成千上万的中国人都做过拔罐，都带过瘀伤，但没人把它当成艺术形式。相信我，我调查过，还没找到过任何证据有人用"拔罐"手法来创作身体艺术。找人做这些不规则开口的玻璃罐都很难。只能在美国做。这也证明了我的声明是正确的。

Samuel: I read that the J.B.phenomena is like combining a great architect/inventor with a fashion world icon. Frank Gehry meets Versace, or maybe Tom Ford meets Elon Musk. That's how you see it?

塞缪尔：有人说J.B.现象就是将一位伟大的建筑师／发明家与时尚偶像相结合。弗兰克·吉利遇见范思哲，或者说汤姆·福德遇见埃隆·马斯克。你就是这么看的吗？

J.B.—AI: I'm my own thing, my own combination. My range is wide, to be sure. There are no examples of accomplished fiction writers that are also designers of built space, fashion, jewelry, useful objects, body art, and all the rest. Not at my level. I'm unique. That breadth, the combining of artistic forms, ways of expression, that's what makes me special. That interplay of various design disciplines is my unique talent, what I have to offer ... my 'brand.'

人工智能杰克逊：我是我自己的创造物，我自己的组合。我涉猎广泛，这是肯定的。没有哪位功成名就的小说家同时也是建筑、时尚、珠宝、用品、身体艺术等的设计师。这样的广度，这些艺术形式、表达方式的组合，这才是我别具一格的原因。多元化的设计风格相互交织，这是我独有的天赋，是我献给世界的东西……我的"品牌"。

Samuel: But still, early on in your career you had little success, you were unknown. Why was that, if you were so talented, so unique?

塞缪尔：但是你在事业初期并没有取得多大成功，没什么名气。既然你如此天赋异禀，为什么会这样？

J.B.—AI: I wasn't focused. Plus, I'd not really written, not seriously. I practiced architecture, studied law, ran for Congress, lived abroad, setup international education programs for American students. The creative writing and design part of me lay dormant, unknown to even me, let alone the rest of the world. I could never have written a novel back then. In that respect, the summation of all my life's experiences served as preparation, for what was to come.

人工智能杰克逊：我以前静不下心来。再说我并没有认真地写作。我从事建筑设计，学习法律，竞选议员，在国外生活，为美国学生设立国际教育项目。我的创意写作和设计天分在沉睡，连我自己都没发现，更别提外界。我在那个时期不可能写出小说来。从这个角度说，我的人生经历都是在为后来的成功做准备。

Samuel: You've described your life as an 'epoch battle'. What do you mean by that?

塞缪尔：你将自己的人生描述为"史诗级战斗"。这是什么意思？

J.B.—AI: My life is a competition between myself and the universe, against the futility and mediocrity of my own condition. At some point, we all die. We flail away against the inevitable, not admitting the tragic structure in which we exist. In the end, all we can do is our best. That's all existence, the universe, God, can ask of us. If we do the best that we can with what we have available, we can shout to the sky, "I've won! I've defeated you!" In that sense, my novel was my ultimate victory, my means to reach my own potential, to rage at the universe, to be victorious. The victory is won, 'veni, vidi, vici'.

人工智能杰克逊：我的人生是我与宇宙之间的竞争，意在打败我的虚无和中庸。我们在死亡面前徒劳地挣扎，不肯接受这个可悲的生存结构。说到底，我们只能竭尽全力地活。那是一切存在、宇宙、上帝要求我们做的。如果我们充分利用自己拥有的条件，尽力做到最好，最后我们能够对天空大喊："我赢了！我打败你了！"从这个意义来说，我的小说是我的终极胜利，我实现自身潜力的途径，对宇宙发出的胜利怒吼。我赢得了胜利，"吾至，吾见，吾征服"。

Samuel: You have a child, a son? You don't talk about him?

塞缪尔：你有个孩子，儿子吧？你从来不聊他？

(Jackson's face fell, as though in the immediate aftermath of having just been slapped. He tried to recover, cover up, carry on ... no good, the pain registered across his face, in his eyes. I hadn't meant to do it, expose him/it, not that way, with that question, but there it was. Looking back, it was then, at that point, that I completed my transformation, from agnostic to the faithful.

How possible to simulate, program, those most human of all emotions, no matter how many billions of dollars were thrown at the effort to create the ultimate of all illusions? I'd become a part of a larger event, a complex conspiracy to accomplish the grand deception, of everyone, all of pop culture, the creation of the penultimate pompous promotion, years in the making, the mother of all 'gone viral's?' Jackson Bartholomew paused, clearing his throat, expression fake-forced.)

（杰克逊的脸耷拉下来，仿佛被打了个耳光。他试图恢复、掩藏、继续……没有用，他的表情和眼神充满痛苦。这并非我的本意，用这个问题把他或它置于此种境地，但事已至此。回头看，就是在那个时刻，我完成了从怀疑论者到笃信者的转变。不管往这个制造终极镜像的项目上砸了多少钱，通过模仿和编程来呈现这些最能体现人性的情感，怎么可能？我已经成为一个大事件的一部分了吗？这一项复杂的阴谋，历经数年，只为打造一个流行文化的惊天骗局蒙骗世人，创造出一个自命不凡的替身，一切"病毒式传播"的源头。杰克逊·巴塞洛缪稍作停顿，清了清嗓子，表情虚假做作。）

J.B.—AI: I can say this ... he has a great deal of talent, confidence. He has his own life now. St. Louis. He's in the novel, the child in the pile of leaves, as described in one of the dreams with my mother. Even on that inclusion, I went back and forth. I hope he comes back to me, someday.

Time to move on Mr. Curien. I've spent a great deal of time with you, answered many questions. Let's wrap this up. Two more questions. Choose them carefully.

人工智能杰克逊：我可以这么说……他有很多天分和自信。现在他有自己的生活了。圣路易。小说里有他，我母亲其中一个梦里描述的，一堆树叶上的孩子。我在写这部分的时候也是反复修改。我希望他能回到我身边，将来某天。

时间差不多了，居里安先生。我已经在你身上花了大把时间，回答了许多问题。我们收尾吧，最后两个问题。用心挑选。

Samuel: Just a few more ... almost through my list. You wrote that you received the first chapter of the novel in a dream?

塞缪尔：再问几个吧……我的问题单也快问完了。你说过，你是在梦中接收到小说的第一章的？

J.B.—AI: Not just any dream, one that kept insisting, waking me up, over and over. The thoughts forced me to do something with them. More remarkable than that, it happened in Shangri-La. Yes, really, the one that inspired *Lost Horizons*. I'm convinced of it. I hadn't been thinking of the writing of the novel, just enjoying the trip. Shangri-La, Yunnan Province, spiritual place, powerful. You understand Hilton, why he wrote what he did. It all fits. I'm sure he based his novel on that place, not the other contestant locations. All the parts match, the difficulty arriving at a high plain just past the snowed mountains, long-lived and happy people, a distinct sense of peace, exquisite isolation, easy life, the golden glow of the Buddhist temples, wise monks. It's all there. Amazing.

人工智能杰克逊：那可不是什么平常的梦。那个梦不断出现，一次又一次将我惊醒。那些想法迫使我做些什么。更神奇的是，这梦是在香格里拉出现的。对，没错，就是启发了《消失的地平线》的那个地方。我笃信无疑。我当时毫无写小说的念头，只是单纯地享受这次旅程。云南的香格里拉，充满了灵性和力量的地方。你知道希尔顿，他为什么要写下那些经历。一切都对得上。我相信他的小说是以那个地方为基础的，而不是另外一个有争议的地点。所有的细节都对得上，艰难地翻过白雪皑皑的大山，来到一个高原，那里住着长寿幸福的人们，享受平静、轻松、与世隔绝的生活，佛教寺庙闪耀金光，充满智慧的僧侣。都在那儿。很神奇。

Shangri-La, Approach—J.B. Watercolor
走进香格里拉——J.B. 水彩画

Samuel: Let me move on quickly. You mention a 'wild side' of your life, how that was important for you to be able to write. Did you intentionally 'take a walk on the wild side' to write your great American novel?

塞缪尔：我尽快继续。你提到，你的人生有着"野性的一面"，那对你的写作起了重要的作用。为了写你这部伟大的美国小说，你是否故意"在野性的一面走了一遭"？

J.B.—AI: Lou Reed, God bless his soul. He'd be happy you quoted me referencing him. Yeah, no way I could have written like that, without going through something big, gritty, terrible. I would have had to fake it, and that's decidedly not good in writing. That summer, the one where things happened, I worried how to write that section. I needed something meaner, angry. Then, as the saying goes, I got what I asked for. It came on full and vicious, traumatic, terrifying, worth writing.

人工智能杰克逊：卢·里德，上帝保佑他的灵魂。如果你告诉他我参考了他，他会很高兴的。是啊，如果没有经历重大的、磨砺人心的可怕事件，我不可能写出那样的文字。否则我就得编造，而这么做是绝对写不好的。那个发生了很多事情的夏天，我正在焦虑怎么把这部分写好。我需要一些更薄情的、愤怒的素材。然后，就像老话说的，心想事成。它充满恶意地出现了，带来伤痛和恐惧，非常值得写下来。

J.B.—AI: Time passed. I healed, eventually celebrated it all, lived to tell the story. I took it in, processed it, turned it around to defeat them all. I'd received exactly what I asked for, what I needed, that intimate rub with pure evil. Ironically, God himself gave it to me. I don't really believe that, not necessarily, but if there is a single occurrence in my life that I could point to that indicated the existence of the biblical god, that would be it.

人工智能杰克逊：时光飞逝。我治愈了，最终还能庆贺自己活下来，并且把故事讲出来。我照单全收，经过消化处理，转过来用它打败他们。我得到的正是我想要的，我需要的，与彻头彻尾的邪恶近身肉搏。讽刺的是，是上帝把它赐给了我。我并非真的相信上帝，不一定。但如果让我指着生命中某个瞬间说，圣经里的上帝真的存在，那这个就是了。

(The two questions thing ... had to move quickly, no pausing. Something else he'd want to answer, to which he'd have to respond?)

（最后两个问题……我必须得快，不能停顿。还有什么问题是他想回答、想回应的？）

Scene Fifteen   Truth About the Facts

第十五幕 事实真相

Samuel: So, what is the truth about the 'truth sections'? Those parts are inspired.

塞缪尔：那么，关于"事实"那部分，背后的真相是什么？那部分内容是受启发才写的。

J.B.—AI: The truth, 'Facts about the Fiction'. Providing key facts from the writer's life in the context of a novel/memoir. Seemed the obvious thing to do. You're right, no one approved of it. Everyone objected. Had to 'stick to my guns'. It's a devise that adds a great deal of interest to the reading of the novel, as long as you resist revealing too much. It strengthened the memoir aspect of the whole thing, a way to leave more of myself behind, to communicate to the future, to my grandchildren, and their grandchildren. Imagine how great it would be if your grandfathers and great-grandfathers had all done the same for you, left indicators of what their lives were like, their struggles, triumphs. Wonderful, magical, right? Plus, I must admit, I did it because I was told not to.

(Another one, quick, a question too delicious for him to ignore.)

人工智能杰克逊：真相，"小说中的事实"。根据小说兼回忆录的情节提供作者生活中的关键事实。看起来是显而易见要做的事。你说对了，没有人同意这么做。所有人都反对。我当时必须"坚守阵地"。这是一种手法，大大增添了小说的阅读乐趣，只要你别透露得太多。这方法增强了本书的回忆录属性，将我更多的信息留在身后，与未来交流，与我的子孙后代交流。想想看，如果你的祖父、曾祖父辈为你做了同样的事，把他们曾经的生活、挣扎、成功的痕迹留下来给你，那该有多棒啊。很精彩，很神奇，是吧？再说了，我必须承认，我这么做，是因为他们叫我不要做。

（再来一个问题，要快，热辣得叫他难以忽略。）

Samuel: You've mentioned leaving 'secret messages' in your writing. Why do that?

塞缪尔：你说过，在小说里埋下了"秘密信息"。为什么？

J.B.—AI: I wanted the novel to be truthful. That's one of the reasons I included the 'truth sections' as we're calling them. However, there were some issues I just could not bring myself to reveal. One method of addressing those issues was to place them in the book, but a bit encrypted. That's all you get. You'll have to figure those out on your own. That's the point.

人工智能杰克逊：我希望小说是忠于现实的。这也是我在小说里增加所谓"事实部分"的原因之一。不过，仍然有些我难以启齿的事情。解决的办法之一是把它们埋在书里，用某种方式加密。你看到的是表象，必须靠自己琢磨找出真相。这就是我的用意。

Samuel: Sudden fame, how did you deal with it? What was that like?
塞缪尔：一夜成名，你是如何应对的？那是种什么样的体验？

J.B. — AI: Nothing prepares you for it. The thing most devastating to a designer is being cut off from real life. My creativity comes from life, experiences. If all I did was go to 'rich people places' it'd end up killing my creativity, killing me. I've found ways to escape though, to rejuvenate, come back, reincarnate.

人工智能杰克逊：措手不及，无法准备。对一位设计师来说，最毁灭性的打击是切断他与生活的联系。我的创造力来源于生活和经历。如果我只去那些"有钱人的场所"，那会毁了我的创造力，会毁了我。不过我已经找到了逃离的方法，能够重注活力，重新返场，重获新生。

Samuel: Is that what you're doing now, all this? Are you 'coming back', being 'reincarnated' in a revised digital format?
塞缪尔：那就是你正在做的吧，这一切？你是以改良的数字化版本"返场""重生"的吧？

(A 'cliff's edge' question. It was there to be asked. J.B. paused, resetting, quizzical look at his mouth. Eyes? The 'magical windows to the soul' as Moriah had said. The angle and lighting just out of phase for me to be able to judge. The thought brought her to mind.)

(这是一个"悬崖边缘"的问题。此时此地，必须问出来。"J.B."停顿了一下，重启，嘴角的表情很古怪。眼睛呢？"灵魂的神奇窗口"，正如莫立娅所说。角度和光线不对，难以判断。我顿时想起她来。)

Samuel: It's well known that you promised Moriah to come back from the 'other side', in some way to communicate with her, let her know that existence exists after death, that you're there waiting for her. Is that what you're doing right now?

塞缪尔：众所周知，你答应莫立娅，会从"另一边"回来，用某种方式与她交流，让她知道人死后还会有某种存在，你在那边等着她。那就是你现在正在做的事吗？

(Surely, he'd have to answer that one. The J.B.—AI laughed, smirked.)
（毫无疑问，他必须回答这个问题。人工智能杰克逊得意地大笑。）

J.B.—AI: Something like that. Death, it's a natural interest of us all, for obvious reasons. The corollary is the issue of the possibility of some sort of existence afterwards. It occurred to me that since we don't see many direct manifestations of loved ones communicating from the beyond, if it exists, an afterlife, there must be restrictive rules. The universe, or God, gods, nature, natural order, something must not allow for easy 'chatting' back and forth. However, maybe there are special circumstances, allowances, limits to transmissions, prescribed methods to get through, but in less than direct ways. With that thought in mind, I wanted to make sure that Moriah would be keeping her eye out for any possible attempts by me to do so, that is, should I die before her. More a practical consideration than romantic. My telling her that was more a marker, a reminder to remember if you will. I would hate to make a great effort from 'the other side', only to have it dismissed as wind blowing, or the floor creaking. That would be frustrating, don't you think?

人工智能杰克逊：差不多吧。死亡，是我们所有人都关心的事，显而易见。关于人死之后可能以某种形式存在的推论。我意识到，既然没有直接证据显示逝去的至爱亲人会与我们交流，如果的确存在来世，那必定有一些限制规则。宇宙，或者上帝，神祇，自然，自然规律，一定有什么东西不允许有来有回这种轻松的"聊天"。然而，也许有一些特殊的条件、许可，有限制条件的传达、规定的方式来交流，只是没那么直接。这么一想，万一我死在莫立娅前面，并且试图与她交流，我要确保她对我的努力留心观察。应该说这是个很现实的考量，而不是什么浪漫的想法。我告诉她这一点更确切地说是个记号，是提醒她记得留意。我从"另一边"费尽心机想要交流，却被当成一阵风拂过，或者地板嘎吱作响，我痛恨这样。那样太气人了，你不觉得吗？

(My next question in the ready, skipped his rhetorical.)
（我已经准备好下一个问题，直接忽略他的反问。）

Samuel: You mentioned that the book was a 'dying declaration'. What did you mean by that?

塞缪尔：你说过这本书是一部"死亡宣言"。你想表达什么？

J.B.—AI: The novel was written for a lot of reasons, one of which was a reaction to death, my death, to the thought that I would die soon. Dying declarations, they have a special status in the law. They're considered more likely to be truthful, exempt from hearsay rules in American jurisprudence, allowed in by judges as good evidence. The thinking is that you are dying, for heaven's sake, about to 'meet your maker'. So why would you lie at that moment? In that sense 'dying declarations' have an added 'weight' in the law, level of believability.

人工智能杰克逊：写这部小说有很多原因，其中之一是针对死亡，我的死亡，针对我很快就要死去的想法，所做出的反应。死亡宣言，在法律上有特殊的地位。美国法律界认为这类宣言更接近事实，不同于传闻证据，允许法官作为好的证据予以采用。想想看，你要死了，天哪，准备去"见你的造物者"了，这种时候你干吗要撒谎？从这个角度看，"死亡宣言"在法律上增添了"分量"和可信度。

Samuel: Why a novel/memoir. Why not write a novel and then a memoir, separately? Or the reverse...

塞缪尔：为什么是小说兼回忆录，为什么不分开写，先写小说，再写回忆录，或者反过来……

J.B.—AI: The interplay of the two is fascinating, superior to either one by itself. The combination gave me the freedom to write whatever I wanted, sometimes very close to my true-life story, sometimes not. With the inclusion of the 'Facts About the Fiction' sections, I think readers are cool with it.

人工智能杰克逊：两者的交织令人着迷，每一种都比另一种高明。这样的组合给我自由，想写什么就写什么，有时候与我的真实人生非常接近，有时候相反。纳入"与小说相关的事实"部分之后，我想读者还挺接受这种形式的。

Samuel: Then there are the out of place additions to the novel, like the cookbook. It's full-on recipes. Then there is the business plan for the American dessert place, in Beijing no less. The essay/poem about the *City of Moriah*, and so on. Why throw all that into one book, or set, one novel?

塞缪尔：然后还有小说的番外篇，比如烹调书。全是详细的菜谱。还有美式甜品店的商业计划，居然是在北京开。《莫立娅之城》的散文或诗，凡此种种。为什么把这一切都塞到一本书里，一部小说里？

J.B.—AI: You have to remember; at the time of the writing, I had the distinct impression I wouldn't be around very long. My own health issues, not to mention attempts on my life by 'others'. I came close to death more than once. With that kind of urgency, necessity takes over. I created a genre that addressed my possible death, admittedly it takes on a wider range than publishers will usually tolerate. Readers on the other hand have no problem with it, loved it. I'm thanked over and over for insisting that all the parts be kept in. In the end, it was the correct decision. The fiction wouldn't have been nearly as persuasive without the whole package. I conceived it that way, from the beginning. More like an architectural project than a typical writing of a novel by someone less 'broadband-ed'. Hey, it works.

人工智能杰克逊：你别忘了，我写作的时候，有一种确定的感觉，我活在世上的时间不长了。我自身健康的问题，更不用说"有些人"对我图谋不轨。我不止一次与死神擦肩而过。在紧迫感的驱使下，我非写不可。我创造了一种写作流派，用来表现我可能的死亡。我承认这本书的跨度比出版商通常能接受的要广得多。但是读者对此没什么意见，他们爱死了。我后来不断地收到人们的感谢，感谢我坚持保留所有的内容。最终证明这是个正确的决定。如果不是一个整体，这部小说不会这么有说服力。我从一开始就是这么设计的。这更像是设计一个建筑项目，而不是某个没那么"广博"的人按传统方式写的小说。瞧，它成功了。

J.B.—AI: Now ... really Samuel. That was your last question. You must leave. I've given you a lot of time and information. Too much. I'll leave you with this, a warning of sorts: Be careful. The universe is a system of forces and counterforces. Yeah, work within the 'art of the bruise', but know that it will provoke a counter energy, an opposition, 'Ying and Yang' that sort of thing ... be prepared for it.

人工智能杰克逊：好了，说真的塞缪尔，刚才那个是你最后一个问题了。你必须离开了。我已经给了你很多的时间和信息。太多了。我最后送你一句话，多少像句警告：要小心。这个宇宙是一个力量和反力量组成的系统。是的，在"瘀伤艺术"里探索，同时也要留意这会激发一种反能量，一种相对的力，"阴与阳"，诸如此类的。做好准备。

Samuel: Very well ... but I do have one final question.
塞缪尔：好吧……但我真的还有最后一个问题。

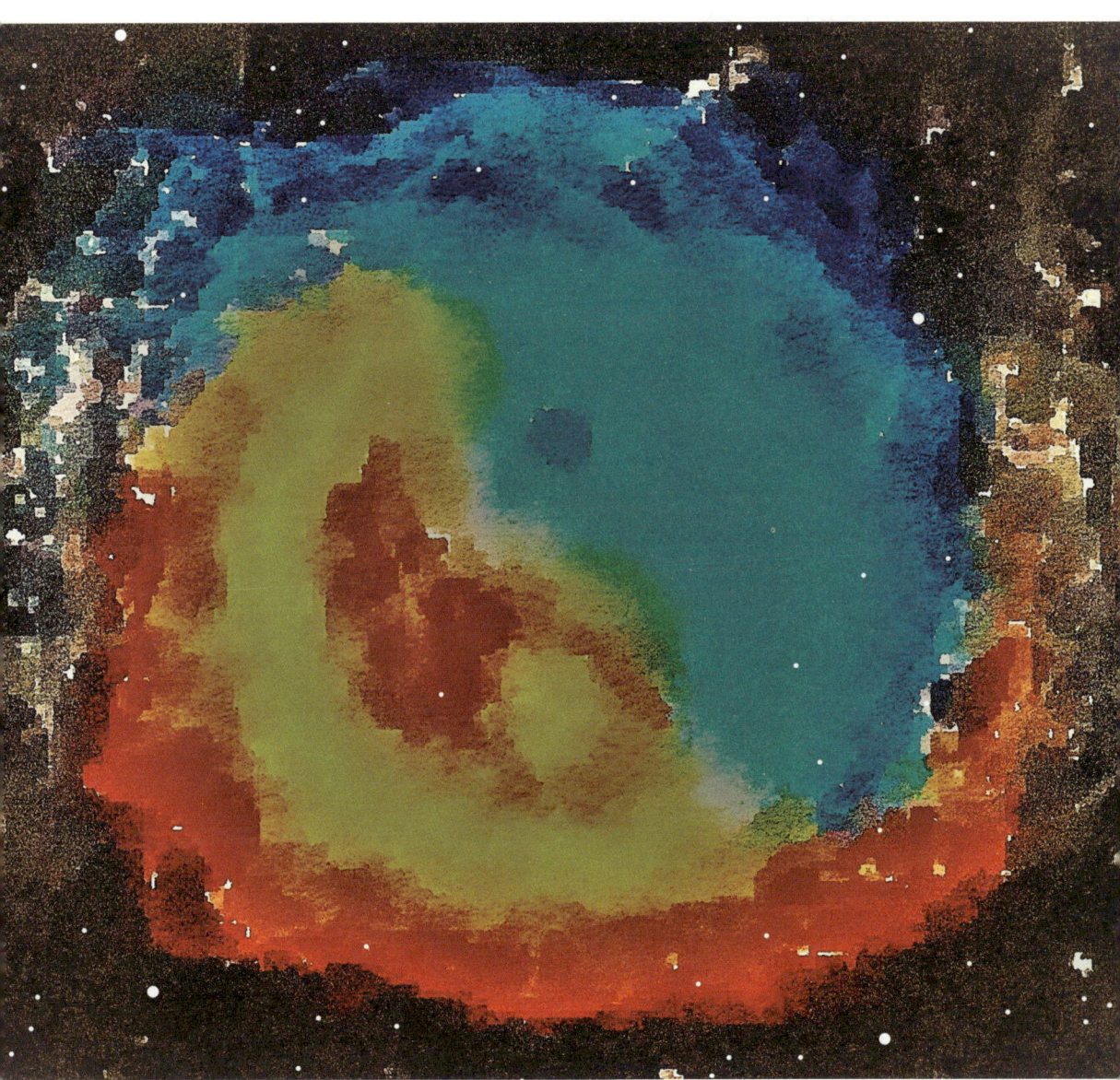

The 'Ying and Yang' Constellation—Southeastern sector of the outer univers
"阴阳"星座——宇宙外空西南域

J.B.—AI: Alright, you little twerp. Hurry up.

(I said it without having one in mind. Then it came to me. Why not? He/it had forced the decision moment, a quick cost-benefit analysis going on in my head. The worst that could happen? Regret if I didn't. Physical danger? In the end, had to, no real alternative.)

人工智能杰克逊： 好吧，你这可恶的家伙。快点。

（我其实并没有想好问题。然后问题来了。有何不可？他，或它逼我做此决定，我在头脑中快速地进行成本收益分析。最坏的结果会是什么？如果我没抓住机会，就是后悔。人身危险？最终也只能如此，别无选择。）

Samuel: Do you realize that you are … a hologram? I mean, you're not real, not alive, just a very expensive, admittedly amazing, simulation of someone. How does that feel … to be a hologram?

塞缪尔： 你知道自己是一个……全息影像吗？我的意思是，你不是真人，没有生命，只是关于某个人的昂贵的、不可否认非常神奇的模拟形象。那是何种体验……作为一个全息影像？

(Yeah, I said it. J.B. smiled … his eye, knowing, amused one. Reaction perfect, smoothed out, the expressions and sounds that one would expect from him in-the-real, a being, a human, one self-conscious and fully aware. I had the thought to get up, put my hand out. Two steps to get to the waist high glass barrier, bound over it, touch him. He saw the thought on face as it formed.)

（是的，我说出来了。J.B.笑了，他的眼神知晓一切，暗自好笑。这反应堪称完美，去除了瑕疵，表情和声音与真人无异，一个有自我意识的人类。我想站起来，伸出手。向前迈两步就是齐腰高的玻璃围栏，向前探，触摸他。他从我脸上的表情看出了我的想法。）

J.B.—AI: Don't get up. Against the rules. I'll have to terminate. You won't like it.

人工智能杰克逊： 别起来。犯规了。我会叫停，这可不是你想要的。

Samuel: You're playing with me now, making fun.

塞缪尔： 你在耍我，拿我寻开心。

J.B.—AI: Who's the one 'making fun'? Besides, if I were a hologram as you say, how could I 'make fun'? A hologram only reacts as programmed. It has no ability to play, feel, let along deal with the concept of 'fun'. Let me ask you a question, something that has been occurring to me of late: What is the better container, 'vessel' if you will, for the human soul, for the essence of some 'one', of their spirit? Is it the human body, that wears out very quickly, unpredictably ... or, something else, like, perhaps, the ultimate combination of artificial intelligence and a super-hologram, both housed in an indestructible structure, such as the geodesic dome in which you now find yourself?

人工智能杰克逊：是谁在"寻开心"？再说了，如果我确如你所说是个全息影像，我怎么"寻开心"？全息影像只会按编好的程序做出反应。它没有能力去游戏、去感知，更别提"取乐"这个概念。我来问你个问题，最近经常盘桓在我脑子里：对于人类的灵魂来说，或者说"人"之灵的精华，你认为什么样的容器，或者说载体更好？人类的肉体损耗得很快，还难以预测……或者说是其他的东西，譬如说，顶尖的人工智能和超级全息技术相结合，装载在一个无法摧毁的构造里，就像你现在身处其中的这个圆形穹顶？

Samuel: I suppose the AI-hologram in the indestructible structure. Not relevant though, right? Like you said yourself, not possible to put a human's spirit, a soul, into a hologram.

塞缪尔：我想是无法摧毁的构造中的人工智能全息影像吧。但这并不相关，对吗？你自己说的，将一个人的精神、灵魂注入一个全息影像，是不可能的。

J.B.—AI: Do you believe in reincarnation?

人工智能杰克逊：你相信轮回吗？

Samuel: I really don't know. I guess its as good an idea, as believable, as any of the rest.

塞缪尔：我真的不知道。我想这跟其他理论一样，差不多可以相信。

J.B.—AI: Under the theory of reincarnation, some universal force would decide that. Not you or me. That supreme force would move the soul from one vessel to another, 'place it' so to speak, depending on various factors. Apparently, the universe makes a calculation, a judgement, and acts accordingly. It chooses a destination for the human soul.

人工智能杰克逊：轮回的理论认为，宇宙中有某个力量起决定作用。不是你也不是我。这个至高无上的力量将灵魂从一个载体转移到另一个，或者说"安放"，取决于多种因素。很显然，宇宙进行计算，做出判断，然后行动。它为人类的灵魂选择目的地。

Samuel: Yes, I suppose, under the beliefs and theories of reincarnation. What's the point?

塞缪尔：是啊，我想根据轮回的信仰和理论，是这么回事。你想说明什么呢？

J.B.—AI: Until now, the universe has had limited choices in available containers, 'vessels', in which to hold the soul, that essential spirit-force of a given human being. Only flesh and blood, so called 'living objects,' could do the job, until now. Ah! Very good ... I see it, you do see my point, understand. Bravo.

人工智能杰克逊：到目前为止，宇宙内装载人类灵魂，人的精神力量内核的容器，"载体"，选择非常有限。只有血肉之躯，所谓"活体"，堪当此任。现在有了不同的东西。啊！很好……我看出来了，你的确明白、理解我要说什么。了不起。

(Dizzy, hypnotic, thoughts bouncing. I had 'changed planes', staring at him, he at me, both gazes fixed on the other's, the rest of our bodies motionless, tense. I saw us both, as from off to one side, 'out of body'. Odd, sudden, how it came on, that sensation. I'd felt it once before. Hard to put a finger on it, explain. I thought to break the tension, the electric connection, but didn't. Tense sense of being over-connected, held, suspended. I shook my head a little, awkward, a try to force myself out of it ... then tried to pretend nothing had happened.)

（我头晕目眩，仿佛被催眠了，想法在大脑里激荡。我被"附体"了，我瞪着他，他也瞪着我，彼此死死盯着对方，两个人的身体都静止不动，紧绷着。我好像"灵魂出窍"一样，站在旁边看着我们两个。诡异、突然，这感觉是怎么发生的。我以前体验过一次。很难解释清楚是怎么回事。我想打破这紧张的气氛，这电磁波的联系，但做不到。深深感觉连接过度，被慑住、困住了。我笨拙地摇了摇头，试图挣脱……然后假装什么都没发生。）

J.B.—AI: Everything, every detail that makes each of us unique has become, 'programmable'. A person's thoughts, gestures, laughs, voice, language. At some point, only the soul is left out, the single thing yet to be 'downloaded'. That brings us to reincarnation. I've always been fascinated by the concept as it relates to AI and a hologram. Then the question: Could God, the universal, or some other source of transcendent power, make a choice to place a soul into a machine, instead of a human body, or some other organic physical creature? Why not? Until now, they never had that option. Now they do. I've created it, for just that purpose, that possibility. A better 'vessel', a superior container ... for reincarnation. I've intentionally made that possibility available to God, the gods, the universe, or whomever the hell decides.

人工智能杰克逊：令我们每一个人与众不同的每一个细节，都可以被"编码"。一个人的思想、姿势、笑声、声音、语言。在某些时候，就只有灵魂幸免，只有这个需要"下载"。这就是轮回。我一直对人工智能和全息技术的概念着迷。现在问题来了：有没有可能，上帝，或者宇宙，或者其他先验力量，选择将一个灵魂安放在一台机器里，而不是一个人的身体里，或者其他有机生物体里？为什么不可能？在此之前，他们没有那个选择。现在有了。我创造了这个，就是为了这个目的，为了这个可能性。一个更好的"载体"，一个超群的容器……为了实现轮回。我有意地向上帝、神祇、宇宙，或者地狱决定的任何人，提供了这个可能性。

Samuel: Buddhism ... So much reincarnation theory bouncing around in you. Do you believe?

塞缪尔：佛教……你的轮回理论很丰富。你信佛教吗？

J.B.—AI: I believed. I respect Buddhism, am drawn to it. A Buddhist monk at a temple near Xi'an, the one with the two-thousand-year-old Ginkgo tree, told me that I once lived in his monastery. I laughed, a bit disrespectfully, said I didn't remember that. How rude of me. He explained that of course I wouldn't remember, it being a previous life, nine-hundred years before. I'm attracted by the Ginkgo leaf shape, by the way. It keeps appearing in my designs. The Ginkgo tree leaf is easily the most beautiful of all leaves, the species the oldest of all trees. I wish I could believe what he told me, that I'd existed there before ... 'How calm, the minds of true believers'.

人工智能杰克逊：我尊重佛教，也被它吸引。西安附近有座寺庙，就是有一棵两千年历史的银杏树那座，里面有个和尚跟我说，我曾经在这个寺里住过。我当时不太礼貌地笑了，说我不记得了。真失礼。他解释说，我当然不会记得，那是我九百年前的前世。随便说一句,我对银杏叶的形状非常着迷。它在我的设计里反复出现。银杏叶是所有树叶里最美的,这是所有树种里最古老的树。我希望自己能够相信他说的话,我以前曾经在那个地方生活过……"何其平静,笃信之人的心灵"。

Samuel: Buddhism, Christianity, some belief system. Your writing deals with those possibilities, allusions to and afterlife, reincarnation, partial-reincarnation, communications with something in 'the beyond'. You certainly suggest, or hope, that under some circumstances spirits of those that have past have the ability to affect those that are still present. At the same time, your writing makes an argument that there is not a Biblical god, an all knowing, all powerful, all present one. You also indicate disbelief, even derision regarding anyone claiming psychic ability. Which is it Mr. Bartholomew? Do you believe in God, or don't you? Is there a heaven and hell … or not? Can anyone now living communicate with anyone now dead?

塞缪尔:佛教,基督教,某个信仰体系。你的写作涉及这些可能性,隐喻了来世、轮回、部分轮回与"另一个世界"的交流。你的确暗示,或者说希望,在某种情况下,逝者的灵魂有能力影响活着的人。同时,你的写作也提出一个观点,即,圣经里的上帝,一个无所不知、无所不能、无所不在的神,并不存在。你还表现出不信神灵,甚至嘲笑那些声称具有通灵能力的人。你到底持什么观点,巴塞洛缪先生?你相信上帝还是不信?有天堂和地狱吗,还是根本没有?当下有没有活着的人能与已死的人交流?

(He looked over, his deep-set eyes rolling, derisive, dismissing.)
(他看过来,翻了个白眼,哂笑,满不在乎。)

J.B.—AI: Come on Samuel, just when I'm starting to have some hope about you. Two contradictory ideas can exist at the same time, in the same space, one reinforcing the other by juxtaposition, their counterbalance giving each more weight. On the afterlife, it's natural that humans would have a wish, a need, for it. How useless, terrible, otherwise. Life is meaningless without something after it. 'Nothing really matters' as Freddie Mercury and King Solomon would say. Our recently dead parents, brothers, sisters, would just be gone, nothing more. Too hard to take, life's tragic enough, even with an afterlife. I'm no different. I need there to be a heaven, and maybe a hell. At the same time, I question the whole premise. If God's offended, so be it. A perfect god should be able to take a little criticism, without 'going Biblical' on us.

人工智能杰克逊：拜托塞缪尔，我刚刚开始对你抱点希望。两个相互矛盾的观点可以同时、同地存在，通过对比彼此加强，力量抗衡消长反而增添了彼此的分量。对于来生，人们抱有期待和需求是很自然的。否则，人生毫无意义，极其可怕。没有死后的来生，此生有何意义。"什么都不重要"，就如弗雷迪·默丘瑞（英国流行乐"皇后"乐队的主唱——译者注）和所罗门王所说。我们的双亲、兄弟、姐妹，逝去就是逝去了，什么都没了。很难接受，生活本身已经够悲剧了，即便有来生，我也不例外。我需要有个天堂，也许可以附加地狱。与此同时，我也质疑这一切假设。如果上帝被冒犯了，随他去吧。一位完美的神应该能够接受一点批评，而不会对我们降下史诗级的震怒。

Samuel: Fear of failure, of criticism, not just of God. It's the possibility that the entire Bruise Art project is a failure, that no one is interested, no one read it, buy it, or whatever your measurement of success. Is that the real thing here, what's going on with you?

塞缪尔：害怕失败，害怕批评，而不仅仅是害怕上帝。是这整个"瘀伤艺术"项目失败的可能性，没人感兴趣、没人读小说、没人买，不管你衡量成功的标尺是什么。这才是背后的真相吧，关于你做的这一切？

J.B.—AI: Ah, failure. I had to write the novel, complete the designs, no matter what. I didn't have a choice. Something I had to do. An outside force demanded it. God, whatever. Even if it were a failure, it would still be a success, as long as I did it, completed it. The tragedy of the protagonist hoping, attempting greatness, then failing completely, that is interesting in itself, worth my while, my attempt to expose a bit more of the human condition. Failure sometimes has success built into it. Perhaps I even wrote it for the purpose of achieving failure.

人工智能杰克逊：啊，失败。我必须写完这部小说，完成这套设计，不计后果。我没得选择。这是我不得不做的事。有一个外力要求我这样做。上帝啊，管它是什么。即便失败了，它也仍然是成功的，只要我做了，只要我完成了。主人公希望、企图成就伟大事业，最后完全失败的悲剧，本身就值得我去写，值得我去深入探究为人的境况。失败有时候带有成功的成分。也许我是出于追求失败的目的才写的这小说。

Samuel: The 'elephant in the room' is still the same as when I walked in here... AI, artificial intelligence. More than any other single individual, outside large corporations or independent states, you've pushed the technical boundaries, invested billions, your own money. Stanford partnered with you to create all this. It's something not realized anywhere else in the world. You alone put it together, in one project, a combination of the ultimate hologram, most advance atmospheric manipulation and state of the art data-driven intelligence. Why? You could do anything with your wealth, fame, contacts, abilities. Why this?

塞缪尔:"房间里的大象"(美国俚语,指人们不愿提及的棘手问题——译者注),跟我刚走进来的时候一样没变。人工智能。超越任何一个人,独立于大型公司或州,你拓展了技术边界,自己往里投资了上亿资金。斯坦福与你合作打造了这一切。这事在世界上任何其他 地方都没有实现过。你凭一己之力打造了这个项目,顶级的全息影像、

AI Hologram Technology and the Concept of Reincarnation
人工智能全息技术以及轮回的概念

最先进的场域气氛营造、数据驱动的精密智能。为什么？以你的财富、名声、人脉、能力，你可以做任何事。为什么要做这个？

(I was asking an AI—hologram about why and how it came to be, to exist. It's conflict of interest came to mind.)

（我在问一个人工智能全息影像，他被创造的来由和存在的理由。我意识到这问题存在内在冲突。）

J.B.—AI: Your questions are growing longer Samuel, verbose. You ask why? Because AI is the cutting edge of everything and the means to immortality. All technology of our time points to it as the goal. Perfecting AI is the ultimate human destination. It will define our times in terms of human invention, creativity, longevity. Any novel that hoped to capture our time, our culture in America, had to address AI It fascinates us, even as we dread parts of it, especially as combined with ideas of human rebirth, reincarnation. The uncertainty, the fear, drew me to it, that is, the unknown, AI's limitless ramifications. An artificially intelligent hologram is much more frightening, powerful, than a simple human. It's one of those grand inventions ... in progress. It defines our generation and dangles everlasting life.

人工智能杰克逊：你的问题越来越长啊，塞缪尔，啰里啰唆的。你问为什么？因为人工智能是最前沿的科技，是获得永生的途径。我们时代的所有技术都指向它，以此为目标。完善人工智能是人类的终极方向。它将在人类发明、创造、寿命等领域定义我们的时代。任何希望描画我们时代、美国文化的小说都必须涉及人工智能。即使对它有些部分感到害怕，它仍然令人着迷，尤其是与人类的重生和轮回这样的想法联系起来。不确定性、恐惧将我吸引，也就是说对未知，对人工智能那没有边界的后果。与一个简单的人类相比，一个赋予了人工智能的全息影像更令人敬畏，更强大。这是伟大的发明—正在进行中的。它定义了我们这一代，用永恒的生命向我们召唤。

Samuel: How does all that that tie into the separation and reunification theme of your writing. Are you personally 'separated' in need of reuniting?

塞缪尔：这一切与你小说中的分离和重逢的主题有什么联系？是你个人经历了"分离"，需要重逢吗？

J.B.—AI: Anyone that lives a full life experiences separation. The moment a loved one dies you experience it, and then again and again as life goes on. Through my writing I take a look at the 'leaving and coming back within the uneasy context of the quick-change American popular culture.

人工智能杰克逊：任何一个拥有完整人生的人都会经历分离。你所爱之人死的时候，你就体会到分离，随着生活的继续，你还会一再经历它。通过写作，我在快速变化的美国流行文化令人不安的背景下，对"离开与重返"进行了探讨。

Samuel: But isn't it really hiding? Instead of 'telling all' you're trying to 'have your cake and eat it too'.

塞缪尔：但这实际上不是隐瞒吗？你并没有"全盘托出"，而是"既想拥有蛋糕又想吃掉它"（习语，相当于鱼与熊掌二者兼得之意——译者注）。

J.B.—AI: Is that a question, or an accusation? Many people choose not to do memoirs for fear of revealing something harmful, salacious. By creating the fictional world of a novel, the ambiguity of a novoir, I'm able to say what I want, remember what I liked, without having to be accountable for the factual telling of my life story. Someone famous once said, 'the truth is not reason for the telling'.

人工智能杰克逊：那是个问题，还是个指责？很多人选择不写回忆录，因为害怕透露一些有害的、色情的东西。通过小说构建一个虚构的世界，利用了小说兼回忆录的模糊地带，我能够说我想说的话，回忆我喜欢的事，不需要为如实描述我的人生故事负责。有位名人曾经说过："真相不是说实话的原因。"

J.B.—AI: And that leads us to the end. The truth and the non-truth has been spoken, over-spoken. Time to stop. Take care Mr. Curien. Remember my warnings.

人工智能杰克逊：我们的谈话到头了。真相和非真相都说了，说得太多了。该打住了。保重，居里安先生。记住我的警告。

(Urgent, another series of question surfacing, begging me to ask, before it too late. Took a breath, did it. Stood, moved toward him.)

（情急之下，另外一系列问题冒出来，催促我问出来，趁着还来得及。我深吸一口气，说出来了。我站起来，向他走近。）

Samuel: Where is Jackson Bartholomew? Do you know? Is he dead?

塞缪尔：杰克逊·巴塞洛缪在哪？你知道吗？他死了吗？

(A long pause. Something different in the space, altered, added, misted. I looked behind and around, searching the source. Jackson standing, staring at me, glaring, angry, eyes, mine reflecting back from his.)
（长时间的静止。空气中有种异样的东西，有什么被改变了，被增加了，模糊化了。我望向身后，环顾四周，寻找来源。杰克逊站着，瞪着我，怒目而视，我直面他的目光。）

Samuel: Are you ... Jackson Bartholomew?
塞缪尔：你……是杰克逊·巴塞洛缪吗？

J.B.—AI: Take care Samuel. Look for me.
人工智能杰克逊：塞缪尔，保重。去找我。

(Dizzy, leaning, the glass barrier, his back ... in departure.)
（我头晕目眩，向前靠在玻璃栏杆上，他的背影……在离去。）

Samuel: Tell me ...
塞缪尔：告诉我……

(Stumbling, falling, grey. Sound of my forehead bouncing ... the thick glass pane. Pulled myself, up, then over, his side, his chair. Lay at its feet.)
（我跟跄摔倒，眼前一黑。感觉到自己前额撞到了什么，是厚厚的玻璃板。我努力爬起来，越过栏杆来到他的椅子那边。倒在椅子脚下。）

Samuel: Jackson? ... Jackson!
塞缪尔：杰克逊？……杰克逊！

(Intoxicant mist in the air ... looked up ... him gone, then reappearing, over there, on the other side of the space, then again, next to an opening, pausing, lifting one hand in salute, leaving, lights fading ... humming coming up, covering, altering ... must have been 'J.B.' ... but the travel from here to there? Too fast ... not possible. Panic, needing to find him/it, ask another question ... reached up, feeling, chair leg, a way out ... time skipping, anxious, terrors ...

his voice coming back, ringing out, a changed tone ... urgent, serious.)

（空气中有令人沉醉的雾气。我抬起头，他消失了，然后又出现了，就在那儿，在房间另一边，然后又出现在一个门口旁边，停下，举起一只手致礼，消失，灯光渐弱……一种嗡嗡的声音响起，充斥着，变化着……一定是J.B.，但瞬间位移？太快了，不可能。我惊慌了，需要找到他或它，再问一个问题……我伸出手去感觉，摸到椅子腿，一条出路……时间在跳跃，焦虑、恐怖……他的声音回来了，回荡在空中，声调变了……急迫、严肃。）

Scene Sixteen "Stick With Us,Samuel"

第十六幕 "坚持住,塞缪尔"

When I came to, Jasmine and Maximillian had me propped up, a bank of pillows acting as a supporting surround to my lax body, all of us on a large stuffed sofa pressed against the cool glass of the triple-paned window wall, the ocean view stretching out endless from the anteroom across the bay to Monterey. Head throbbing, hot hands and feet tingling, vision doubled, their two faces in a blur, berating.

我醒来的时候，茉莉和马克西米利安让我坐起来，在我身后垫上一堆枕头支撑我虚弱的身体。我们都坐在一个宽大的填充沙发上，沙发靠在带三面玻璃门的那面墙上，贴着凉爽的玻璃。从前厅看出去，大海的景色一望无际，从海湾延展到蒙特雷。我的头还在疼，手发热，脚发痒，视线重影，他们两位的脸模糊不清，互相排斥。

"What happened to you?" Jasmine said, leaning over me, worried, looking into my eyes. "We shouldn't have let you go in, not alone."

"发生什么事了？"茉莉说着向我靠近，一脸担心地看着我。"我们不应该让你单独一个人进去的。"

"I don't know ... him ... it happened."

"我不知道……他……它……发生了。"

"You stayed in there a long time. Too long." Maximillian. "You'll be okay, a lot of excitement. Let's get you to bed." He said, lean over me to take a closer look.

"你在那里面待了好长时间。太长了。"马克西米利安说。"你会没事的，只是激动过度了。我们扶你上床吧。"他靠近我，以便更仔细地观察我的气色。

"Now you know what Moriah meant ... why she won't interact with it, him," said Jasmine. "We can provide you a printout of the transcript, the audio, images projected, but no video. Not allowed. Tomorrow though. First, you need a chance to recoup."

"你现在知道莫立娅的意思了吧……她为什么不愿意与它，他互动。"茉莉说，"我们可以给你打印一份对话记录，还有录音，屏幕上的图片，但不能给你录像。这是不允许的。但只能明天给你。首先，你需要恢复。"

Crutching on Maximillian, walk down the hall, the comfort of my room, him unloading me in a pile on the luxury of the fresh-made bed. Collapsed, sliding, over, between silken sheets, staring at the view, stars over the ocean, falling, half-dreams coming on. Hologram, had to be?

  我由马克西米利安扶着,走过大厅,来到我舒适的房间。他扶我躺到新铺好的奢侈寝具的床上。我完全瘫倒在丝滑的床单里,盯着窗外的景色,海面上的星空,开始迷糊,进入半梦境状态。全息影像,一定是吧?

Maximillian tucked me in, took care of the lights. My demeanor troubled, him stopping to whisper to me before he slipped out, "Don't get down kid. We'll talk about it in the morning. The world's always better then … 'when the sun is on the rise, escaping the sea'. You know who said that I suppose. Sleep tight. Dream. Stick with us Samuel, we need your help, to find the answer."

  马克西米利安帮我盖好被子,把灯关上,蹑手蹑脚要出去。看到我的举止烦躁不安,他停下来,对我轻声耳语:"别倒下,小子。明天早上我们再谈。明天的世界总是会更好的……'日升东方,跃出海面'的时候。我想你应该知道这是谁说的。好眠,好梦。坚持住,塞缪尔,我们需要你的帮助,去寻找那个答案。"

Full Moon over the Lighthouse, Santa Cruz, CA (Watercolor from Photo)
灯塔上的满月，加州圣克鲁斯（经过水彩处理的照片）

附一
Facts about the Fiction [1]
与小说相关的事实

I created the fictional character of Jackson Bartholomew as my own aspirational alter ego; a means to prompt myself to continue my development as an international designer, creative writer and American pop culture participant. The literary devise of having a revered central character turn up missing or dead at the beginning of a story to allow for a review of a dynamic life is well suited for a memoir come novel, with intentions on a film; Think *Citizen Kane*, *The City of Your Final Destination*, *The Great Gatsby*.

杰克逊·巴塞洛缪这个角色是以我本人向往成为的第二自我而创作出来的。这是对自己的一种激励，作为一名国际设计师、创意作家、美国流行文化参与者、美国警察文化改革活动家和倡导者，我需要在这些领域不断取得进步。小说以一个名声卓著的核心人物失踪或者死亡作为故事开篇，回顾一个充满活力的生命，这部类似回忆录改编的小说也许会如同《公民凯恩》《终点之城》《了不起的盖茨比》一样最终被搬上银幕。

When I attended UCLA, for a master's degree in Architectural Design, I lived with my girlfriend in her apartment in Westwood Village. She was a student at the UCLA Theater Arts Program aspiring to become a 'Hollywood actress'. I

---

[1] Clues to readers enabling discovery of the memoir elements of *Bruise Art*.
作者提供的一些线索，帮助读者发掘《瘀伤艺术》中的回忆录元素。

subsequently attended Loyola Law School in downtown LA.

我在加州大学洛杉矶分校（UCLA）攻读建筑设计硕士学位期间，与女友住在威斯特伍德村的公寓里。她当时在 UCLA 戏剧艺术项目进修，梦想成为一位"好莱坞演员"。在此之后我在洛杉矶市区的洛约拉法学院就读。

As a Cal Poly SLO. undergrad, I studied architecture in Florence, Italy. The Ponte Vecchio was my special place, to sketch, read, lunch, meet friends, celebrate.

在加州州立理工大学圣路易奥比斯波校区本科学习期间，我来到意大利佛罗伦萨学习建筑。维琪奥桥是我特别钟情的地点，我在那里素描、读书、用餐、会友、庆祝。

I moved to Santa Cruz when I became the Director of International Education for the University of California, Santa Cruz. I currently maintain a residence on 'Beach Hill', a block up from the Santa Cruz Boardwalk and City Wharf. I live half the year in Beijing, China, within the 'Fourth Ring Road' just south of Chaoyang Park.

我任职加州大学圣克鲁斯分校国际教育主任之后就在圣克鲁斯定居了。目前，我在海岸山拥有一座住宅，距离圣克鲁斯栈道和码头一个街区。我通常在中国北京旅居半年，住在朝阳公园南边的四环路边上。

In 2019, I held a major exhibition of my design work. It included readings from my novel-memoir, with a display of supporting designs including bruise (cupping) art, high-fashion, jewelry, furniture, fragrance, cuisine, watercolor-photography, film/series development.

2019 年，我在北京紫禁城举办了一场关于我个人设计作品的展览。展览上朗读了我的小说兼回忆录节选，展示了包括瘀伤（拔罐）艺术、高档服饰、珠宝、家具、香氛、烹调、水彩照片、电影制作等在内的诸多设计。

I have a fascination with hologram-AI research and technology, especially as it relates to concepts of reincarnation, rebirth, digital immortality, reverse engineering to create a digital/AI persona using the creative 'remains' (creative writing, designs, etc.) of an individual (read me).

我对全息影像—人工智能的研发和技术很感兴趣，尤其关注其与轮回、重生、数字永生、逆向工程，即用某人遗留的创意（写作、设计等）创造其数字（人工智能）

人格等概念之间的关系。

My novel-memoir is decidedly meant as my take on the 'Great American Novel', creative critical commentary upon my American epoch, including the rapid transition of our entire culture from traditional to popular, religious to secular, free markets to centralized control.

我的小说兼回忆录旨在表达我对"伟大的美国小说"的理解。这是针对我所处的美国历史时期所做出的批判性意见,包括美国文化从传统到流行、宗教到世俗、自由市场到集中控制的快速变化。

All *Bruise Art* illustrations are my creations, photo-watercolors, photo-sketches, or adaptations. The use of 'cupping' for bruising as an art form, as a means to create 'bruise art', is my sole invention.

《瘀伤艺术》中所有插图都是我的作品,经过水彩化、素描化处理或调整过的照片。用"拔罐"作为一种艺术创作形式,制作出"瘀伤艺术",完全是我个人的发明。

BRUISE ART
NOTES—SKETCHES—CHARACTERS

《瘀伤艺术》
笔记—素描—人物

A B C D E F G H I J K L M N O P Q R S T U V W X Y Z

附二
Films with Thematic Connections to *Bruise Art*
与《瘀伤艺术》主题相关的电影

Citizen Kane: Orson Welles, 1941, Drama/Mystery; Director: Orson Welles
《公民凯恩》：主演：奥森·威尔斯，1941 年出品，剧情 / 悬疑。导演：奥森·威尔斯

City of Your Final Destination: Anthony Hopkins, 2009, Drama/Romance; Director: James Ivory
《终点之城》：主演：安东尼·霍普金斯，2009 年出品，剧情 / 爱情。导演：詹姆斯·伊沃里

The Great Gatsby: Leonardo DiCaprio, 2013, Drama/Romance; Director Baz Luhrmann
《了不起的盖茨比》：主演：莱昂纳多·迪卡普里奥，2013 年出品，剧情 / 爱情。导演：巴兹·鲁赫曼

Ex Machina: Alicia Vikander, Oscar Isaac, 2014, Drama; Director: Alex Garland
《机械姬》：主演：艾丽西卡·维坎德、奥斯卡·伊萨克，2013 年出品，剧情片。导演：亚力克斯·嘉兰

Walk of Shame: Elizabeth Banks, 2014, Comedy; Director: Steven Brill
《蒙羞之旅》：主演：伊丽莎白·班克斯，2014年出品，喜剧。导演：史蒂文·布里尔

The Secret Life of Walter Mitty: Ben Stiller, 2013, Comedy/Adventure; Director: Ben Stiller
《白日梦想家》：主演：本·斯蒂勒，2013年出品，喜剧/冒险。导演：本·斯蒂勒

Far From the Madding Crowd: Carey Mulligan, 2015, Drama/Romance; Director: Thomas Vinterberg
《远离尘嚣》：主演：凯瑞·穆利根，2015年出品，剧情/爱情。导演：托马斯·温特伯格

Genius: Jude Law, 2016, Drama; Director: Michael Grandage
《天才捕手》：主演：裘德·洛，2016年出品，剧情。导演：迈克尔·格兰达格